THE CRYPTO KING'S MUSE

THE CRYPTO KING'S MUSE

FRANCESCA FROST

FROST HOUSE

This is a work of fiction. Names, characters, organizations, places, events, and incidents are either products of the author's imagination or are used fictitiously.

FROST HOUSE

Published by Frost House, Morristown
www.francescafrost.com

GIRL FRIDAY PRODUCTIONS

Edited and designed by Girl Friday Productions
www.girlfridayproductions.com

Cover design: Emily Weigel
Project management: Emilie Sandoz-Voyer
Image credits: Eugene Partyzan/Shutterstock (woman), Crypto360/Shutterstock (earring)

ISBN (paperback): 979-8-9939338-0-1
ISBN (ebook): 979-8-9939338-1-8

Library of Congress Control Number: 2026903350

First edition

What is needed is an electronic payment system based on cryptographic proof instead of trust.

—Satoshi Nakamoto (bitcoin white paper, 2008)

The Crypto King's Muse Playlist

- **Trustfall**—P!nk
- **Money Changes Everything**—Cyndi Lauper
- **About Damn Time**—Lizzo
- **We Do What We Can**—Sheryl Crow
- **Inner Light**—Elderbrook
- **Crazy (Radio Mix)**—TEEMID, Joie Tan
- **Ghostkeeper (Edit)**—Klangkarussell, GIVVEN
- **Bejeweled**—Taylor Swift
- **High Infidelity**—Taylor Swift
- **I Won't Back Down**—Tom Petty
- **Turn On The Lights, again..**—Swedish House Mafia, Anyma, Future, Fred again..
- **I Hear a Symphony**—The Supremes
- **In a Manner of Speaking**—Nouvelle Vague, Camille
- **Bang a Gong (Get It On)**—T. Rex
- **In the Moment (Adriatique Remix)**—RÜFÜS DU SOL
- **In And Out Of Love**—Rivo, Armin van Buuren, Sharon den Adel
- **Hide U (Tinlicker Remix)**—Kosheen
- **Set Me Free**—Armin van Buuren, SACHA
- **Mountain Jam**—Allman Brothers Band
- **Not Your Man**—Teddy Swims
- **Love Of My Life**—Harry Styles

- **Always**—RÜFÜS DU SOL
- **Faded**—Alani Allen
- **shoreline**—chole moriondo
- **Alive (Anyma Remix)**—RÜFÜS DU SOL, Anyma
- **Innerbloom**—RÜFÜS DU SOL
- **Power of Love**—CYRIL
- **Take Me Home, Country Roads**—John Denver

Chapter One

. . . bitcoin, beats, and bubbles

THE APARTMENT'S SILENCE WRAPS AROUND ME LIKE A warm blanket, but it feels heavy, suffocating, like the weight of numbers I can't outrun. I pad in semidarkness from the kitchen to my desk, the bitter smell of coffee churning the queasy knot in my stomach. A ghost of hesitation hovers as my fingers type into the Zoom meeting already underway. My gaze flicks to the time in the corner of my screen: 4:36 a.m.

"Charlotte, your royal lateness graces us." Jen's voice breaks the silence, yanking me into the razor edged world of cryptocurrency. The words are teasing, but my mind is too wired to play. I manage a small smile, masking the growing tightness adding to the simmering anxiety under my ribs. Around me, a grid of faces flickers on-screen—women scattered across the world, bound by ambition, necessity, and the desperate pursuit of digital gold. This isn't a hobby. This is survival.

"Bitcoin is up," Vivian advises, voice crisp. "We should hold and let the rally strengthen." A fellow New Yorker and founder of a blockchain company, she's always the first to jump-start our trades, her sharp read on the market steering us to the next opportunity.

"I'm with you," Marta chimes in from Guatemala, her voice competing with the soft cries of a baby in the background. Natasha's agreement follows, but something nags at me. My spine straightens. My instincts flare.

"I don't know," I cut in, pushing against the easy optimism. "This feels like a dead-cat bounce. The volume's too low—"

Jen, ever methodical, interrupts. "I'll check the charts. Five minutes." Unlike the rest of us, Jen is a professional, trading cryptocurrency from her residence in Switzerland.

The screen reflects a mosaic of differences. Each person is here for a different reason, but my own stands stark against the backdrop of my thoughts: a crushing debt born from the ashes of a once thriving business.

"Natasha. What's in the wineglass?" I tease, hoping to break the tension now.

"OJ and prosecco." Natasha grins, tech music pulsing faintly behind her. Dressed in a cotton T-shirt and shorts, she embraces chaos in Belarus, which sharpens her art and trading instincts. "Bitcoin, beats, and bubbles, Charlotte. You should try it."

We're as different as the countries we live in, I think: Natasha in Belarus; Marta in Guatemala, exhausted but resolute, one arm wrapped around her baby while her other navigates trading software; Jen, razor sharp in Switzerland, her mind working at a speed none of us can match. And Viv—my best friend, the only one who knows just how deep my debts run.

We're not casual traders. We're infiltrators in an arena built by men, rewriting the rules before they even realize we're playing. The crypto markets don't sleep, and neither do we.

Vivian and I found this group just before the pandemic—two outsiders at a bitcoin conference in a sea of men. Months later, when the world collapsed, we forged our own empire from the wreckage, built on mutual grit, necessity, and a shared belief in the power of cryptocurrency. Women brought together in defiance of a system that barely notices us.

For Marta, this is a revolution—bitcoin's promise of economic equity. For Natasha, it's art and code entwined in something the world doesn't yet understand. But for me, it's simply survival. This group, this screen, these early mornings—they're my lifeline against the relentless debt that feels like it's carved into my very bones.

Viv had been my rock. With a decade of business experience, her strategic advice helped me build an empire, a business based on curating and styling lavish wardrobes for the elite—a ticket to their red carpets, gala events, and whispered exclusivity. The fees were staggering; the clientele, even more so. But then, the pandemic struck like an earthquake.

The world I had so meticulously built began to crumble. My team, a cadre of fiercely talented stylists, needed their wages even as our client roster evaporated overnight. Our offices in Milan, Paris, and Manhattan—once the jewels of my crown—became massive liabilities. Signed contracts with designers loomed over me as unforgiving creditors. And the numbers? They were no longer just red; they were hemorrhaging. Hundreds of thousands of dollars in the hole. I was drowning in financial chaos.

Anxiety became my shadow, my unwelcome constant. I spent my days clutching the phone like a lifeline, calling every contact who might help. None did. I renegotiated leases, contracts, and private loans while I slashed payroll with a shaking hand. But no strategy could undo the cascade of ruin. Eventually, I froze, paralyzed by the unrelenting weight of failure.

Then, one tequila soaked night with Viv, our drunk despair transformed into a frenzy of creativity, leading me to an idea so absurd it shouldn't have worked: cryptocurrency. What began as crazy brainstorming solidified into action. Within weeks, I had gathered this coalition of financially hungry women, Zooming from all over the world, united by risk and a flicker of hope.

With Jen's expertise, YouTube tutorials, and Udemy courses, we forged our own digital salvation. We learned to ride the volatile trading waves, sketching strategies together that turned collective fear into profit. The virtual space became more than a meeting; it was my sanctuary. While my life dangled on a precipice, a daring leap into digital gold gave me a jump start to outrun the ruin clawing at my heels.

Jen's voice cuts through my spiraling thoughts. "Trading volumes are low across the board. This surge? It's a correction, not a rally."

The others nod, their enthusiasm for a bitcoin surge tempered, as I tighten my grip on the coffee mug and remind myself to keep steady. Crypto has mood swings. It takes all my emotional strength when trading these markets not to be pulled under.

"We stick to the plan," I say, my voice firm. "Buy in the west, sell as the day progresses in the east. We ride the clock."

Natasha pipes up, rushing to direct the group. "Great! Plan's locked. Now we chat. I need my social fix."

"Not today, babes," Viv cuts through with lively urgency. "I have some news for Charlotte—huge news. We'll talk tomorrow, promise." Her tone carries an edge, something sharp beneath the excitement.

A chorus of protests rises—"No cliques!" "So unfair!"—as the screens wink out like stars.

The call ends, but my world doesn't quiet. My skin prickles. My debts loom too large.

This morning, I was already at my desk long before the others had logged in. I had seen the bitcoin swing because I was trading even before the group met. Yet no matter how much I made, it was never enough to quench the raging inferno. Since the cryptocurrency exchanges never close, in desperation I found myself venturing deeper into the riskier waters of cryptocurrency options trading—a solitary, high stakes gamble.

Options trading gave me an adrenaline rush, which fueled my ability to hyperfocus and generate high returns. It was thrilling and terrifying, and each trade brought me closer to either redemption or ruin. But it wasn't sustainable, and I needed to find another way out of this labyrinth.

My phone lights up. Viv's name. I exhale sharply before answering.

"Listen," she says, her voice alive with danger. "I've found something incredible for you."

A spark ignites in my chest, equal parts hope and fear. Viv *knows*. She's my keeper of the keys, the only one who knows just how close I am to the edge.

"Will I make a lot of money?" The desperation in my voice is undeniable. "I can't keep this up. One wrong trade, Viv—just one—and I'm done."

"You'll make more than enough," she says. "It's with Riverbank, a cryptocurrency trading platform that's relocated to the Caymans. Billionaire founders. They're looking for someone to connect them with luxury brands and NFTs. It's perfect for you."

I pause, the name catching in my throat. "Riverbank," I repeat, half to myself. "Who are the founders?"

Her hesitation crackles over the phone before she answers. "One of the founders is Duane Blacklock."

Everything stops. The room tilts. The name slaps into me like a wrecking ball. "No." My voice is small, choked. "It can't be."

"It's fine, Charlie," Viv rushes to reassure me. "You look

completely different. He won't recognize you. And he has no idea about the book."

The book.

"What are the chances?" My voice is hollow, unsteady. "Of all the people . . ."

Viv barrels on, relentless. "This job could save you, Charlotte. They are offering huge salaries. And you've talked for months about wanting more women in crypto—this is your chance to bring fashion and bitcoin together. The money, the connections. It's everything you need.

"One of the big loans is coming due," she adds, her voice softer, threading through my defenses. "Since you can't get the money from your dad, this is your best bet."

The mention of him slams the door on my hesitation. I grit my teeth.

"No, I can't count on my dad," I say flatly. The anger is sharp and familiar. He has all the connections in the world—powerful financiers, old-money titans, the gatekeepers of wealth. And yet when I had fallen, he hadn't reached out a single hand to catch me. I can't rely on him. I never could.

I shake my head. *Don't think about it. Just keep moving forward out of this stranglehold of debt. Whatever it takes.*

"I'll go," I say finally, the decision burning in my throat. "I'll find out if this is worth it. Can you set it up?"

"I'll handle the introductions," Viv promises. "Give me a day."

Gratitude swells in my chest, tight and overwhelming. Despite everything, despite all the pain, problems, and risks, I have people who support and believe in me. A group of friends and fellow traders who have my back.

"Thanks so much, Viv." My voice cracks despite myself. "I can't thank you enough."

"Charlotte, we have to look out for each other," she quietly reassures. "That's what we do."

I end the call, feeling weighed down by my decision. The ghosts have stirred. A past I had buried, clawing its way to the surface. Riverbank. Duane Blacklock.

Salvation—or another circle of hell?

Whatever happens, I'll face it.

Because I have to.

Because I always have.

Chapter Two

. . . a little chaos

I CLIMB INTO THE UBER AT THE BUSY GRAND CAYMAN International airport, the air filled with the loud chatter of tourists and the hum of aircraft engines. I'm not nervous per se, but I can feel an adrenaline infused thrill pulsing through my veins. The warm embrace of the Cayman Islands weather intensifies my excitement along with Viv's words from our chat last night.

"Charlotte, you're an expert on luxury brands, you're a whiz with cryptocurrency, and you can learn NFTs. This is your chance. This is for you after all that happened: the betrayal, the deaths, and the debt. Go dazzle them and show them why more women should be in cryptocurrency. And, babe, can we have a video chat so you can help me pick out something to wear for my upcoming business trip?"

Viv's endearing lack of faith in her own fashion sense, even as she bolsters my confidence, makes me smile.

As the Uber navigates the bustling streets, I find myself admiring the sprawling green parks and lush palm-lined business district. It's a breath of fresh air after New York's dreary cold. Relief washes over me, signaling things are going to get better, until I remember the book. Anxiety rushes through me. *No, it's okay,* I reassure myself. The book is published under a pseudonym by a small indie publisher and will probably—will definitely—fly under the radar. Shaking my head as if I can physically scatter the unease, I tell myself that nothing will come of the book. I force my thoughts back to the beckoning view of powdery white sand and mesmerizing blue coming up in the distance.

The car stops at the entrance of a sleek two-story office building, its modern clean lines a delightful complement to the surrounding tropical beauty. I feel a wave of relief realizing it wasn't beachfront, thus sparing me the potential discomfort of conducting business with sand between my toes. Checking my reflection in my phone's camera mirror, I apply a fresh swipe of lipstick and brush my long brown hair off my shoulders.

I'm wearing a simple yet elegant Armani suit with a V-neck white blouse underneath and strappy black Louboutin sandals. The subtle sparkle of my gold Rolex and the glint of my Cartier gold hoops serve as a silent testament to my personal knowledge of the luxury brands the Riverbank founders hope to partner with. I want to make it absolutely clear that I understand these brands intimately. With that thought, I step out of the car and into the sun drenched lobby of the office building, murmuring my anchor phrase, "a little chaos"—the quiet code that tells me I've got this, that I can absorb whatever volatility awaits me and still deliver.

As I walk into the main office after checking in at the lobby, I feel the low key vibe, the busy hum of people working. The expansive room flaunts floor to ceiling windows on three sides, offering a serene view of the turquoise ocean beyond. Sunlight reflected from the water's surface streams through the windows, casting a hypnotic shimmer, filling the room with an otherworldly glow. A faint tropical aroma of coconut hangs in the air, mingling with a hint of something sweet—perhaps a fruit smoothie or freshly baked cookies.

The office features rows of large, sleek tables in a modern layout. Lively conversations pulse along with rhythmic tap-dancing on keyboards as a group of twentysomethings focus intently on their computer screens or chat with colleagues.

I notice him on the opposite side of the room. He's talking to someone. As I make my entrance, the typing stops, and all heads turn to follow me. Even at thirty-seven, I'm aware of my beauty. I don't blush; it's a reaction I'm all too accustomed to. My five-foot-ten height, mahogany brown hair, sapphire blue eyes, and facial symmetry had earned me a job at sixteen. It was how I'd supported my mother and brother when my father walked out on us. But after all these years, I had learned to enjoy it more when I was accompanied by someone even more attractive and the stares were for them.

Duane Blacklock, the man I'm here to see, pulls away from the desk he's leaning against. His piercing eyes lock onto mine as he slowly walks toward me. Each of his features feels intentional—the sculpted jaw, lashes impossibly thick against his sun lightened hair, and a mouth that promises cruelty and tenderness in equal measure. He's wearing jeans—Ralph Lauren, I think, from the fit—held up by a soft black leather belt, a crisp white linen shirt, and tan loafers without socks. *Loafer guy.* His half smile softens his more severe features, rendering him rather handsome. It's a transformation that can be very deceiving. A sudden flush of warmth spreads through me. His broad, almost imposing figure is . . . intimidating. Is my excitement turning into anxiety?

"Mr. Blacklock, I'm Charlotte Gordon-Lennox. It's a pleasure to meet you, and thank you for seeing me." I stretch out my hand as his long fingers reach for mine. His hand is large with a tight grip, a little painful, warm, a little sensual. *What the fuck?*

"It wasn't me who invited you here, Charlotte," he responds tersely. "May I call you Charlotte? My partner, Oliver, was impressed that you were willing to come down and see our operation. And to make it work on such short notice, with so little fuss."

Okay, harsh tone, tight grip, he's definitely unfriendly. But I need to make the right impression. I decide to lighten the tone and reply laughingly, "Oh, my friends often refer to me as 'Charlotte Gordon Little Fuss,' Duane. May I call you Duane?" I ask, my eyes twinkling as I parody his formality.

He gives me a curt nod as if he's a king granting permission, just as a lively young man in jeans and a gray T-shirt bounds up, hand outstretched to shake mine. His grip is firm but casual. "I'm Oliver. Nice to meet you, Charlotte. What a good sport to come see us like this. We have a place arranged for you to stay overnight, and we'd like to show you the team and layout and spend some time talking."

Oliver looks about six foot one with well cut chestnut hair. His attractive face has sensitive green eyes that look directly at you when he speaks. As he leads me around the room, introducing me to the team, pointing out computer screens with active trading volumes, and explaining what each person is doing, his nervous energy is palpable.

Riverbank, the cryptocurrency derivatives trading platform loved by traders worldwide for its user-friendly interface and impressive capacity to handle millions of dollars in trades, is their creation. Duane and Oliver had written the software code for the platform while they were still freshmen studying computer science at Carnegie Mellon. They'd arrived at college having owned and traded bitcoin, Ethereum, and other alt coins while in high school. There were other strong cryptocurrency trading platforms around, of course, but what set Riverbank apart was the sophistication of their software, designed to trade cryptocurrency derivatives. It had taken the world of digital gold by storm, and within a few short years, over $100 million was traded daily on their platform, making them billionaires before they were thirty.

I quickly realize that I'm probably the oldest person in the room. There are three or four other women in the office, but my style and my manner of dress make me stick out like an adult on a playground. This is who I am, I remind myself. This is what they want me to represent.

As if picking up on my thoughts, Oliver comments, "You look like you spent your career in fashion, as your résumé indicates." Oliver and I face each other in a glass enclosed conference room. Duane, at the head of the table, watches me with a sharp, focused look. I know this is the perfect job for me. I have all the skills to connect luxury brands with cryptocurrency. And they seem to like me—well, Oliver anyway.

"But do you understand cryptocurrency?" Duane's tone is sharp, his question a challenge.

"I understand it's a form of gold, only digital, that it's digital gold, meaning it exists on the internet," I begin. "Just like gold, it's a store of value. And the bitcoin software protocol limits bitcoin mining to a maximum of twenty-one million bitcoin—"

"That's basic knowledge that most people understand," Duane cuts in dismissively. "What's the harder stuff about cryptocurrency?"

"I think you're referring to the blockchain technology," I venture, looking from Duane to Oliver, who nods in agreement. "That's a bit trickier."

I continue, explaining how the "crypto" in cryptocurrency refers to cryptography, a branch of mathematics. Cryptography is concerned with codes, unbreakable codes, that make cryptocurrency immutable, or unable to be hacked. The digital code for your bitcoin cannot be figured out or hacked, as it exists on the blockchain. Bitcoin is highly secure. What gets hacked are the platforms or wallets if people don't secure their private keys.

"Go on," Duane's arrogant voice instructs.

Really, is this how it's going to be? Why is he interrogating me? I was no stranger to being dismissed because of my looks. It came with the territory. But this feels different. Regardless, I force a smile and press on.

"The limited supply of bitcoin, capped at twenty-one million coins by the protocol, leads some to predict that each coin might one day be worth $250,000 or more. Then there's Satoshi Nakamoto, the mysterious inventor of bitcoin, who posted the protocol in 2008 outlining how digital currency would work via blockchain technology. People could download the protocol's software on the internet and start mining or creating bitcoin. Satoshi was the biggest miner of bitcoin in the first two years. But after posting on her blog in 2009, she vanished," I explained.

My last words hang in the air, followed by a prolonged silence. "Various theories exist about who the real Satoshi Nakamoto is, but personally, I believe Satoshi is a woman who disappeared because of the amount of bitcoin she had amassed."

Duane's voice pierces through the silence—low, harsh, and menacing. "What evidence do you have for that, Miss Gordon-Lennox?"

Caught off guard, I feel my face flush and stammer out my reasoning while trying to control my confusion.

"If you read a lot of crime novels like I do and understand basic human motivation—I mean, I'm not a psychologist—but it's the most likely explanation. That is, bitcoin is based on community. At its core, cryptocurrency empowers people by eliminating a third-party intermediary, such as a bank. It levels the financial playing field by allowing people in developing countries to have access to finance. These seem like nurturing concepts to me, which I associate with women. But no, what I said is just a theory. I don't have any actual evidence."

Oliver's clapping brings an abrupt end to the interrogation. He stands up, walks over to me, and extends his hand. "Well done, Charlotte. Well done. Your sentiments about cryptocurrency align very much with ours. You'll have to forgive Duane. He's our technical operations person, so he wants people to understand the nuts and bolts of the technology."

"That's okay, Oliver," I reply, giving him my most gracious smile. It's time to regain control.

"Normally I might feel like Duane's questioning me so much because of my looks, or because he doubts my comprehension of this intricate technology. But that's precisely the asset for Riverbank. With me, you get a package of beauty and brains," I say with a soft laugh.

I cast a glance at Duane. He stares coolly back at me.

"Exactly," Oliver exclaims, smiling and looking to Duane for agreement. "Charlotte, we'd like you to come to a gathering we're hosting tonight to meet some people. Riverbank wants to become part of the local community, to understand its needs, so that we can invest in its future. It's at the Atlantic, eight p.m. I'll walk you out."

Turning to Duane, I extend my hand and offer a friendly smile. He does not smile back. His impassive look leaves me with a slight sweat on the back of my neck and a sudden urge to escape the room. *There's something so intense about him,* I muse. He could use a full strength Xanax, a triple scotch, or a vigorous workout . . . in the bedroom. His mysterious aura pulses with something strange, magnetic, provocative. I continue to feel his gaze on me as I exit the glass room and walk down the hallway with Oliver.

"I've known Duane since we were roommates at boarding school, then at college," Oliver begins. We are descending the stairs to the front entrance. He's looking at me with a friendly, intent smile, as if he can sense my reaction to Duane's less-than-friendly questions.

"Duane's intense," Oliver says offhandedly, "but incredibly loyal underneath it all. He and I are mavericks, as you've probably realized. He has his idiosyncrasies, though, and they've led him to be defensive. That's all it is. See you at the gathering tonight."

Chapter Three

. . . the arrogance of it

"RELAX, CHARLOTTE. IF ANYONE RECOGNIZES HIM IN THE book, you're anonymous, so they can't link it to you. And small publishers aren't exactly churning out bestsellers. But c'mon, babe, tell me about that interview!"

I'm in the condo Riverbank arranged for my interview visit, phone on speaker, stippling concealer along the faint scar at my hairline, getting ready for tonight's reception. The book has just been published. What had I been thinking, writing that thing? I pause, brush poised, and glance through the floor to ceiling glass at the ocean, now a tumultuous, steel gray abyss. Exactly. That's what the book was—a riptide. I hadn't been thinking; I'd been feeling. A storm of anger as wild and unpredictable as the ocean churning outside these windows.

Writing the book had been therapy for navigating my descent into chaos. It had helped me heal.

"They are so different," I confide to Viv. "Oliver is quirky, but he's open and friendly. Duane is intense and not really approachable. He doesn't talk very much, but you can tell they respect each other tremendously. They're like brothers, really.

This job would be fantastic if it weren't for the messy business of my book. I have all the skills and connections in fashion and luxury they need. The salary is ten times more than I thought. I could clear my debts without any more hellish high-risk trading. It would be such a win-win."

Viv's laughter, coming from the phone, fills the room. "Of course it would. You've been through the gauntlet with your own company. You're tougher than you look. You've got an optimist's heart. And we both know your incredible resilience. Fuck Duane and keep up your impressive full-court press. Are you flying back tomorrow?"

"That's the plan," I reply. "I have this reception or party or whatever it is tonight and then my flight's at eleven a.m." I cap the concealer, slip into my heels, and watch another set of waves break against the reef.

"Just remember, you've got this," Viv reassures me. "This job is going to fit you like an haute couture Chanel suit."

"Or maybe a baggy Kardashian leisure outfit?" I counter. "Thanks, Viv, you're my rock. I promise I'll work my magic with your wardrobe for your business trip when I'm back."

The Atlantic is a series of gleaming glass-and-steel structures in a secluded horseshoe arrangement located in the Seven Mile Beach area of the island. It's a fifteen acre private oasis complete with a helicopter pad, a marina, a two star Michelin restaurant, and all the amenities. In the two-story lobby, I feel like I'm in a rainforest. Moist plants in all shades of green cling to the entire height of one wall. Checking in with the concierge, I observe men in black suits with discreet earpieces near the entrance, the elevator, and the large teak doors. The steady drip of water falling from the wall adds to the ominous quiet. Is the extra security for exclusivity's sake or something more?

As I enter the White Garden through those massive doors, I'm greeted by a gentle gardenia fragrance and a sizable crowd. Small groups of people cluster among shimmering greenery and lit paths. In the twilight, the white flowers seem to glow from within, as if hiding secrets of their own. As I weave my way to the bar, I notice Duane. He's with a young woman with long blond tresses in her early twenties in a short, bright purple dress. They're laughing. He's handsome in the kind of way that makes strangers stare. Bloody hell. It's good that he doesn't laugh around me. It would be too hard to ignore him then. A pang of curiosity hits me. Is that his girlfriend?

As I sip my champagne, Oliver materializes at my side. "Come, let's mingle," he suggests, his calm confidence making his office attire of casual jeans and shirt seem effortlessly stylish. We make our way through the crowd. Lowering his voice, he tells me a few things about each person before he introduces them. This feels so easy as I realize Oliver has the skills of a seasoned diplomat.

"Director of Economic Development, very big on bringing high-tech businesses to the island."

"Youth and Family Services, wants to see more vocational schools for high school kids."

"Women's Business Council, thinks we need computer coding night classes for women."

There's a succession of faces and names that I easily remember, for the first half, anyway. My years in the fashion industry, attending galas, charity events, and navigating the frenetic social scene of New York, have honed my skills for remembering faces and names. It had been essential in building my client base.

I quickly understand Riverbank is forging close ties in the community. "I'm impressed that you really want to invest in programs here," I say.

"We want to share Riverbank's success with others and

cultivate a workforce for the tech industry, which is really everyone's future. C'mon. I'd like you to meet our parents. They're here for tonight's event."

"I would love to. What do you mean by 'our'?" I ask as he leads me through the increasingly crowded gathering.

"They're my parents, of course, but we all consider Duane a member of the family. We're like brothers, and they've become his parents, too." I nod, biting back the obvious question: What the hell happened to Duane's parents?

Mr. and Mrs. Mitchell stop their conversation to look at us as we approach. They are an attractive couple in their sixties and look very fit. Mrs. Mitchell gives her son a quick hug, releasing him as Oliver shakes hands with his dad.

"Hello," I greet them, offering my hand. "I'm Charlotte Gordon-Lennox. I'm here interviewing at Riverbank."

"Oh, Charlotte, I'm Margaret." His mother has Oliver's lively, sensitive hazel eyes. "You're so beautiful . . . and smart if you're here for an interview. So good to see more women in blockchain and cryptocurrency."

"I'm Charles, Oliver's dad, and Duane's adopted dad, although not really. We say that because he's such a member of the family. I don't think you could separate those two if you wanted." Oliver's dad has a natural smile and a sort of professorial look with the gray at his temples and his tweed blazer. I like him instantly.

"I'd describe them as incredibly enthusiastic about cryptocurrency," I say.

"Yes, a shared love of digital gold and very different personalities is the secret of Riverbank's success. Oliver is like his mother—open, accepting, optimistic. Duane's inside his head more, analytical but creative, intense but good at reading people."

I smile in agreement, musing to myself. *I don't know whether I would use those exact words. Maybe arrogant, short-tempered, aggressive?*

"Do you live here?" I ask, wanting to know them better.

"We've both cut back on our work schedules, so we're spending more time here. Charles just retired as chairman of the engineering department at a Boston university. And I work part-time now, doing research in a computer science department," Margaret explains.

"You can't beat the weather here compared to Boston," adds Charles.

"Wow. So you're both in STEM fields. I imagine Oliver must have science in his DNA. But where did Duane's tech talent come from?" I ask.

"I've no idea," Charles laughs. "But Duane's been coding for a very long time. It rubbed off on Oliver early on, but was driven by Duane's passion. Eventually, our daughter Lily became interested as well. She's here somewhere, asking Duane's advice on her PhD."

Before I can respond, a crisp British voice rises above the murmur of conversation from the front of the gathering. One of the hosts lifts his glass, and heads turn in his direction.

"Friends, thank you for joining us this evening as we welcome Riverbank to the Cayman Islands," he calls out, his vowels precise. "Here in this little corner of Britain in the Caribbean, we're proud to be part of the islands' evolution into a financial and technology hub."

There is a ripple of polite laughter, then applause and the clink of glasses. A small Union Jack flutters on a pole near the terrace steps, catching in the warm breeze.

I thank the Mitchells and slip away toward the bar set up near the edge of the terrace where I spot Oliver.

A massive gardenia bush bursting with small, white fragrant flowers secludes Oliver and me from the rest of the crowd, their exotic scent hanging heavy in the warm air. We're talking about the Cayman culture and the difficulty of finding tech workers when Duane makes his way over to us.

He hands Oliver a cold beer and me a full glass of champagne. We clink glasses, but I pause to let out an inaudible sigh as Duane, not missing a beat, says, "There are a lot of photographs on the celebrity websites of you attending all those exclusive social events. Was that business or pleasure?"

I'd been feeling relaxed and so comfortable with Oliver, allowing my curiosity to roam about Riverbank, the Caymans, and the Mitchells. As I'm met with Duane's intrusive question, the feeling evaporates. I struggle to control my irritation and anger at what he's suggesting, hoping it doesn't show on my face.

"Appearances can be deceptive. I'm far from the superficial person those photos might suggest," I respond quietly. "Those events were not about partying but about cultivating business relationships and securing publicity for my brand. It might look glamorous, but when you peek behind the curtain, it's not quite the fairy tale it seems. But you and Oliver know that, right? What hurdles did you face launching Riverbank?"

The best defense is a good offense—or was it?

Oliver exchanges glances with Duane before cautiously admitting, "Our families chipped in a bit to kick-start the platform."

"That was helpful," I say encouragingly.

Duane interrupts before I can ask more. "We want to hear about your start-up experience, Charlotte. You can't say living the high life wasn't fun, especially with all that free-flowing champagne and cocaine," he challenges with mock incredulity.

Heat climbs my neck as I try to arrange my face into neutral. I meet his gaze, vault shut, impassive. "It wasn't like that," I say, sanding each word smooth. "And for the record, I don't do drugs."

His response is all too predictable. This is what he had been like that first time. At the conference. Dismissive and condescending. Thinking back to that event, I feel my composure slipping. I'm usually able to hide my temper in most circumstances. But my skin prickles with a simmering anger, which makes me speak too quickly.

"Duane, you couldn't be more wrong. I didn't have a dime of family money when I started my business. Every night was a new event, another designer to pursue for a dress to wear in return for a name-drop, every weeknight, and weekend, not forgetting the fashion weeks in New York, Paris, and Milan, twice a year. All this to get my business up and running. I worked hundred hour weeks for a decade. Not so different from what you're doing now, I imagine."

I can't stop. This has been building all day; Duane has gotten in my head.

"All that hustle just to get my brand on the map. I spent days scouting for talented stylists who could build wardrobes to complement each client's style," I say, recounting my journey. "Then there was managing appointments, handling difficult clients, and pushing to develop an app."

I halt, feeling as if I've fallen into Duane's diversion. I look from Oliver to Duane, lean in, and lighten the atmosphere with a conspiratorial grin. My ability to pivot my emotions when they are too heated is my secret weapon. "But hey," I say, "that's the entrepreneurial life we signed up for, right? Create, problem-solve, eat, sleep: rinse and repeat."

As if on cue, the tension dissolves. Their expressions mirror my knowing smile. *Perhaps my candidness will pay off,* I muse. I hope they finally recognize my value: a unique blend of fashion, crypto, and entrepreneurial spirit.

I leave them to mingle with other guests. Even if it doesn't lead to a job offer, networking is never a waste of time. I find myself conversing with Riverbank's director of development and the head of the business alliance. The company has pledged financial support to after-school computer programs for middle graders, even creating a separate group for the girls. Despite their maverick tendencies, their philanthropy is sincere.

A crescendo from the gathering builds—the chatter, the music, the energetic movements. Time for a graceful exit. I'd mastered the art of not arriving first or leaving last. I can feel Duane's gaze on me as I navigate the crowd. Each time I look over, he looks away. I doubt they expect a formal goodbye from me. So why is he watching me so intently?

My evening unravels as I bid farewell to the last group. A hand catches mine. Voices around us pause, and all eyes turn toward the man who's announcing my name so forcefully.

"Charlotte!" A tall, tanned man in his late forties with graying hair at the temples is giving me his "can't look away" smile.

"David," I say, removing my hand from his grip. David Delacroix: a past lover and former business partner.

The day's events—the interview, Duane's grilling, the barrage of unfamiliar faces, and the relentless pressure to be on the whole day—make me hunch my shoulders. Fuck, this day could not have one more surprise.

"What are you doing here?" My tone is not friendly.

He lowers his voice, using it as an excuse to step in closer. "I have business with Riverbank."

Business with Riverbank? How could that be?

"You're lying," I say, and quickly turn to go.

He catches my arm this time. "Wait. You know Riverbank is spending money left, right, and center to get their name out there. I'm part of a venture group deciding whether to invest in them." I realize this is probably true.

I free my arm. "David, we've got nothing to talk about."

"Come on, Charlotte. We were going to marry. We have history."

"Yes, we do have history, but it's the bad kind." I need to set him straight.

"Let me drive you home," he proposes, ignoring my clear dismissal. "We can talk or maybe grab a drink at the lounge."

As my head begins to shake no, he quickly adds, "Please. You owe me that."

"I don't owe you anything. You, on the other hand, owe me every month I lost thinking we'd build a family." I fight the tears forming at the back of my eyes. I force myself to maintain eye contact with him. Don't run. Do not let him force you to run.

"We had something good, Charlotte," he persists. "You can't deny that you love me."

"No. I. Don't." I emphasize each word with disgust.

"What about this?" He moves closer, trying to draw me into a kiss. Filled with rage over stolen time I can't get back, I reach out and slap his face. Then his hand comes up to . . . what? Grab mine? Hit me? I can't tell. Someone pushes him away and steps in front of me. It's Duane.

"Is everything all right?" He's looking into my eyes intently, ignoring David. His molten eyes pull me like an undertow.

I step back from both of them instinctively. "Of course. I'm fine. This is David Delacroix, a VC investor from Switzerland. He's interested in Riverbank." My gaze meets Duane's with a calm demeanor. I cannot have any drama negatively impacting this job offer.

"Hey, great to meet you, Duane. I've got a meeting scheduled with your team in the coming days." David reaches out his hand. I can see he's absolutely relieved at the shift in focus.

But I don't want David Delacroix meddling in what could potentially be my new world. Desperation rises in me. I want, I need, to shut this down.

Interrupting quickly, I turn to Duane. "There's something crucial we need to discuss." I keep my voice calm but assertive. "I noticed you were about to leave," I lie. "Would you mind dropping me off at my condo."

"Not at all. Do you have your things? Good," he responds as I nod yes.

He steers me past David, through the dwindling crowd, to a waiting parking attendant who soon returns with a black McLaren Artura Spider. Not the brand's signature papaya orange that shouts pedigree—this one is midnight and mirror-slick. It's rare, ruthless, and exactly what a tech king would drive. He opens my door, then drops a bombshell. "You know, Riverbank has a firm policy prohibiting fraternization."

"What? Excuse me?" I don't understand what he said. Then, his meaning becomes clear, and I laugh.

"Do you really think that because I asked to talk to you privately that I'm hitting on you?" I don't even try to hide my bemusement and surprise. "Duane, as you just saw, I prefer to date older men. You're a little young for me. No, I genuinely have something I need to discuss with you."

"So, you and Delacroix . . . ?" he asks incredulously.

"No," I clarify. "We were involved, but not anymore."

"Why was he trying to kiss you, then? And why did you slap him?" he persists.

I ignore the questions. This is becoming too personal, too quickly. I slip into the convertible. As Duane pushes some buttons and the top retracts, I draw out and fasten my Hermès scarf—classic orange in design—over my hair. The silk is cool and familiar against my skin. Duane's glance flicks to it, unreadable, as we pull away, accelerating into the warm darkness. We ride in silence. He lets the speed climb, handling the car with obvious ease. I remember something about him spending a summer in college on the amateur race car circuit.

He looks over at me. I have to raise my voice above the rush of the wind.

"You're impressive behind the wheel. I really like this."

The quiet night, with the wind washing over me, broken only by our headlights, gradually settles me. I finally relax after an exhausting twelve hour ordeal. The unexpected encounter with David and his insistence on rekindling our relationship isn't shocking, not really. That's how things had always transpired when I tried to cut ties with him. But this time, instead of all the emotional frustration, anger, and hurt, I feel indifferent. Regret is the only lingering emotion. Finally.

When I think of David, I always chastise myself for having been so foolish. After Matthew, I had resolved to steer clear of all relationships, and I did, for a long time. David had offered me solace during my company's downfall amid Covid, as the market for private stylists evaporated. Gradually, our professional camaraderie had transformed into something more personal. I really wanted to marry and have a family. His family was pressuring him for the same thing. But he prefers his independent, carefree life. It was hard for me to accept that he would never settle down or start a family. He liked to believe otherwise, but I understand him better than he understands himself.

Duane pulls up to the condo walkway. He shifts in his seat to look at me. His features stay hidden, but sitting so close I notice a citrus, almost bittersweet scent coming from him: bergamot.

"I'm surprised you like me driving fast," he says. "Most women spend the whole time telling me to slow down."

"But you're obviously in complete control of the car. It was really thrilling," I say.

"You were quiet," he comments.

"Well, it's amusing. Did you really assume when I asked you to drive me home that I was making a pass at you?" I ask, laughing. "I'm so much older than you. You're what, twenty-seven, twenty-eight?"

He ignores my question. Instead, he says, "People with similar chemistries attract each other. Maybe that's what you're feeling?"

I tug the edge of my scarf, letting the silk slide through

my fingers as I ready myself to explain the book situation to Duane. Telling Oliver would have been easier, but I had needed Duane to escape from David at the party, so Duane it is. My apology sits on the edge of my tongue, a well rehearsed concession to clean up the mess I've caused, but before I can begin, his voice slices through the air, steering us in an entirely different direction.

"He's too old for you."

I freeze, blinking at him in disbelief. The weight of his words hits me, but they don't seem to register. His bluntness—the arrogance of it—has caught me off guard. As their meaning sinks in, burning stirs, rising to the surface, and quickly melts my numbness.

I tilt my head slightly, raising my scorching eyes to meet his. "He's eleven years older," I say, my voice hard with defiance. "I don't think that makes him too old for me."

I know I should focus on the actual issue—the book and this job that hangs by a thread—but his words dig under my skin. Something in the way he speaks about me, about my choices, as if he has a right to decide what's best for me, triggers something deeper. My pulse quickens, and before I can stop myself, I push forward, the sting of his opinion feeding the flames inside me.

"You know, Duane, I'm sure with your intelligence, good looks, and wealth, you've had many affairs, which you feel allows you to lecture me. Perhaps you've left a trail of heartbroken women, each convinced they were special, only to be discarded when you got bored. But here's the thing—I wouldn't know, would I? Because your personal affairs are exactly that, personal. They're none of my business, just as my love life doesn't concern you."

His eyes narrow, but his smirk doesn't fade. Instead, it deepens, almost as if he's enjoying this. "Touchy subject, is it, Charlotte?"

"It wouldn't be if you kept your unsolicited opinions to yourself." My voice trembles, my control slipping. A mixture of anger and seething—a deeper frustration I can't quite name—clutches at my chest. The once warm night air has become a cloying tension, choking me.

Duane leans forward, his gaze suddenly more intense, like he's searching for something in my face. "You must admit, if he isn't married by now, he's very unlikely to be at his age. Shouldn't you be with someone who actually wants to settle down? Have a family?"

His voice sounds mocking, but I also detect a hint of concern; I can't be certain. My heart beats faster, and I'm infuriated he can make me feel this way—off balance, confused, vulnerable, all in the same breath.

"You don't know him." My voice is lower and fierce. "And you know nothing about me, or what I want, or why I've made the choices I've made."

The tension between us feels unbearable. There's heat in his eyes now, a spark that wasn't there before, and for a fleeting second, I wonder if I've pushed too far. But then something shifts in the way he looks at me, his expression softening, just barely.

"And what is it you want, Charlotte?" he asks, his voice quieter, almost daring.

I open my mouth to respond, but the words catch in my throat. I don't know if I can answer him, not honestly. Not when every part of me feels like it's at war—the part that resents his audacity, for his thinking that I'm attracted to him, for passing judgment about my personal life. I hate that he makes me feel so exposed. He's gotten under my skin in a way that no one else has.

"I just want this job, Duane," I say with resignation. "Just a job. Thanks for the ride. I'll wait to hear from you and Oliver."

I quickly exit the car and enter the building. I don't look back.

Chapter Four

. . . covers pulled over my head

"I'M FUCKED. THAT'S IT. I KNEW SOMETHING WOULD MAKE this job crash and burn."

"You don't know that." Viv's calm voice holds conviction and concern.

We're having a late dinner at a West Village bistro around the corner from the stately walk-up where I rent the second-floor apartment and Viv the first floor with the garden.

"Well, you tell me. The cofounder of my dream company, aloof, unfriendly, and borderline hostile, intervenes with an old boyfriend, drives me home, carefully mentioning his company's strict nonfraternizing policy as if I'm out to seduce him, and then lectures me about my love life. What the fuck?"

"He has movie-star good looks, I mean, super hot," Viv says, scrolling on her phone and viewing the few images available of Duane.

I absentmindedly agree. "Yes, I remember thinking that too when I started reading up on him for the book. His intensity makes him compelling."

Attempting to organize my internal chaos, I finish with,

"I just want the job, Viv. No more romance, or in the case of David, what turned out to be just a sexual affair. Duane Blacklock hasn't changed from the first time I met him at that conference two years ago. But I need this job. I still have loans to pay off, and I don't want the stress of the derivative trading any longer."

And then there's my parallel plan, quiet, precise, expensive. Late-afternoon reminders for injections, an upcoming secret appointment, a line item in my budget labeled "future," nonnegotiable. There's a part of me that resents even making a plan like this, as if I failed an invisible test. Then my better self shows up—the one who survived the collapse, rebuilt, kept going. She doesn't care about pride; she cares about outcomes. She says *Pay the bill. Book the slot. Protect what you want.*

"Hey, little sister."

I look up to see my brother, Danny, pulling a chair up to our table. Danny is my older brother, a little taller than me, medium build with copper curly hair and the delicate features of our mother.

"Glad I tracked you down yesterday. What's good here?" he asks as he waves down a waiter.

"Oh, Danny." I lean over to give him a big hug. "Thanks for coming. It's been too long."

"Yeah, well, you know."

Yes, I did know. Danny is an orthopedic surgeon at Hospital for Special Surgery, the New York orthopedic mecca where pro athletes and worn out weekend warriors go to be rebuilt. Although he's an established attending and finished with his grueling surgical training, he has a wife and young family needing his time when he isn't with patients.

We are only eighteen months apart. Even though he's older, I had been the one to look out for him when the divorce wreaked its devastation. He had struggled terribly at the local high school. By taking on more modeling jobs, I'd been able to contribute money to send him to private school. There he got the attention he needed and had flourished.

And here he is now for me. Despite his casual demeanor, I know he accepted my invitation to dinner because of Matthew's anniversary tomorrow.

"Charlotte had a fantastic job interview," Viv announces before I can signal her not to say anything.

"What's that about, Carlie?" Dan raises an eyebrow.

I pause as he uses my childhood nickname—my mother's nickname—for me.

"I will tell you if you promise not to call me that."

He beams at me as only a tormenting older brother can.

"It's a cryptocurrency company in the Cayman Islands. They want me for my fashion connections, and you know I've been interested in bitcoin these past few years."

"Sounds perfect for you. I'm seeing so much about the use of blockchain in medicine for maintaining medical records and patient privacy."

Despite feeling I can tell him anything, he doesn't know about my business debts and financial struggles. With all the emotional demands of his patients and now his young family, he doesn't need my problems and worries dragging him down.

His food arrives, and we continue our relaxing banter, exchanging the comforting details of daily life, all three of us drawing closer.

That's Danny's gift, I think. The secure feeling and stability he brings to all his personal interactions. I was so thankful that he had taken a year off after high school to help me nurse our mother through the end stages of her cancer. By that time I was earning a six figure income from modeling and was making enough to pay for help so she could pass away at home as we all wanted.

"Listen, Carlie," he says suddenly. "Kate and I want you to

come and be with us and the kids tomorrow. We don't want you to be alone."

"Hope you have more success than me," Viv comments. "She's refused all my invitations."

"Not necessary," I say firmly. "This year Matthew's death will be easier. I'm going to sleep late, have a session with my personal trainer who kicks my ass, and then spend the rest of the day reading up on NFTs. I'll be fine. Truly."

Truthfully, I want to just stay in bed with the covers pulled over my head tomorrow, but I made plans to force myself to ignore my underlying sadness, which lessens each year on this day.

My workout leaves me too tired to even read about NFTs. I'm in bed by nine p.m. And in the blurry descent from awareness to sleep, I'm engulfed in floating memories, this time feeling Matthew as a positive glow instead of anger.

Applying the approach of looking only at what's in front of me, the weekend passes. I keep busy, and hope and anxiety for the Riverbank job only hijack my thoughts five or six times a day, instead of hourly. I understand and believe strongly in cryptocurrency. It could change the world. It was changing the traditional banking system. And it pairs with my greatest strengths, my knowledge and expertise in fashion. I am the perfect candidate for the job.

But if I'm honest, it's mostly about the money. With the steady salary they're offering, I can slash through my debt in no time, and once the anxiety and paralyzing concern about money are relieved, I can start to move forward. Start dating and focus on my personal life. Landing this job would be like winning the lottery, even if Duane Blacklock was a part of it.

Remembering Matthew and obsessing about a dream job

at Riverbank, those feelings intertwine and have me recalling when Matthew and I were first married. It had been simple, fun, a high of happiness and contentment for both of us, for the first year anyway. Each of us rushing home to talk about our long workdays over dinner or going out to see friends but always ending the day back in bed, wrapped around each other. I tell myself I will have the love of a good man. I will meet a man I can trust and count on. I have to believe that. I just need to become financially stable first.

I'm up early Monday morning as usual to join the trading group, but today I determinedly ignore my solo riskier trading with hopes that I will soon have another option. *Oh, please let me have another option,* I silently plead.

The morning trading session with the group does not go well. More and more people are investing in Ethereum because transactions on its platform can be processed faster. As a result, Ethereum's value is rising higher.

"I know," Viv snaps when I mention the stagnant bitcoin as we gather in front of our computers on Zoom.

Bitcoin isn't slow because it's broken—it's slow on purpose, like a safe that only opens on a schedule. And Ethereum isn't faster because of hash rate; it doesn't use mining anymore. It runs a different way now, and it's built more like a busy city—lots of things can happen there besides moving a coin from one person to another. As I ponder, still in my crypto trading mindset, I consider a shift in strategy. Maybe we should lean more heavily into Ethereum and lighten our bitcoin position. On Ethereum, other people can build useful things, not just a single digital coin like bitcoin.

I can't help but reflect on the rapid changes in the industry as we all sign off for the day. Exhausted, I retreat to bed for my usual two hour post-trading nap. My phone's incessant buzzing stirs me. And as I wake, images from my dreams linger—is it Matthew, laughing joyfully on our wedding day, leaning in to whisper to me? My focus returns as I sift through levels of awareness, and the image morphs. It's Duane, looking at me with his signature half smile, leaning in for a kiss.

I slide the phone to answer, slightly bewildered. "Hello?"

"Charlotte? This is Angela from HR at Riverbank."

An hour later, Viv is at my apartment, and the pop of a long-saved bottle of Billecart-Salmon fills the room.

"Excelsior and congratulations, Charlie! This job is meant for you. Things are finally falling into place, and you deserve it."

"Excelsior, Viv! Your success too, since you found this for me. Imagine falling asleep and waking up to news of being hired as head of luxury brands at Riverbank?" I giggle, pointing to the time on my phone. "We're turning into Natasha with our morning bubbly."

We sip champagne from my finest flutes. I can feel the happiness mixed with relief settling over us. "I guess this was my last trading session for a while," I muse, already missing my bitcoin crew.

Looking around my apartment, I can't help but smile. I moved here following Matthew's death, leaving behind our large, well furnished Tribeca apartment, our first home as newlyweds. This new place is truly mine, smaller and more charming, without the lavish amenities of a luxury building, but a warm, welcoming space for Danny and his family during holidays.

"I'm keeping this apartment while I'm in the Caymans," I say. "I'll be earning enough, and this can be our communal space."

And now the Caymans. I'm ecstatic—truly, this job is a way forward. I've done the math a dozen times: salary plus bonus should be an eventual clean line through my debts with time and patience. Fingers crossed. Relief loosens something in my chest every time I picture it. But the thrill sits beside a bright edge of fear. It's a different life—salt air and new streets, driving on the other side of the road, a complete set of new people. I know no one there. I'll miss Danny's Sunday drop-ins, Viv's emergency cappuccinos, New York's sirens and steam. Still, the last few years taught me I'm even more resilient than I thought was possible. When the ground falls away, I find another way to stand. I can do the unknown. It's become one of my strengths.

"Well, I should hope so. I plan to use it as a hotel for my friends when you're not here," she says, winking.

"Besides," I add, "I'll be traveling frequently for fashion events. I'll keep you updated on my schedule so when I'm in town you can hopefully make time for me."

Viv, ever my standard-bearer, puts down her champagne and hugs me. "Charlie, I'll always have time for you. We're family."

Chapter Five

. . . shadows and edges

THE CAMERA LIGHTS BEAT DOWN ON ME, AND I CAN FEEL the heat intensify in my dress as I sit sideways in the chair. Glancing over, I notice Oliver, who is seated in front of me and to my right, looking comfortable in his regulation black T-shirt, jeans, and sneakers. Duane, standing behind me and the farthest from the camera, leans his outstretched hand against the wall. Clad in his white shirt, jeans, and a midnight navy blazer, he probably feels the heat the most, even in loafers without socks.

"And that's a wrap," calls Angelo as he steps out from behind the camera. He's a fit, attractive man in his fifties with a full head of hair sprinkled with gray, combed back neatly. Known for his magic with the lens, Angelo has earned recognition from top models and designers in the industry.

We've worked tirelessly all morning and through lunch to capture these press-release photos. I want to change the images usually associated with Riverbank, which emphasize the tech savvy aspect, to focus more on the founders and people in the company. Tech is binary; people are real. Although Oliver and Duane have been accommodating, I know they're reaching their limit, regardless of how the photos turn out.

I'd been eager to start at Riverbank once I'd been offered the job. I'd signed my contract, cleared security, and moved into an apartment close to work within a few weeks. The photo shoot is my first project for a press release announcing the addition of fashion to the Riverbank endeavors.

I relished the opportunity to see my old friend Angelo, a preeminent fashion photographer. We'd spent the time during the shoot bantering about our wild past and reminiscing about the craziest events. Our laughter and chatter helped to distract everyone during the tedious process of taking photos and kept the atmosphere light, which was precisely our aim. Angelo and I knew what it took to make a successful photo shoot; we were seasoned professionals.

Gathered around the camera, we watch as Angelo clicks through some of the shots.

"*Mia carina*, Charlie, you're gorgeous," he croons. "The other two are just okay."

Everyone laughs, and I quickly plant a grateful kiss on Angelo's cheek. While the crew begins dismantling the lights and camera equipment, I leave to oversee lunch arrangements.

"Join us in the dining room when you're ready," I call out. Riverbank has a talented chef who cooks healthy meals five days a week in the elaborate kitchen and dining area. No soda, candy, or empty snacks here—only deliciously prepared, nourishing dishes. Oliver, Duane, and I make our way toward the tantalizing aromas of roasting chicken and freshly baked bread.

"Thanks for being such good sports, you two. These photos will elevate the press release and maintain the high standards associated with Riverbank's buzz," I say appreciatively.

"As long as I can be myself, I don't mind any PR event," Oliver replies. "I just can't pretend to be someone I'm not. Thank you for understanding that, Charlotte. See you two at lunch."

I stop and turn to Duane. "And what about you? Did you feel comfortable taking your place at the back, away from the spotlight, where you seem to prefer to be?"

It was true. In recent weeks, I had observed Duane's inclination to step aside, lingering at the back and remaining on the edges, except when engaged in one-on-one conversations. Unlike Oliver, who was a constant presence in the office and seemed to be everywhere. True, Duane was head of operations and steered the coding and programming of the platform, and as such, he was part of the back office. But he acted like a hidden cofounder.

Ignoring my question, Duane counters, "Is he one of the older men you like to date?"

I can't quite decipher whether he's serious or not. "Are you talking about Angelo? Are you joking? I've known Angelo since I started in the business. He was very kind to me when I had my . . . my . . ." I cut short my sentence, not wanting to delve into personal matters.

"No, Duane, I'm not dating him." I sigh. "We're good friends, and this was him doing me a big favor, that's all."

The frustrations of the day are starting to wear me down. Once again, I feel uncertain around Duane. Unable to contain my emotions any longer, I blurt out, "Why do you always ask me so many questions about myself?"

"I'm not sure why," he responds with surprising honesty while I look at him. "I guess I've never met anyone like you. I'm trying to figure you out," he says slowly.

Our gazes meet as people pass us on their way to the dining room.

"To see if you can trust me?" I ask, contemplating his words. "That's what it feels like."

"If you want to determine whether you can trust someone, Charlotte, you have to look at their actions, not just their answers. But I suppose I'm protective of Oliver. I want to ensure that you respect who we are and don't misrepresent us to the world. Oliver has his vision for this company, and we are both committed to cryptocurrency."

"Listen, I understand Oliver and his desire to use blockchain and bitcoin to make the world a better place, decentralize finance, and provide secure access to money for people in undeveloped countries, just like we have in the US. But I don't understand you, Duane. You're trying to figure me out? Well, I don't get you," I say before I can stop myself.

Realizing the audacity of my statement, I rush to explain and soften what I've said. "I mean, you and Oliver are both incredibly intelligent. Probably the smartest people in the room. And you're both clearly passionate about cryptocurrency and its potential to change the world for the better. But Oliver speaks out and is always at the forefront, expressing his passion. So why are you never alongside him, representing Riverbank, giving interviews, or speaking on panels?"

"So, you want to know why I'm not speaking on a panel? Is that your question?" Duane asks, his face unreadable.

"Yes—I mean, no, no, that's not my question," I stumble, my nerves getting the best of me as I think of how we had been on that panel. Bloody hell, why had I mentioned a panel? "My question is, why are you always in the shadows?"

A stillness settles between us. I hold his gaze, staring into obsidian eyes that contrast so strikingly with his blond hair. His expression remains impassive, impenetrable.

"We each have our role to play, Charlotte, no matter who we are," he replies curtly, and without another word, he turns and abruptly leaves me standing alone in the hallway.

"What the fuck?" I fume under my breath, frustrated by his refusal to acknowledge his inclination for secrecy. "Well, I have bigger things to figure out than Duane 'Shadows and Edges' Blacklock."

Chapter Six

. . . the way anyone would for family

SWIVELING IN MY CHAIR, I SIGH AS I EXCLAIM TO MY NEARBY team, "This is so frustrating. None of my friends can help."

I've been at Riverbank several weeks now and feel I'm proving my competence more every day. I feel like I belong, and it's exhilarating to realize my expertise works so well for such a completely different field.

I'd already finished several projects within my first few weeks. The successfully completed photo shoot had been key, along with the next significant project—cultivating a top fashion designer to become an ambassador for Riverbank. After many meetings, phone calls, and contract negotiations, Delilah Stevens had finally come on board.

Delilah had disrupted the traditional concept of cocktail attire. Her sophisticated outfits for informal evenings ranged from luxurious fabric shorts paired with flowing kaftans to silky shirt dresses cinched with masculine belts. She'd established herself at the top of her game and earned immense respect from the fashion world since her first runway show a decade ago.

Public relations had suggested the idea of flying Delilah down to Riverbank's headquarters for a live-streamed discussion between her and Oliver, with me moderating. We could use clips from the footage for various social media campaigns and upload the final version to the internet.

However, Delilah is a diva and incredibly demanding.

I'd been handling her with extreme care. I don't give up easily, yet her latest request was proving impossible to fulfill. She'd insisted on a private jet to pick up her stylist and photographer from two different locations. Riverbank had already arranged for private jet travel for the designer and her entourage. But my team couldn't find another jet willing to make two stops on such short notice. And everything was scheduled to kick off tomorrow at noon. I had spent the entire day making phone calls, desperately trying to solve the problem. I even took a deep breath and called several wealthy friends who owned private jets, asking for a favor. Unfortunately, my Hail Mary attempts had failed.

Delilah's assistant had just informed me that Ms. Stevens wouldn't appear if her hairstylist and photographer weren't present.

I sense the mounting stress among my team as the deadline looms. I suspect part of it comes from how I feel—unnerved and unsettled. These are familiar emotions from my younger days, waiting for my dad to show up for important events like my high school graduation or my reception for the college honor society. The impending disappointment. And every time, he had let me down.

Nope, not going to wallow in that. I have more resilience now for problem-solving, I remind myself. I've learned to make decisions with more optimism.

I stand up and walk around the bustling room filled with people working diligently at their computers, the sound of incessant typing filling the air. I sit down in my chair, leaning back and gazing up at the ceiling, my mind racing: contacts, favors, brokers I swore I'd never call again. There has to be a way. I push back from my chair and pace, searching for options. Lost in the blur of logistics and pressure, I turn too sharply and collide with Oliver.

"Charlotte, we're receiving fantastic responses on that press release. We've been inundated with interview requests regarding our partnership of crypto with luxury brands," Oliver says, giving me his quick, easy grin.

Duane steps up beside him, and the impact of his presence hits harder than the collision with Oliver. His eyes settle on me—steady, unreadable. Watching me. Always watching me. And I can't decide if it makes me want to stand taller . . . or run.

Taller it is, I decide, and turn to each with a confident smile as I say, "Yes, we were truly fortunate to have Angelo. He's one of the best. And the team did an excellent job with social media and in reaching out to key business journals. What did you think of the press release, Duane?" I ask, hoping to preempt his questions.

We stand gathered by the dramatic ocean view, computer sounds and work voices surrounding us as a female version of Oliver, tall, with blond hair and a friendly smile, rushes up in a whirlwind of energy to join us.

Lily is Oliver's twenty-four-year-old sister, who I had seen Duane speaking with at the Atlantic reception the day of my interview. Oliver had introduced us several weeks earlier when she stopped by Riverbank while visiting her family.

A candidate in the artificial intelligence PhD program at the University of Toronto, she had an engineer's mind and loved fashion. We had really hit it off on our first meeting, spending way too much time discussing the head designers at the different fashion houses to the neglect of my work that day. Now she wraps her arms around me in a big hug, unceremoniously pushing Oliver and Duane to the side.

"I absolutely need your help. My career hangs in the balance. Only you can advise me. It's so important."

Laughing as I return her hug, I explain, "Perfect. I haven't been able to solve my 'find a jet' problem, so maybe I can help you solve yours."

"Let Charlotte do her work and find her jet or whatever the hell she's looking for," Oliver scolds as he moves to the side to talk with Duane. Meanwhile, Lily takes out her phone and pulls up photos of three different dresses.

"I have a departmental dinner with the chair and the professors and their spouses, and I want to look and feel confident. Which of these dresses should I buy to wear to the dinner?" she asks, stopping to take a breath. "If I don't wear the right dress, the night will be ruined as well as my standing as a PhD candidate in the department."

We laugh together, both knowing her hyperbole is part of her style and reflects her enthusiasm for everything she does. It's infectious.

"I'm sorry, but none of them," I say, laughing again, this time at her expressive look of dejection. "But I'll find a more flattering dress for you. Don't follow fashion, Lily. Create your own style. Something that suits you.

"Look at this beautiful blue-green dress," I say as I pull up a popular website and scroll through quickly. "Black can be a harsh look. You're young. You should wear color. Keep it no shorter than mid-thigh—something like this."

I spend the next few minutes showing Lily some choices on curated websites, which she's vocally excited about. Satisfaction and a sense of something good envelops me. We scrutinize the dresses on her phone.

"I'm going to order these two. Thank you, thank you, thank you." And as she hugs me again, she says, "You are so lucky to spend time around Duane and Oliver, my two favorite people."

She notices my unbelieving glance over at Duane and

continues. "No, Charlotte, you don't understand. He's so great. When I was waiting to hear from PhD programs, he spent the entire day hiking with me because I was so anxious. And he reviewed and made fabulous suggestions to improve my dissertation proposal. And he always, always remembers my birthday with a gift."

I give a soft laugh and roll my eyes.

"Yes, I know. He has his quirks," she says.

"That's one word for him," I venture in a low voice as she continues.

"He won't ever let me post any photos of him, not even at family gatherings, or selfies of us, like when we reached the top when we were hiking, I had to post a photo as if I had reached the top alone. Once I posted a family photo of his birthday, and he literally became someone else, someone unfriendly and cold, and insisted I delete it immediately. But he, even more than Oliver, has never let me down."

Duane looks up from his conversation with Oliver as if he has heard this last part and walks over to us. Oliver follows, telling Lily they have to leave to meet their parents. Lily gives me yet another hug and a quick kiss on the cheek to Duane. She walks away with Oliver after promising to let me know which dress she chooses, leaving me alone with Duane.

"She's wonderful," I say, "and she's certainly a big fan of yours."

"Lily's my family, along with Oliver and his parents. I would do anything to protect them," Duane says, voice edged with that rare heat he lets out when he means something.

"To protect them? Are they in danger?" I tilt my head, unsure if he's confessing more than he intends.

"No, I didn't mean it that way. Just that I would do anything for them. The way anyone would for family."

My throat tightens. *Not my family.* My father would never. Matthew certainly didn't.

"It's funny," I whisper, the realization breaking loose before I can catch it. "You talk about family more than any man I've ever known."

"I'll admit, family is very important to me. Nothing unusual about that, Ms. Gordon-Lennox," he replies, voice edged like a blade. "Perhaps you just know the wrong men."

The words land like shrapnel. My skin burns hot, flushed with humiliation, as heat stings behind my eyes. He doesn't know what he's said—how easily he's struck bone. My father walked out, not even turning around when I cried for him. Matthew betrayed me, leaving me grieving and broken. They both taught me the same lesson—I wasn't enough to keep them. Not worth the fight. Later the men I let close—men who smiled at me, held me, even said they loved me—just confirmed it. When it mattered, none of them chose me.

And here I am again. Attracting the wrong man, the dangerous man, the one who will leave me hollow. Yes—I do choose wrong. Over and over. The wrong men. And maybe that's because there's something wrong with me. Maybe there's some flaw stitched into my very being. Maybe love slips through me because I'm incapable of holding it. Broken. Unworthy.

I force myself to look down before he sees too much, before he sees the hurt in my eyes. But it's too late—his gaze lingers, sharp, unreadable. He takes a step closer, as if to reach me.

His nearness unsettles me—his scent, his presence seem to press against my skin and make my body betray me even now, aching for something I swore I didn't want.

No. He doesn't get this. He doesn't get *me*.

The pressure in my chest bursts. I can't let him see, can't let him touch this rawness.

"Is that what you think, Mr. Blacklock? That you've already worked me out so neatly? Don't flatter yourself. My life isn't nearly that simple, and you know far less about me than you imagine."

I brush past him, shoulders rigid, as my voice falters with a quiet self-reproach, every syllable a confession of my own failures.

"You've no idea."

I return to my desk, the whitecapped ocean still rolling outside the window, but the sparkle of my laughter with Lily has drained into confusion and unease. Duane's words echo in me, leaving me unsettled, out of my depth, unsure where I stand with him—or myself.

Fred approaches with his usual unhurried stride. Solid. Dependable. He's a big, quiet man in charge of office security and responsible for the private bodyguards assigned to Duane and Oliver. He deals in facts, not feelings.

"We're sending a Riverbank jet to pick up Delilah Stevens's stylist and photographer first thing tomorrow. They'll be here by nine a.m.," he says, plain as stone.

Relief floods me, sharp and dizzying. I spring up and throw my arms around him. He stiffens immediately, his body all rigid lines of discomfort.

"How? Why? Who—how did this happen?" I bombard him with questions, finally releasing him from the awkward embrace.

He shrugs and says, "I don't know. PR told me to pass along the message."

As he steps away, I lower back into my chair. The ocean keeps moving, restless. One crisis solved, tied up neatly with a jet and timetable. Fred's bluntness feels safe, almost comfortable in its clarity. But Duane? He leaves me unmoored, chasing shadows, tangled in questions with no answers. And I can't decide which unsettles me more—his chaos, or my hunger for it.

Chapter Seven

. . . small asks don't move markets

"DAMN, DAMN, DAMN, AND BLOODY HELL," I SWEAR TO VIV and to no one in particular as we talk on the phone that night. "He is so conceited, arrogant, superior, and annoying."

"Be careful," Viv cautions.

"I know, I know. I need this job, and honestly, I do love it, but for some reason, he exasperates and infuriates me every single time I see him."

"Be careful, not just about your job, but about him. Your kind of exasperation sounds like the 'I'm exasperated because I like him' kind."

"What are you talking about? It's not that at all. He's just very different. He asks so many questions and acts so arrogantly. I'm too old for him. Besides, he doesn't trust me.

"Listen, Viv," I say, shifting gears. "My agent called. The book's moving. It's getting passed around on podcasts and women-in-tech panels as a sharp little satire—short fiction—about the industry's worst habits. Even though I never used Duane's real name, he's only thinly disguised. Readers have made a short list of who they think inspired the main character, and sometimes Duane is on it."

I exhale. "And that's why I'm rattled. I feel terrible about writing the book and the way I portrayed him as a villain. He was dismissive and insulting to me on that panel, but I'm not a cruel person, and I genuinely regret writing that thing. He's right not to trust me."

"Well, it isn't just about him," Viv consoles. "You wrote a compact, fictional account that is a composite for effect. It's funny and ferocious. You call out the system—funding blind spots, ego theater, the boys' club filter and how male VCs underestimate a two-trillion-dollar fashion industry—not a real person. That's why it lands: People laugh, then think. I think it's great."

"That's not helping, Viv," I wail. "The worst part is, I asked them to pull the book but because it's starting to gain attention, they won't. I signed a contract. Ugh."

Sensing my growing distress, Viv changes the subject. "What have you done about the jet?"

"Can you believe it?" My mood brightens. "The head of security came to my desk to let me know they were able to secure a private jet. The stylist and photographer will be here on time tomorrow when Delilah arrives for her hair, makeup, and photos. When I tried to find out who provided the jet, Fred was vague. I still don't know who my fairy godmother is for that one."

"Excelsior!" exclaims Viv, using our cheer for a winning event.

"Excelsior!" I echo, filled with gratitude.

"Your idea to have Delilah and Oliver discuss their thoughts about fashion and cryptocurrency and women is really good."

"Yes, things are falling into place. It's been so long since I've worked at something that made me feel relaxed and competent. I always had self-confidence in our crypto trading group, but the high-risk trading by myself left me on edge and unsure of myself every day."

"Well, let's see how Delilah does sharing the spotlight tomorrow," Viv warns, chuckling.

"Look for some clips of the discussion on social media and let me know what you think."

I am about to end the call when I remember something. "Hey, Viv, did I leave my orange Hermès scarf at your apartment? You know the one my mother gave me? I can't find it anywhere."

"Not here, Charlie. And if it were, you'd have it back—orange isn't my color."

The moment the interview with Delilah and Oliver wraps up, a palpable sense of relaxation sweeps over everyone on set, like the gentle ocean breeze rustling through the majestic palms framing our open-air space. Our vibrant discussion about NFTs in the realm of fashion has resonated, leaving the media crew buzzing with excitement as they look at the monitors. Their equipment flashes off the sleek glass-and-steel facade of the office building behind us, temporarily blinding me as I don sunglasses to look at the footage.

With the warmth, sun, and greenery, Delilah had shed her diva antics to enthusiastically share her vision for working with Riverbank. I glance around, my team's smiles bright, their excitement contagious, as we decide what to use for the social media posts. Oliver, ever the friendly and approachable figure, has set a comfortable tone throughout, his laughter competing with the distant waves crashing just beyond our view as he relaxes in a director's chair.

Is it the right moment to introduce my next big idea?

Yes, absolutely.

I take a leap and pitch my idea to Oliver—Riverbank attending the Met Gala. Sure, official sponsorship is off the table this late in the game, but I need to make him understand the significance of Riverbank attending fashion's most prestigious event. My plan? Secure Oliver's approval to approach Anna Wintour, *Vogue*'s legendary editor in chief and the supreme ruler of the Met Gala, to put him on the invitee list as my guest.

The idea is simple, yet powerful—Oliver, the well-known cofounder of Riverbank, and me, head of luxury brands, making an appearance together. It would be a bold declaration of the partnership between cryptocurrency and fashion.

I slide into the chair next to him and lay out the plan. He listens with operational calm, chin in hand. "That's . . . ambitious," he says at last, thumbs pressed together as if testing the edges of the idea. "You mean Anna Wintour herself?" His tone is teasing, but I catch a flicker of genuine admiration.

"I know it's late, but I can make it happen. I'm not saying Anna and I are best friends or anything, but we've worked together enough for me to make a solid intro. Her guest list is tightly curated—celebrities, power players, change makers. If this happens, it could open doors that Riverbank can't even knock on right now."

He gives a low whistle. "I don't think anyone in crypto has done it before—appearing at the Met Gala." A quick, impressed grin. "Disruptive in the right way."

A slow smile spreads across my face. "Exactly."

He tips his head, amused. "You do realize you never do small asks?"

"Why bother? Small asks don't move markets."

A laugh bursts from him, quick and genuine. "Dangerous."

"Effective," I say, crisp.

"All right," he says, rapping his knuckles once on the table. "Green light."

I can't stop the smile that breaks loose. I keep it personal, chin up. "Good call."

"Also," he adds, pointing at my name on the table document, "I'm calling you GL from now on. Gordon-Lennox does the heavy lifting. 'Charlie' sounds like Sunday brunch. 'GL' is the version who moves walls and sentiment."

"GL it is," I say. "As long as you don't make me regret getting you on the red carpet."

He smirks. "Deal. But if this blows up in my face—"

"You'll be too busy wishing you'd hired me sooner."

"Confidence. I like it. Just don't make me regret this."

"Noted."

You won't regret it, I want to blurt. *If anything, you'll regret underestimating me.* But I smile instead, unwilling to give away how much approval from these cofounders matters to me.

Oliver stands, and as I half rise too, he says, "Speaking of connections . . . Duane's dinner party tomorrow night? Are you coming?"

I glance down at my phone, praying for an interruption. "I don't think so, no," I say, keeping my voice light. "He hasn't asked me."

"Oh, he will," Oliver says confidently. "He told me he was going to. You should be there. Don't overthink it."

I hold his gaze as he moves away, wondering just how much he and Duane discuss me. He must sense my thoughts, because he chuckles and stops, his expression turning serious but still friendly. "Look, Duane and I are best friends. We talk about everything together. I know he can be arrogant, but he developed that as a form of protection. Come by."

My thoughts are racing as I try to focus on all he's said. And the weight of his recent investment in my project presses in on me. "I'll think about it."

"Don't duck out," he says with a wink, walking away and

leaving me in the bright green and yellow outdoor surroundings. I replay the conversation in my head.

Unbelievable. A dinner party? At Duane's? Anxiety washes over me as I think about what this means. Oliver just committed a massive sum to my project—I can't exactly say no, despite Duane's well-known distrust of me. At least with Duane busy playing host, he won't have time for his favorite pastime: grilling me.

Returning to my workspace, I find Duane waiting, sitting on the edge of my desk, his long legs stretched out, watching me with his relentless gaze, lingering, taking me in, piece by piece. His intense focus makes me falter. He stands as I approach, too tall, his broad shoulders casting a shadow over my space. I feel confined. We're so close I can see the fabric of his white button-down shirt stretch across his chest as he moves, and I catch the faint rustle of it—a whisper of friction.

"I'm having some people over for dinner tomorrow night," he says, his voice deep and measured, yet carrying an undertone that chafes my nerves like sandpaper. "I want you to come."

It's not a request. His eyes lock on mine, daring me to say no.

I swallow, my mouth parched. Damn, he's so in control, so self-assured, and yet there's a slight tension in his jaw as his lips press together. Thank God Oliver gave me a heads-up; otherwise, I might have crumbled right here, right now.

I hesitate, my thoughts scrambling for an excuse, conscious of how messy it could be to mix business with personal affairs. His gaze doesn't waver. I'm acutely aware of how there's a slight scent of bergamot in this space, how his presence makes it hard to focus on anything other than his body so close to mine. A palpable aura emanates from him; my heart's racing; my face feels flushed. *Oliver's also invited me, which makes it lean more toward professional than personal, right?*

With a deep breath, I nod, offering what I hope is an effortless smile. “Of course. I'd love to,” I say, willing my voice to stay steady. His eyes flick to my lips, and I fight the urge to lick them, feeling a warmth settle in my core.

“What can I bring?” I ask, eager to appear unaffected, knowing he doesn't need me to bring one bloody thing. I've got this. I straighten slightly and flash a friendly smile, casual and gracious—that's the goal. *Just casual and gracious.*

His lips twitch, and for a split second his gaze softens even as the electricity hums between us. “Just yourself,” he murmurs, his voice sending a cascade of pins and needles over my body, causing a momentary pause. Then, with slow, deliberate steps, he moves past me as the brief brush of his arm against mine accelerates my breathing. I exhale unsteadily once he's gone as I ungracefully collapse into my desk chair. *Damn him.*

Chapter Eight

. . . dangerous stuff

TOSSING THE WHITE JEANS ONTO THE ALREADY MOUNTAINous pile of blouses, cocktail dresses, strapless midi gowns, and even a silk pant suit sprawled across my bed, I finally pull out the off the shoulder periwinkle blue sundress. It's a favorite—timeless, soft against my skin, and the perfect shade to bring out the intensity of my blue eyes. But as I hold it up, my hands tremble slightly. *What am I doing? It's just a dinner. A simple dinner.*

I smooth the dress across my hips and catch my reflection in the mirror. The flush creeping into my cheeks is unmistakable. *Why is this so hard?* I've been to countless events—galas, red-carpet premieres, high stakes business dinners—and never thought twice about what to wear. My heart thuds in my chest, betraying my unease. *It's not just the dinner. It's him.*

When I finally arrive, Kurt, Duane's imposing security guard, meets me at the elevator door entrance to his apartment. He nods, with his usual polite but unreadable expression, and as I step inside, my breath catches.

The apartment is stunning. A wall of glass windows frames

a view of the ocean, as the soft glow from statement chandeliers casts gold reflections onto the polished marble floor. A faint scent of eucalyptus lingers in the air, mixed with something warmer—like oak and vanilla. Distant strains of my favorite jazzy Sheryl Crow song play softly in the background. Occasional clinks of glass and murmured voices drift in from the terrace.

As I glance around, the space feels achingly personal in a way I didn't expect. Sleek charcoal and cream furniture dominates the open concept living area, every piece arranged with precision. On one low glass table sits a chessboard mid-game, the pieces perfectly positioned as if waiting for someone to return. Nearby, I recognize some book titles lining a minimalist steel-gray bookshelf—*The Art of War, Dune, Digital Gold.* A single abstract painting in shades of yellow and red hangs above the fireplace, its bold streaks of color reminding me of its enigmatic owner. *Is it a De Kooning?*

It dawns on me why I'd been so worried about my outfit. This isn't the grand dinner party I'd envisioned, filled with familiar faces from work. Instead, it's an intimate gathering, small and cloaked in exclusivity. My instincts were right—Duane, ever the elusive figure, wouldn't host a large, chaotic shindig. This is curated, deliberate, his fingerprints in every detail.

My pulse quickens as I gingerly place the champagne on the smooth surface of the entry table. *Does this gift feel thoughtful or try-hard?* I shake off the doubt and step farther inside, the hum of voices growing louder. From my vantage point in the living room, I catch a glimpse of the other guests, maybe a dozen, in small groups on the terrace. Their laughter is inviting, and the vibe friendly. I take a deep breath and smooth my hair, quietly intoning my anchor phrase, "a little chaos"—my reminder that I can walk into the noise, stay grounded, and still run my own show.

"Hey, Charlotte." Duane's voice is low and warm, his greeting accompanied by a rare, breathtaking smile. It transforms his face, softening the sharpness of his features. My heart skips a beat as I realize how much more devastatingly attractive he is when he lets his guard down. His usual intensity is replaced by something far more disarming.

"Let me introduce you around," he says, his hand brushing lightly against the small of my back as he guides me toward the group. The heat from his fingers stays, even as he moves away.

"Thanks for having me," I manage, hoping my voice doesn't betray the flutter of nerves rising in my chest. Duane looks different here—relaxed, completely at ease in beige linen shorts and his signature crisp linen shirt, the sleeves rolled up to reveal tanned muscled forearms. He's barefoot now, a pair of Prada driving moccasins discarded by the terrace door. The sight of his bare feet somehow feels deeply intimate, like I've stepped into a part of his life few others get to see.

He introduces me to the other guests, as I piece together their connection to him. Old college friends, some colleagues from Riverbank, and I wonder if he has a girlfriend among the women present. There's Deb, a leading programmer; Chad from finance; and Joe from PR, whose face I recognize. Oliver is here, too, leaning casually against the railing, his girlfriend Tessa by his side looking at me with a mix of disapproval and unease.

The small group is close-knit, their conversation peppered with shared memories and inside jokes. Yet there's something unspoken in the air, a tension that seems to orbit around Duane, as though the others are acutely aware of the mystery that clings to him, part of his shadow.

"Charlotte, so glad you're here," Oliver says warmly, his tone genuine, though Tessa offers only a perfunctory smile. I return it with polite detachment, drawing on years of practiced charm to hide my discomfort. Her hostility doesn't faze me—it's the kind of reaction I've learned to expect. My tactic is always to maintain a pleasant demeanor, but not overly friendly—a hard-learned lesson from my early career days when I had tried to make every woman like me. Women like Tessa always seem to view me as a threat, and I can never quite figure out whether it's envy or distrust.

Duane returns with two large glasses of rum punch, one of which he hands to me. His fingers graze mine as I take the glass, and I feel a spark of electricity sear my arm. His gaze jumps to mine as if he felt it, too. "Dangerous stuff," he murmurs in a husky voice as if he isn't talking about the drink at all.

I tilt the glass to my lips, catching the tang of fresh lime and sweet tropical rum on my tongue, but sip carefully, knowing its strength. The heat of the alcohol settles and loosens my nerves. The scent of salt water drifts up from the ocean, mixing with the faint aroma of grilled seafood wafting from the kitchen. The party is intimate but vibrant, laughter spilling across the space with the sunlight as we settle onto the white-cushioned couches on the terrace.

Inevitably, the conversation shifts to cryptocurrency.

"Oliver, when are you scheduled to testify before Congress?" Deb, from programming, asks.

"Testify? Regarding what?" someone asks.

"There's a congressional committee meeting to discuss the regulation of the cryptocurrency industry, and Riverbank has been asked to present its perspectives," Deb explains.

"But do you want regulation?" I ask, with a perplexed glance around the group. "I was under the impression that cryptocurrency enthusiasts preferred it unregulated, free from government interference."

"Not exactly," Duane says, stepping in to clarify. "True, the backbone of bitcoin is the blockchain, which excludes government or banks from monetary transactions, unlike traditional financial systems. However, for cryptocurrency to go mainstream and be accepted in the US, we have to cooperate with the government for regulation. We're looking for guidelines that safeguard investors without impinging on the decentralized foundation of cryptocurrency."

Chad, who has known Oliver and Duane since their teens, is sharing amusing tales from their boarding school days. Stories of Oliver's lackluster sporting skills, Chad's notorious record of girls in his room, and Duane's initial arrogance when he arrived as a junior.

Sensing something's not quite right, I turn my attention to the conversation. "I mean, seriously," Chad continues, "Duane was so haughty the first three months after he arrived, if you'd called his name, he wouldn't bother to respond. It was infuriating." I notice Duane and Oliver exchange an uneasy glance.

Duane's conceit wasn't a surprising revelation, maybe a bit excessive in that setting. Why would they exchange looks over that, I wonder? And why are there always questions surrounding Duane? Whether he's asking them, or they're being asked about him?

"Yeah, and who was that mysterious 'uncle' who would randomly appear at your rowing meets but was notably absent at parents' weekends?" Chad asks. "You know, that guy with the British accent, always dressed in a blazer and tie."

Duane's laugh smooths away any troubling undertones. "He's just my uncle. A distant uncle."

"Distant? I'll say. We never even knew his name."

I watch the group from the sidelines, my eyes drifting to Duane again and again. He looks different here: more open, less sharp edged. The rum punch has worked its way through all of us, and everyone is tipsy. The friendly banter flows.

"Hey, Duane," Oliver calls out, gesturing with his glass. "We've rented a villa on St. Bart's in February. You should join us."

"I've never been, but it's supposed to be phenomenal," Tessa chimes in. "The weather, the beaches, the clubs . . ."

The group starts to buzz with enthusiasm about the French Caribbean playground. I glance at Duane, catching a flicker of a smile—relaxed, disarming, in a way that makes me wary.

"What about you, Charlotte?" he asks, his tone deceptively casual. "Ever been to St. Bart's?"

Taking a sip of my drink, I absentmindedly consider his question. "It's a fabulous place," I reply. The next words slip out on their own. "I had my wedding there."

Chapter Nine

. . . not now, not like this

ONE LINE. PIN PULLED. IT'S AS IF I'VE THROWN A GRENADE into the middle of the group. My stomach drops. *Damn it, Charlotte, this is why you don't mix personal and professional. This is why socializing with coworkers is off-limits.* The friendly atmosphere, the rum punch, and the small gathering have slowly dissolved my guard.

"Wait," Tessa says breathlessly, breaking the silence. "Charlotte, you're married?" Her voice carries a mixture of surprise and disbelief.

"Not anymore. That was . . . a lifetime ago," I say, the words rushed and brittle. My fingers tighten around my glass, and I force a laugh, hoping to lighten the tension. It doesn't work.

When I glance up, Duane is staring at me. His eyes burn with something unreadable—searching, maybe, but not his usual anger. I feel the blush creeping up my neck.

Chad glances between Duane and me. "You two are quite a pair with your cryptic pasts and secrets."

Duane looks at Chad intently, and then leans back in his chair, relaxing, a slow boyish smile spreading across his face.

"Secrets? I don't have any secrets. I'm just a nerd chained to my computer."

His handsome gaze slides back to me suggestively, deliberate. "What about you, Charlotte? Any more secrets you'd like to share?"

Sensing his attempt to downplay Chad's comments, I join him in claiming innocence. "No secrets here. Just a working girl trying to make my way in the world."

The group laughs as Chad stands up, saying he needs another drink. Duane turns in his chair as he studies me. His grin deepens, his expression both amused and intrigued. "That's not what I'd call you, but okay."

I lift my glass toward him in mock acknowledgment, a small smile tugging at my lips. "Did you just step in to rescue me, Mr. Blacklock? Or was keeping the prying questions away more for yourself?"

Ignoring my comment, he asks, "So, Ms. Gordon-Lennox, the perfect wedding in paradise and it didn't stick? You didn't tell me you were married."

There he is, Mr. Shadows and Edges, interrogating me as he hides on the side.

"I didn't realize I owed you a full biography," I shoot back, keeping my tone light but my defenses sharp.

He chuckles, low and deep. "Fair enough, but don't think I missed the part where you called St. Bart's 'fabulous.' Sounds like a pretty luxe heartbreak."

His comment makes me flinch, but I recover quickly. "Not everyone has the luxury of being a mystery wrapped in shadows, Duane. Some of us actually have to live our lives."

For a moment his expression shifts—something raw and vulnerable flashes in his eyes. But just as quickly, he smirks, the mask slipping back into place. "Touché, Charlotte."

The group's chatter picks up again, and I'm pulled into a conversation with Tessa, who pumps me for information about my wedding. I carefully change the conversation with pleasantries. But I can still feel Duane's presence at my side. It isn't just his aloofness and how he lives on the edges. Questions and mystery swirl around Duane and his life, a constant fog that never burns off. Why haven't I noticed this before?

Feeling more relaxed, I stay on the terrace with a few others, helping to clear away dishes and food before we move on to dinner. From inside, boisterous voices echo, growing louder and more animated in sync with the escalating consumption of rum and now whiskey. The party is in full swing.

Just as the noise seems to reach its peak, a thundercloud suddenly looms overhead, catching everyone off guard. Within seconds, a torrential downpour drenches everything and everyone on the terrace. Stunned and laughing, everyone scatters in all directions, shielding themselves with empty plates or towels. Soaked and breathless, guests cheer as most remember they have a stash of beach clothes to change into from earlier.

Water runs in rivulets down my face and neck, soaking through my sundress and turning the fabric sheer. The rain feels cool against my skin, a sharp contrast to the warm tropical evening. My hair clings to my face as the breeze picks up, carrying with it the salty tang of the ocean, and I shiver.

Hearing the commotion, Duane steps outside, his bare feet splashing gently against the wet tiles. He laughs as he surveys the drenched scene. When his eyes land on me, they soften with a flicker of something I can't quite name. Without a word, he reaches out and brushes wet strands of hair from my cheek, his fingertips warm against the cool droplets on my skin. I resist the urge to turn my face into his touch.

"You're soaked," he says, his voice quieter now, tinged with something deeper. Something carnal. His gaze lingers, tracing the curve of my collarbone where the water glides down. I can feel the heat of his eyes as his gaze slips down to my breasts, the firm nipples poking through the wet fabric, even as I shiver under his scrutiny.

I manage a helpless laugh, gesturing to my dress, now clinging to my body in ways that feel far too revealing. "I'm afraid even as Miss Gordon Little Fuss I can't stay here like this," I admit, my cheeks flushing as I glance down at the fabric sticking to the delicate lace of my lingerie.

Duane's lips curve into a faint smile, his gaze not leaving mine. "I think you look perfect. But come with me," he says, his tone leaving no room for argument. He gestures for me to follow as he steps inside.

The hallway leading to other rooms is dimly lit, the muted glow from the terrace casting long shadows across the walls. Walking carefully, I trail behind, my damp footsteps slippery on the polished marble floors. When Duane opens the door to his bedroom, embarrassment heats my core. As we stand in the doorway, I realize he's fully dressed while I'm essentially naked. I feel vulnerable, exposed, and inexplicably I move to shut the door.

He grips the side of the door, not letting it move. "Relax, Charlotte." His voice is low, commanding. My thighs tighten at his tone, and he keeps my gaze as if he wants me to understand all his instructions.

"This is my room. I want you to change in here. Look in the second drawer for one of my T-shirts. I'll be back with some shorts."

He pulls the door shut, and I turn to examine his room. The space is surprisingly understated. The king-size bed is dressed in, yes, crisp, white linens, the kind that look impossibly soft, while a low bookshelf holds a collection of novels, some with titles in a language I don't recognize. There are built-in drawers against one wall, while two glass walls with sliding doors lead out to a terrace. Sheer curtains billow gently in the rain-tinged breeze.

I move to pull open the drawers. As I rifle through neat stacks of mostly white T-shirts, a vibrant orange color peeks out from beneath. Curious, I lift it out.

It's my scarf.

The scarf from that first night when Duane drove me back to the condo in his convertible. My scarf has been here, with him, all this time.

Relief surges through me at the sight of it—a piece of my mother I thought gone forever has suddenly returned. But the relief is tangled with disorientation. He knew this was mine. He must have. Why keep it? Why hide it in his drawer, close to his bed, folded among his own things?

Heat prickles my skin, my pulse erratic. Does it mean he thinks of me when he sees it? That he wanted to keep some part of me close? The idea sends a shiver spiraling through me, wonder mixed with fear.

But then the anger comes, sharp and hot. How dare he? To keep this without a word, without returning it. To claim it in silence as though he has a right to me.

I sit on the edge of the bed, the heavy silk lying across my lap. The fabric is soft and familiar, but my thoughts twist and tangle. This is dangerous. If he feels something for me, if this is a sign, everything becomes complicated. This job is my lifeline, my stability. It's the one chance to climb out of the wreckage of vast debt, to stand on solid ground again.

He's younger. He's a playboy billionaire who doesn't want what I want. Marriage. Children. A real life tethered to something lasting. He's probably infatuated, thrilled by the idea of a chase, addicted to winning what he shouldn't want. And me? God help me, I can feel the pull, the fire in my chest at the thought of being wanted by him.

I want to storm out there, hold the scarf up, demand an explanation—a way to gauge my next move—but the thought knots my stomach. I feel slightly drunk. If I confront him, if I give this meaning, I can't pretend anymore.

With trembling hands, I bury the scarf beneath his T-shirts, as though burying my own turmoil with it. I reach for one of the shirts, slip it over my head, and whisper to myself, *Not now. Not like this. Not ever.*

His knock on the door startles me. I crack the door just enough for him to pass me a pair of shorts. Giving a quick thank-you, I immediately shut the door even as he tells me dinner is ready. I have the clothes I need, but embarrassment lingers. This time from finding my scarf.

The shorts are Versace, likely left behind by a model girlfriend, but what matters more is that they fit.

Chapter Ten

. . . that's how I end up in trouble

AS I STEP INTO THE DINING ROOM, CHAD CALLS OUT, "Charlotte, you're lucky he only dates models, otherwise you'd spend the night trying to make his shorts fit."

The amusing mental image, combined with the alcohol, makes everyone erupt into laughter, and I join in, though my mind is still partly occupied with the scarf.

We all gather at the dinner table to eat crunchy gazpacho soup followed by fresh fish and vegetables. The servers move effortlessly around us, refilling wine glasses, gliding in and out of the candlelight. Conversation loosens as the courses arrive—stories, jokes, little bursts of laughter rise and fall as the outside sky deepens from blue to ink. By the time the last bites of fish are gone, the table has that satisfied hush of people who've eaten well and are reluctant to move.

Dessert appears—warm brownies, melting scoops of ice cream—a few people linger over coffee and chocolate. Eventually the caterers slip out with their last trays, leaving everything quieter, more intimate. I notice a cluster of empty dishes near my elbow and gather them up to take to the kitchen, calculating how much longer I should stay.

I'm surprised to find Duane at the kitchen island as I enter. I walk away from him to the sink, and before either of us says anything, Oliver strides in. He's animated, his voice friendly, jovial. "Hey, Cel, we're heading out, but what a fantastic party!"

He has clearly had too much to drink, but something else catches my attention. Cel? Is that a nickname for Duane? They shake hands as Duane joins in the laughter, clearly recognizing Oliver's intoxicated state.

"Well, hell-lo, Charlotte," Oliver says, his voice brimming with delight as he notices me at the sink. "Has he told you yet?"

"Told me what?" I echo, looking from Oliver to Duane, curiosity piqued.

"How he has the biggest crush on you," Oliver blurts out.

"Okay, Ol, time for you to go," Duane quickly intervenes, steering Oliver out of the kitchen.

My face flushes a deep shade of pink. *Is that why he's kept my scarf?* Exhilaration fills me. I take a deep breath to calm my racing heart and inhale the lingering freshly baked brownie scent. A tingle runs down my spine, and my whole body feels on fire.

But I quickly reel myself in. No, this cannot happen. This job is too critical to risk complications from a personal relationship. My mind is screaming warnings by now—he's too young, too arrogant, too dangerous to my carefully constructed plans.

I turn to the sink, placing the last of the dishes inside. I should leave. I begin to look around for my belongings, desperation and confusion slowing my moves. I can't think straight. I have to get out of here.

But before I can take a step, I feel him—his presence commanding, inescapable, as he leans against the doorway, jaw sharp as a blade, brown eyes melding into obsidian. I feel my pulse fluttering wildly in my throat.

"Let me explain," he murmurs. His voice is a husky thread that wraps around my senses.

"No need," I say, shaking my head, keeping my gaze fixed on the floor, trying to be as still as possible. I don't dare look at him. "Oliver was drunk. He didn't mean it."

"What he said is true." His words brush my skin. I feel goose bumps rise along my shoulder.

My gaze jumps to his. The charged silence stretches between us. He's staring at me with that unrelenting intensity that always makes me feel like prey trapped in some wild animal's den. My lips part, but no words come out. I should walk away, but I don't.

His usual fierce aura has transformed into something magnetic, electrifying the air until it feels like I could spontaneously combust.

He doesn't lunge, he doesn't rush. Instead, he moves in slow, deliberate inches, as if daring me to stop him. And I should. I really should.

"I thought you were seeing someone," I whisper, the question barely escaping.

"I'm not."

"I thought you had a girlfriend." My voice is unsteady.

"I don't."

"I thought you liked models."

"I do. But I like you more."

With those words, he's in front of me, his eyes locked on mine, physically dominating the surrounding space.

"Any more questions, Charlotte?" he coolly challenges as his hands move to rest on the counter on either side of me, hemming me in against the sink.

In one sweeping move, he crushes his lips to mine, gripping my shoulders and pulling me close. The force of it steals my breath, my fingers grip the counter to keep from sinking into him completely. His hands slide to my waist, holding me in place, his touch firm and unyielding.

Without thinking, I rise up onto my toes and raise my face to meet his, our bodies lining up, long against long. His mouth is hot, tasting of whiskey and heat—a slow burn that floods my senses. His scent—bergamot and clean skin—wraps around me, dizzying, until the room falls away. He parts my lips, his tongue sweeping into my mouth, and I respond without thinking, my arms winding around his neck, fingers diving into his thick hair, anchoring myself to him as if I could stay in this kiss forever.

Warmth spreads from my lips, trailing all the way down to my core. It's been so long since I'd felt this type of exhilaration, this sense of unadulterated pleasure. A quiet moan escapes me, and it's like a switch flips. His grip tightens, his body pressing against mine with unmistakable intent.

But just as quickly, a nagging realization breaks through the haze. I should not be enjoying this. *I cannot be enjoying this.* I push lightly against his chest, breaking the kiss, even as he struggles to hold me closer, our breaths ragged, our lips swollen.

"Duane," I whisper, my fingers still fisted in his shirt.

Our eyes meet as he eases his hands from my arms but doesn't step back, the silence between us heavy.

"I . . . I don't know what to say."

His throat works. "So you don't want this?" The question comes out low and rough, his hands curling into fists at his side, as if he's restraining himself from hauling me in again.

"You know this is a terrible idea for so many reasons."

He lowers his forehead to mine, his breath warm against my mouth. "Tell me you don't feel this," he murmurs.

I don't answer. I can't.

Instead, I continue, my voice almost pleading.

"I work for you. My entire future hinges on my position at Riverbank. There's the no-relationship HR policy. This complicates everything." I try to keep my voice steady, even as my heart pounds in my chest. I can feel my body trembling.

He exhales, a faint rueful sound. "I knew things could get complicated. I wanted you the first week. I fought it. I accused you of trying to seduce me—because it was easier to make you the problem than admit I couldn't stop thinking about you. I was antagonistic because I was losing, Charlotte. To you. As for that 'no fraternizing' rule? It doesn't exist. We have disclosure and governance, not puritanical vows. I wrote the handbook. If it needs a new page, I can author it in an hour."

I blink. "You're saying policies bend for you?"

"I'm saying I set the policies." His tone is edged, unapologetic. "You wouldn't report to me. We disclose to legal, shift your report to Oliver, and let HR choreograph the optics. I will not let a line in a manual decide my life. Or yours."

He straightens to his full height, and the room shrinks around the shape of him. It should feel like pressure, but it feels like shelter. That's the danger.

"Sometimes, you have to give things a chance based on how you feel, not just according to some premeditated plan," he says, his eyes softer now, steady on mine.

My vulnerability sets in. At thirty-seven, I have to make the right choices for my life. This is my reality.

"Actually, that's how I end up in trouble," I say, untangling myself from his embrace and taking a step back.

Undeterred, he bridges the gap once again. "I want to kiss you again, but not until you want me to. Tell me you don't feel it when I'm near you? I've felt it since the day you walked into our office and everyone turned to look at you. It's not going to go away."

Damn it, how did he know what I was feeling? We stand in silence, studying each other.

I let out a soft sigh. In the end, it's always the same feelings, the same doubts. Nothing is guaranteed. People disappoint you. How can I rely on him? How can I trust him?

Moving around him, I gather up my things and go to the foyer elevator. He follows me as I press the button.

"So, Duane, I'll say good night, and we'll pretend this never happened," I say firmly. My body is flushed and trembling. Even now there's an energy pulling me back to him.

He leans down and brushes his lips lightly against my cheek. I step into the elevator, watching the door close as he says, "This is not the end, Charlotte."

Chapter Eleven

. . . was she into cryptocurrency

DUANE: *Hey Charlotte, I have something of yours you left at the party.*

His text pops up on my phone the next morning.

ME: *Oh, hey Duane. Is it orange and underneath a pile of white T-shirts in your drawer?*

DUANE: *No, Charlotte, that's finders keepers, losers weepers.*

ME: *Duane, it's more you should "tell the truth and shame the devil."*

DUANE: *No, Charlie, it's definitely "What's mine is mine, and what's yours is negotiable."*

ME: *D, the only definite thing is you're using my nickname.*

DUANE: *Charlotte is prettier.*

ME: *Thanks. My mother loved Jane Eyre.*

DUANE: *My mother loved . . .*

Three dots, then . . .

DUANE: *. . . cryptography.*

Cryptography? His mother was into codes and math equations?

ME: *Cool, so it runs in the family. Was she into cryptocurrency, too?*

Silence, then . . .

DUANE: *I have your dress and will return it after my housekeeper has it cleaned. D.*

A wave of confusion washes over me as I toss my phone aside. Did I make it too personal in asking about his mother? We had been bantering playfully, and then, crash, he goes radio silent. Just a typical exit from Mr. Shadows and Edges.

While I'm lacing up my sneakers for a run, my phone rings. I see with a little disappointment it's not him. It's Vivian.

"Hey, superstar," she greets me.

I laugh. "Sounds like good news if you're calling me that!"

"It's great news. Your last round of trading and your regular deposits have put you on track to clear your debt by the end of the year. Keep it up."

A lightness bubbles up within me. "I can live with that

time frame. This job has literally saved me financially. I'm finally sleeping at night for the first time in months."

"So, how's it going?"

"That's what's so great. I'm really good at this, and I've hit all my project goals so far. The next big event is the Met Gala, and then I start working on the Riverbank cryptocurrency conference. I have a great team, and I love the weather down here. You have to come visit me when you're back from pitching your business in London."

"You're still dealing with loafer guy?" she asks, making me wince.

Vivian, with her mad internet sleuthing skills, had dug up everything she could on Duane for the novel. His past seems nonexistent.

"You were a lifesaver, Viv, finding information to help me fictionalize Duane and lampoon tech culture for the book. But honestly, he's not all bad when you get to know him," I say.

"And yet I remember how he treated you. It's even on YouTube as part of the conference uploads. There forever, for everyone to see."

We end up chatting about everything and nothing—Viv's blockchain company, her upcoming trip to London to raise more capital. She's delighted with the business outfits we pulled for the trip. I fill her in on the fertility preservation procedure I've scheduled, keeping the details simple. "Mornings at the clinic, a quick shot at night. I'm a little puffy, a little moody, but fine. One day at a time."

"Hey," Viv says, my shieldmaiden, warm and steady. "You're doing the brave, boring parts of taking care of your future. I'm proud of you."

I swallow. "Thanks. It isn't the answer, just a hedge, but I need to hear that.

"Last thing," I add. "Can you do a deeper scrape on Duane?

Photos, obscure mentions, school newsletters, early yearbooks. And . . ."

"And before sixteen, there's still nothing," she finishes for me. "It's like he appears at boarding school fully formed. Bizarre," she says, confirming the sinister feeling of mystery that surrounds him.

Chapter Twelve

. . . loafer guy

MY ASSISTANT WAITS AT MY DESK BRIGHT AND EARLY ON Monday morning. Everyone notices Jeannie with her violet streaked blonde hair, a gauzy peasant blouse, vintage jeans, a macramé belt, and a hush of clinking bangles. It's a lovingly thrifted, retro-hippie look—decidedly not designer—but every choice is deliberate. In her interview, she coolly diagnosed my blind spots and sketched a fix before I'd finished my coffee. Beneath the boho layers is a whip-smart, savvy operator who gets things done.

"These just came for you," she says, gesturing toward a large bouquet of lilies of the valley. The delicate scent quickly envelops the surrounding air. "No note, hand delivered. They must've opened the flower shop at the crack of dawn and harvested a whole field of those little white bells to create a bunch this big."

I know immediately where they came from, but the question that puzzles me is . . . *how did he know?*

"And," Jeannie continues, "I heard through the grapevine that it was Duane who arranged his private jet to pick up Delilah's stylist and photographer when the Riverbank jet wasn't available."

"Jeannie, you're truly fabulous. You help me so much," I confess, with heartfelt sincerity, suspending my surprise until I can grasp what the hell all this means.

At that, Jeannie straightens up and replies, "Just let me know if you need any more lowdown."

It's as if Duane is slowly taking over my world. Do I want that? No, I need to stay committed to my plan: pay off my debt, regain my emotional stability, find a reliable, successful older man with whom to start a family. I always thought I'd meet the right man, marry, and let the rest unfold. I did not picture myself building a safety net I wish I didn't need. It hurts—this admission that timing is not on my side—but choosing a hedge isn't a surrender. It's love pointed forward. And yet, it's maddening to be at the mercy of a clock I can't see. I've carried myself through worse. I'll do what I have to do, pay what I have to pay, and give my future the runway it deserves. And in the middle of it all are Duane's thoughtful gestures—the jet, and now the flowers.

I search for Duane in the office midmorning, intent on thanking him, but to no avail. He isn't due back until later. By two p.m., I spot him entering a conference room with a group of people and jump to intercept him when he exits.

"Can we speak in private?" I ask.

"Hello, Charlotte." His slow smile makes me smile, too. "I'm afraid I've got back-to-back meetings. I have another one starting in just a few minutes. But if it's privacy you want, I could pick you up for dinner tonight at eight?"

"Impressive resourcefulness," I respond and relent. "Then eight it is."

"And Charlotte, I'll have the top down, so don't forget to bring a scarf."

"What about you? Have you ever been married?"

We're sitting at a secluded outdoor café having dinner. Not the place I'd intended to be so soon after Saturday, yet I feel relaxed, enjoying his intense, coiled, masculine presence next to me.

He'd asked me what it's like to be married, but I deflected the conversation back to him.

Laughing, Duane confesses, "Me? No, but I want to marry and have kids someday."

He swirls his whiskey glass, looking somewhat embarrassed. "I can't believe I just shared that with a woman. Most of the women I've dated wanted nothing more than to marry a rich man, preferably a billionaire, and have kids. But the conversation was off-limits precisely because I knew that's what they wanted."

"Perhaps that's not what they wanted at all," I counter. "Maybe they aspired to be a business partner or your muse, but you never knew because the conversation was off-limits."

"My muse?" Duane looks at me with a twinkle in his eyes. "Do you want to be my muse, Charlotte?"

Damn, those eyes can be so dreamy when he teases.

With cool detachment, I say, "Absolutely. Who wouldn't want to be your muse, Duane?"

As I lean in across the table, my voice drops to a more sincere tone. "You're smart, talented, gifted, really—incredibly competent, and powerful. I even sense traces of kindness and compassion lurking somewhere beneath that confident exterior," I add, lightening the mood.

His triumphant smile is the perfect response. "That's why we should be together. You get me."

I straighten, careful to maintain my poise. "Let's not forget, we're together tonight because this was the only way you'd agree to meet, so I could thank you. For sending your private jet to help me with Delilah and for the bouquet of lilies of the valley. They're my favorite flower."

"I know," he replies. "I overheard your conversation about flowers with Delilah after her interview. You forgot to mention 'eavesdropping' in my list of talents."

This is so fun, so easy, but somewhere inside I know I have to make my position clear. I'm conscious of the growing fondness I have for him. His kiss on Saturday has lingered too much on my mind. I had felt his excitement when he kissed me, but he was so in control at the same time. He had been the one in charge, and it had been utterly seductive. His physical presence is intoxicating, enveloping me, even as we sit here, engaged in casual conversation. All the more reason to draw the line now.

"Listen, Duane," I begin, striving for honesty. "I really like you, and because of that, I need to be straightforward. I'm saying this without any hubris, but I've been in this situation countless times before. It's the thrill of the chase and the eventual rejection that seem to draw you to me. You're fascinated by who you think I am, but it's not really me."

"So, the real you is hidden somewhere?" he asks calmly, in a mocking tone.

I flush, realizing how silly I sound. "No, it's not like that. What I mean is, every time I've let myself be drawn into a relationship with someone who's infatuated with me, it's proved to be fleeting." *Ephemeral, but still long enough for betrayal and hurt,* I think, but don't say.

"Charlotte, I don't routinely have crushes or become infatuated. Yes, I've dated a lot of beautiful women, but those relationships didn't go anywhere because I didn't want them to. This is different. There's something here, at least for me, and I think we should give it a chance."

I ignore his last comment, changing subjects and grabbing the muse idea. "You know, I think I could be a fantastic muse. In that role, I could inspire you to consider testifying before Congress alongside Oliver."

He studies me silently as I continue, seizing momentum. "At your dinner, you spoke with such vision and passion about the need for regulation. You understand the intricacies that could shape credible laws without infringing on the liberties that cryptocurrencies represent." I speak rapidly, not allowing him to object. "With both of you testifying, you could make a stronger case for legislation that favors cryptocurrency. That's the goal, isn't it?"

Duane leans back, a sly smile playing on his lips, his eyes narrowing slightly as if he were savoring the taste of every word I just said. "Ah, so that's what being my muse means to you. Making a crusader out of me, dragging me before Congress. Is that how you'd inspire me, Charlotte? To turn me into a public figure, a way to make me vulnerable by putting me under scrutiny?" He pauses, letting the silence stretch just long enough to create tension.

"Why not? You're a cofounder of this wildly successful cryptocurrency platform. You understand this world inside and out, and I'm sure Oliver would appreciate your support. It must be hard for him to be the face of Riverbank all the time. I bet he's already asked you to step up. This is your vision, too, and perhaps it's time you assumed your rightful place at the head of the company."

"Or maybe this is your play to see how far I'd go for you."

His words hang in the air, a subtle challenge. I tilt my head, refusing to let his enigmatic demeanor derail me.

"Well, if I'm to be your muse, Duane, then I would expect you to let me do more than just inspire you on your terms. Real muses challenge. They push. They stir something raw and uncomfortable in the person they're inspiring. I wouldn't be content just standing by, smiling while you play it safe."

Now he's looking at me, his eyes piercing me with lightning bolts. I remember the look from the interview when I talked about Satoshi Nakamoto. "You think I play it safe?"

"Yes," I say, not backing down. "You're always putting up this armor, deflecting with arrogance and mystery. You're smart, and very good at hiding behind that sharp tongue of yours, but a muse can't work with that. You want me to be your muse? Then you have to give me something real beyond this witty sparring and these half-truths."

For a moment, silence hangs between us, thick with unspoken words. Duane's eyes flicker with something I can't quite place—is it amusement or something deeper, more intimidating?

"You're asking a lot, Charlotte. Letting people know you can be . . . complicated. It doesn't always work the way you think it does. Sometimes it's less about breaking down and more about choosing which parts of yourself to reveal."

"So which parts of yourself are you revealing to me now?" I ask, my tone softening, intrigued by the shadows of mystery he's casting.

He looks me over for a long moment with his slow smile before answering. "Maybe the part that's intrigued enough to take a risk. Or maybe the part that enjoys this dance we're doing—the push, the pull. Or maybe"—his voice drops—"the part that wants to make you realize that I'm not just chasing for the thrill of rejection."

My core clutches as I gasp. I feel confused, as if I've stumbled and lost my balance. Oh, hell. He's staking a claim. For me.

He capitalizes on the silence caused by my growing anxiety to take control of the conversation. "Charlotte, I can't recall any other woman encouraging me to do something like this. Encourage me for a shopping spree in Paris, sure, but to testify before Congress? No."

I seize his words, relieved to be back on solid, boring ground. "Does that mean you'll consider it? I can assist you in your presentation to Congress. I know Riverbank has public relations consultants for that, but I could provide some feedback. I have experience being on . . ." My voice falters, then I quickly recover to finish, "Speaking in public."

The earth shifts under me once again as I remember that, yes, I have public speaking experience. The infamous panel. Back when he didn't know me, he'd managed to kill me silently with humiliation in front of a professional audience.

The feelings flood back. Desperation, humiliation, brokenness—endless brokenness—and finally anger.

A few months after horrendous life events had caused me to crash out, I was struggling. Struggling to come to terms with all that had happened, losing Matthew and something even more precious. I hadn't been sleeping. I cut my hair short and let myself go, my daily makeup and carefully selected outfits abandoned, too difficult to continue.

But despite it all, I was slated to appear on a technology panel at a major cryptocurrency conference. Bolstered by Viv and Danny—pushed, really—I'd managed to get out of bed the last few days before the conference and focus on something for the first time in a while.

That day as I dragged myself onto the stage, I realized I was the only woman, as usual, with four young, aggressive-looking Mark Zuckerberg wannabes in hoodies and sneakers. Well, one of them had on slacks and a dress shirt and loafers—Gucci, I thought. Then during the discussion, loafer guy launched into a dissection of why there were so few women in tech.

I shouldn't have been there. But I had invested heavily in developing a sophisticated mobile app that made my business wildly successful, and the sponsors felt this qualified me as a "tech person."

Loafer guy then turned to me, asking me to explain how my app worked: Was it C++, HTML5, or Java? Did the developers use ReactNative, or had they experimented with Flutter, a new trending cross-platform technology? With my exhaustion, my emptiness, I was a panicked face before a firing squad.

I had no answers. But loafer guy had a lot of technical, throat slitting questions that would not end.

As he threw question after question like flaming arrows from his quiver at me, I sat there, unable to defend myself, weary, distraught, looking like shit, and totally ambushed. Finally, as the flames died down, and I finished burning at the stake, the moderator stepped in to shift the questioning.

That night, I returned home seething with a fury that, for the first time since my life fell apart, sparked a will to fight back. I channeled my rage into writing a wickedly witty novel about a woman's experience in the start-up world, featuring a thinly veiled Duane as the villain. Six months later, my biting depiction of a fiendish tech genius was signed as a book deal.

Jolted back to the present, I realize Duane's responding to my suggestion about testifying before Congress.

"Where have you been?" he asks quizzically, noticing my distracted look, and then says, "Yes, I'll consider it."

Chapter Thirteen

. . . he always loves a winner

OLD KING COLE GREETS ME FROM HIS GOLDEN THRONE BEhind the bar of the St. Regis hotel in Midtown Manhattan. I'd taken a flight in for an important meeting scheduled for the following day and had managed to get Danny and Dad together for drinks. I allow myself a pause, soaking in the warm glow of the Maxfield Parrish panel behind the bar before I see Danny already seated in one of the plush banquettes.

He looks in a hurry and quickly jumps up to embrace me, announcing, "If Dad keeps us waiting as usual, I'm going to bolt. Kate's had a shit day with the kids and needs me at home."

I respond in a soothing tone, "That's not a problem. I understand your family needs you. If you want, you can leave now, and I'll explain the situation to Dad."

He settles back into his seat, gesturing to a waiter. "I'll give him a few minutes. How do you manage it, Carlie? You've always been the peacemaker, ensuring everyone feels heard and stays calm."

"Well, I don't exactly feel calm," I admit, my own nerves

showing through. "Seeing Dad always makes me a little tense, too. But he's our father, so we have to at least try."

Danny brings up old, unhealed wounds. "Even after he essentially left us high and dry during our childhood? When he used his midlife crisis as an excuse to chase after a bunch of young girls?"

"I know they were young, Danny, but they weren't teenagers. Dad isn't some kind of creep."

"Really? And what about his refusing to fund our education? Or provide us with a home after Mom passed away? Or visit you in the hospital in Paris, and then again when—"

"The man has issues," I interrupt before he can dig up something even more painful. "I'm probably more aware of that than anyone else. But let's talk about you for a bit. You look fit. Have you been running? How do you find the time?"

He seems relieved at the change in subject. "That's the beauty of a good marriage. Kate understands how stress can pile up at the hospital and even at home. She ensures I get time to run at least five days a week."

I smile. "Danny, you've got yourself a gem. Mom would have adored her."

Just as I place my order with the waiter, our father arrives.

He stops before greeting us, focusing solely on the waiter, and requests his drink in a curt tone. "I'll have a dry martini, olive, no twist, and make sure it's very chilled."

My father, Julian Gordon-Lennox, still has the classically handsome features that seem to draw everyone's attention, even in his early sixties. As a child, I remember watching women instinctively lift their hands to their hair, wanting to appear as appealing as possible whenever he graced a room with his presence. He knows the effect he has and exploits it. In my eyes, this is one of the reasons he never really grew up. Because he never needed to.

"Good to see you two," he says, shaking hands with Danny

and giving me a cool kiss on the cheek as he slides in to sit next to me. "You've really knocked it out of the park with your new job, Charlotte. Cryptocurrency is beyond my comprehension, but my partners understand it, and they say you're doing extraordinarily well."

His words hang in the air, reminding me my father always loves a winner, but not so much if you're down on your luck or struggling. With a deep breath, I prepare to navigate the rest of the evening.

"That's because Charlotte does know crypto. She knows it very well, and she's legendary in fashion," Danny declares, his voice edged with unnecessary force. I grab his hand under the table and gently squeeze.

"Okay, okay, you don't need to convince me," my dad says. "So how much are they paying you?"

"Dad, please," I plead just as Danny erupts with, "That's none of your business."

We all fall into an uncomfortable silence, broken only by the arrival of our drinks. I try to divert the conversation to a more positive topic. "Dad, Danny's going to be featured in *New York's Top Doctors* next month."

"Well, congratulations! I'm so proud of you, Dan," he exclaims, looking at his son with evident pride. "Didn't I always tell you that you should become a doctor? I recognized your potential from the start."

Danny and I exchange glances but remain silent. It was actually our mother who had first recognized his passion for understanding how things worked, how he liked to put things together, and his compassion for people. She had been the one to guide him toward medicine.

"Dan, could you make sure to get a dozen copies of the magazine for me to give to my friends?"

As we're talking, a female voice cuts through. "Well, there you are, Julian."

We look up to see a woman, around my age, standing by the table. Dad stands and greets her with a full kiss on the lips. "Kids, meet Sabrina, my girlfriend. I hope you don't mind. I asked her to swing by to pick me up for dinner. We have Broadway tickets and an early dinner reservation."

"Total asshole," Danny mutters under his breath.

After brief introductions and small talk, they prepare to leave. "Dad, I'll be here for the Met Gala in a couple of weeks. Let's get together then."

"I'll be here, Charlotte. You know you can always count on me," he replies.

Left alone, Danny and I sit in silence, nursing our drinks, recovering from the episode. I can sense Danny's upset and wait for him to speak. When he does, his concern is about me, not Dad.

"Why do you always do that?" he asks, frustration clear in his voice. "You're always trying so hard to maintain a relationship with him when he's clearly not capable of it. Just like all those older men you date. None of them is dependable. You know that. You need someone who adores you, someone who won't let you down when it matters."

"Danny, David's no longer in my life. I am trying to find someone who truly cares for me, someone who puts me first or at least has a valid reason when they can't," I reassure him. "I'm tired of Dad's weak excuses and selfishness, too."

"I don't mean to lecture, but as your big brother, I worry about you," he adds with genuine concern. "How's everything else going with you?"

"Everything's good, really. I love my job and the people I work with. Plus, I'm more financially stable now than I've been since my business collapsed."

"Good for you. And by the way, Kate wanted me to remind you about the twins' birthday party."

"I'll be there. You know you can always count on me," I say, making us both laugh ruefully at our dad's empty expression.

Chapter Fourteen

. . . no problem, sis

THE CRUCIAL APPOINTMENT THE NEXT DAY IS NOT A BUSINESS meeting but a personal one: a procedure to harvest and freeze my eggs. I'd never thought it was necessary when I was married, but with my love life on hold, I feel the need for a safety net. The injections were excruciating, and the hormones sent my moods on a roller coaster. Thankfully, it would all be over by day's end. I plan to recover in my apartment over the weekend and head back to Riverbank on Monday.

Only Viv knows about my plans. She called early yesterday from London to wish me luck and promised to call over the weekend to check in.

The procedure is simple enough, but when I wake from anesthesia, I'm besieged by nausea that swiftly leads to vomiting. My head pounds, and severe cramps rack my body. And I can't stop vomiting. Medical staff swarm around, hanging bags of fluid and attaching EKG pads to my chest. Eventually, they wheel my bed into a private room, where over the next few hours, I gradually start to feel better. Yet the doctor won't discharge me without someone to accompany me home.

After I spend a futile ten minutes trying to convince the doctor I'm fine, Viv calls.

"Why are you awake? It must be midnight where you are," I ask.

"I've been on the phone with your doctor and his staff all day. You've had a severe reaction to the anesthesia. Danny's caught up in emergency surgery, your dad's MIA as usual, so I arranged for someone to take you home. Otherwise, they're going to admit you to the hospital. We're talking ambulance ride and everything."

"Oh, Viv, you're a lifesaver. I've been arguing with the doctor about not wanting to stay here. Who did you find?"

"Well, I told them he's your brother, so play along."

"My brother?"

"At least I didn't say he's your husband."

"Thank goodness for that. Who's coming?"

"Hey sis, how are you feeling?" A wall of broad shoulders and immaculate charcoal wool fills the doorway as he follows the doctor into the room, his presence shrinking the space around him.

"Charlotte, your brother Duane has signed the release papers for you," the doctor announces.

"We are going to have a very serious chat about this," I hiss into the phone, ending the call despite Viv's protests.

"Uh, hey, Duane, thanks for, um, coming to get me," I stammer. Oh, bloody fucking hell. This cannot be happening. His polished perfection makes me even more aware of my hospital gown and disarrayed state. I feel vulnerable and so exposed.

"No problem, sis," he says, a wicked little grin playing at his mouth, clearly enjoying how the balance of power has flipped. "Let's get you home."

The IV is disconnected, and I dress with the help of the medical assistant. The doctor comes back into the room with

Duane to go over discharge instructions. He plants himself next to the doctor, radiating that contained Blacklock force field while I sit on the bed. I steal glances at him as he asks about follow-up and emergency telephone numbers to call if needed. The doctor instinctively interacts with Duane, sensing he's the one in charge.

Once we're alone in the elevator, Duane preempts my questions.

"You're staying at my place tonight," he says in his "don't argue with me" voice. "The doctor said you needed supervision for at least the next twelve hours. I have staff there, so if there's any further complications, there's someone to help. I assume you don't have anyone at your place?"

I'm too drained to protest. I feel exhausted. "I . . . I don't know what to say. I'm so tired I can't think. Okay. I'll stay at your place until tomorrow morning. I just want to sleep."

His driver's waiting for us. I gingerly settle into the back seat of the large SUV with Duane's help. My head rests on the back of the seat, my eyes closed. Duane sits close to me, but not touching. We ride in silence.

His apartment is in a luxury high-rise in the Meatpacking District. The elevator opens directly into his penthouse. There may be views of the Hudson, but I don't notice. I'm vaguely aware of floor to ceiling windows looking out to a river and blurs of serene, modern, beautiful rooms, including a gleaming grand piano in the living room.

Does he play, I wonder, my thoughts hazy.

"Let me show you the guest room," he says in a low voice. "My housekeeper has made some chamomile tea and sandwiches. The doctor said you should eat since you've had nothing all day. Then you can sleep."

His voice is so kind, so soft. He leads me down a corridor to a spacious bedroom decorated in calming pastel greens and yellows. Someone has already placed a tray with a teapot, cups, and a plate of sandwiches on a bench.

"Sit here." He ushers me toward a couch, pouring me a cup of tea and handing me a sandwich. "Eat this and then one more."

I eat mechanically, the sweet warmth of the tea soothing my ragged throat. My fatigue is overwhelming, causing me to almost doze in my upright position.

"Can I sleep now?" I beg.

Even in my haze, I register his response. "Yes, darling, you can." Then he gently picks me up and lays me on the sheets, already pulled down on the bed.

I feel him brush my hair back over my ear as he whispers: "Sleep well, my muse."

Chapter Fifteen

. . . she wanted her bed next to his

I WATCH HIM TALKING ON HIS PHONE FROM THE KITCHEN doorway. Tall, commanding, with a magnetic stillness that makes him stand out in any room. I had quickly oriented myself to the surroundings of the unfamiliar bedroom when I woke. After freshening up in the bathroom, I wandered down the hall, drawn to the kitchen by his voice. As I move toward him and catch his eye, he ends his call.

"Hey."

"Hey."

"Do you want some coffee?"

"Yes, please," I say with a soft smile, sliding into a chair at the counter.

"Feeling better?" he asks as he pours coffee into a mug. "I don't know how you take your coffee."

"Much better, thank you. All I needed was sleep. Lots of milk, no sugar."

He joins me at the counter.

"Duane, I can't thank you enough—"

"Charlotte, I hope you realize—"

Our words jumble together, talking over each other.

He's quick to speak again. "Viv didn't have a choice. She had to call me. I'm just glad she did."

I shoot back, "I love Viv. She's my best friend, and I'm going to wring her neck."

We look at each other in a silent standoff as I study him, letting him study me.

"Why didn't you have children when you were married? You could've avoided that procedure," he says suddenly. His words are unexpectedly sharp and accusing.

"Why is there nothing about you anywhere in the world until you went to boarding school?" I volley back in defense.

He seems to catch my defiance. "Oh no. You don't get to change the subject. You always change the subject, deflect the question, or outright ignore what someone asks."

That mysterious Blacklock force field has taken on a sinister, angry feel. I don't like it.

But then I agree out of nowhere. "You're right." I don't want to argue with him. I need to change this tug-of-war we experience every time we're together. He's my boss, I'm making things too personal. The tension in the room drops.

I take a deep breath. "Let's start over. I just want to thank you. I know you probably dropped something important to come help me. It was so kind of you and totally unexpected."

"C'mon," he softens his tone to match mine. "From what I've gathered talking to Viv, she would have come if she could."

"Yes, she would have, and so would my brother, but he doesn't have the freedom most people have."

"And what about your parents?" he continues.

I shake my head. "My mother's dead, and my father is always a no-show. That's how he operates."

"Well, I couldn't leave my muse in distress. There's probably some unwritten law against it. It might even get me exiled from Olympus."

I find myself laughing. "Yes, it doesn't sit well with us muses when our inspiration is not appreciated. Because I've inspired you to do so much," I say sarcastically.

"Yes, you truly have, Charlotte. You have no idea," he confesses.

I mirror his sincerity. "Well then, I'm glad."

"As for this other stuff," he continues. "I asked you once what it's like to be married, and you ignored the question."

"I know I did. It's complicated."

I pause. *Do I really want to do this? Once I start, where do I stop? Is he someone I want to share this with?* But I know I want to know more about him, and one of us has to open up. He's really been kind to me despite his ever present hostility and arrogance.

"I'm not divorced, Duane. I'm a widow," I say simply, knowing its effect.

He stares at me.

Yep, that shuts the conversation down. Every . . . single . . . fucking . . . time, as I knew it would. What could anyone say?

I wait.

"And I did like being married, for a while anyway." I fill the silence, trying to provide an answer to his previous question.

I wait some more.

His face looks utterly stunned as he struggles for words. "He . . . died? How? What happened?" His voice is incredulous, demanding immediate answers.

This is why I prefer not to discuss my marriage or widowhood, or whatever I was. It's so fucking painful, and it always brings along a whirlwind of questions.

"He died from Covid. He was one of the first cases in New York in January. He had just returned from a business trip to Italy and went straight to the hospital from the plane."

"Holy shit," he says. "Charlotte, I . . . I'm sorry."

And this is exactly why I don't talk about it because now the floodgates are open.

"The doctors weren't certain what it was; they didn't diagnose Covid until later. It was so early in the pandemic. He and his mistress. They were together, both were ill . . ." I begin to ramble, never knowing how to put the story together because I never want to examine it.

"It wasn't a business trip. I didn't know about them. The shock of seeing him so sick and then learning of his affair. She was hospitalized too, but she survived." I know I'm probably not making any sense. I just want to tell him the facts, so that he knows what happened, and avoid telling him how it felt.

"He died after a week on a ventilator. They had to tell me in the hospital that they were together because she wanted her bed next to his as he was dying. She was ill in the ICU, too. I didn't know."

"Charlotte, I'm so sorry," he repeats.

And this is why I don't like to discuss it, because I'm becoming angry.

"I was going to say no," I continue, my voice harsh and choking. "I was so hurt and angry and overwhelmed. He was dying, but I saw that we both loved him. So I was there in that room in the ICU with her in a bed next to his, and we watched together as he died.

"It was such a clusterfuck. You have no idea. That wasn't all that happened. I get so angry when I talk about it. All the pain and betrayal and sorrow come back. I don't know what to do with these feelings."

He rises from his chair and pulls me into his arms, holding me tightly against his chest. I can feel his heartbeat, the silkiness of his cotton shirt, and smell his familiar scent of bergamot and soap.

"I know, Charlotte, I do know. I'm sorry. It's okay."

He's stroking my hair and saying quietly, "It's okay, it's okay."

And it all makes me sob harder. It hurts so much again,

right then, after it had not hurt for so long. I'd never cried like this with anyone, even in the moments it was happening, even all the time I'd been with David. I thought those feelings had lessened with time until they were gone. But here they are, crushing me, and I feel so heavy, so beaten down. When would it ever be over? I feel like this is my punishment for not being a better wife, for being unaware Matthew was unhappy and wanted something, someone, else.

Duane's stillness and strength seep into me the longer he holds me, a quiet strength rising through his chest and into my bones. His heartbeat thuds steadily beneath my cheek, his shirt warm and already damp where my tears have soaked through.

The apartment is hushed except for the low breath of heat vents and outside shudders of wind fifteen stories up. I breathe him in. The word "mistress" still tastes like metal in my mouth; the word "death" sits heavy in my chest. But with my head on his sternum, his heartbeat steadies the wreckage.

He tightens his arms, and my body answers before my mind does, turning toward that shelter he makes around me. When I shift, I feel the slow, certain press of him against my core, and a small sound escapes me.

I know what I do to him. I know what he is doing to me. Grief is cold, but his hands are warm at my back, and my sense of wanting him flares there. I press closer. Loss may haunt the room, but desire is louder.

He quickly releases me and moves back, saying harshly, "Fuck, I'm sorry, Charlotte. You must know how much I want you."

I look at his chest where my tears have drenched his pressed white shirt and then up at him, his eyes smoldering swirls of obsidian.

"You're so tall," I marvel, wiping my nose with my hand.

"I know. My father was six one. I'm six three," he responds

matter-of-factly, his voice husky, and looks around to hand me a napkin from the counter.

His voice, his nearness, his warmth, make it hard for me to speak. Whatever this is growing between us, it feels risky. I could lose him as a friend, and my job. I need time. We both do.

"I don't think you should be by yourself today," he says suddenly. "Let's go look at some art and distract ourselves or go for a walk on the High Line. Let's get out of our heads for a while."

I nod. He lifts my chin with his thumb and forefinger to look up at him. I must be a mess, my face blotchy, tears filling my eyes. "Yes?" he asks.

"I'd love to get out of my head, even for a little bit," I agree.

We grab our coats and leave his building, walking over a few streets to climb the stairs up to an urban sanctuary of unexpected loveliness and greenery. "This is such a great area," I say with satisfaction.

"The highlight is being near the river," Duane answers, shoving his hands into his pockets as I think about how it would feel to hold his hand in mine.

"That reminds me," I say, stopping a little in front of him and turning to face him. "Why did you call your company Riverbank? Most cryptocurrency platforms have names that are techy, with crypto references, like Coinbase and Binance. Riverbank sounds the opposite of tech, more nature and earth.

"Does it have to do with the cosmic flow like a river of zeros and ones, which is the internet?" I continue. "Or is it a play on the word 'bank,' meaning blockchain is the opposite of a centralized bank?"

Duane is laughing now. "No, not at all, but may I use your explanation next time I'm asked about our name? It's much more intense and thoughtful."

"Only if you tell me the real story behind choosing it," I tease, at the same time saying *fuck it* to myself and lacing my arm through his as we continue walking. It feels like the most natural thing in the world. He moves closer to me.

"Spill," I demand.

"Well, it's part of this boring history about the emergence of cryptography in this country."

"Quit stalling," I persist. "I love history."

"Riverbank refers to Riverbank Laboratories, where cryptography was first studied in the US. It started after World War I and only three or four people initially worked on crypt analysis, as it was known then. Have you ever heard of it?"

I shake my head. "No, I had no idea."

"One person," he continues, "was Elizabeth Smith Friedman, and she is rightly considered legendary for her work developing many of the principles of modern cryptography, which led to the creation of blockchain and thus cryptocurrency. She originated many of the cryptographic tools for cracking enemy codes during World War II. She was finally honored in the NSA Hall of Fame."

"A woman?" I say. "How great is that?"

"Much of her work was assigned to her husband and overlooked until recently. But I always knew about her," he adds.

"Because your mother loved cryptography?" I ask, remembering our text exchange. Then I quickly realize how he had shut down after he had mentioned it. But it's too late.

His obvious pleasure in talking about the original Riverbank vanishes, and he is quiet.

Moments later he's grabbing me and kissing me fiercely, his intensity blurring everything around me. He feels angry, so angry. His lips are igniting a combustion between us so intense I can't breathe. I cling to him as he tears his lips away with a hushed growl in my ear. "This is what you do to me. I talk about things I shouldn't. Only you, only you, and I can't fucking control it."

People move around us as we stand in the middle of the

walkway, frustration radiating off him as he continues to hold me. Someone says "Get a room" in irritation. He moves me off the crowded walkway to the side.

I want to say something. To tell him I understand. That his anger is okay. That I know that kind of anger, the anger of hurt and possible betrayal, but who had betrayed him? Instead, I just stand, leaning my head on his shoulder, my arms wrapped around him. "Let's go," he commands. Grabbing my hand, he leads me down to the street.

When we arrive outside his building, I stop. "I should go back to my place," I say, worried about what might happen if we go up to his apartment.

I'm attracted to him, to his mystery, his strength, his body. This would never be anything more than a fling with him. I'm at a different stage in life. I want a family. He's young, and it's natural for him to want to be with other women. He's been with a lot of women, from the rumors and from what he's told me.

He pulls out his phone as it buzzes and reads a text. "Fuck, I forgot I have a meeting. Let me call my driver, and we can drop you off on the way."

"Do you . . . do you know where I live?" I ask, realizing he probably does.

He's already talking on his phone. He hangs up with a nod yes to my question as his driver pulls up to us. I silently get into the Belgravia-green Range Rover with tinted windows. Sitting next to each other for the few minutes' drive to my place, we don't speak. He steps out of the car when I leave and gives me a cool kiss on the cheek, saying, "Talk soon." Then he gets back in, and the car drives off.

It's all so quick, efficient, clinical. Had I only imagined those tender moments, his passion, his sympathy for the events with Matthew?

As I shut the door to my apartment, I find myself leaning

against it, confused and exhausted. After a few minutes, I push myself away to crawl into bed. Embarrassment at having him know about my procedure, anger at his admonition about having kids, all slowly change to warm feelings about him. He truly cares. He'd dropped everything to come get me, even taken a call from Viv, a virtual stranger.

But then the doubts begin to creep in, insidious little thoughts that gnaw at my confidence. *Does he see me merely as a mother figure? Did he lose his mother when he was young?* I don't know because there's no damn information online about him. He's not just in the shadows, he's a damn ghost. But the way he'd kissed me, and had held me this morning, his desire was so clear. That was no mother thing.

There are these moments when he can be unbearably arrogant, passing judgment left, right, and center. He's like a knife with sharp edges, slashing casually at those around him. I've been on the receiving end of his harshness. And I've witnessed him treat others the same way. But this time with me, he was different. *Who is this man?*

Chapter Sixteen

. . . seek a beautiful, available woman

RETURNING TO RIVERBANK AFTER DUANE'S UNEXPECTED rescue, the push and pull between us coils tighter. I attempt to limit my interactions with him at work. Yet despite my coolness toward him, Duane asks me to wait behind several times after a meeting and invites me to dinner. I stand firm and decline, making up excuses, or give a solid no and leave quickly. There's always a tension between us, an anxious expectation that I might say yes. An anticipation of what we would each feel if I were to submit, to surrender and say yes to him. He accepts all my no's without challenge, but there's a mocking look in his eyes. As if he senses my struggle and knows I want to say yes. As if he knows it's only a matter of time before I say yes.

One day I venture into the Pit, the nerve center of Riverbank's digital empire, where Oliver and Duane have their computers set up alongside the relentless hum of programmers as they troubleshoot the platform's problems. In the sun-soaked room, with light pouring in from large windows, their faces appear bathed in shifting patterns of binary code and cascading numbers. There are inaudible murmurs of problem-solving, the staccato rhythm of keystrokes, and the occasional sharp exhale of frustration or triumph.

The Pit smells of heated circuitry, faint traces of Red Bull, and the unmistakable warmth of bodies that have sat too long in the same spot engrossed in their work. Some of the coders sit for twelve or sixteen hour shifts, headphones on, immersed in cryptographic precision, fixing the latest bug to ensure the security of transactions on the platform. There's a subtle yet constant whir of cooling fans blending with the muted chatter of developers debugging critical flaws in the system.

The Pit's narrow, with tables close together, so I navigate around and almost over people if I need to speak with someone. I always find myself in unusual proximity to people entering or leaving the area. The first time I came here, everyone looked up as I entered, and the cacophonous tapping of a dozen people typing at furious speeds abruptly stopped. I decided to act like a sorority girl entering a fraternity and gave a small, casual wave—"Hey guys, how's it going?"—hoping to create a feeling of me as a big sister.

Nope, definitely not a big-sister feeling. The response was more ogling, bordering on eye-fucking as I maneuvered myself through tight spaces around seated men, being forced into close physical contact.

By the third time, everyone has calmed down, and I enter almost unnoticed. This time, after speaking with the top coder for a non-tech-friendly explanation of how the metaverse operates to explain to one of my clients, Duane suddenly appears. Thankfully, I'm at the other end of the Pit and rush to the door to avoid speaking to him. I'm walking—actually, I'm fleeing—down the hall when I hear Duane call my name.

Bloody hell. Is this my own *Groundhog Day* where I have to keep going over my refusals again and again? I'm frustrated—exasperated, really—with this situation. I know his persistence bothers me because I'm fighting my feelings for him. When he calls out, I stop and turn around. *Okay, you've got this: casual and gracious. Inspire him, charm him, keep it light,* I tell myself as I walk back to him.

He stands there with his sly smile, his deep-set eyes following me.

"Hey, I can't believe the level of techno expertise in that one small area," I confess, making small talk to avoid his questions. "Whenever I'm there, I get seduced into thinking I actually understand cryptography and blockchain."

"Yeah, I've been seduced since I was eight or nine years old. Mathematical coding, writing software programs, countless hours on the computer. It was a world that swallowed me whole, an intoxicating maze of logic and mystery. A mystery I felt compelled to master. A mysterious chemistry similar to my feeling for my muse," he says, glancing again and again at my mouth.

I swallow, steadying myself. "Well, Mr. Blacklock, I'm not a complicated code, or an unknowable equation, so as your muse, I don't see the similarities. But I do see you like to drench everything in crypto and computer metaphors."

His lips curve, slow and deliberate. "Oh, but Ms. Gordon-Lennox, you are, by your very nature, a cipher. Seductive. Impossible to crack, and yet, here I am—an addict needing another hit."

The air between us becomes thick, humming with a dangerous kind of voltage. "And so, is this you wanting to master me, too?" I tease, but my voice is breathless.

His expression becomes grim; the easy playfulness melts into something raw. "I need to do something." The words are a rough whisper. He leans in, so close I can feel his heat pressing against the space I no longer control. His breath skims my skin, igniting every nerve ending. "I can't sleep. I exercise for hours in the gym, hoping exhaustion will claim me. I can't focus. I start on something and then, suddenly, it's hours later and I've done nothing. Nothing but think about you."

Silence.

"Charlotte." His voice is edged with command, a chain pulling me into him. His eyes, burning embers, flash with golden flecks, like raked coal. And then, his fingers close around my arms—possessive, electric.

Shadows and Edges Duane has arrived.

Heat coils inside me, an unwilling thrill at the way his touch brands. He wants me. No, he needs me. More than that, he needs my submission.

"Duane, you want my help? Here it is," I say, my tone cool despite the wildfire spreading through me. "Keep busy, practice gratitude, develop a disciplined schedule, and—most importantly—seek a beautiful, *available* woman." I let the last words land like a slap.

A low growl rumbles from his throat, his frustration etched into the hard set of his jaw. "You willingly share your inspiration but not my bed." His voice groans with accusation; his restraint is paper-thin. The tension crackles as intensity scorches the air between us.

"Muses, by their very definition, are elusive. Unobtainable," I say, even as my pulse betrays me, hammering a desperate rhythm against my ribs. And then, before he can close the distance, before I can lose myself in the pull of him, I turn to leave.

"I came to see you for another reason," he calls out. "Oliver's parents are here. They wanted me to ask you to join us for dinner tonight. They want to see you. Margaret told me three times to make sure you come. What should I tell them?"

Why is everything with him such torture to me? I want to see the Mitchells again. It would be such a pleasure. But a pleasure tempered with the pain of Duane's presence. I give my head a slight shake. No. I won't give up a chance to see them. I can handle Duane.

"Please tell them yes and let them know I'd love to see them again."

Chapter Seventeen

. . . death ground

MOORED IN THE ATLANTIC MARINA, THE YACHT IS A VISION of understated luxury, its polished deck gleaming under the fading light. The air carries a salty tang, mingling with the faint scent of lemon wood polish. The gentle lapping of waves against the hull creates a rhythmic murmur, easing my tension. I feel myself slowly relaxing.

It's a sunset dinner around the island. Fortunately, I had texted Lily to get the details.

"Charlotte, so good to see you," Margaret Mitchell greets me, enveloping me in a surprisingly fierce embrace. She pulls back, studying me with an assessing gaze. "You look lovely, but a little too thin. Are the boys working you too hard?"

"Knowing them, they are," Charles Mitchell adds, giving me a quick kiss on the cheek.

"GL. Finally," Oliver calls from a plush seating area on the lower deck, where he sits with Lily and Duane as Margaret and Charles join the group. His tone is teasing, but his eyes flick to Duane. "My girlfriend bailed on me, so Lily's my date. And Duane, well, he can be yours."

The warm evening air turns thick. "Oh, but that's a conflict of interest on so many levels," I say smoothly, sidestepping the tension. "Didn't he tell you I'm his muse now? We made a deal weeks ago."

Duane's expression doesn't shift, but his glass tilts in a muted acknowledgment—approval, possession, or both.

Oliver chuckles. The sound is softer than usual, edged with something unspoken. "Well, that would account for the change I've noticed," he says, his eyes flickering between us.

Heat rises along the back of my neck, prickling under my hair. I turn toward the sea, as if the horizon can steady me. "You mean because he's agreed to testify in front of Congress with you?" I ask, my heartbeat turning loud in my ears: *What change?*

"That," Oliver answers lightly, "and because we plan to plaster Riverbank's name across a stage in Austin at our crypto conference in a few months. Sponsorship. Panels. Cameras. The whole circus."

Duane sets his glass down. "We're not calling it a circus."

"Fine," Oliver replies. "A professionally lit circus."

"Austin," Lily repeats, brow creasing. "Is that the conference where everyone pretends they understand NFTs?"

Oliver's smile is quick. "Not everyone. Some of us actually do."

"Explain it," Lily says. "Like I'm five."

Oliver opens his mouth—then glances at me, as if inviting reinforcement instead of sparring.

I exhale, grateful for the subject that isn't *us*. "Think of an NFT like the authentication card inside a Birkin bag," I say. "People can copy the photos. They can even copy the look. But the card—the provenance—proves which one is real, which one is yours. And sometimes it comes with perks: access, invitations, special treatment."

"That's a good first start." Duane's gaze stays on the water, but his voice cuts in—quiet, decisive. "Now learn to explain what a metaverse is—without making it sound like you joined a cult or you took hallucinogenics."

His words are simple. The warmth they leave behind is not.

"All right. Next lesson: 'metaverse' without making people roll their eyes." Oliver lifts his glass an inch as we all laugh.

The yacht glides away from the marina, its powerful engine a low purr beneath my feet. I watch as the shoreline slowly fades, replaced by the vast inkiness of the ocean. The dining area is art deco elegance—bronzed lanterns flicker golden light across modern beige leather seats, and crystal glasses gleam under their glow. A staff member in crisp white offers drinks and delicate appetizers as laughter spills from our group and we watch the changing pattern of private estates and parks on the shoreline slide past. The moment feels stolen. It's an oasis of ease, as though none of us has a past or shadows trailing behind us.

I step away, drawn to the edge of the deck, where the water stretches out, unsettled and unknowable. Charles comes to stand beside me, his presence a quiet anchor.

Without thinking, I ask, "What happened to Duane's parents?" My voice is low, the words nearly lost to the slapping waves.

He hesitates. The pause stretches too long.

"It was a tragedy," he says finally, his voice weighted with something I can't name. "Only Duane can tell you the details. But it left him . . . driven. It consumes him."

I glance sideways, my heart pounding. "Driven? Consumed?"

Charles turns his gaze to the roiling waters. "Do you know the concept of *death ground*?"

"Death ground?" I echo.

"Yes. It's the idea that when you're backed into a corner, when retreat is no longer an option, you either fight, or you die. Duane has been on death ground since he was a teenager. Too young, too inexperienced at first, but he's forged himself into something else. A sort of warrior, fighting a battle no one else understands."

A chill passes over me. The yacht, the warmth, the flickering candlelight—it all feels too fragile now, too temporary.

I swallow. "Is that why he stays in the shadows? Always on the fringes?"

Charles lets out a breath. "I don't know, Charlotte. And I'm probably saying too much. But whatever happened made Duane who he is today. Extremely loyal. Responsible. Family comes first."

I turn the words over in my mind. *Family comes first.*

"I can see those parts," I murmur. "So why do you think he hasn't married or had a family of his own?"

Charles shrugs, leading me back toward the others. "He likes dating. I assume he's still exploring his options."

The dining table glows under amber light, the sea wind riffling the linen as we join the group, who are now sitting down to dinner.

Lily is laughing, her wineglass tilted playfully in one hand. "Taylor Swift has a song about meeting the band and not remembering if she has a man. That's my tagline," she says with a grin.

"She's brilliant," I say. "But my favorite of hers is less playful, the one that warns that the slowest way to kill someone is not to love them enough."

The words hang there, a quiet challenge.

I glance up. Duane's gaze drills into me with a thousand unreadable thoughts.

A slow, deliberate heat rises in my chest.

I smooth my expression. *Play it off, Charlotte.* "Do you have a favorite song?" I ask almost playfully. Almost.

We all wait as Duane sets down his fork, his movements measured, deliberate.

"My favorite song?" he repeats. Then, with a faint smirk: "I think most people here can guess. It's about not backing down, even at the gates of hell."

The table shifts back into chatter, but I feel the cold ripple run through me. His choice isn't casual; it's a revelation. He didn't pick a love song; he picked a battle call. Tom Petty's "I Won't Back Down." Death ground, Charles said. No retreat. Fight or die. That's been Duane for fifteen years. When you live on death ground, you step lightly and keep to the edges, follow clean sightlines, control exposure. Concealment is a survival skill, not a romantic game.

Then I hear it—the quieter chord beneath the defiance. Not "save me." Not "fix me." He's been living in ruins, waiting for the war to end—or a reason to end it. My throat tightens. Could I be that reason?

Lily's exuberant chatting continues in the background, flitting from topic to topic as she sips her wine. Beaming, she turns her attention to me, pulling me back into the conversation.

"Charlotte, what got you interested in cryptocurrency?"

I turn from staring at Duane, forcing a small smile.

"An English course," I answer, causing surprise. Lily lets out a laugh, and everyone stops to listen.

"I wanted a break from Hardy and the Brontës," I explain. "So I took a course on British crime fiction, hoping for a deep dive into P. D. James. But my professor went on a tangent—about the mystery of Satoshi Nakamoto."

There's a pause. Then, Oliver stiffens. Duane stills.

The atmosphere shifts, subtly but undeniably.

"I fell down a rabbit hole," I continue. "From Satoshi to bitcoin to blockchain to the cryptocurrency ecosystem. By the end of the semester, I was hooked. After that, I began trading."

"What's the mystery about Satoshi, again?" Lily asks.

"No one knows who he or she was. Satoshi invented block-chain technology, which is the foundation for digital gold, posted a paper online about how it would work along with the software to mine bitcoin, and after a year disappeared, never to be heard from again."

Oliver takes a sip of wine. "But does it really matter who Satoshi was?" he asks casually. "At this point, the technology speaks for itself. Most crypto enthusiasts focus on the revolutionary technology created."

I feel Duane carefully watching me.

"It matters," I say evenly, "because the world buries the accomplishments of women. I think Satoshi was a woman. And I think she should be given her due."

Silence.

Then Duane speaks, his voice low, sharp edged. "But what if she didn't want people to know? What if she understood the world too well? Good is fragile, Charlotte. There will always be forces waiting to destroy it."

A chill curls down my spine. "Ouch," I say lightly. "That's a bleak view."

Oliver, ever the diplomat, scrapes his chair back with a grin. "Ceasefire, geniuses. The sun's doing its last great trick." He lifts the bottle toward the whole table, not just me. "Top-ups before we go topside?" He splashes a little into my flute and winks. "Hydration, Gordon-Lennox. Sparkling and French."

I laugh despite myself. "Doctor's order, is it?"

"Kid brother's orders." He taps the rim of my glass with his. "C'mon."

We step onto the upper deck. The air is cooler here. Salt mist freckles my skin. The rails give off a faint, sun-warmed-resin smell, and the teak is smooth under my palm. Far out, a knife thin blade of gold slices the velvet blue sea. The yacht engine hums a steady note under my feet, and muffled conversation softens as the wind shifts.

Oliver angles his body to the water, not me. "You've changed," he says, easy, matter-of-fact, like he's giving a status report. "Brighter. More . . . alive. It's good. For you—and Cel, for him." He tips his chin. "He listens when you talk. That's new."

There's that nickname again. *What is that about?* "Thanks," I say. "And thanks for defusing back there."

He snorts. "Please. You two were about to invent a new branch of philosophy over dessert. I'm just here to keep the ship upright." He bumps the rail with his fist, boyish, then pushes off. "I'm going to rescue Lily and then check to see if there are blankets down below. Wind's picking up."

Before I can answer or ask about the name, another presence slips in—Duane. He steps between us with unhurried certainty, claiming the space at my side, one hand resting on the rail just inches from mine. He doesn't acknowledge Oliver directly. He doesn't have to.

"Wind's shifting," Duane remarks, his voice calm, even. "We'll feel it when we round the point."

It's nothing, really—just an observation about the weather. But the way he says it, the weight in it, settles like a line drawn in the sand.

The wind whips a strand of hair across my cheek, and before I can move, his fingers catch it, brushing it back deliberately, grazing the curve of my jaw. The touch is nothing—and everything.

His gaze locks on mine, and I feel it—what it means to be his muse—not inspiration as an abstract thing, but a possession, a devotion, a claim. He sees me as the fire that sharpens his edge, the light in his hidden shadows, the reason he moves forward. And I, God help me, want that.

He leans closer, his breath hot against my ear. "My muse,"

he whispers, raw and low. The words ignite me, dragging a shiver down my spine.

Then his mouth is hovering over mine, so close the salt on my own lips feels like it belongs to him. For one reckless beat, I believe he'll kiss me here, with Oliver and Lily just feet away and half the crew ready to witness it. The risk, the recklessness, make my pulse pound with a ravenous hunger.

And then—

"Charlotte, you have to see this pod of dolphins!" Lily's bright voice cuts through the night. She's leaning over the railing, waving me over. "Hurry! They're leaping as if they're performing just for us!"

I jerk back a half step, my skin burning, my breath uneven. My mouth is still parted, waiting for something that didn't happen. I force a smile, willing my pulse to slow as I turn toward her.

Lily bounces on her toes, reaching for my hand. "C'mon—you'll miss the whole show!" she laughs, tugging me toward the rail, blissfully unaware.

I let her pull me, pretending to focus on the dolphins' white arcs breaking the now orange-pink water. *Pretend. Distract. Breathe.*

But I can still feel him behind me, his gaze heavy on my back, searing through the pretense. As if he knows precisely what almost happened, what nearly undid me.

The horizon has disappeared behind an invisible curtain. And so has my resistance.

Chapter Eighteen

. . . falling into the same hole

THE ROOM IS CRAWLING WITH PEOPLE, AND I FEEL A LITTLE claustrophobic as I strain to tune out the background chatter and concentrate. I focus my thoughts on tomorrow, Sunday, when we have our dress rehearsal before the gala on Monday. Then the room will be packed with double the crowd, I remind myself.

I'm sitting on a high stool while Christine, my makeup artist, fine-tunes my makeup under a ring light. The social team hovers nearby with phones and an iPad, filming test shots—profile, three-quarter, flash—so they can decide what reads best for posting the night of the gala.

The Mark Hotel is the ideal place for preparing for Monday's biggest night in fashion. We have four rooms reserved: mine, Oliver's, a dressing room, and one for Oliver's private security. We're just a few blocks away from the Metropolitan Museum of Art, where the Met Gala will be held.

Everyone's engrossed in photos of me during the dress fitting, trying to settle on the perfect eye makeup look. A media agency photographer clicks photos while assistants adjust microphones, lights, and reflectors, capturing every moment of my preparation. Another person steps back to film the photographer and his crew as they photograph me. This is another fresh angle for Riverbank to post fashion amid the cryptocurrency content on their social media account.

I'm anticipating Oliver's arrival for his tuxedo fitting, which is scheduled at five p.m. uptown at Tom Ford. I'll be at Giambattista for, hopefully, my final dress fitting at the same time. Midafternoon exhaustion is creeping in and, despite knowing it may keep me up all night, I reluctantly request an assistant to bring me a cappuccino.

Thinking about the dress gives me a surge of energy. I'm smitten with what the designer and I have chosen: a strapless royal blue silk dress that drapes beautifully around me. It's breathtaking. The elegance and sophistication of my dress can't compete with the flashy outfits the celebrities will wear, but I know it makes me look stunning.

Amid all the chaos, my phone rings.

"Charlotte, it's Oliver. I know it's the last minute, but I've decided to skip the gala. It's just not me. I've never been the tux and red carpet type. I always insist on being myself, not playing a part that doesn't fit." His voice is firm, assured, very unapologetic.

As his words hang in the air, I stifle the urge to shout "Are you fucking kidding me?" Instead, a moan escapes my lips, and I hear Oliver say "Charlotte, are you all right?" As I quickly grasp that no matter what I say, Oliver won't change his mind, my heart sinks somewhere to the lowest part of my body. I don't want to upset him and risk damaging our relationship.

Suppressing my disappointment and irritation, I take a moment. I'd spent months on this. A.W. will not be happy to hear someone is backing out of her carefully curated guest list. As unappealing as it is, I have to attend the Met Gala solo.

"Of course, Oliver. I understand completely. I wouldn't

want you here if you feel uncomfortable. I'll let Anna's assistant know. She may be upset, but you bought pricey tickets and Riverbank made a generous donation on top. I think that will soften the blow."

Even though I don't believe a single word I've just uttered, I think I sound convincing.

"GL, you're such a professional. From the day you walked into Riverbank, I knew you were the perfect choice to introduce crypto to the fashion industry."

"Thanks, Oliver. I appreciate your letting me know. I have these rooms at the Mark . . ." My voice drifts off, questioning.

"Don't worry, Riverbank will cover all expenses. Just go out there and represent us with your natural glamour and elegance. See you when you get back." And just like that, he hangs up.

Bloody fucking hell. I restrain my screams as my mind races about what to do next. In a desperate move, I pull up a number on my phone and hit dial.

"Hey, Dad, how are you? Are you in the city?" I know Anna might be okay with my dad as a substitute. After all, he's a big name in elite New York circles, with a glittering reputation on Wall Street. I propose the idea of his accompanying me to the gala and wait for a response.

"I'm sorry, honey, but I have plans."

"It's on Monday night, Dad. It won't interfere with your weekend plans," I lie.

"Well, Sabrina's sister is coming in on Monday, and we're planning to do some things with her."

"But can't Sabrina spend some time with her sister without you? Then you'd be free to help me."

"Really wish I could, kiddo, but I don't want to disappoint her. You know how these things are. Sabrina is relying on me. I don't want to let her down."

I bite back my response as silence fills the air. So he doesn't want to disappoint Sabrina, but he has no problem letting me down.

"All right, Dad. I get it. Thanks for answering. Talk soon," I say and hang up.

Why the hell had I made that call? I feel like such a fool, always taking the same path, only to end up falling into the same hole. My disappointment quickly morphs into anger before settling into resignation. At least I had given him the chance to help me. It seems he doesn't want that kind of relationship. Why is that so hard for me to accept?

Suddenly, the Met Gala's requirement of a recent Covid test for each guest comes to mind. They are due today. Anna's team probably hasn't received one from Oliver yet, which means they know he isn't coming.

I'll fall on my sword and let them know about Oliver later. I feel my shoulders slump as the weight of this event and the tiredness I've kept at bay push my posture down. For now, I need to get through this final fitting.

Chapter Nineteen

. . . and your guy is taller

I RETURN TO THE HOTEL AFTER NINE P.M. I'M PHYSICALLY drained, but thrilled with my dress. At the same time, a sense of melancholy washes over me at the thought of attending the gala on my own. *But people do it all the time.* Still an image flashes before me: one solitary figure—me—ascending the Met's sweeping stairs while glittering pairs arrive around me. I briefly consider asking Duane, but quickly realize that someone who values anonymity would never agree to walk a red carpet.

On top of that, I haven't spoken to him since the dinner with the Mitchells. Our encounters at work were brief and usually from a distance. He seems incredibly busy, and so am I. Despite receiving several bouquets from him, I haven't acknowledged any of them. I'm not sure why. It's rude, yes, but a lesser evil compared to the risk of becoming more involved. He knows too much about me already, and I need to stick to my game plan of finding someone ready to commit and start a family.

Suddenly, the Tom Ford showroom number pops up on my phone.

"Charlotte, it's Damien from TF. That handsome young man who showed up for the fitting didn't leave his number. We knew from your assistant's call that it would not be Oliver Mitchell."

"Handsome young man? I—" I start to say, "I don't know anyone like that," but stop myself.

"The tuxedo will be ready for a final fitting tomorrow, late, around seven or eightish, I guess. But it will be done in time. Can you pass on the message?"

"Do you mean Duane, Duane Blacklock?" I ask in disbelief.

"Yes, that's him. Will you let him know? Such clean lines and weaponized shoulders, with that lethal blond hair/dark eye combo—like a king and villain at once. And your guy is tall."

My guy? Since when was Duane my guy? I apologize for the late request and shower him with thanks, and pass every compliment along to TF.

I hang up and dial Duane.

"Hey Charlotte. I'm down here checking in. Is there a particular room you want me to take of the four they have under the Riverbank name?"

"Oh my God, Duane. Are you here to take me to the Met Gala?"

"Yes, I am." His voice is a verdict, solid and final.

A yelp of sheer joy escapes me. "Oh, thank you. Thank you so much. You must have been a Boy Scout. Grab room 434. Swing by my room, 432, and we can get something to eat while I thank you some more."

I still had to call A.W.'s assistant. It was nearly ten p.m., but it's Met Gala season and everyone works around the clock. By the time Duane knocks on my door, I've pleaded my case for Oliver's name to be replaced with Duane's on the invitation list.

My argument is straightforward: Does it really matter which cofounder is attending? I sweetened the deal with a promise to make another generous donation to the Costume Institute. According to her assistant, this should appease Anna.

The Mark is buzzing. The gala vibe has set in, and I spot celebrities with their entourages scattered throughout the dining room. The lacquered bar glows at the far end, its shelves lined with bottles like jewels. The faint perfume of truffle butter and charred steak mingles with the green-floral scent of the massive arrangements scattered through the room. Duane joins me at a small table at the edge of the dining room.

"Hey, my gorgeous muse."

"Oh, Duane," I sigh as he settles into the secluded spot with a clear view of the main dining room. "If I'm your muse, you are my King Arthur, saving me from climbing those red-carpet stairs alone."

"Well, I was indeed a Boy Scout on my way to becoming an Eagle Scout. Scouts take these things seriously."

"What, the Boy Scouts of America take muses and the Met Gala seriously?" I tease.

"Yes, because remember the scout motto is 'be prepared,' and my personal addendum is 'for anything.'"

His voice is deep, even, and playful, a smile dancing in his luminous eyes. My stomach drops as I realize just how handsome he is. I feel the heat rising from my neck to my cheeks and look down, hoping he doesn't see my growing appreciation in my eyes. The thought that his infatuation with me is turning into a shared delusion momentarily silences me.

I see his hand reach out as he places it on mine. I look up as he commands "Charlotte" straight into deep brown eyes that pull me in, igniting a tightness in my core.

We move on to talk about his time in college, his friendship with Oliver, his admiration for Oliver's parents, starting Riverbank, and the sleepless nights required to bring it into existence.

I let him talk, nodding in encouragement, but every word he speaks is half lost to me. My senses are too sharpened, too drawn to him. It's as though the entire room has receded, leaving only Duane at this small table, his presence impossible to ignore.

His long fingers curl around the cut-crystal whiskey glass, the amber liquid catching the chandelier's light. Each time he lifts it, the muscles of his forearms shift and tighten beneath his rolled sleeves, a detail I can't seem to look away from. I'm aware of the subtle masculinity in that motion, the easy strength that lives in his body, in the way he holds even something as ordinary as a glass.

My gaze slips to his profile—the clean, aquiline line of his nose, so proud and aloof, and then to his mouth. That mouth could be severe, cutting, imperious. But now it softens into the trace of a smile as he speaks, and the effect is my undoing. My heart catches, beating hard against my ribs, though it doesn't know whether to race forward or stop altogether.

His hair—dark blond with a streak of sun through it—falls slightly into his eyes. It looks carelessly styled, but I can imagine the weight of those strands between my fingers. I swallow hard, the thought so intimate it makes me warm under my light sweater.

I should look away, remind myself to keep control, but when his gaze meets mine, everything in me stills. The din of the room fades; the chandelier's glitter dulls. There are only his unrelenting eyes fixed on me with a gravity that makes it impossible to pretend I'm not caught.

The waiter glides in with our food, the clink of silverware breaking the spell for the moment. I'm grateful for the interruption, though my hand trembles as I pick up my fork.

"And what about you, Charlotte? What was college like for you, and what led you to start your company?"

We talk about my time at NYU, choosing to remain in New York for my family, majoring in English literature because it allowed me to work from anywhere, any place I traveled for a photo shoot. It was hectic balancing work, classes, exams, and paper writing, but my mother and brother were counting on me.

Now he's the one asking a lot of questions, which I answer, provided they steer clear of my marriage.

But there's still one question I need to ask. "I'm stunned that you came to fill in for Oliver. It's so kind of you. But you dislike being the center of attention. What made you decide to attend?"

"Well, I sent you flowers, which you ignored." A quick half smile when I wince. "And I wanted to see what this could be between us. I hoped you might welcome an alternate founder since you were in a bind. And Charlotte"—his voice lowers—"I've known many women, but I've never known anyone like you."

I look down, turning the champagne flute. Heat rises in my cheeks. Twenty again. Ridiculous.

"As your official muse, I should hope so. How else can I inspire you? It's my role to be different. Is there anything you need inspiration for?"

"Yes," he says slowly, waiting until I look up. "But it's rather personal. It's about this amazing woman I have a crush on."

I laugh softly, shake my head. "Duane, think this through. You feel this way now, but that's what a crush is—it's fleeting. In a few weeks, you'll meet someone closer to your age with more in common, and she'll sweep you off your feet."

The air shifts. He leans in, tension gathering across his shoulders like a storm front. "You can't dismiss this, Charlotte. This is about who you are and how I'm so fucking attracted to you."

His voice dominates now as he leans over to raise my chin to look at him. "And before you go there—no, I don't have mommy issues. What I want with you isn't nostalgic. It's adult. It's now. And the things I want to do to you are not things anyone would do to their mother."

My pulse jumps. Electricity skitters over my skin. I pull back, try for air.

"I want you because you're direct. You say what you mean. You don't wait three hours to text back because some book told you it's 'high value.'" His mouth tilts. "You answer. You show up early. You apologize when you're wrong. That's rare."

"Basic human decency," I murmur, as I try to breathe.

"You don't play games. I'm done with dopamine hunters who want clout and chaos. I build things that last. I need someone who understands sustained effort. You do—because you've lived it. And you're so confident. You walk into a room and it stops. Not because you're loud but because you're sure."

I stare at the droplets rolling down my water glass, because the intensity of his eyes might drown me.

He exhales; the thread doesn't break. *Mr. Shadows and Edges, apparently, also does floodlights.* "You challenge me. You tell me to testify before Congress and then dare me to be better. That's not maternal, that's catalytic. You want a life. Not just another 'good time all the time.' You want purpose, a home base, a family. You think in decades, not weekends."

"And the obvious?" I ask, arching a brow.

He doesn't blink. "Your beauty is not the obvious thing to me. It's the problem. I can't not look." He shifts close, voice rougher. "I am unbelievably attracted to you, Charlotte. It's not theoretical. It's chemical. I sit across from you and my body decides before my brain weighs in."

I glance away. Searching for a little distance. The waiter drifts by and mercifully vanishes. The room hums.

"You've had . . . a lot of women," I say, aiming for neutral and missing. "How do I know this isn't just the chase?"

"Because I didn't chase." His grin is boyish, shy. "You walked into our office and I decided. I sent you flowers. You ignored them. I came anyway."

"That is not how crushes work," I murmur, trying not to smile.

"It's how I work." A small shrug. "And if we do this, it won't be because I'm trying to be fourteen again. It'll be because two adults chose it with open eyes. What I'm promising you is no games. No hidden agendas. If you tell me to slow down, I slow down. If you tell me to stop, I stop. If you need me to stand where the light hits, I'll stand there—no matter how much I hate it."

"Big words, Mr. Blacklock."

"Big stakes. I'm all in, Ms. Gordon-Lennox."

Then he does the smallest, most lethal thing: He reaches and rests two fingers lightly on my wrist, where my pulse is a trapped bird.

"Say you'll at least stop arguing with the calendar," he murmurs. "Let's find out what this is without pretending birthdays are barricades."

He holds my gaze as waves flutter somewhere deep in my core, his words, his commanding touch electrifying my body, and then the moment passes.

"We're here for the next few days. Let's see how we feel after spending some time together." His tone is reasonable and relaxed.

He helps me up from my chair and lightly takes my hand to lead me through the dining room to the elevators. We're silent as we make our way to our rooms, but he still holds my hand. We arrive at my room, and he leans against the doorframe as I unlock it. I turn to look at him.

"Good night, Duane. Thank you for dinner. I enjoyed it."

He's looking at me, reaching out to place a strand of my hair gently behind my ear.

"You are my muse, Charlotte, which you say means 'elusive and unobtainable,' but this is not the end. Good night."

I close the door, feeling a wave of confusion wash over me. *What am I feeling?* The evening had been unexpected with all his confessions of why he wanted me. He had been direct, open, authentic even, his usual disdainful defenses abandoned. I feel so aware of him. Physically aware. His touch is as dominant as his words.

I'm drawn to his voice, deep and precise. The way he speaks—assured, without uncertainty—has an unremitting pull. And then I know what I'm feeling. Disappointment. Yes, disappointment that he didn't kiss me, and a hidden thrill knowing that this isn't the end.

Chapter Twenty

. . . perfume, sweat, and fabric steamers

I TRY TO SLEEP IN LATE, KNOWING THE GALA WILL STRETCH into the early hours. But by ten a.m., the whirlwind begins. The media team floods in first—the lighting expert voicing concerns about angle glare, the videographers adjusting tripods, the sound tech checking levels, and the social media specialist, fingers flying, preparing updates for X, Instagram, and TikTok, all under the Riverbank brand.

At eleven a.m., my makeup artist and stylist arrive, their entourage trailing behind, dragging silver suitcases bursting with their tools of transformation. The room instantly thickens with the sharp bite of hair products, the musk of warmed-up foundation, and the tang of fresh citrus from someone's open container of juice.

I pause and order a high protein, low carb breakfast of scrambled eggs, avocado, and a green juice blend, knowing I'll barely get a chance to eat during the evening's event.

"Move, move, move—she needs to be in the chair now," my stylist directs, hands flying as she gathers my hair, her fingers deft but firm. I lower myself into the grand chair before a massive vanity mirror set up by the hotel for guests attending the gala. Thank goodness one of the rooms I managed to reserve was a Manhattan suite. The luxurious space with ebony, nickel, and sycamore furnishings is exceptionally large. Still, there's little room to move around. And cables snake across the floor, making a silent trip hazard among all the movement.

Someone adjusts the overhead rig, creating a glow that sends shadows rippling across the bustling space, as the stylist's assistants add more fixtures around the mirror. The sudden brightness casts an unforgiving spotlight on my face. There's a frantic dance of bodies behind me—brushes dabbing, hands twisting, tools clattering against countertops.

A Spotify playlist thumps electronic dance beats, heavy bass vibrating through the walls and setting the pace for the room's relentless energy. Someone swears under their breath as a brush topples to the floor and rolls away. A phone vibrates against the vanity, unanswered, lost in the din of overlapping voices and movement.

Suddenly, Duane's beside me, his presence cutting through the controlled chaos. His reflection in the mirror is a stark contrast—calm, steady, unfazed. "I'm heading to the gym. I'll be back by three," he murmurs, voice low, words brushing against my skin like silk.

"This type of chaos isn't really your scene," I reply, unable to turn my head as an assistant lines my eyelids with quick, precise strokes. "Remember, photos at four. We head to the Met at five sharp, even though we're not due until six thirty. Thanks for sticking around." He smirks, winks, and vanishes, leaving behind a faint whisper of bergamot and clean skin.

As the last blending sponge brushes across my face, I scroll through Instagram, X, and TikTok. The team has been diligent, posting snippets of my transformation. I'm relieved that the clips, especially those early moments, which aren't the most flattering, last only three to five seconds. The candid photos, on the other hand, saw a rush of likes.

By three fifteen, waves of chocolate brown hair frame my face, the weight of perfectly placed curls flowing over my shoulders. A stylist spritzes a finishing mist, the scent cloying, suffocating. My gown—sapphire blue, shimmering like liquid—hangs on the door, the silk fabric alive with movement from the lights.

"Five minutes!" someone calls, tension spiking.

The room smells of nerves and excitement, a heady mix of perfume, sweat, and fabric steamers. Bodies close in to help me dress, my undergarment bustier laced up by quick-moving fingers pressing into my ribs. The feel of the dress sliding over my skin is almost electric. Fingers now carefully zipping up the long back, my body weighted in silk satin, reminding me of just how little room I have to breathe.

The team huddles in a corner, strategizing social media angles. Across the room, I notice Duane getting his hair done. But when I approach, he's already gone.

"Where did he go?" I wonder aloud.

"He's got such perfect hair, I barely had to touch it," the stylist comments.

A warm flush creeps up my cheeks as the intimate moments of his dinner party and our physical touches over dinner last night flash before my eyes. The way he kissed me, like he was going to devour me. How he grabbed my arm with his commands. The aura that envelops me when I just stand next to him.

Snap out of it, Charlotte. I mentally shake myself. Tonight is vital for fashion, for Riverbank, for me. I need to shine and make every second count. I shove my Duane daydreams down with all those other unexplored feelings.

At four p.m., Duane appears, his tux and white tails tailored to perfection across his broad shoulders, his presence commanding. The room stills for a heartbeat as all eyes—mine included—sweep toward him. The sharp angles of his jaw, the crisp line of his collar, the way his gaze sweeps over me like a slow-burning fuse leave the entire room spellbound.

He's intoxicating as he comes close. "Here I am, prepared for anything."

His voice is a quiet hum beneath the chaos, a promise, a challenge. Laughing, I grab his arm, leading him to the corner cluttered with lighting gear and the chosen backdrop.

We stand side by side, the photographer directing us with quick commands: "Grab her hand." "Move closer." "Put your arm around her." "Turn toward him."

The camera flashes burst, each pop freezing time for a fraction of a second. Duane's fingers skim my waist, light but firm, sending a bolt of heat up my spine. I press my lips together, focusing. But I feel him, his presence, his heat, his undeniable pull. His scent is all around me, freshly showered, that distinct scent of bergamot—crisp and tangy. I feel vibrant and alive. Shimmering.

"You two look stunning together!" an assistant gushes.

Champagne corks pop in the background. With Duane by my side, I lift my glass, my voice strong despite the fire under my skin.

"Five hours of dedication have brought us to the threshold of fashion's greatest evening. Your talent, professionalism, and camaraderie have been indispensable. To my incredible team, my family—thank you. Cheers to us!"

The clink of glasses rings out. Embraces, laughter, and congratulatory kisses flow throughout the room. Duane leans in, our lips meeting in a kiss that lingers a second too long, the taste of champagne on his breath, the heat of his body too close, too familiar. A shout—"Hey! No messing up the makeup!"—shatters the moment, and I am pulled away, rushed back to the vanity for last-minute touch-ups.

Then suddenly, we are in the hotel lobby. As the elevator doors slide open, the air shifts—this is the calm before the storm. The murmur of celebrities mingling, the hotel's iconic black-and-white floor barely visible, the press just beyond the glass doors, the waiting world poised for the spectacle.

Duane, looking slightly perplexed, asks, "Why are all these famous faces gathered here?"

"It's the Mark," I begin to explain. "The unofficial red carpet for the Met Gala. We don't leave until Anna does.

"Okay, I need you to remember a few things," I continue. "First, no phones or photos are allowed inside during the gala. Anna's already a tad upset with me for tweaking her guest list, so we need to be on our best behavior. And your security can't accompany us. The Met ensures everyone's safety. Your security detail can rejoin you at the end of the night."

"I've got it covered," Duane reassures me.

Soon, all eyes are on Anna, poised at the Mark's main door, her tiara glittering. As she steps out onto the carpet with its large, black **M**, camera flashes explode like fireworks. The crowd stirs. The Met Gala has officially begun.

And so have we.

Chapter Twenty-One

. . . felt like an initiation

WE WAIT JUST OUT OF SIGHT UNDER A TENTED PLAZA AT the Met Museum, like actors in the wings before opening night waiting for our cue. The roar from the photographers lining the grand staircase swells every time someone steps out, then drops again, like surf against stone.

"Is my hair all right? Anything out of place? You've got to be my mirror now," I say, turning to look in Duane's eyes, letting him check my appearance.

"Also, the carpet isn't red this year."

"What? No phones, no photos, no red carpet? Is this a scam, Charlotte?" he teases, grinning. "And by the way, you look stunning. Your hair is perfect, and there's nothing out of place, down to your little finger."

His playfulness is infectious. I give a deep curtsy, almost kneeling before him, and reply, "Thank you."

He takes in a sharp breath and growls, "I want you kneeling at my feet all the time."

Before I can react, we are on the stairs, and I'm hit by electrifying waves of energy—flares of light exploding in the air like fireworks, punctuated by the relentless clicks of cameras and the low hum of voices. The air smells like a cocktail of city cement, expensive perfume, and pure, unfiltered excitement.

I look to my left and there he is—his tailored tux clinging to him like armor, smiling that half smile that I feel deep in my core. He extends his hand, and as our fingers lock, I feel a surge of reassurance. The surrounding chaos suddenly seems manageable, and I feel like we were meant to do this together. I look at Duane. We silently laugh, our eyes meeting over the heads of two costume helpers fussing over a celebrity's gown in front of us. Thankfully my dress is well-behaved.

With him beside me, we climb the famous Met Gala staircase. Each step is an act of both rebellion and conformity—rebelling against professional failure because I'm here even though my company has failed, and yet conformity to the expected public pageantry of the fashion world. I catch glimpses of familiar faces in the crowd—designers, models, photographers—and feel the pressure of countless eyes, dissecting, adoring, critiquing us.

The scent of roses wafts over me from their meticulously wound placement on the banister. It's funny how amid all this surreal madness, the simplest things keep you grounded.

"Smile," he whispers, and I turn just as another volley of camera flashes goes off. My cheek muscles are beginning to ache. This is intoxicating; this is thrilling. I've climbed these steps before, but it feels new with him next to me. My heart pumps adrenaline through my veins like fuel in a race car speeding toward the finish. As we reach the top of the stairs, we pause for one last round of photographs. I'm aware of every inch of myself—how I hold my clutch, the angle of my chin, the posture of my back.

We turn toward each other, the noise of the crowd fading as if someone's turned the volume down. As we look at each other, his lips move to my ear.

"That climb, the adrenaline, the spotlight. Un-fucking-believable. I haven't felt this on fire since . . . well, that first time I ever felt truly on fire with someone."

A thrill shivers through me, my heart pounding in response. "Ah, Duane, first times. They're imprinted on us forever, aren't they?"

His eyes track my face as if he's memorizing every line. I can feel the pull of him, like his body has its own gravity. "Every step up those stairs with you felt like an initiation, like we're getting closer to something rare and ours alone. We're on a path together, with all the excitement and fear and anticipation."

I lock eyes with him. The intensity of the moment and feeling this searing connection to him make me confess, "Each camera flash felt like a spark, setting me on fire. That we were going to combust together."

His lips part in a knowing smile. His hand finds the small of my back, pulling me an inch closer into his aura. "Ah, but you're not just a spark, you're my muse. You've ignited me to be more than just who I've been, to become a better man, the man I'm supposed to be."

I place my hand on his chest, feeling his heartbeat, feeling it beat faster with my touch. "To be someone's muse is to be their north star, guiding but never reachable. Do you think you could handle ever reaching your north star?"

"What if being consumed by my north star is my destiny?" His voice is a husky whisper, every syllable a touch, every word a caress, a sound I feel deep in my core.

I take a quick breath in. "Then I suppose we're on a divine path together."

His gaze brightens, a warm flare in those espresso irises. "Shall we?" he asks, gesturing toward the museum's grand archway, and to what's about to unfold between us.

"Absolutely," I respond, aware I can't stop what this has become. I can't stop this, and I don't want to.

Chapter Twenty-Two

. . . not your usual type

I SLIP AWAY FROM THE CHAOS OF THE GALA, MY STILETTOS clicking softly against the marble floors as I make my way toward the ladies' room. The air is cooler here, quieter, a reprieve from Duane. There's something about him tonight—something magnetic, intense. I need a moment to breathe, to clear my head. As I reach the hallway, I spot a familiar figure leaning casually against the wall near the entrance to the bathroom, her muted metallic dress glinting under the soft lighting.

"Grace?" I say, my voice rising in disbelief.

She turns, and as soon as her eyes meet mine, a wide smile spreads across her face, as she reaches out for me. "Charlotte." Her warm voice has a trace of a French accent. We embrace. The scent of her perfume is rich, floral, intoxicating, and instantly brings me back to Paris, to those heady days when I was strutting down the runways and she was quietly but fiercely making her mark behind the camera.

We pull apart, and I can't help but laugh. "What are you doing here?"

"I could ask you the same thing," Grace says, her voice filled with mischief. "But you . . . of course, you belong at an event like this. Fashion. Art. The Met." She looks me up and down appreciatively, her penetrating eyes gleaming. "And as always, you are perfection."

I shrug, trying to downplay the compliment. "You look stunning. But really, what brings you to this madness?"

She sighs, a soft, wistful sound. "I'm here because of *him*," she says, rolling her eyes slightly. "Of course, he couldn't attend without his talented assistant director by his side."

I nod slowly, realizing who she means. Grace works for one of the biggest French directors in the business, a legend really, but anyone who knows her knows she's the real genius behind his success. And more than that, she's his lover, but somehow never quite his equal in the eyes of the world.

"You're still working on *his* films?" I ask, my tone gentler now.

She shrugs again, her lips curving into a bitter smile. "Yes. Still in his shadow. But this last movie . . . Charlotte, this one was different. I gave everything, every ounce of myself, to this project. I wrote half the script, directed the crucial scenes, poured my soul into the story." She pauses, her voice dropping to a whisper. "This . . . this has to be it, my moment. He has to give me the credit I deserve, finally. Don't you think? After all these years?"

There's a flickering vulnerability in her eyes that I haven't seen in a long time. Grace, always so confident, so strong, now waits for validation from a man who takes her brilliance for granted. My heart aches for her.

"He has to," I say firmly. "There's no way he can keep hiding you in the shadows. You *are* his films, Grace. He can't deny that anymore."

She presses her lips together, as if trying to hold back a flood of emotions. "I hope you're right," she murmurs, "because if he doesn't . . . I don't know how much longer I can keep doing this."

We stand there in silence for a moment, the weight of her confession hanging between us. Then she takes a deep breath, shaking off the seriousness with a practiced ease. "But enough about me," she says, her voice lighter. "What about you? You seem . . . different. Happier. And who is that drop-dead gorgeous man you arrived with?"

I feel a flutter in my stomach at the mention of Duane. "His name's Duane," I say, trying to sound nonchalant. "He's . . . well, a friend. A complicated friend."

Grace raises an eyebrow, her lips curving into a teasing smile. "A friend? Charlotte, he looks at you like he's ready to burn the world down for you."

I feel my cheeks warm, the intensity of her words striking me more than I want to admit. "He's . . . intense. But he's younger, you know. I'm not sure he's—"

"Age?" Grace interrupts, her eyes narrowing playfully. "Since when does age matter to you? Besides, he doesn't seem younger. There's something about him—he has gravitas, a presence. Unlike Matthew or David, who were charming, yes, but boys compared to him."

I let out a soft laugh, shaking my head. "What do you mean?"

"Come on, Charlotte." She leans in, her voice dropping to a conspiratorial whisper. "He's dark, brooding . . . not your usual type. He's serious. He seems self-assured and competent," she says, her eyes studying my face closely. "And it's obvious that he's into you."

I've always felt Duane's aura, a physical attraction, pulling me to him whenever we're in the same room. But she's right. There is a gravitas to him, a sense of seriousness and responsibility. The words feel heavy. I had never felt that about Matthew or even David.

Grace's confidence in me has always been unwavering, but her confidence in Duane leaves me feeling unsettled, yet excited. Hearing her—someone I respect, someone who sees people for who they really are—makes me appreciate that there is a depth to him. "Maybe . . ." I say softly, my voice trailing off. I feel a strange tension in my chest, like I'm on the edge of realizing something that's been hiding in plain sight.

Grace tilts her head, studying me for a moment longer before she speaks. "Don't deny it just because you're scared, Charlotte. You deserve someone who takes you seriously, who sees you for the incredible woman you are. Maybe Duane's that person. And if he's not . . . well, at least he's not afraid to show that he cares."

She loops her arm through mine, pulling me gently toward the ladies' room door. "Come on," she says, her voice playful again. "I need to freshen up before I face the crowd again. I'm working on a screenplay for a new movie, a romance. The key will be to have the male and female leads really fall in love with each other on-screen."

I nod absently, my mind spinning. As we walk, I can't help but think about how different Duane is from my past lovers. I've been so focused on him being younger and therefore not really wanting to settle down and have a family. But there is something deeper there, something I hadn't allowed myself to fully acknowledge until now. Grace's words echo in my head, and I wonder if maybe, just maybe, there's more to Duane than I've been willing to see.

As we return to the table, I see Duane look up, his eyes finding mine immediately. There's that intensity again, his shadow and edges pulling me in, making the rest of the world melt away. Grace is right—he does have a depth that I've overlooked. For the first time, I see Duane as Grace described him—serious, accomplished, mature. He's not a playboy, not just a thrill, but someone of substance. Could he be something more?

I introduce Grace to Duane, and they exchange pleasantries. Duane is familiar with her work and the movies she's made. And I see how she considers his words and responds as if talking to a colleague, not a tech playboy. As she goes to leave, she gives me a subtle nudge, her eyes sparkling with amusement. "You weren't lying," she whispers. "He's intense. And he's definitely into you."

Chapter Twenty-Three

. . . as of tonight

GLANCING AROUND THE CROWDED ROOM FOR IMPORTANT connections for Riverbank, I notice Duane speaking to Anna's assistant. I don't recall them being acquainted. Duane has a secretive air about him, a trait I find intriguing. It reminds me of how I used to hide my own secrets from the world, like the horrifying moment I first noticed blood streaming down my leg, the agonizing cramps taking my breath away.

"You're shivering. Are you cold?" Duane's voice pulls me back from the memory. He's next to me now, the dance floor thinning out around us as the DJ fades into a softer track.

"They're playing our song." He offers his hand, and I let him draw me in as "I Hear a Symphony" by the Supremes fills the room—subtle tinkling, then a bright rush of harmonics.

"Our song?" I tease, settling my palm against his shoulder. His arm wraps my waist, firm and warm.

"As of tonight," he says, his voice close to my ear. "Did you know this was Diana Ross's favorite song to perform?"

A laugh catches in my throat. "You know so many details about music."

"I do." His smiles, small and private. "My mother loved telling me all about her favorite groups. She always had music on—the Allman Brothers, the Stones, Fleetwood Mac, Motown classics. She'd turn the volume up and literally glow, eyes shining, like the chorus lit her from inside."

"You got your music from her," I say softly.

He doesn't reply, only leads me into a twirl and pulls me back, our bodies pressing together in the rhythm of the music. The world around us seems to fade away into silence. His face comes closer to mine, and he's staring into my eyes. His look radiates power, harshness, impatience. I see luminous amber eyes, and then he's crushing my lips, his mouth consuming my tongue, consuming me like he can't get enough, igniting a heat within me that spreads down to my core and then slowly rises up to spread throughout my whole body.

With my hands in his hair, his lips continue to explore mine, along my cheek and then down my neck. I am about to melt. It's a sense of vertigo, of the room spinning. And at the same time I can sense him holding back, and it only makes me feel even more on fire. I have to force myself to pull away, breathless, feeling a loss of control. But then he tilts my chin up, and his look pins me open, like he's seeing the girl and the woman, the armor and the ache, all of me with nothing between us; the naked truth is almost unbearable, and I have to look away, too exposed to hold his gaze.

"I. Want. You. Now," he growls, his voice a husky whisper. I can only manage a wordless nod in response.

There's a sense of urgency as we move back to our table. I hastily gather my things, and we slip out into the crisp May evening. It's a short walk down Fifth Avenue to the Mark. He takes my hand, holding it to his lips, sending a jolt of electricity through me. Is this happening too fast? I haven't felt yearning like this since the early days with Matthew. It seems like a lifetime ago. But no, I can't ever remember feeling this way before.

For several seconds I hesitate, arguing with myself. It's too fast. I don't know who this man is. But my questions are a deceptive charade. I know what I want. I want this.

We pause on the sidewalk near the entrance to Central Park, with the hotel just around the corner. I reach up to encircle his neck, pulling him down for another kiss. This time, I make our kiss tender, languid. I trace my lips over his, his cheeks, his nose, and back to his lips. He willingly opens his mouth, letting me explore until he pulls away, whispering, "We need to be alone."

We enter the hotel surrounded by small clusters of spectators hoping for a glimpse of their favorite celebrities. The lobby buzzes with the A-list crowd and their entourages. I catch myself daydreaming about a passionate elevator ride, something out of a *Fifty Shades* scene.

But the elevator's packed, bodies pressed shoulder to shoulder, perfume and alcohol thick in the air. I'm pinned against Duane's side, his hand braced on the small of my back, the heat of him seeping through the fabric of my gown. I feel rather than see his gaze slide down to my mouth, and my pulse kicks in.

I gasp as Duane starts to loosen his bow tie, fingers working the knot, then popping open the top buttons of his shirt. A woman in a sleek metallic gown next to him lets out an appreciative whistle. He tips her a lazy, captivating smile—but his eyes stay on me. "Oh darling, this isn't for you," he drawls just as the elevator doors slide open on our floor. He catches my hand and pulls me out into the hallway as collective sighs of disappointment follow us.

"You're such a flirt," I tease, feeling a thrill that his charm has all the women entranced, but it's me he wants. I begin to question why. He should be chasing the young, glamorous women we've just left behind. *Stop overthinking, Charlotte, enjoy the moment,* I hear Viv saying in my head as he unlocks the door to his room.

Chapter Twenty-Four

. . . now we're in it

I DROP MY BELONGINGS ONTO THE ENTRY TABLE. "WOULD you like a drink?" he asks, approaching a well-stocked bar, while a slow, sultry samba fills the room with sensuous vibes.

"I'll have some champagne," I reply, intrigued by the music. "Who is this?"

"Nouvelle Vague," he answers as the Billecart-Salmon cork pops over the champagne glasses.

"Charlotte," he starts, voice strained, "despite everything I'm feeling for you right now, I want to take this slow." He hands me a glass, and we clink our flutes together, studying each other. As we sip our champagne, the tension between us fills the room.

I break the silence first. "I feel like whatever happens next, we're going to be lost."

He gently takes the glass from my hand. "No," he counters. "It doesn't matter what happens next. We're found. I found you, and you found me.

"Now turn around so I can get you out of that dress," he commands.

As I turn, he delicately sweeps my hair to the side, placing tender kisses from my earlobe down my shoulders, slowly unzipping my dress. The fabric pools like a royal blue lake at my feet, and I step out of it, spinning around to face him in my pale blue bustier and panties. I step toward him, my gaze locked onto his as I slowly unbutton the rest of his shirt, whispering, "Darlin', I think this is for me."

He shrugs off his waistcoat and shirt, stashing his cuff links into his trouser pockets. As I reach for his zipper sliding down his pants, he swiftly discards his shoes and steps out of his clothing.

Now we are face-to-face. I lean into him, pressing soft kisses along his chest, teasing his nipples. I can feel him stiffen beneath my touch.

Suddenly, he grips my arms, pulling my head up to claim my mouth in a deep, explorative kiss. I kiss him back as his teeth nip at my lower lip. I'm aware of my breathing, aware of his fingers on my face, the way his mouth tastes warm but rough, the pressure of his rippled chest muscles against my bustier.

I'm desperate to feel his skin against mine. I fumble with the hooks behind me, stretching to shed the last of my clothing.

He senses my struggle and turns me around, skillfully unfastening the stubborn hooks. As my bustier joins the trail on the floor, he kneels, pulling down my panties. His lips trace a warm path down my back. I gasp out his name. He stands, his hands tracing a path from my hips, over my breasts. I lean back into him, feeling him press against me.

"Duane," I mutter, reaching toward him as he pulls his underwear off. We are facing each other now, both bare, raw, and unguarded. The simple utterance of his name escapes my lips again. As his hands cup my breasts, he whispers, "Lola, you are simply so beautiful. I want you more than I've ever wanted any woman."

Lola. Yes, I'll take it. It makes me feel sexy, his.

Our lips meet in a fiery kiss; my hands roam freely across his skin, eliciting a low moan. Suddenly, he scoops me into his arms, carrying me toward the bedroom as I try to melt my body into his.

He lays me down on the white silk sheets, his mouth exploring the length of my body with a heated fervor that sears my soul. My moans echo through the room as his lips latch onto each nipple, coaxing them into hardness. He covers them with wet kisses, making my core clutch tightly. His descent continues, each kiss, each lick further stoking the rising inferno spreading from deep within me outward to every nerve fiber.

He places open-mouthed kisses along my stomach, making his way down below my navel, intermingling biting kisses and sucks to my skin. My body feels electrified, waiting on edge as his mouth finally finds my quivering folds. I arch my back in pleasure, a low groan escaping my lips as his tongue expertly teases my sensitive skin. His tongue slowly licks from the top mound to my entrance as I combust into a searing bonfire.

"I want you inside me," I manage to say.

"Not yet, Lola. You're not ready for me." His voice is a growl as he looks up at me from between my legs, keeping his gaze steady on mine. I feel embarrassed, uncomfortable, looking at him from this position. "No," he says, sensing my need to look away. "Eyes on me." He's *so bossy.* But I think I like it.

His mouth finds me, teasing and claiming in turns. The slow pull of his lips and the deliberate swirl of his tongue send sparks shooting through every nerve. Pressure builds and shifts, a rhythm of pleasure that blurs into something wild and uncontainable.

I can't keep track of what he's doing—only that he's everywhere at once, unraveling me, dissolving me. My body arches helplessly as he anchors me in place, one hand firm at my hip, the other pressing me down as if to hold me inside the storm.

The world collapses into pure sensation. Heat radiates out in waves, white light bursting behind my closed eyes, my body trembling, convulsing, surrendering completely to him. I cry out, clinging to the bliss as it crashes over me, fierce and unstoppable.

He moves momentarily, retrieving something from the bedside drawer. As he climbs back on the bed, I hear the rip of a packet and watch as he rolls the condom down his rigid cock. He comes forward to kiss me, and I taste myself as his mouth invades mine. Everything he does is to let me know he's in charge.

He pulls away to look at me. "You are so beautiful, Lola, and you taste so fucking sweet." His words, his appreciation of my beauty and the carnality of his statement, send shivers of confusion and longing through me. As his knee nudges me open, I quickly adjust my position to accommodate him. His gaze is heavy, smoldering with desire and anticipation. I return his look with a slight smile, a silent invitation. His words rumble against me as he plunges into my warmth. "Fuck, Lola, you are so wet."

"Don't be gentle," I urge. We are in this now, raw and honest, an experience I've never had before, and I sense a freedom, an abandon to bare myself and my desires now, with him.

"I'm not going to be gentle. I know what you need, Lola, know what you want. This is you and me, darling."

And then he is thrusting deep into me, filling me up, his pace faster and faster, his hips pistoning as he roughly pounds into me, punishing my body, and I'm crying out in pleasure and pain. He pushes my knee up against my chest to get even deeper, and I hover at the edge, his position purposeful, pushing and rubbing, but it's not enough. His movements are powerful, rhythmic, while my inner walls respond in kind, gripping him tightly.

I sense he's in control but holding back, and I realize he's waiting for me. Urging me. "What do you need?" My body thrashes. I don't know how to let him know. He's in charge, but I still resist. Then he's demanding. "Tell me, Lola, say it." And as everything builds, he asserts his control, moving his lips to the angle of my neck and shoulder, and bites down deeply, hard, releasing me to come as he marks me. Searing pain. Then, I'm shimmering, feeling so high, trying to grasp the paradise in front of me until I'm calling out his name. And then "Lo . . . la . . ." swells up like thunder as he shouts my name, and our bodies vibrate with final shudders.

I follow the soft rhythm of his breath with my own, my fingers playing idly with his hair. "Duane," I whisper, "that was amazing." He shifts beside me, pulling out of me and then lying so close that our faces are mere inches apart. "You're an incredible lover," I murmur. "You made me feel so . . ." In response, he cups my face, drawing me into a tender, chaste kiss before he gets up. I hear him pulling off the condom as he goes into the bathroom.

The silence envelops and gnaws at me, a creeping dread. Did he feel the profound connection like I did? Was this just a physical encounter for him? Does he feel the private world we just shared? I hold my disappointment at bay, waiting for his response. He soon returns, sliding into bed beside me, pulling me close, my back to his front, his face near my ear.

"Lola, it's all I wanted," he confesses, his voice a low rumble of exhilaration. "You, so stunningly beautiful, all the glamour and the photographers and the rush of our entrance. And then to spend the night with you. I've fucking wanted you for so long. Now we're in it. And it's incredible."

Relief washes over me, replacing the dread that had lingered moments before. He did feel the connection. We lie there, his arm around my waist and my hand on top of his, not speaking, his head against my shoulder.

"You called me Lola," I say, tasting the name again. It still feels like heat under glass.

I feel his flicker of a smile. "I did."

"What is she to you?" I ask, pretending lightness and failing. "Because when you said it, I felt . . ." I search for the shape. "Like a private jewel. Hidden. Kept. A little wicked."

"Dirty sweet?" he offers, amused and tender all at once.

I nod.

He reaches, tracing a finger down my throat. "Lola. For when the world isn't invited in. For when you want me to lead."

I turn my face at an angle to brush tenderly over his lips.

"Has it always been that way for you?" he asks.

I don't want to talk about this. I can't. I never could. Not with any lover, not even Matthew. He's turning me onto my back and looking at me, his fingers on my chin, moving my face, forcing me to look at him. "Listen, I like to control things in the bedroom. That's who I am, and I think you like it that way, too. But you have to talk to me to let me know. What about you?"

"Me?" It's a single word, but I have to force it.

"What gets you off?"

"I think you can guess what it is."

"The pain?"

I nod but don't want to explain, and he doesn't push.

Chapter Twenty-Five

. . . disappointed me only once

"DID YOU GET THEM TO PLAY THAT SUPREMES' SONG?"

He grins like a mischievous child, proudly admitting his part in the evening's musical surprise. We're lying in bed, my face on a pillow looking at him, as he moves his fingers slowly over my neck, my shoulder, my breasts, stroking my hair, constantly layering goose bumps over my skin.

"But how? Everything is always so tightly orchestrated at that event."

"Everything has its price. I offered to make another irresistible contribution to the Costume Institute if they could indulge my wish."

"Duane, that's the sweetest thing anyone has done for me."

"I told you," he responds, his smile infectious, "music is a big part of my life."

"What type of music do you like?" The conversation flows naturally, an intimate moment providing the perfect backdrop to delve into the unexplored territories of our lives.

"All types," he responds, "but I guess I always default back to rock and roll."

"Is that what your mother liked?" I asked, curious about the woman who raised the man beside me. He doesn't reply. Instead, he proposes, "Are you hungry? Let's order some food."

I feel the curtain descending. The window into his personal world is closing once more. But I'm not upset. I have patience. I understand that truly knowing this man is a journey worth every moment.

"It's two a.m."

"I know. But this place is the epitome of service." He reaches for the phone and orders scrambled eggs, croissants, and a pitcher of orange juice. Covering the phone, he asks, "Do you want tea or coffee?"

"Chamomile tea and maybe some avocado," I say as I make my way to the bathroom.

Warm water cascades over me as Duane joins me in the solitude of the shower. I feel his hands soaping my back. "You're a little sloppy with those suds," I tease, thankful I'd put my hair up.

"Turn around," he commands. His hands begin to trace patterns on my front, provocatively stroking my breasts while watching my reaction. I close my eyes, sighing in pleasure. The sensation of his soapy hands moving lower causes a ripple of anticipation. His hand makes its way between my legs, urging them apart.

"So thorough, Mr. Blacklock," I manage to joke, even as desire clouds my senses.

"Lola, you have no idea." His voice is husky as his fingers begin their intimate exploration.

With a slow, deliberate nudge of his foot, he parts my stance wider. My pulse hammers, the ache between my thighs sharp and insistent. I clutch his forearm for balance, but really it's keeping me from unraveling completely.

"Stay still," he orders, his voice low, a blade of sound against my ear. His hand moves with devastating precision, circling, pressing, claiming, until every nerve is strung tight as wire. "That's it, Lola. You feel that? Give it to me. All of it. I own your pleasure."

The command tears through me. My body convulses, surrendering, breaking under the sharp edge of his control. His name rips from my throat as I shatter, and the marble and steam blur into white heat.

He doesn't let me collapse. He catches me, holds me upright, then pivots, caging me between his body and the hard marble wall. Water pounds over us, relentless, as his mouth seizes mine—not a kiss, but a taking. His tongue forces entry, his breath hot, demanding, until I'm dizzy, gasping, consumed.

I wrench back just enough to lather my hands, sliding them across his chest, down the ridges of muscle to where he's already straining, hard and merciless. His sharp intake of breath makes me smile, a tremor of defiance. "I like to be thorough, too," I whisper.

He clamps down on my wrist with a playful glare. "Not here. Rinse off. Then back to bed." His tone leaves no room for choice, only obedience.

I look at him, my eyes wide in amusement. "You want to again?"

His smirk is shadow and hunger all at once. "You started this, and I'm so hard and crazy for you, Lola. Yes, again."

"What happened?" he says.

We're talking again, in low tones, our bodies tangled around each other, another interlude in these dreamlike hours together.

My hand instinctively goes up to my forehead scar, where his fingers are touching me. "I fell from the stage during a Paris runway show when I was twenty-two." My voice is a whisper. He waits.

"The very end of the runway collapsed due to poor construction, and I collapsed with it, breaking my arm and cutting my face."

"My God." He rises up on his arm to look at me.

"Everything healed, but I was left with this scar on my forehead, ending my modeling career. That's why I always look put together. I can hide it that way most of the time."

"What did your father do to the agency when he found out?"

"My dad? He sent me flowers when I was in the hospital. But he really didn't do anything. I remember he had some big deal going on, so he couldn't come to Paris to check on me."

"What the fuck? You're so young, injured in a foreign country, and he didn't come to help you?"

"It was actually a turning point for me. I realized I needed to do something else. Start my own business. The first few years were difficult as I tried to support myself and decide what the business would be, but then it all came together."

"I'm sorry, Lola. I don't know your dad, but it was such an asshole move of him not to be there when you were injured." His tone is tight, harsh.

"It's complicated." It's the only thing I can think of to say. How can I explain the difference between what I want my dad to be and the reality of who he is? Even I couldn't understand, or more importantly, accept it, and I've had a lifetime to try.

"What about you?" I ask. "Did your parents ever disappoint you?"

He turns onto his back, looking up at the ceiling. "In some ways, they disappointed me only once."

I laugh. "Well, that's a rather quixotic thing to say."

"What do you mean by 'quixotic'?" he asked. "Really, Lola, 'quixotic'?"

"Don't change the subject . . ."

"I have to. That's room service at the door, and I'm starving."

—✶—

I wake, his soft lips warm on my skin, kissing my cheek and nuzzling my ear. He smells of toothpaste and a fresh citrus scent. The same scent I have now after our soapy shower together. I open my eyes and wrap my arms around his neck. "Come back to bed, darling," I beg.

He looks like he belongs in another era—a king, a warrior, something mythic in the way he holds himself, just out of yet another shower, with damp hair, already dressed in a denim shirt and jeans. I lean up on one arm in bed to watch him. "Where are you going?"

He slips on his Prada loafers and grabs his exquisitely tailored Cucinelli blazer, then sits on the edge of the bed.

"I have a quick meeting this morning. It won't take long, and when I get back, I want to take you shopping."

I'm intrigued by both statements.

"Oh, Duane, you're so kind, but even though I love fashion, I don't really shop to relax or have fun. What's your meeting about?"

I'm exploring what he feels comfortable sharing with me. I realize that in the past few days he's begun to tell me more about himself, but this time his answer makes me anxious.

"There's a book circulating that pretty much depicts me as the main character. We're working on a way to stop publication."

"You need to stop publication because it's unflattering of you?"

"No, Charlotte." The "Lola" is gone, his voice tight. "It has nothing to do with whether I'm a villain or a hero. It's just too much publicity about me that I can't control. The author is anonymous, so it's taking some time to find out who they are and shut the book down."

I sit up in bed, holding the sheet up to cover my breasts. "But why do you want to hide, Duane? Why is it so important not to be known and to stay in the shadows?"

He looks at me and laughs softly. "After all the very intimate things we did last night, how we were so thorough exploring each other's bodies, this morning you're feeling modest?" he asks, looking at the sheet clutched to my chest.

"You have a beautiful body, Lola. Don't ever hide it from me." And he leans forward to remove the sheet from my hands and tenderly kiss each breast.

"You can't touch me like that and just leave," I say sternly. "And I know you're avoiding my questions. I hope someday you'll trust me enough to share more of yourself."

He pulls away from me and grabs his phone, wallet, and keycard from the table.

"It's not that simple," he says in an apologetic tone. "I can't talk about my parents. And it's important that no one knows about me, for now."

He comes to the bed, leans over, and gives me a deep, long kiss. "Back soon, baby."

Chapter Twenty-Six

. . . so many nicknames

BLOODY HELL, I THINK, MY HEART POUNDING IN A STATE OF panic. Why on earth did I write that ridiculous book? This is the first man I've felt something for since Matthew. The revelation feels like a ticking bomb, ready to detonate at any moment when he finds out it's me behind that book. I have to tell him. Explain the anguish, the rage, the chaos from Matthew's betrayal and subsequent death, and even tell him about the final heartbreak that crushed me.

My phone is practically buzzing off the table from an influx of text messages. Congratulations from Oliver and others at Riverbank on the fantastic coverage and social media engagement. Our team's posts have accrued tens of thousands of views: an assortment of me, styling and getting ready for the gala, the dress fitting, the makeup and hair sessions. But a select few are of me and Duane. Those, unsurprisingly, have drawn the most attention.

We make an attractive pair. A titan with blond hair, and deep-set espresso eyes, he complements my height, dark hair, and bright blue eyes. I find myself focused on a particular photo on my phone. Both of us look at ease, me turning slightly to gaze up at him as he looks down at me.

I mutter an expletive under my breath. Holy fuck. It's so clear. The customary polite veneer shared between couples is absent, and our intense chemistry, our mutual longing and passion, is totally exposed. There for everyone to see.

I begin to grasp the extent of his sacrifice in accompanying me to the gala. His carefully crafted anonymity has been cast aside in that one photo. All for me. And how have I repaid him? With a concealed betrayal lurking in the shadows. The painful reality is that I have publicly depicted him as an arrogant, conceited, intolerable tech villain. I had convinced myself that the book was humorous, that the comedy softened the blow of my descriptions of him. But deep down, I knew it wasn't true. I had deluded myself to make my cruelty seem justifiable.

I go over all my thoughts and feelings with Vivian when she arrives at the hotel room to help arrange the return of my dress. We talk as we carefully stuff the extravagant designer gown into its massive dress bag.

She insists I can't tell him now, reminding me of the book's popularity and the financial windfall it's bringing in. Thanks to my agreement with the indie publisher, the majority profit is mine.

"But Viv, I really like this guy. I feel awful for betraying him twice. First with the book, then by not confessing that I wrote it," I say.

She tries to reassure me, saying what's done is done and pulling the book won't help. She advises to let things play out while I get to know Duane better. When she asks if I'd discovered anything else about him, I can only admit his determination to remain an enigma.

"He's so private. He doesn't want anyone to know anything about him."

She chuckles, making her own observation. "Goddamn,

Charlie. He must really care about you. For someone so desperate to keep to the shadows, showing up at the Met Gala is an unusual move. His appearance earned forty-seven thousand likes on social media, making him more famous than ever as the cofounder of a successful cryptocurrency platform. Welcome to the celebrity world, indeed."

I cease my struggle with the dress bag, contemplating Vivian's words.

"He refers to me as his muse. He makes me feel cherished." I feel my eyes light up with a dreamy glow.

Vivian embraces me tightly. "You deserve to be adored."

Just as Vivian lifts the dress bag to take it to the reception desk for return, Duane steps into the suite.

"Hello," he says, reaching out to Vivian with a friendly hand. "You must be Vivian. Finally, I get to meet the woman who seems to work magic from anywhere in the world."

"It's a pleasure, Duane. And thank you for coming to Charlie's aid when no one else could," Vivian responds.

"Charlie? So many nicknames, eh?" he says, looking at me with a half-concealed smile. He crosses over to me and plants a kiss on my forehead.

"Ah, I can explain that," Vivian chimes in, amused. "At work, she's Charlie. But her brother insists on calling her Carlie."

"Charlotte, Charlie, Carlie . . . and here I am with no nicknames."

Vivian shoots back, keeping the playful banter going. "I wouldn't be so sure. Haven't you guys been dubbed the Kings of Crypto?"

"Vivian . . ." I warn, not wanting things to go south.

"Yes, I've heard that one, also Bitcoin Billionaires, but neither are entirely accurate. We've also invested heavily in Ethereum," Duane concedes.

"Is that because of Ethereum's flexibility and adaptability?" Vivian asks.

"Indeed. Its software protocol blockchain is open source, so developers can build applications to run on the Ethereum blockchain. That makes it more than just a cryptocurrency."

"Oh, I know," Viv says. "And you can execute smart contracts on the Ethereum platform, which bitcoin can't. Transactions are faster too, making the Eth platform cost-efficient," she adds.

Deciding to end the impromptu crypto class, I intervene. "That's enough for today." Although I'm tempted to dive into the discussion, I hold back. I don't want Duane to feel like my friends are after him for financial insights.

Changing the subject, I say, "Weren't you going to take me shopping?"

Chapter Twenty-Seven

. . . a decadent sprawl of silk

STANDING OUTSIDE A FEW MINUTES LATER, DUANE TAKES my hand, leading me toward Madison Avenue. "Where are we off to?" I ask, trying to keep the atmosphere light.

"To atone for my past crime," he replies mysteriously.

I have no clue what he's talking about, but decide to play along. "I'm intrigued."

We stroll down Madison in comfortable silence, his arm snug around my waist. As if echoing my thoughts, he murmurs, "We're a perfect physical fit." His touch is intoxicating, and I can't get enough of him. He must feel it too, as he whispers, "I can't get enough of you." The words send a warm rush through me. I silently pray that whatever this is, it continues.

Finally, we stop in front of the elegant Hermès store. "This is it," he announces as a doorman ushers us inside. Suddenly, it clicks. "This is about my scarf!" I exclaim.

An attractive woman with a subdued but obvious Hermès scarf elegantly wrapped around her neck approaches us. "Mr. Blacklock, what a pleasure. I'm Hélène. How may I assist you today?"

"Hello, Hélène. I'm looking for a scarf for my girlfriend," Duane explains.

Girlfriend? That's pretty bold. We've spent one night together and certainly haven't discussed what this is. Before I can say anything, he leads me through the store, bypassing the enamel bracelet section, until we finally arrive at a stretch of pristine glass display cases adorned with scarves that could only be described as wearable art.

"What colors does mademoiselle prefer?" Hélène asks.

"Let monsieur choose," I playfully deflect, looking at Duane.

"You should pick one that you like," he says.

"You're not off the hook that easily. You stole my scarf, so it's your job to pick a replacement."

"Consider my punishment accepted," he says, eyes lit with amusement and a glint of challenge as he moves with slow precision to the display cases.

He leans against the counter as if it were built for him, all effortless dominance and indecent good looks. His fitted black tee clings to his muscled chest and toned biceps, while the fabric of his jeans stretches taut over the lean curve of his waist, hinting at the strength beneath.

"Something to complement her eyes," he murmurs, ensuring I hear him.

Hélène unfurls scarf after scarf—deep sapphires, powder blues, stormy teals—layering them over the counter in a decadent sprawl of silk. The sheer volume of them is almost absurd. One catches the light and shifts from sapphire to violet, an optical illusion in fabric, as his fingers brush over the delicate silks with the same reverence he's used on my skin.

I hang back a little, watching him intently. The luxury of the fabrics is evident, but it's Duane's thoughtful consideration that steals my attention. He discards another as I watch him smile slightly.

"You're enjoying this," I say, caught up in the excitement of the luxury.

"I like spoiling you." His voice is casual, but there's a gleam in his eyes that makes my stomach flip.

When he finally chooses, he holds the scarf up, tilting his head. "Yes," he murmurs. "This one."

I step forward, but he pulls it back, a playful glint in his gaze. "Ah ah ah," he teases, twirling the silk around his fingers before handing it to Hélène. "Not until later."

"Duane—" I start, but he silences me with a slow, deliberate brush of his lips over mine.

"When we're alone," he murmurs against my mouth. "I want to put it on you myself."

His fingers ghost along my jaw, tilting my chin up as his lips hover just a breath away.

"And when I do, you'll have nothing on." He moves his fingers to trail down the inside of my wrist, featherlight.

Hélène places the iconic orange bag in Duane's hands. She exhales a soft laugh as she watches, sensing the tension suffocating the air between us. "Enjoy your selection, monsieur and mademoiselle."

As we exit the store, I swallow hard and find my voice as I reach out and touch his arm.

"Duane, I already love this scarf, sight unseen, because you chose it for me. But I need my orange Hermès back. It was my mother's . . . she gave it to me when I was sixteen. It's a special piece of her that I still have in this world."

He pulls me close and murmurs, "Of course. I love your scarf because it reminds me of you. But now that I have you, I don't need it."

His confession unleashes everything I've been feeling. Tears stream down my face, my emotions in the last twenty-four hours raw and exposed. The relief of Duane's last-minute appearance, the excitement and intensity of the event, happiness at seeing Grace and concern for her struggles for recognition, and then the incredible night with Duane. He knows my desires. Incredibly, pleasure and pain are what he wants, too.

My thoughts come full circle back to my mother, to that impromptu conversation about relationships, what men and women share, how no one really knows what's between them, and her explanation of why she had remained married so long to an unfaithful husband.

Duane lifts my chin, his gaze warm, gentle, searching mine. "Lola, what's wrong?"

I can't articulate my thoughts—the potent mix of happiness and sadness, the memories of my vibrant, loving mother. It's too much to explain.

I can only say, "I guess I miss my mom."

He pulls me into his chest, his lips against my hair, and says, "I know the feeling, Lola. I know the feeling."

Chapter Twenty-Eight

. . . leave it alone

AFTER A SOOTHING SHOWER AND A LONG NAP, I FEEL REfreshed. When we meet in the hotel lobby, Duane immediately pulls me close, his hand snaking around my waist as hotel guests bustle around us. He kisses me deeply, whispering "You look radiant" into my ear. I find myself lost in the moment, words flowing freely from my lips. "You make me feel that way," I admit, our lips colliding in a kiss that becomes deeper, urgent, as he explores my mouth with his tongue, my fingers threading through his soft hair.

For our evening out, he'd suggested casual attire. So I'd chosen boot-cut jeans, my Luccheses, and a snug blue-gray T-shirt, my hair hanging loose below my shoulders. I'd never considered casual as an excuse to go makeup-free, so my face bears subtle touches of foundation, blush, and eyeshadow that accentuate my features and hide my scar.

As we arrive at Casa Cipriani, I'm struck by the crowded dining room. We're led by the maître d' through the throng of diners to a secluded corner banquette. I cast a questioning glance at Duane, surprised by the empty table next to ours.

"I bought us some privacy," he explains with a grin. "It's quieter this way."

I settle into the plush cushions, briefly wondering what it cost him to buy this kind of seclusion here on a packed night.

Our dinner is divine, complemented by a delicious vintage wine. Duane is an easy companion tonight, regaling me with sly start-up stories. I trade back with fashion war tales—the photographer tantrums, the midnight fittings, the shoes that drew blood, the extreme exotic locations. He's an attentive listener, often reaching across the table to hold my hand as we laugh together.

As we finish our second bottle of wine, I lean toward him to whisper conspiratorially, "Where are we going? Because I think I've already lost those blues."

"Yes, but this will keep them away," he assures me. "We're going to a concert."

At the mention of a concert, my heart sinks slightly, fearing the intimacy we've built would be shattered in a boisterous crowd. But he quickly dispels my worries. "It's a small, private performance, maybe fifty people," he adds, as if reading my thoughts.

A concert, music. I swirl what's left in my glass. "Tell me something. Your name—Duane. That's not an accident, is it? As in Duane Allman?"

He goes still, eyes on me, saying nothing. The newly created hush around our table deepens.

"Tell me more about yourself," I try, gentle, offering him an opening he can step through or not.

A door slams shut behind his gaze. He leans back, summoning the check with a glance. "We've had too much to drink."

"Or maybe you feel comfortable with me," I counter calmly, not reacting to his sudden hostility. "I know I feel really good right now being here with you, just talking and getting to know you."

"Leave it alone, Charlotte," he snaps.

"Duane, what's wrong? Anything you share with me stays with me. I get that you don't want to discuss your parents. I respect that. But please, don't become a ghost now," I plead.

He sighs, turning back to me after calling the waiter. "I'm not a ghost, Lola."

His warm breath hovers near my ear, layering goose bumps along my neck and shoulders. "I'm very real," he murmurs, voice a low promise, "and I'll show you how real later—when it's quiet, when it's just us, me in control, your body under mine."

Chapter Twenty-Nine

. . . is that what you need

I FIND MYSELF AT A CONCERT, OF ALL PLACES, IN WHAT APpears to be a recording studio. It's furnished with plush seating, accommodating barely thirty-five people, arranged in a semicircle. The celebrity at the heart of it all is a world-renowned pop star strumming his acoustic guitar in solitude. I recognize some of his older pieces, but many are unfamiliar to me—new, raw, and mesmerizing.

Between songs, he chats amiably with the audience, sharing snippets of his life, personal anecdotes, and his perspective on world events. There's something so human, so relatable about him in those moments.

Once the performance ends, he remains to mingle with the crowd. My heart leaps with surprise and excitement when I see the performer recognize Duane. As they embrace, patting each other's backs, I watch from the side, another veil surrounding Duane mysteriously lifting before my eyes.

Duane turns to me, catching my arm and drawing me into his circle. "John, meet Charlotte, my girlfriend." The musician's hand lingers a little too long in mine.

"Pleasure to meet you, Charlotte. Duane, she's a stunner." John winks, causing a flush to spread over my cheeks.

Ignoring the flirtation, I quickly respond, "I really love your new songs. And the whole concert, actually."

He invites Duane and me to his place the next night, where he is hosting a jam session with other musicians. But Duane, placing a protective arm around my shoulders, declares, "We're leaving tomorrow. And even if we weren't, hands off, my old friend. Charlotte's with me."

His protective words, his confident laughter, his hand on my lower back as John guides us out, has me blushing as I realize Duane is staking boundaries.

Back in my hotel room, everything feels dreamy and slightly unreal. I'm lightheaded and euphoric, maybe from the excitement or the wine, maybe from Duane's presence. I discard my T-shirt, shaking my hair loose. Duane closes the gap between us as I feel a thrill of anticipation. His touch is soft but purposeful, kissing my bare skin and tracing a path down my back, expertly unbuttoning my jeans. His skilled movements have me chuckling. "You're quite coordinated," I tease.

With a light "hush" he pushes me back onto the bed and removes my boots. I do as I'm told, lifting my hips up as he pulls my jeans down and off, struggling a little to maintain my balance. Our laughter echoes in the room, a comfortable sound in the charged atmosphere.

Stripped of my jeans, I turn to face him, my heart pounding as I remove my jewelry. His eyes never leave mine, his gaze hot and expectant. Left in nothing but my blush pink lace undergarments, heat surges from my core up to my chest, spreading everywhere. I'm on fire.

His deep, husky voice breaks the silence. "You're breathtaking, Lola. And so fucking sexy."

Desire pools low in my belly, my body reacting instinctively to his words. Every part of me burns with need. My gaze still locked on his, I whisper, "Undo your shirt."

Watching him unbutton his shirt, I catch my breath, my gaze drinking in the sight of him. As he works his shirt free from his jeans, I reach forward to undo his belt, followed by the button on his jeans. With his shirt off, he leans in, his lips tracing a tantalizing path across mine, down my neck to my throat. My breath hitches as he rubs my breasts through my bra, teasing my nipples until they're taut.

"Allow me," I say, my hands finding their way to his muscular chest. I trace my fingers over his firm pectorals, feeling the heat radiate from his skin. Slowly, I kneel before him, my lips meeting the center of his chest, teasing my way down to the edge of his jeans.

"Remove your shoes," I instruct, sitting back on my haunches. In response, he slips them off, his jeans following in a fluid movement. He hooks the waistband of his underwear, but I stop him.

"No, let me."

Keeping my gaze locked on his, I push his shorts to the floor, releasing him. Taking him in my mouth, I stroke him, my hands on his hips as my tongue explores. I can feel him, hard and throbbing, his panting breaths growing heavier as he runs his hands through my hair, massaging my scalp.

"God, Lola, that feels so good," he moans.

Moving my mouth along him, I feel a responsive throb deep within me. Suddenly, he groans, pulling me up to meet his mouth. His tongue pushes into my mouth with a desperate urgency as he grips my ass, lifting me off the floor. My legs instinctively wrap around his waist as he lays me down on the bed, bending one knee up against my chest, his voice husky with desire.

"Look at me, Lola," he demands.

I meet his eyes, pupils blown wide as he thrusts into me

with a powerful movement, eliciting deep groans.

"Tell me you want this." He's above me, eyes glowing like charcoals, locked on mine.

I feel weightless under him, even as his pace quickens. Duane in charge, demanding—I feel exposed, yet safe.

"I want this; I want you. Make it harder; give me more. Fuck me, Duane."

My words seem to fan the flames between us. His male scent of citrus and sweat mingles with my light floral perfume and fills my senses. He closes his eyes, lost in the moment, bringing me closer and closer to the edge. But the release doesn't come. I wrestle against his hold, and he grips me tighter, sensing my body struggling to climax.

He moves down, sucks my pebbled nipple into his mouth, firmly swirls his tongue around its tautness, and then bites. Pain erupts, coursing through my body and mixing with the pleasure of him inside me. I let myself go, losing myself in him.

"Lola," he groans, his voice a desperate plea.

I climax, clinging to him as he finds his release with a shudder.

In the afterglow, he lies still inside me, his arms framing my face as he pulls me closer. We bask in the shared ecstasy, the room filled with the sounds of our heavy breathing. He rolls onto his back, pulling me against him. In the drowsy quiet, he asks, "Is that what you need to get off?"

Relief and shame flicker. He wants to talk about this again. He wants to go there.

This part of me I tried so hard to show Matthew but ended up hiding, sensing how unacceptable it was to him. I had struggled so long with shame and at the same time anger because this was me, this was who I was.

I force myself to meet his eyes. "I need an edge," I say. "Not cruelty. Not harm. Pressure. Control. The pain that turns the noise off. It was never talked about, so it never happened. I felt . . . wrong. Like asking made me less."

His hand stills on my shoulder, then his thumb starts tracing idle circles on my back, lazy, possessive. "You're not wrong," he says. "You're mine."

Something loosens in my chest.

He tips my chin so I'm looking at him. "I like ruling in the bedroom, Lola. I like setting the pace, the terms. I like being your king there. But a king who serves his muse. We'll talk before, during, after. I'll ask. You'll answer. We'll adjust. That's how a kingdom runs."

My voice is small and shaky. "You make it sound . . . simple."

"It is. Desire is allowed to be simple." He kisses my knuckles, one by one. "What you want is what I want to give you. Don't hide from me."

Chapter Thirty

. . . the greater risk lies in our being lovers

THE SIGNATURE FLIGHT LOUNGE AT THE MORRISTOWN PRIvate airport hums with an understated elegance, echoed by the expensive furniture and charming reception staff. I rest comfortably in an overstuffed fondant colored leather armchair, my eyes tracing the outline of jets beyond the expansive glass wall as the late-afternoon sun creates patterns across the carpeted floors. Duane's busy at the desk. The past few days have been a whirlwind of excitement and delight, but they already seem remote, just memories.

A knot of anxiety forms in my stomach as Duane and I prepare to board our flight back to the Caymans. Kurt, Duane's bodyguard, steps forward, offering, "Let me put your luggage on board, Ms. Gordon-Lennox."

"Thank you, Kurt. But please call me Charlotte."

My mind churns, a storm of thoughts swirling around our impending return. What am I doing? Involved with a man eight years my junior, withholding secrets from him, luxuriating in the way he makes me feel, and neglecting my ultimate goal—children. The ticking of my biological clock echoes in the silent moments, a relentless drumbeat propelling me forward. But toward what? A husband, a marriage, children, or a single life filled with solitude and loneliness?

I think back to when I was Duane's age, not quite thirty, when the future felt endless, an open runway. That's probably how he feels. He isn't looking to settle down, marriage, children—all the things I yearn for.

What does he want? My mind wanders back to last night. The passion between us is like a tsunami, always leaving me euphoric and breathless, and I know he feels the same. But am I nothing more than a sexual conquest to him? That's what he desires, I think painfully. The connection between us is so intense, so unique, it intensifies every part of me. It's all physical, I remind myself, and because of that, it's sure to burn out quickly. But he also gives me what no lover ever has. It's not something I can talk about with him, but he knows, he understands, he's so attuned to my body.

"Hey, what are you daydreaming about?" Duane approaches me after checking us in. His voice is a deep, soothing hum that pulls me in. He perches himself on the armrest of my chair, a smile playing on his lips. "Thinking about us . . . together . . . last night?"

His question catches me off guard, and I find myself blushing. How does he know? He bends down with a light kiss as he whispers in my ear, "Because I've been thinking about last night all morning. It's a four hour flight back to the Caymans, and this jet has a bedroom."

His kiss becomes a trail of nuzzles down my neck as he gently pulls on my hair, lifting my face to meet his. His lips possessively take mine, demanding entry into my mouth. I'm ablaze. I can feel my pelvic muscles clenching, a familiar warmth spreading through me. I pull away, gasping, "Duane, I, uh—damn, how do you do that?"

"Your body is attuned to mine, baby. I want to claim every part of you."

His words make my heart race, and I yearn to surrender to him, to lose myself in his scent, to tangle my fingers in his soft hair and let his exquisite body consume me. But I pull back from him just in time to see a male figure of impressive stature, athletic in build, approach Duane and greet him enthusiastically. I recognize the man as one of the twins who had made it big with a cryptocurrency trading platform. Duane introduces me, and I keep my peace, listening attentively to their intense discussion.

"Riverbank is set to testify before Congress in support of more cryptocurrency regulation, isn't it?" he asks Duane. "You and Oliver are on point; we need to make crypto mainstream through SEC oversight. It's high time we move past the FTX fiasco and draw institutional and mainstream investors back to the crypto world."

Duane agrees. "But the CTC might serve investors better. The SEC tends to be a bit heavy-handed, and we need regulation that won't choke the life out of the industry. Especially when there are plenty of countries that have an open door policy for crypto without the burden of oppressive regulations."

The conversation concludes as Duane's friend indicates that his flight is ready. He shakes hands with us. "That was quite a picture of you two at the Met Gala," he says, winking. "Good job getting crypto introduced to the fashion world."

After we're alone, Duane explains, "The Gemini trading platform came out on top after the FTX crypto winter. They've done everything by the book, setting an example for the rest of us. Oliver and I have kept a close eye on them, and we've modeled much of Riverbank after their platform." Now he winks at me, stealing his friend's humor. "But rest assured, we're going to outshine them."

Kurt returns, indicating that it's time to board. I find

myself stepping into a Gulfstream G650ER, the most opulent jet I've ever set foot in. Its interior, with individually spaced seats, is all sleekness and luxury. I take in the leather couch facing a large flat-screen TV. As Duane takes a moment to chat with the pilots, an attendant introduces me to the jet's layout and its various features.

We both settle into the comfortable beige seats, adorned with tan leather accents, as we prepare for takeoff. Once we hit cruising altitude, I unfasten my seat belt and gesture for Duane to join me on the couch.

I notice two more men accompanying Kurt at the front of the plane.

"More security? Should I be worried?" I ask as the flight attendant hands Duane a whiskey and me a glass of champagne.

"Not at all. It's just the usual uptick in security as Riverbank garners more press attention."

"Oh, all because one of the elusive founders attended the Met Gala?" I tease.

"Yes." He hesitates. "I'm not one for public photos. There's a heated debate on Reddit; our followers are blaming Riverbank, Gemini, Coinbase, and others for the disaster that is FTX. Just being cautious."

"Have I put you in danger?" I ask, more worried about the implications of my book than our gala appearance.

"I believe the greater risk lies in our being lovers while working at Riverbank. Or maybe I should just make you my official muse, which would override any HR policy," he teases.

I move over to curl up in his arms on the couch, offering him a faint smile. Yet, uneasiness settles over me. An all too familiar feeling of uncertainty. What implications would our relationship have for my position at the company? And the damn book. I have to tell him about it. My anxiety calls for action.

"Don't worry," he assures me, his arm enveloping me in a

warm cocoon. "The two of us will figure this out. Oliver and I are going to be off site with a media coach for the next few weeks practicing our planned testimony before Congress. It's on us to make sure every answer is bulletproof. We'll be in and out of the office until the DC trip, but you won't see much of me during the day. Our evenings are nonnegotiable, so clear your calendar."

"Duane"—I keep my voice low and serious—"we need to talk."

Chapter Thirty-One

. . . the luxury of time

I'M INTENT ON MAINTAINING MY COMPOSURE AS I PREPARE to address him. I move out of his arms to the other side of the couch. I want to look him in the eye, to remain firm and unemotional. But I can never trust myself to do what I think I'm going to do. Before I can control myself, I find myself expressing my feelings, my voice laced with an unexpected anger.

"Duane," I start, "whatever this is between us, it isn't part of my plan. And before it develops into anything else, I think we should stop things now."

He stares back at me, his expression inscrutable, his poker face in place. "Why?"

"Why?" I echo. I then forge on with words that I know will cause him pain, but have to be said. "Duane, you're a player. You've had five girlfriends over the past two years . . . that I know of. And at your age, that's fine. But I'm searching for more than that."

He sits quietly, his face still revealing nothing. "What is it that you want, Charlotte?"

I rush through my words, desperate to get them out.

"I want different things. I'm eight years older than you and you're technically my boss. I love my job, and I don't want to jeopardize it due to our personal relationship."

"What different things do you want?"

I draw a long breath; the cabin hums around us, a soft, steady vibration. Cold air whispers from the vent above my temple. The faint scent of jet fuel and citrus cleaner lingers. "I want to get married, have a family. I've tasted success as a model, as the CEO of my own company, and even as a wife. Now, I'm in the world of cryptocurrency, empowering women in a way I've always yearned for. But despite all of it, I long for a family. Time is running out for me in a way you can't yet comprehend."

"What if I want the same things? Marriage, kids, a family?"

I shake my head. "I don't believe you. You're young, you've had no long-term relationships, you're still dating—a lot." My judgmental tone softens. "You're under the influence of our physical attraction."

He slides closer, and I lean back a little, my position already cornered on the couch. The ice in his glass clinks once he sets it into the holder. "I've never felt with any other woman what I feel when I'm with you," he says, voice low, threaded with the engine's hum. "It's not just about the physical. You steady me."

"But that feeling might not last. In six or eight months, you might be ready to move on, and I will have wasted precious time."

"Charlotte"—his voice is the commanding Duane now—"you don't get to decide my future for me. I know my past, but I've been craving something different. I want us to be exclusive." His fingers find the inside of my wrist, heat sparks, quick as the wingtip lights blinking outside. "This feels special. We've known each other for months, and what's between us is stronger. No other woman has ever made me feel the way you do. You know it. I won't promise forever at forty thousand feet, but I know you feel the same."

I pull my wrist free as gentle turbulence shimmies the ice in his glass. "I can't afford to wait. I've been through a lot, endured so many hardships. You wouldn't want to deal with all that emotional baggage. And you have your own secrets. I know enough about you to know that."

"We both have secrets, but I believe in us. We can build a strong enough relationship to trust each other with them." His voice is insistent, not loud.

"So how can we envision a future together, a marriage, children, when you're such an enigma? I'm left with so many questions that you seem incapable of answering," I counter as my gaze traces the oval of the window, where frost feathers the edge like lace.

"I'm working on that," he replies, following my gaze. He pulls the cashmere throw from the armrest and drapes it across my knees without asking. "You're changing me. I'm stepping out of the shadows. I attended the Met Gala for you. I'm preparing to testify before Congress because of you. You're my muse, my inspiration, my creative force. You ignite the best within me. Being with you allows me to let go of struggles I've carried for far too long."

"What struggles, Duane? What have you battled in the past? What continues to haunt you?" Our hands rest near each other on the throw's fringe. I spread my fingers until they almost—almost—touch his.

He hesitates. "I can't discuss that now. But I want to. I intend to. You light my soul. You make me want to be a better man. Just give this some time."

I shake my head. "I don't have the luxury of time."

"Come with me," he suddenly says, scooping me up in his arms and eliciting a squeal from me as the throw drops to the floor. His voice is a soft rumble, a low note in my ear as he carries me toward the back. I know what's back there and rush to say only half-heartedly, "Duane, stop," as I try to wriggle from his arms. He just grips me tighter as I say, "This can't be solved with sex."

He ignores my professed unwillingness. "This bedroom has a rather sizable bed, never christened, never shared, with anyone."

My breath hitches in my chest, my heart pounds as I hungrily sink into the feel of him. "What were you waiting for?" I murmur, wanting all of this, all of him.

"My muse, Lola, my muse," he confesses.

Chapter Thirty-Two

. . . more than just a moment

MY BREATH CATCHES AS A PIERCING THRILL SETTLES IN MY core. Duane's aura of danger and mystery permeates the cabin as he lays me on my stomach on the bed. I can't tell whether I'm feeling excitement or fear.

"Stay," he commands. And I decide it's both. Definitely both.

I feel his weight as he kneels on the bed behind me, then leans over, seizing my wrists and pinning them above me. "Keep them there or I'll tie them up."

He moves his mouth to my ear as his scent—bergamot, soap, something that is only him—surrounds me. "Answer me, Lola. Words. Use your words," he whispers.

"I . . . uh . . . I will," I quickly stammer. Embarrassment makes me want to giggle, but I manage to hold back.

He raises the skirt of my dress and slides my panties down, and I feel both embarrassed and a growing sense of warmth and wetness between my thighs. This is turning me on. I'm so aroused, and that makes me uncomfortable, bringing back the laugh. A laugh that is promptly stifled as I feel a painful smack on my ass.

I let out a soft yelp and try to move, but his hand is between my shoulders, holding me down. He straddles me, my thighs tight between his legs.

"I want to give you this pain with your pleasure," he says.

His voice is next to my ear. "Do you want this? Do you trust me, Lola?" he asks.

I'm lost in his dominating presence, in knowing he's in control. My breath settles. This is what I want, what I've wanted for a long time, but could never admit or let my lovers know. But Duane knows.

I answer him. "Yes, I trust you. I want this."

Each smack becomes more and more painful. One cheek, then the other. I push my face into the covers, trying to muffle my cries as tears coat my face. I'm not sure how much longer I can take it. And as I ready myself to tell him to stop, the pain starts to change, merging into something less pain and something more pleasure. The heavy pain becomes an unbearable lightness of desire rising from my core and spreading outward.

I'm aching now for him to enter me. To fill me up and relieve my growing tension. He raises me up, bending me over as he takes me from behind. Each powerful thrust accentuates the heat and agony he's given me there. And I want more of him. More of him moving inside me. His rhythm pulls me along with him to that unreachable edge, making my spine tingle until white lights explode behind my eyelids, and I cry out his name as his body tightens, and he goes over the edge with me.

We collapse onto the bed, Duane resting on top of me. We breathe heavily, the endorphin rush flowing through every part of my body. He rolls over onto his back, pulling out, and grabbing me to rest next to him, my head nestled against his chest. As our heavy breathing evens out, he says, "I didn't use a condom. I'm sorry. Too much in the moment. I get checked routinely, and I haven't been with anyone since the last time all my tests were negative."

"My tests are all negative, too, and I'm on the pill, so that's not an issue," I say. "And I would call that more than just a moment," I add, feeling myself blush even as my face is hidden.

I feel his fingers brush my cheek, and then they lift my face to look at him.

"Lola, how much of your need to end this thing between us is about not trusting what we do in the bedroom?" His fingers hold my face as he searches my eyes, his gaze intent and questioning.

"Did you like what we did just now? Did I hurt you?" he asks.

We'll talk before, during, and after . . . the rules of his kingdom.

"No, it was painful at first, but then I could let go and feel the pleasure," I admit.

"You could forget everything and let go because I was in charge. That's what I want to do for you. When it's just us, just you and me, alone and intimate, let me take care of you. Let me give you what you need."

He brings my face up to his and kisses me slowly, tenderly, lavishing attention on my mouth, my lips, as he kisses along the length of my jaw to nuzzle my earlobe. "I need to care for you," he murmurs.

Then he's turning me over, examining my ass as he rubs soothing cream over the throbbing area. It feels good. His hands cool my burning skin. When he's finished, he bends down and places a kiss on each cheek. He pulls up my panties and arranges my skirt. Then, standing, he adjusts himself and his slacks. Sitting back on the bed, he pulls me into his lap and strokes my hair.

"Lola, I want to be your lover. The one you've been waiting for."

He sees me.

What would that be like, to have him care for me? Is he someone I could count on?

I remember Matthew began pulling away early in our marriage. I didn't know why, only that the distance left me unsettled, anxious, always guessing. I stopped asking for what I wanted in the bedroom, silenced by his withdrawal. His quiet, his absence, scorched me. I tried to push through the sting of rejection, but every effort I made seemed to drive him further. His business trips stretched from the occasional week away to monthly, then every two weeks, until finally, he was gone almost every week.

Despite all that, I continued to make sure we stayed connected through sex on his terms. He had wanted that. And I had even become pregnant. How could he possibly be having an affair if he was still sleeping with me, I had reassured myself. I'd allowed my reasoning to push my suspicions away.

Pulling my thoughts back to the handsome man now sitting beside me at forty thousand feet, I touch the sculpted muscles of his forearm.

"Duane, this isn't a good idea, this thing between us." I continue my objections. "I can't be with someone who has secrets. Matthew had secrets, David betrayed me, and though I know you are not them, you have the most secrets and mystery surrounding you. I literally think of you as Mr. Shadows and Edges."

"Lola." His voice is low and husky. "You have yet to see all the edges I have. They are sharp but pleasurable, I assure you."

At his words, his lethal energy surrounds me, spreading a heatwave through my core to the rest of my body, and I feel breathless. I'm shaking my head, physically trying to disperse this magnetic quality engulfing me.

"No," I insist. "What we had this week was great—actually, more than that. It was fabulous, unbelievable even, but when the plane touches down, it's over. You go back to your life, and I go back to mine. Let's not ruin what we have professionally. I want to keep this job and remain on good terms with you."

The anger, demands, raised voice, whatever I had expected, don't materialize. Duane leans back, never looking away. I can't read him. His poker face is in place. He squeezes my hand, which I realize he's been holding through this entire discussion, and then lets it drop.

This has to be for the best. My life is my choices. I didn't know Matthew or David, not really. And the simple truth is, I need to know the man I'm with. To have him open to me, to know all of him.

Chapter Thirty-Three

. . . a brief reign

THE REMAINDER OF THE FLIGHT IS SPENT IN SILENCE. DUANE is engrossed in his computer, while I scroll through the newsfeed of the Met event on my phone. At least that went smoothly. Riverbank at the Met Gala has garnered all the positive publicity I anticipated. My spirits lift with a feeling of pride. The event has been a glowing success even with Oliver canceling at the last minute.

We land several hours later under bright sunlight and gusty winds welcoming us in a pleasant seventy-eight degrees. As Kurt pulls up in front of my apartment building, Duane pulls me into a tight hug. Feeling tears brimming in my eyes, I whisper into his ear, "Thanks for a wonderful time, for being my king, even if only for a brief reign."

He tightens his hold and whispers back, "Lola, this is not the end," before letting me go.

Kurt leaves my suitcases inside the entry door as I walk away from the car, refusing to look back. By the time I get to my apartment, tears stream down my face and I'm sobbing uncontrollably. I collapse onto my bed and bury my face in my pillow, curling myself into the smallest shape I can.

Why are you crying? my inner voice challenges. *You did this. You want him to be the one, but he isn't. You don't truly know who he is or whether this relationship is real.* I chastise myself until I finally succumb into a fitful sleep.

The harp ringtone of Vivian's call wakes me. The dull roar of the ocean soothes in the background as purple tendrils layer the horizon over the balcony. My eyes feel swollen, and my pillow is drenched.

"So, Charlie, are you thoroughly and satisfyingly fucked by that heartthrob who happens to be your boss?" Vivian teases.

"Oh Viv," I wail. "It's over. I ended things before they could go any further."

"Wait, let me get this straight," Vivian says. "You've got this tall, blond genius who's been constantly at your side, showing up for the emergency at the clinic, lending you private jets, appearing like a king at the Met Gala, the hottest man there, and after he shows how much he adores you, you decide to let him go? If you did drugs, I'd swear you were high."

"It's more than that. He took me to a private set with a celebrity guitarist and the whole time absolutely lavished me with his intense attention," I confess.

Vivian's voice loses its playfulness. "Carlie, what's going on? Don't you like him? Aren't you attracted to him?"

"It's the exact opposite, Viv. There's an undeniable chemistry between us. He has this aura that just descends on me. He knows how to please me. He's probably the first man who ever has."

"He's absolutely stunning," she blurts out.

"He adores you," she continues in shock.

"He's incredibly intelligent," with frustration.

"And he's so wealthy," nearly yelling.

"Do you understand that he's head over heels for you? Is that clear?" Her voice is coaxing now.

"Yes, yes, I understand. But I want a family, marriage, children. He's barely thirty. Men his age aren't ready for those commitments."

"Did you ask him?" Her tone has softened.

"Yes, I expressed my desires, and he agreed he wanted the same. But I know it's merely his infatuation speaking."

There's a pause. "Should we bring up the *L* word here?" Viv asks carefully.

"No, absolutely not. His infatuation, calling me his muse—it won't last. He claims he's been with countless women because he's been searching for someone like me. But I need a reliable partner, someone who'll stick by me through all the shit life throws at you. This man harbors too many secrets. I hardly know him, and I don't have the time to invest in discovering who he truly is."

"Charlotte," Viv's voice turns stern, "that's called trust. You need to trust him. This will be true for anyone you meet."

"But even if I trust him, how can he trust me? I wrote that reckless book, and it's only a matter of time before he discovers the truth. We both have secrets. You can't build a relationship on deceit. And when I think about Matthew and his betrayal . . . and the, the loss . . ."

My voice falters, but I push through the pain. "And the wasted time with David. I'm not sure I can ever trust anyone again. It all goes back to my dad, Viv. You know he was never reliable, and he hurt my mom over and over."

"Well, you could tell him about the book. You have control over that," Viv offers quietly.

"You're right," I concede, my voice barely above a whisper as I reflect on my past disappointments. "I'm sorry, Viv, but I can't discuss this anymore. You're my best friend, and I know you want what's best for me, but Duane isn't it. I'm exhausted. Let's chat tomorrow."

And with that, I end the call.

The following weeks at Riverbank drag on. I feel like I'm sleepwalking through life. I show up for work, attend calls, conduct meetings, strategize with my team, but it's as though I'm observing someone else's life.

I'm relieved Duane's not around. As he had told me, he and Oliver are attending off site coaching sessions in preparation for their testimony in front of the House panel on cryptocurrency. He's gearing up to take center stage, and I'm genuinely happy for him.

The second day after arriving back, flowers begin arriving at my apartment. Each evening, the concierge greets me with a smile and another stunning bouquet as I return home. First, it's lilies of the valley, then white roses in a large vase. A spectacular array of hyacinths and tulips follows, then a crystal bowl of pink peonies, and finally, orchids in a blue and white ceramic basin. The lilies of the valley hold a place of honor next to my bed, their delicate scent haunting my restless nights as I lie tossing and turning, their aroma stirring up thoughts of Duane.

On Saturday, instead of flowers, a box arrives with a note from him.

Old tech for a new, cherished muse. These songs inspire me. D.

Inside is an iPod. As I remove the thin slab from the box, nostalgia fills me for this piece of tech art. Its lightness is striking. The silky smooth rounded edges and matte metallic finish resemble an artifact from the near future. It has a playful red cover. He must have searched for this one, because I know they stopped making them several years ago. Scrolling through the album list, there it is: Allman Brothers, *Eat a Peach.*

I think about somehow sending it back, but instead, I connect it to my Powerbeats and let the music accompany me on my run. It makes me feel closer to him, and I know this is his intention.

After the second bouquet, I had sent him the safest thing I could: "Thank you for the flowers."

He replied, "You're welcome. I miss you."

I leave it there. Anything more feels like I'm opening a door.

On Sunday, he sends another message: "I know your quiet is you being careful but what I feel for you matters more than all these other things. I hope you like the music."

Damn, the quiet relief—*he gets me.*

Chapter Thirty-Four

. . . the past is data, not destiny

"CHARLOTTE, HOW ARE YOU?"

I whip around at the sound of my name echoing down the Riverbank corridor, eyes landing on the last person I expect or want to see—David Delacroix, my ex-lover. There he stands in his custom-fitted shirt and jeans, his athletic physique making him appear closer to thirty-five than his true forty-eight years. His tanned face is a picture of charm and ease.

"I've come looking for you. Can we talk?" he asks.

What is he doing here?

He says, "I had a meeting with the head of venture capital. It looks like my company might be striking up some deals with Riverbank. I'll be around for a while, so expect to see more of me. You're looking great. There's something different about you."

Inside, I think, *Yes, there is something different. I'm free of your deceitful grasp. I feel lighter.* However, I opt for a colder reply. "The team you're collaborating with is completely separate from mine, David. Trust me, our paths won't cross."

Ignoring my clear rejection, he reaches out and touches my arm. "C'mon, Charlie."

I rip his hand from my arm. "Don't you dare call me that."

Unfazed, he presses on. "We shared something unique, Charlotte. We both want the same things. I'm ready to settle down and—"

Cutting him off, I shoot back, "No, David, you were never going to give me what I wanted. For six months you filled my ears with false promises about wanting a family, claiming we were the perfect couple due to my legacy background and your lineage and wealth."

"Our backgrounds do fit together," he retorts.

"So did you and Christina, right? My friend? Who I caught you with . . . in our bed?"

He waves a hand dismissively. "She was my final fling before I fully committed to you. I'll admit, commitment scared me. I've been free for a long time."

"Too long," I retort. "You'll never commit. You'll always have a wandering eye. You used me because your family pressured you to settle down. I couldn't see the signs because I wanted marriage and a family so desperately. You exploited that. Shame on you, but even more, shame on me."

Suddenly, his smile falls away, replaced by a scowl. He grabs my arm again, and this time his nails dig into my skin. I wince as I try to break free.

"You bitch," he spits out. "You have no idea what you're giving up. Ever wonder why all the men you've been with cheat on you? Matthew, me? You're going to end up alone. No husband, no kids, just your career. You're someone no one wants."

His words strike me like a slap in the face. He knows my fears, my vulnerabilities, and used them to control me. Each time I pushed him to announce our engagement or start planning our wedding, he manipulated me, using veiled threats to keep me in line.

But the memory of him with Christina, my friend, in our bed, had finally sparked enough anger to cause me to pack my bags and leave him for good. He never cared for me—his infidelity was the final blow. I was just his convenient solution to pacify his family's expectations. As I yank my arm free from his grasp, I tell him, "David, *you're* the only person you're ever committed to. It's *you* who will end up alone."

A palpable heaviness lifts from me, a sensation I can't quite pinpoint but feel deeply—in my heart? My soul? I don't know, but the transformation is immediate. I feel lighter. I think of Duane. When someone genuinely cares for you, there's a calming, grounding feeling of security and trust—trust that you won't be betrayed.

"Is everything okay, Charlotte?" Oliver interrupts as he comes along the corridor, stopping in front of us. His eyes widen at the sight of my arm. "You're bleeding," he notes with evident concern, eyeing the marks left by David's nails.

Turning to David, Oliver issues an abrupt command: "I don't know what's going on, but you need to leave. Right now. Permanently."

"Wait, what?" Panic laces David's voice. "Oliver, I can explain. Charlotte, tell him."

I offer Oliver a look of gratitude. "Yes, I agree, Oliver. David should leave for good."

David begins a hurried explanation but is quickly cut off.

"Wait here. Security will accompany you to the front door," Oliver says, dialing security without breaking eye contact with him.

"But Oliver," David starts in his most charming voice, "that's not necessary."

While Oliver's talking, I search my pockets for a tissue to wipe the blood trickling down my arm. Finding none, I start to excuse myself to the restroom just as Oliver ends his call with security.

"Are you really okay, GL?" His worry is apparent.

"I just need to clean up," I say, trying to smile reassuringly and gesturing to my arm.

Inside the restroom, I grip the counter as waves of anxiety crash over me. The realization of David's threat, the potential harm he could've inflicted, and the miraculous timing of Oliver's arrival all sink in. I'm strangely comforted by Oliver's protectiveness.

As I emerge from the bathroom, I see Oliver leaning against the wall, typing on his phone. His normal stance is so casual and relaxed compared to Duane's. Just an inch or two shorter than Duane, he's leaner with a strong, defined nose and slightly arched eyebrows, which give him an aristocratic look. His chestnut brown hair is thick and styled back. His eyes are light green that deepen to emerald with excitement. He looks up while I'm studying him and moves to stand next to me.

"It's my day to stop by for a few hours and check in with the staff here while Duane gets coached by the media team. I'm glad I ran into you, GL. All good?" he asks, looking at the faint red marks on my arm.

"I wasn't expecting to see you here today," I admit. "But thank God you came around that corner when you did."

His mouth tightens. "No one puts their hands on you like that and keeps a badge. David won't be back."

A strange mix of embarrassment and relief swirls in my chest. "Thanks for stepping in, and for making him leave. My mistakes always seem to resurface."

Oliver's expression softens, a brotherly steadiness in his gaze. "If we were judged solely by the people we dated in the past, none of us would pass the test," he says quietly. "The past is data. Not destiny."

Later in the afternoon, under a brooding gray sky that casts a somber hue into the usually sun-filled rooms, I sit in the Pit, discussing the concept of metaverses with Rick,

Duane's second-in-command. I need a simplified way to explain the technological aspects of what a metaverse is to my luxury clients. My encounter with David has left me uneasy, and the dreary weather resonates with my mood. Rick, ever the professional, takes off his headphones and smiles at me, ready to answer my questions.

Explaining the basic workings of a metaverse is far below his pay grade. He's been coding since he was ten, famed for marathon sessions that could last sixteen to twenty hours, with only short breaks for sleep. I suspect that he microdoses—small, daily doses of LSD for stamina and creative insight. But whether it's drug-assisted or pure genius, Rick is a force in the Pit, headphones on, immersed in EDM, relentlessly debugging the Riverbank trading platform.

We had bonded over a spontaneous discussion about electronic dance music and discovered shared experiences at several concerts. To my surprise, despite his highly mathematical mind, Rick possesses a fabulous ability to explain complex cryptocurrency concepts in nontechnical terms.

Whenever I'm around him, I can't help but notice Duane's watchful gaze. His workspace, shared with Oliver, is nestled within the Pit, a place few other employees venture into. As I cross the threshold of this forbidden zone, all eyes turn my way, their curiosity palpable. Duane's absent but that doesn't stop the sea of curious glances. Nonchalantly, I return their nods, pulling up an office chair next to Rick. The sensation of being in a fishbowl is strangely familiar—but hey, it's nothing compared to a runway walk in a swimsuit that barely covers anything.

After discussing avatars, virtual reality, and NFTs at length, we find ourselves chatting about Rick's latest EDM finds and favorite tracks. I'm in the midst of asking for a playlist, when Oliver approaches.

"Hey, Charlotte. Can I talk to you for a few minutes?" he

asks, wheeling a spare chair over with his sneaker, nodding me into the huddle.

"Well, isn't this cozy?" Rick jokes.

"Duane and I want you to move your workspace here with us," he says. "Your area is bringing in a lot of business for the company, and we want to be close for discussions."

A blush creeps up my cheeks as my thoughts spin. The invitation feels less like convenience and more like a move onto their chessboard. Being so near Duane's desk each day would mean his gaze on me, his presence threading through my work whether I want it or not. *Is this protection after David? Am I to be a showpiece in a pit of tech men? Or is this simply Duane's way of keeping me tethered?* The lines blur until I can't tell if I'm wanted for my skills, my appearance, or because he refuses to let me drift from his orbit. Would this be a kind of surrender? I don't know if I fear it or want it more.

Oliver continues to layer on reasons. I let him talk until I don't need them.

"Fine," I say, easy, like we're swapping seats at a long lunch. "I'll move my laptop."

I've survived cataclysmic changes, this . . . is a change of desks. Obstacles, to me, are like ill fitting garments—you adjust the seams, change the cut, and keep walking the runway. I can shift into this pit of glowing screens and restless energy even when the reasons aren't clear. My strength has always been in moving forward—and I'll keep moving quietly, steadily—reshaping the space around me until it bends to fit.

Chapter Thirty-Five

. . . are we hedging or holding

I FUMBLE WITH THE KEY BEFORE FINALLY UNLOCKING MY apartment door and dumping my brother's luggage in the entryway.

"This is it. My warm weather cryptocurrency-job hideaway," I declare, stepping aside as Danny and Kate wander in, surveying their surroundings with approving eyes.

"So much light. You can see the water. This is excellent, Carlie," Danny says admiringly.

"Let's not get too comfortable just yet. There's this crazy party today at the Atlantic. It's for everyone from Riverbank, and I think we should go. The Atlantic itself is rather . . . extravagant. After that, we can tour the town," I suggest.

This is Danny and Kate's big escape from routine, but for me, it's a chance to reconnect with Danny. Picking them up at the airport made me realize how much I missed spending time with my brother. We are as different as night and day—he's always calm, slow to anger, but also slow to forgive. I, on the other hand, have a fiery temper, but I'm quick to let go of grudges. And Danny has always clashed with our dad, despite my years of trying to help them bond.

After showing them where they'll be sleeping, we pack our bags with everything we need for a day of exploring local sites—bathing suits, towels, water, sunscreen, and hats.

By the time we arrive at the Atlantic, the party's in full swing. I can hear the thumping music and voices raised in shouts and chatter as we approach the lively crowd gathered around the pool. Swimmers are diving in and out, while a group of programmers engrossed in a beer pong game has everyone's attention. I introduce Danny and Kate to Rick and a few others, with friendly handshakes and general comments about the game, the weather, and Danny's practice in New York. We eventually drift away from the boisterous crowd, heading to the beach, where more people are seated at tables, eating and drinking.

"Shall we get some drinks?" I suggest.

"Wow, Carlie, this place is amazing! Do they organize these events often? This beach is like a private paradise," Kate comments. She's dressed in jean shorts and a cropped top, showing off her toned abdomen even after two children. She's hugging Danny.

They're a beautiful couple, Danny tall and athletic, and Kate with her California girl next door beauty. They're so relaxed and obviously into each other even after five years of marriage. I'm struck by how much they love each other and fit together. I feel an ache of emptiness rising up, a palpable void in my chest, and I quickly reply, pushing the feeling aside.

"Oh, they have something going on here every few weeks. Most of the company's top people and the founders have apartments here. They're rather luxurious," I share.

"Will we get to meet any of your bosses today?" Danny asks.

"No, they're off site preparing for their testimony before

Congress in a few weeks." And there is no way we would be here, I think, if there was a chance one in particular would be around.

The afternoon passes in a blur of delicious fish tacos, a bottle of Ott rosé, and lounging on the beach. I make sure to give Danny and Kate time alone. As they swim and take walks along the beach, I wander around chatting with people. Seeing them spend time together, smiling and bending close to touch each other, I feel a sense of calm and happiness. Our mother would have loved knowing Danny had this love in his life. It's exciting to be around them, feeling their obvious passion for each other.

Danny wants to drive around to look at the island. As we prepare to leave, I suggest we stop by the Atlantic main entrance to show them the sprawling plant wall with its own waterfall. I'm pointing out this marvel when a familiar voice calls my name.

"Hey, Charlotte. I thought that was you."

And there he is. Duane. Right beside me, smiling that irresistible smile. For a moment, we just stand there in silence, until Danny extends his hand. "Hi, I'm Danny, Carlie's brother, and this is my wife, Kate. Quite a place you have here."

Duane steps forward to shake his hand with obvious eagerness, engaging them with questions. Have you seen the beach? Did you get something to eat? Have you seen the complex?

I feel myself blushing as I recognize Duane's full charm at play. He's being so friendly.

"I wasn't meant to be here, but I had to get some things from my place. Why don't you come up and I can show you my apartment."

"I don't think so, Duane," I say. "We wouldn't want to hold you up."

"No, it's no problem. I needed to take a break. I've been training." He gestures to his attire. "Hence the reason for the jacket on the weekend."

"We'd love to see your place," Danny says, ignoring the message I'm sending him with my glare. "I've wondered what the views would be like."

"Excellent, follow me." Duane guides us to the elevator, acknowledging the security staff on our way. He introduces us to Kurt, who holds the elevator door open for us. As we ascend, Danny and Kate pepper Duane with questions about the building and the enclave's layout.

My heart pounds erratically in my chest, rendering me speechless. I'm drowning in my internal turmoil—why am I so flustered? Why is Duane going out of his way to be so hospitable? I know the answer, and part of me is flattered. He still desires me. But I quickly scold myself. *Don't fall for it, Charlotte. There's no future here.* Yet, despite my attempts to stay focused, I find myself drawn to him. His is a ruinous kind of beautiful, the kind of face that could shatter your resolve just by looking at you. Sharing the tight space of the elevator with him, I'm acutely aware of his bergamot scent, his presence, all of it uniquely him.

The elevator doors slide open, and we step into his luxurious, sunlit apartment. Kurt vanishes, attending to his security duties, while Duane plays tour guide. He hovers close to me, careful not to invade my personal space but ensuring he's always within reach.

And then things take an unexpected, intimate turn.

"This is where Charlotte attended my dinner party, and we admitted our mutual crush on each other," Duane announces.

Kate bursts into laughter. "What a lovely story."

Before I can censor myself, I retort, "Actually, *you* confessed *your* crush. I mentioned we weren't compatible."

"That does sound like Carlie," Danny joins in. "Analytical and practical."

"I am too, Danny," Duane says. "That's why we make a great pair. But your sister seems to think our age difference and diverging life goals are stumbling blocks—"

I interrupt. "Duane's numerous relationships are another hurdle. And Danny, your board certification in orthopedics doesn't extend to an expertise in relationships."

Just then, Duane's phone rings—I recognize Oliver's ringtone. He excuses himself and retreats to the kitchen.

Danny turns to me and bumps my shoulder. "So, are you officially the muse of this King of Crypto," he asks, "or just moonlighting as court jester to keep him humble?"

"Neither," I say, nudging his shoulder back.

He smirks. "And Duane options—are we hedging or holding?"

I look up, pretending to consider. "I'm assessing . . ."

He leans in. "Then let me say this about Duane. I've only just met him, but he's nothing like the other men in your life—not like Dad, Matthew, or David. It's evident he adores you. Carlie, we can never predict whether our desires will align today or diverge tomorrow. We don't get such guarantees. But we do have the chance to hold on to those who love us, love them back, and work hard on the relationship."

I give him a quick hug, his words resonating with my hidden emotions. Kate wanders through the open doors. "Shall we call and check on the kids?"

As children's voices fill the terrace during their video call, I'm left to my thoughts. Danny doesn't ever weigh in with a definite opinion about my personal life. He prefers to offer general support for whatever I decide. Could I trust Duane with what I truly wanted—marriage, family?

And yet all these thoughts feel distant, disconnected from my reality. In my heart, I know I've already made a decision. I'm not going to dwell on potential regrets. I miss Duane and think about him constantly. There's an unremitting longing, a physical ache for his presence. But most importantly, he sees me—the real me. That feeling of acceptance and being understood makes me feel secure and empowered. It makes me feel invincible.

Duane returns to the terrace, standing beside me. "I've got to get back. But I can drive you back so we can talk. Danny and Kate can take your car."

"Yes, I'd like that."

"I'm going to grab a few things and then we can head out," he says.

Chapter Thirty-Six

. . . I don't want a half life

WE'RE OUTSIDE THE BUILDING, SAYING GOODBYE. I'VE ENtered my address into the car's navigation so Danny and Kate can find their way back.

"Good luck with your testimony," Danny says, extending his hand for a shake. "Didn't you and Charlotte share a panel discussion once?" he then asks Duane.

Duane looks at me, raising his eyebrows in surprise. "I don't think so. Did we meet before, Charlotte?"

"No, we haven't," I respond hastily. "Danny, you must be confusing him with someone else."

"Likely," Danny concedes. "In my line of work, I gather so much information about my patients, it can get jumbled."

After exchanging effusive waves, Danny and Kate drive off, leaving Duane and me to get into his convertible. He sits for a moment without starting the engine.

"Do you mind if we take a little detour before I drop you off?" he asks, reaching into the back seat and retrieving something orange from his bag.

"Sure," I reply.

"But first, wear this. It's going to be windy," he says, handing me the Hermès scarf that he's kept all this time.

I touch the orange fabric, feeling the cool silk caress my hands, remembering the last time we were together and the way his hands caressed my naked body. I'm trembling and realize I want him to touch me. In my confusion I murmur, "So you're returning my scarf. The guilty always return to the scene of the crime. They crave the thrill of reliving something illicit, something they could be punished for."

He turns to me with a slow smile as I drape the scarf over my hair.

"Am I the guilty one, or are you the one who feels guilty?" he asks.

He's so close. His intense stare and words light my face on fire as I seek refuge in twisting my hands in my lap. Anything to avoid his eyes.

I can't believe he's talking about this.

"Lola," he says. "Look at me."

When my eyes meet his, he continues in a hushed tone. "I know you're scared. About wanting a family and kids, about being with someone younger. About what we do together."

"About you keeping secrets," I say with a frantic need to shift the focus. "Duane, please just drive. I need the breeze and a few moments to think."

He starts the car, and soon we're on an unfamiliar route along the coast. We ride in silence until he expertly steers onto a modest pull-off. The gravel lot has just enough space for a couple of cars, bordered by seaworn wooden posts meant to keep cars from straying too close to the bluff. "Let's get out here," he says.

A few steps beyond the area reveal a breathtaking expanse of the ocean stretching toward the horizon. We walk along a narrow path leading to a rustic bench surrounded by blooming, fragrant wild jasmine bushes. The warm breeze envelops me, offering a sense of tranquility. At this moment, I feel at ease in his company, like anything can be discussed.

"I may feel guilty, wanting to relive illicit feelings, but what intense emotions are you seeking to relive by returning my scarf?" I ask, going back to my comment in the car.

Before we can sit, he encircles me with his arms, dragging me close. He whispers in my ear, "I want to relive our first night in the car, when I drove you home and knew."

He hungrily crushes his lips to my mouth, devouring me with his tongue and small bites on my lower lip. I rise up to put my hands around his neck and kiss him back, getting lost in the way he feels, the way he is dominating me.

An electric surge sweeps through me as I cling to him, my hands entangled in his messy hair. My anxiety melts into him as he slowly trails soft kisses down my neck and back up, kissing my lips, my cheeks, moving along my jawline to bite my earlobe. "Lola," he whispers, wrecked and reverent at once. "Be with me. Not later. Now."

I seek out his mouth, savoring his unique taste of salt and sweet. My hands trail up and down his back. I'm desperate to feel him close. And as his mouth traces a path along my bare shoulder, waves of desire wash over me. I need his skin against mine.

But I pull back, even as he holds both my arms, his deep groans reflecting his inner turmoil.

"Lola, what must I do to convince you to give this relationship a chance? I crave the same things you do. I don't need a muse—I need you. In my bed, in my mess, in my life."

I try to turn away, elated to be so close to him, craving him, but anxious, afraid. Bloody hell. I can't make anything make sense. I can't think clearly. What do I want?

His hands slide down my arms to grab my hands, not letting me move. "Do you feel it? When we're together, when we kiss, when we fuck—don't lie to me. Tell me you want this. Tell me you want me."

"Yes," I breathe. "Yes, but—"

"No 'buts.'" He steps in, chest to mine, forehead to forehead, voice rough. "Tell me what it takes. I'll take the fallout. I'll take the spotlight. I don't want a half life. I want us."

Chapter Thirty-Seven

. . . the weight of heavy chain mail

"THEN, DUANE, I HAVE TO TELL YOU SOMETHING FIRST BEfore we decide anything."

I'm so close, I can see flecks of gold scattered within his deepening irises. His familiar feel surrounds me—intense, but somehow calming.

"Yes, I have to tell you some things, too," he answers.

I can't help it. My curiosity takes over. After months of trying to understand what his secrets are, he's going to share something of himself.

"What is it? What do you want to tell me?" I say.

He drops my arms but doesn't move away. Then he begins to speak slowly, his tone even, controlled, looking directly at me, watching me.

"You can't find anything on me before the age of sixteen because my uncles had the information buried."

He continues his gaze, waiting, silent.

"I had just started high school. I came home and found my parents murdered."

I inhale sharply.

"My uncles were close friends of my mother. They aren't my real uncles, but they stepped in and kept the fact that my parents had a son out of the papers and had enough sway to minimize the media coverage. They got me a new identity and put me into hiding to keep me safe from whoever the killers were."

The words slam into me. My chest feels tight, like I can't draw in enough air. I see him—fifteen, walking into that house to find his parents dead, and something inside me breaks. The boy lost absolutely everything. I want to reach for him, hold him, tell him he's not alone. But fear needles through me at the same time, cold and sharp. *This is the shadow I've felt around him from the beginning.* The silence, the control, the way he watches everything like the world might turn on him any second. It all comes from here. From this.

I ache for him. And yet—my stomach twists. Because his past isn't just history. It's alive. It follows him. And if I let myself be pulled in too close, it will follow me, too. His darkness is both a lure and warning, pressing in on me like the weight of heavy chain mail. I'm caught between the urge to gather him up and the instinct to step away before it consumes me.

I have so many questions, but I don't want to bombard him. I try to calm my rapid thoughts, to focus and think of simple questions.

"So you were the one to find your parents?"

For the first time, he looks away as he says in a detached voice, "Yes, they were in the basement, shot execution style. The killers were professionals."

"But why?" My voice cracks.

"I'll tell you that, but not now. It's too much to go over all at once. But I want to start answering your questions and let you know me. It's my commitment to you, to us."

My face is wet with silent tears. "Duane, I'm so sorry," I say, as I wrap my arms around him and place my head on his chest.

He's stroking my hair as my tears soak his shirt. We both stand together silently.

"I always seem to be ruining your shirt with my tears," I murmur.

"Lola, I love your tears for me," he says. "I wasn't able to cry about it for a long time. Seeing a therapist helped. But even now I don't want to let myself feel the sadness. I just have the anger, and that's what drives me now."

"For what?" I say, pulling away and searching his face. "What is your anger driving you to do?"

"I can't talk about it right now, but meeting you, having you in my life, has changed things. I don't want to hide anymore."

"But does that put you in danger, Duane? Are those people still out there? Will they come after you?"

"I don't know. Maybe. But I have to live my life, and I have to make it safe for both of us. You need to know who I am before you decide. If we are together, I promise I'll protect you."

I'll protect you. The words bind as much as they soothe. Fear prickles, but instead of pushing me away, it coils into hunger. His all consuming shadow isn't a threat alone—it lures, it burns. Pressed to his chest, I feel his strength, the heat beneath the soaked fabric, and I ache for it. I want that power not out in the world, but on me. Claiming me. Consuming me.

The ride back to my place is silent. He gets out to walk me to my door.

"I know you want to spend time with your brother, but just so you know"—he moves in close, his eyes locked on mine—"if he wasn't there I would carry you up to your apartment right now and slowly undress you as I kissed every inch of your body and moved my mouth over all the places I know will give you pleasure until we both explode. There may be some silk ropes, some slipknots, and playthings you don't want but will definitely love because you have defied me, staying away, making me come after you."

I press myself to him as he speaks, fusing my body to his through the thin wrap over my bathing suit, as his voice overtakes my senses. I feel on fire, wet and burning at once.

He moves back and kisses me softly on the mouth. "You have tonight with your brother, but tomorrow night you're all mine."

As I climb the stairs to the second floor, tingling and happy, I remember with a sinking feeling: *I didn't tell him about the book.*

Chapter Thirty-Eight

. . . twenty-seven minutes in

DUANE MAKES GOOD ON HIS PROMISE, AND THE FOLLOWING night I'm nude, lying in his bed wrapped in his arms, sweaty and euphoric from his savage domination of my body. He's gently rubbing my shoulder near my neck, gliding his fingers over the swollen area of his bite mark. It aches but feels good at the same time.

"This will be a week of wearing blouses, thank you very much, Mr. Blacklock. No off the shoulder dresses for me until that fades," I murmur next to his chest.

"I like my marks on you, Ms. Gordon-Lennox. You belong to me. You are mine. My marks designate you as my muse and lover."

"And what are you to me?" I ask teasingly, sitting up and pushing him onto his back. I look down at him. The sharp angles of his face catch the bedroom's fading light as his plush mahogany brows frame his deep-set velvet eyes, their gaze unexpectedly open. His lips are slightly parted, hinting at a smirk. The overall effect is one of balance and symmetry and breathtaking perfection. He's unbelievably handsome.

"Tell me, Lola. What am I to you?" he asks as his eyes roam over my face, my neck, and down to my bare breasts. The air sizzles.

"I'm not sure. I feel connected to you. There's this invisible force field I enter whenever I'm near you. A sense of anticipation of what we could do together."

I pull away as he laughs and reaches for me. "I know what we can do together," he says.

"No, it's not just physical. I mean, yes, I willingly surrender to you in the bedroom, but I feel like you're captivated by me, and that makes me feel powerful and creates this charged field around us."

He's quiet, lying next to me, his face unreadable but holding my gaze.

"You dominate me, Duane, even as you say I inspire you. There's a power between us that feels volatile but inventive, as if we're creating something together."

My words are lost as he pulls me down, his tongue parting my lips, warm and urgent as he devours my mouth and begins to consume my body with his mouth and touch.

For the next several weeks, I spend most of my time at Duane's. We rise early to work out and go for a run along the beach, which is much harder than I ever appreciated. Duane adjusts his pace to mine and slowly, over time, we increase the distance. Occasionally Oliver joins us, and then there's much more talking, more panting on my part, and shorter distances. It feels comfortable and easy, the three of us together, with the satisfying burn of a good workout at the end.

At work, I focus on the upcoming cryptocurrency conference to be held in Austin. Duane and Oliver have plans to attend the World Economic Forum in Davos, Switzerland, being held in June this year instead of January due to Covid. They have a lot of crypto partnerships they want to negotiate and cybersecurity experts to cultivate. Duane asks me to join them, and I eagerly agree.

I've never been to Davos. It's an important venue for learning from world leaders and making influential contacts. I see it as an opportunity for Duane and Oliver to direct Riverbank and cryptocurrency into many other areas besides finance. Heady proximity to smart people, dynamic agendas, and passionate motivations may be the opportunity to tap into the inventive power I feel between the two of us and create something together.

Occasionally, Duane joins me at my apartment, but most days, we end up back at the Atlantic. After a long day at Riverbank, it's easier to call for dinner delivery from one of the on-site restaurants. At times, Oliver joins us, especially if he and Duane finish the day working on the same project.

Oliver and I have fallen into a breezy give-and-take when we're together. I tease him about how he uses his charm to get around people and problems, and he chastises me for encouraging all the young programmers who he says have a crush on me.

"I don't encourage anyone," I say, defending myself. "They are desperate to look at something other than code after hours and hours chained to their computers, that's all."

"Well, on the days you wear pencil skirts and scoop neck tops, not a single line of coding gets completed," he says.

I throw him a look; he grins, pleased with himself, then stage-whispers, "Don't worry, I'll issue a productivity memo—mandatory blinders when Charlotte walks by," just as Duane emerges onto the terrace with our drinks.

The evening is soft. The sun's lowering rays cast a warm glow over us as we settle, famished, into a delicious dinner. We linger at the table, conversation drifting between jokes and real things. Oliver steals the last few bites from my plate; I flick his wrist with my napkin like an annoyed older sister. Duane suddenly says, "Bedtime," a signal for Oliver to leave, and then gets up, carrying dishes inside.

Oliver pushes his chair back but stays a beat, eyes clear. "Charlotte, I just want to say how grateful I am that you're with Duane. You're good for him. I've never seen him this calm and content before."

Duane reappears at the terrace door, undoing the top buttons of his shirt. Oliver jerks a thumb his way, already backing out, grinning. "See? Calmer already." He gives us a two-finger salute and disappears.

Duane grabs my hand, lifting me up to him. "Come here," he commands, leading me to his bedroom.

He adjusts something on his phone, then sets it down on the bedside table as music plays from the bedroom speakers. I don't recognize the song. It's an instrumental, open and airy, with two guitar solos weaving in and out of fluid melodies. Blues-infused passages fade into the background as my senses attune to Duane's mouth and touch.

He undresses me, pulling my dress up over my head and tossing it to the floor. Undoing my lace bra, he leans down, pulling my panties down to my feet. I step out, and they join the growing pile of discarded clothing. He slowly pushes me onto the bed. And the music fills the room, even as I'm quickly caught up in the maleness of his scent, of bergamot and soap.

He undresses, and then his touch becomes more rough and more urgent, moving and positioning me as he wants. And as always, as if for the first time, we are in it together, him pushing me forward until my climax gives him release to follow.

As we lie on the bed, facing each other, studying each other, I notice Duane's expression softening, something lighting up his face, and I'm aware once again of the shifting, ever changing music. We listen together as the tempo struggles to evolve and the guitar players merge and fuse and then pull away from the melody. Duane rolls onto his back, pulling me to him as he softly says, "Twenty-seven minutes in."

And then I hear it. The achingly tender guitar weeping a serene melody, something so gentle, so exquisite, I still to listen more closely. The poignant solo continues for only a few minutes, but it is stunning before shifting again to a wild crescendo as the music ends and the crowd roars. Then I hear a musician call out "thank you" and introduce the other musicians, ending with, "I'm Duane Allman."

The room is hushed. I hear myself breathing. I know this is something important to him, almost sacred. I don't want to break the spell, so I wait.

"'Mountain Jam,'" Duane says, then remains quiet for several seconds before continuing, "The melody might sound familiar. Those several minutes come from an old country tune called 'Will the Circle Be Unbroken,' one of Duane Allman's favorite songs. One he returned to again and again to include in different forms in his playing."

"Did your mother share this song with you?" I ask, needing to connect with him somehow.

"Yes," he says. "And now I've shared it with you."

I move in as close as I can, wrapping my arms around him, holding him tight, burying my head in his shoulder, letting him feel me. Knowing there's nothing I can say.

Chapter Thirty-Nine

. . . sorry, my love

ME: *I'm at the beach. Join me.*

DUANE: *Give me twenty minutes.*

ME: *Are you and Oliver figuring out your plan for the FTX meltdown?*

DUANE: *That. And I thought I'd search your apartment looking for my missing T-shirt.*

ME: *Oh—hasn't Kurt done that already?*

DUANE: *He has not. I've been inspired to follow a different lover's playbook this time.*

ME: *I'm honored. But what if you did find out something about me you don't like?*

DUANE: *Not sure. Am I going to?*

Here's an opening, a natural way to tell him about the book, but I can't bring myself to confess, not as a text message. I dismiss his question with humor.

ME: *Only if you search my apartment. Come find me. I'm wearing a very small, very pink bikini.*

I watch from the water as he makes his way down the path. His pace is leisurely, his gaze scanning the water, not breaking eye contact once he's found me. His shirt hangs open at the front, revealing rows of chiseled muscles—a body I learned by heart last night, slick with heat under my hands.

Twilight has settled around the secluded beach, with only a few lingering souls still around. The fading rays of the sun keep me warm and playful as I revel in the placid water. Duane discards his shirt onto the pile of my belongings. Kurt takes up a spot near the path, casual but alert, gaze sweeping the sand.

I watch as he dives into the water and resurfaces right in front of me. "Hey, where's the pink bikini?" he asks, catching sight of my white, deep-plunge one-piece.

"A little bait, switch, reward."

"False advertising," he murmurs, delighted, as he lifts me into his arms.

"Smart marketing," I counter, looping my arms around his neck. "You still clicked." Our lips meet in a salty kiss as he cradles me in his arms, twirling us in the turquoise water.

"This is what I've been waiting for all day," he admits.

"Me too," I confess, wrapping my arms around his neck and nestling into him. The water laps against our chests as he ambles about, holding me close.

"Now, let me," I instruct, extricating myself from his arms to stand before him.

"Float on your back," I command.

He's standing, the afternoon gold glow surrounding him

in a halo, water droplets burnishing the ripples of his chest muscles, collecting at the V of his lowered waistband, his wet hair like tarnished bronze slicked back from his sharp profile. Molten eyes flecked with gold radiate mystery and intensity. He reaches out to grab my arms, but I step back. A slow smile crosses his lips as he continues to gaze intently at me.

"Yes, command me, you have the control, but just this once," he says as he reclines onto his back in the water.

"Shhh," I whisper, placing one hand under his back and the other around his shoulder. I move him gently across the water's surface, causing him to chuckle.

"You want my submission, Lola?"

"Close your eyes. Trust me."

I can feel his body loosening, becoming heavier in my arms, as he floats in the deepening blue beneath the dwindling light. I softly hum. "Whenever you're near me . . ."

Holding, supporting him like this but refraining from our usual touches, we enter a deep moment together, complete surrender. But these slight touches in the warm, soothing water create a fusion we've never had, even when our bodies have been inseparable in the bedroom. We're now one, sharing the silky sensation of the water, the warmth, me guiding him, lost in the sensation of his surrender. He's become a sovereign of my soul.

His eyes flutter open as he stands upright, pulling me toward him. "Lola, it's like whenever you're close, all the static goes quiet; like everything tunes itself to us. If you left, I'd think it'd go silent."

I reach up to bring his head down for a kiss, water dripping down our faces, tasting salty on our lips. "I'm not leaving," I whisper. "Not now. Not ever."

Later, back in my apartment, we make a different kind of love, him submitting to me as I control the direction and pace, slowly undressing him and exploring his body in a new way.

He moans with low groans and then harsh growls as I prolong the crescendo, only releasing him when I feel his spiral is about to begin. I command his gaze, our eyes unwavering, as I watch him go over the edge as he pulls me with him.

We both collapse, rolling onto our backs as we laugh with a sense of wonder. "What the fuck was that?" he exhales.

I roll over onto my side, my hair spread out on the pillows, my eyes bright. "You look thoroughly fucked, Lola," he says.

We lie there quietly, looking at each other for a long time.

I have to look at him all the time because it's never enough. I'm his muse, and he's my king. He's rescued me from the pain and burden of what happened to me in my marriage, my relationships with my father and other men. I feel light, unburdened, not fiercely strong as I had to be before, but more of a quiet titanium strength.

"Duane, there's something I need to tell you."

He's just stepped out of the shower and is drying off. Discarding the towel, he crawls onto the bed beside me. "So, tell me," he prompts, planting a kiss on my lips before rolling over onto the pillow next to me.

The room is dim, with a cool breeze drifting in through the screen door to the balcony.

"You know, we've met before."

"Really? I'd remember, trust me. You're too fucking beautiful to forget."

"Yes, but the circumstances weren't ideal. It was several years ago in New York."

His phone rings, Oliver's tone piercing the quiet air.

"Sorry, my love. I need to take this," he apologizes, snatching up the phone before stepping out onto the balcony.

Wrapping myself in a silk robe, I head to the kitchen and

pour myself a glass of white wine. I need to get this out in the open. The longer I wait, the worse it will feel. I can't fucking bear the weight of guilt any longer. All the lightness and strength I just felt a few moments ago vanish as I prepare to tell him.

He'll feel betrayed. *But will he forgive me, or will he hate me? Can I make him understand what happened?* How I didn't know him then, how I had been in an altered state, trying to continue on the edge of hopelessness as a void slowly consumed me. He had inflicted such humiliation in a public setting, but it had saved me. His savage cruelty had shocked me back into the real world, my sadness replaced by anger. Anger and rage.

And now—his words echo in my mind. Did he really call me his love? The pit in my stomach battles with a surge of elation. Shaking my head, I chastise myself for being childish. But no, he had indeed called me "my love."

The reality of the situation threatens to crush me. I want to wail and pound my fists at the cruelty of fate. I feel fury at finding the love I've always wanted, only to have him be someone I'd betrayed. It feels like a sick joke.

"Lola, gotta go." He's dressed. "Things are blowing up. I've got to meet with Oliver. I'll see you tomorrow, and you can tell me about how we met before."

He's in a hurry. I can see he's preoccupied with problems at Riverbank. He grabs me, gives me a soft kiss. I kiss him back, making the kiss linger a few seconds longer, wanting to cling to him. He gives me a last hug and leaves me as I turn in misery to pick up my glass.

I gulp down the wine, pounding back my feelings, suppressing a scream of "*Bloody. Fucking. Hell.*"

Chapter Forty

. . . a trifecta of fucking hell

THE REMAINING WEEK AT WORK SETS A HECTIC PACE, AND my time with Duane is cut short. Cultivating fashion sponsors for the cryptocurrency conference is much trickier and time-consuming than I'd originally planned. Riverbank is the main sponsor, so there's a lot of pressure to get it right.

I'd personally invited a number of fashion journalists and highly placed designers. My plan is to host a panel discussion focused on the intersection of NFTs and fashion. The challenge is to ensure the fashion heavyweights understand the nuances of the topic.

I brought a college friend on board who covers emerging fashion for *WWD. Women's Wear Daily* is the definitive insider fashion publication. Vanessa is smart, ambitious, and, with her background as a business major, eager to learn more about cryptocurrency. I hired her as a consultant and arranged for her to attend several workshops on blockchain and NFTs. Since then, she's been hosting informal lunches with potential panelists to demystify the concepts.

Vanessa knows everyone, and people are always eager to

meet with her for the possible media exposure in *WWD*. She has a finance column in the publication and is now writing frequently about cryptocurrency.

"Great news," she gushes during our daily update. "I have two upcoming lunches scheduled. One with Dior's marketing head and another with Cartier's global head."

"Well done," I tell her.

"But listen," Vanessa continues. "Have you heard of this book? It's all about the top movers and shakers in crypto? The author's anonymous and doesn't use real names, but it's a total takedown—very witty, very funny but merciless character assassination. One of them is supposedly your boss. All these photos of you and Duane at the Met Gala have pushed the book into the spotlight. Have you read it? Any idea who wrote it? I would love to break that story."

"No, no. I'll have to get a copy and read it," I say weakly. "Sorry, but I have an incoming call I have to take. Keep up the great work."

I'm grateful for the interruption. I actually do have an incoming call. It's from my agent.

"Charlotte, I don't know how much longer we can keep a lid on your anonymity. The publisher is being threatened with a lawsuit by one of the people portrayed in the book unless they pull it. I think you have to go public and defend the book."

A cold fear seizes me. Is it Duane threatening the lawsuit? Has he found out that I'm the author? I need to tell him I wrote the book, not the publisher, not anyone else. He will never forgive me if he hears it from someone else. I lean forward as if I've been punched, and a heavy sigh escapes me. Do I really think he'll forgive me anyway, no matter who tells him? I straighten up. No, but telling him face-to-face that I wrote the book is the only decent thing I can do right now.

"I don't want to go public," I insist.

Taking command, I continue, "Tell the publisher to pull

the book." Then I add with emphasis, "As I requested three months ago. This lawsuit is a serious threat, and the person behind it will spend whatever is necessary to take the book and publishing house down. Have them send me the paperwork to sign right away. Get them to send a courier down with the papers if they have to, but have it here by the end of the day."

"Okay," my agent says. "I'll get them to see it's finally in their best interest to pull the book. I'll call you back with the details."

I gather up my things in a hurry, preparing to leave. This is just a shit day. I need to be alone to think about how I will tell Duane. Stay calm and think. Whatever I say, I have to speak to him from my heart, and I realize that means finally revealing more about Matthew's death.

When Oliver calls to me as I'm in the atrium, the day has become a trifecta—a trifecta of fucking hell. My heart drops, and panic rolls over me. Vanessa, my agent, and now Oliver. The fates have aligned against me.

I see him coming toward me at a clipped pace. He looks what . . . distressed? angry? yes, angry but also disappointed.

"Charlotte, time to talk. Walk with me." He grabs my arm and steers us down a side corridor toward a service exit. His security team fans out, casual but watchful.

"What's wrong?" *Please let this be about something else, anything else. Please.*

"I know about the book," he says, dropping my arm.

The words knock the wind from me. "Oliver—"

"There are things you need to understand." His voice has a sharp edge to it, and he pauses before continuing. "Duane and I are not good friends or 'like' brothers," he says, voice even. "We are chosen brothers. Junior year, he took detention for me—three weeks—so I could make finals. He protects his people. Duane isn't in the shadows because he's humble or shy or any of that shit. He's in the shadows because he's hiding. It's his story, but I will tell you there are reasons he was forced into a new life when he was a teenager." His mouth quirks. "And yeah, I'm angry."

"I . . . I'm sorry, Oliver," I stammer. "I have tried to help him become more of who he's meant to be."

"By writing a venomous book about him?" He's scowling now. "You're lethal with adjectives. Save some for our critics, not his jugular. We live with threats you can't see. I know what hunts him."

"I wrote the book two years ago. I didn't know him then. I was hurt. Angry. He humiliated me and I—" I stop. "I didn't know him."

I swallow. "They're pulling the electronic edition immediately as well as the print-on-demand. I'm signing papers as soon as I have them."

He rubs his hand over his face and takes a beat. "Listen. There are so many moving parts to what's going on with him right now, events converging to detonate. I'm rooting for you two. Truly. I'm not here to punish. I'm here to keep him breathing. Stay at Riverbank, work things out with him about this book. He cares for you. Everyone can see it."

A stupid tear escapes. "Does he?"

He snorts. "I watched him choose the shadows for a decade. Suddenly he's at the Met Gala and will be in front of Congress because you said 'Come stand in the light.'"

"I'll tell him to his face. I'm meeting him at my place shortly." I'm crying again. "Thank you."

"It's just such bad timing, GL," he says, softening, using my nickname at last.

I muffle my sobs and walk away, shakily wiping my tears as I struggle to get to my car.

Chapter Forty-One

. . . muse kneeling before her king

THE DOOR BURSTS OPEN WITH A SHARP GUST OF WARM AIR as the sun goes behind a cloud. Duane strides in, arms full of vibrant orange bags marked with the iconic H, clutching a champagne bottle. He lets the bags fall onto my couch.

"Lola, I couldn't quite decide if you liked the scarf I picked out, so I called Hélène and she sent three others. Take a look. Choose one or choose them all."

I come out of my bedroom. He's smiling, at ease, eyes glowing. He laughs and grabs me, giving me a deep kiss. I love this: relaxed Duane, delicious kisses. I find myself clinging to him.

"Hey, where are your champagne glasses? Let's pop this while it's cold," he says, his tone light and amused.

I move away and pull two flutes from the cupboard, their delicate chime ringing too sharply in my silence. There's a loud pop, but it isn't until he starts pouring that he notices I'm not talking.

"Lola, is something wrong?" he asks, glancing up from the bubbling flutes. "Hey, you've been crying. What happened?

Talk to me." He takes a step closer, intending to embrace me, but I stiffen and hold out my hands to keep him away.

"I wrote the book, Duane," I say. Forcing my voice to be strong, I meet his gaze. "I'm the anonymous author of that unflattering book about you."

I watch him closely, my eyes fixed on his. All I can hear is the faint fizz from the untouched glasses on the counter. I see the moment he comprehends what I'm saying. His fingers loosen slightly around the bottle, as if his grip has weakened. His pupils dilate, molten iron, the storm rolling in.

He's like a vibrating bow, set to pierce me with a steel-tipped arrow. The tension stretches taut between us. He shifts his gaze from mine, dropping his head as if the weight of my words has physically crushed him.

My anxiety mounts.

His voice, when it comes, is quiet. Deceptively reasonable. "Why didn't you tell me before?"

I squeeze my arms tightly around my body, as if I can physically hold in my spiraling dread.

"I tried, I really tried. That first night . . . when I asked you to drive me to my hotel, but your comments about David made me angry, and I didn't want to tell you in anger."

I'm shivering.

"I meant to tell you when you confided in me about your parents, when you joked about Kurt searching my apartment. I started to tell you we had met before, remember? Last week." My voice cracks.

I cannot read him. He has turned away, his back straight, his arms stiff at his sides. But I can feel it—a fury rising in him like a storm about to break. His shoulders are too rigid, his breath too slow, too measured.

Then he moves.

So fast, I barely register his hands are on me, gripping my arms, shaking me with every jagged, broken sentence.

"But I care for you, Lola." Shake. "I felt you cared for me, too." Shake. "How could you?" Shake.

His hands are firm but not cruel. Still, I feel the stab—not in my skin, but deep in my chest, a wretched and raw pain that spreads through my ribs like a slow, twisting knife.

"I didn't know you then, Duane," I gasp, my eyes burning. "But I do now. And I do care for you. More than care. What we have is special. What I did was wrong. I'm sorry. I'm so sorry."

He jerks away from me as if I've burned him, spinning on his heels to face the windows. Sunlight slants in, dappled and golden, catching in his disheveled blond hair—but it does nothing to soften him. As the sun moves in and out among the clouds, the room loses light, and his silhouette appears cut from steel.

"You wrote that humiliating book about me?" His voice is colder now, low and almost guttural. "The arrogant tech geek—isn't that how you described me?"

"Dua—"

He shakes his head once, sharply, and then moves. Retreating. Seeking distance between us. His steps are fast as he crosses onto the balcony, his breath ragged as he runs his hand through his hair. He paces, restless as a caged animal, the balcony door open, the warm wind stirring papers in the room.

"Lola, I didn't think you could be so cruel." His voice is different now. Low, heavy, grim. "And the danger your damn book has put me in . . ."

I follow him to the doorway, watching him pace, my heart hammering against my chest. "Duane, please, I—"

"How could you? How could you?" He says it again and again, as if the words alone might make sense of it.

Finally, he stops pacing. He sinks onto the outdoor couch, putting his elbows on his knees, running his hands through his hair. He still won't look at me.

I move to him. Drop to my knees before him. A muse kneeling before her king. Tears spill freely, stinging my warm skin.

"Why, Lola, why?" His voice is barely above a whisper, but the rawness of it shatters me. I reach for him, but he flinches; his entire body tenses. My heart drops somewhere to the center of the earth.

"I'm sorry, Duane," I sob. "I'm, I'm so . . . so sorry and ashamed. It was before I came to Riverbank. We met before. You don't remember. I was the only woman on that tech panel you spoke at two years ago."

His head snaps up, eyes blazing. "What panel?"

He's looking at me now, his eyes searching mine, scorching me, confused and desperate. I want to look away.

"When?" he demands. "We've never met before."

Then realization dawns.

"Wait," he breathes. "You . . . that was you?"

I break. A sob rises from my throat as I drop my head, unable to meet his gaze.

"It was me," I whisper. "I was the one you humiliated with your questions about my business app, asking me so many details about the software. Do you remember? You grilled me over and over, making it clear to everyone I had no idea about tech or software, which I didn't."

"But that—that wasn't you."

"It was me. I had short hair. I was a wreck then. I should have bowed out, but I was trying to get back on my feet, and my friends urged me to do the panel. I had sort of dissolved, mentally, after Matthew's death."

I stop, my voice breathless. "And then, when I miscarried, I fell apart completely."

He's clenching his jaw, his breathing unsteady. "You lost a baby?" His voice is so quiet I raise my head to catch his words.

I nod, pressing my hands to my face.

"I was eight weeks pregnant. I was so distraught and stressed by Matthew's death and betrayal, I wasn't eating, I wasn't sleeping. I was going to tell him about the baby when he came back from Italy. But I never had the chance. I gave up on everything. On my pregnancy, on myself. And then, I lost the baby."

Silence.

"You should have told me." His voice is rough, choked with something heavy. "You should've told me everything. We've shared so many things. And the way you present me to the world in that book. Is that how you really feel about me? Selfish, entitled, dismissive of women?"

"No, Duane, no, of course not. I was angry. Angry at the world, angry at Matthew, at myself for not knowing about his affair . . . feeling that I had killed my unborn child. But I took it out on you."

"But you didn't even know me. You knew nothing about me," he says, disbelief in his voice.

"I'm so ashamed, Duane. You're right, I didn't know you. And it isn't who I am, but I was blindsided by such intense anger—sorrow, really. What you put me through on that panel, in front of all those people with all your technical questions . . . it felt personal, and utterly humiliating."

The silence is stifling, even as the breeze picks up and thunder sounds in the distance.

"In some twisted way, it was a wake-up call," I say, almost to myself. "It shook me from my grief and led me to write that book. But it wasn't about you. It was about me, my anger, my pain. I didn't know you, but I wanted to hurt you. Because I was hurting."

I can't breathe. I can't speak.

"Well, if that's what you wanted—to hurt me—you've done that and worse." His words are dull, emotionless. "I thought we had honor and trust between us. You captivated me and brought me to my knees with this relationship, inspired me, made me think I could have a different life with you. But now you've killed everything between us."

There's nothing I can say. He's right. The book is mean, but then I had done something even more unthinkable. By not telling him, I had betrayed him, betrayed us. There's a bitter, acidic taste at the back of my throat, and my chest is so tight I can't breathe.

He rises slowly, towering over me, his face unreadable but his eyes dull, matte, anguished.

"I hope it was worth it, Lola, my love, my muse. You inspired me; you made me want to become the man I was meant to be.

"You were my north star," he murmurs. "And now I'm lost."

I let out a strangled sob as I kneel, crying before him.

He doesn't look at me.

He walks around me. Then the door slams.

And he is gone.

A cascade of cool droplets steams against the warm balcony stone, releasing a fleeting mineral scent with a *pit, pit,* patter sound reminding me of a *Bambi* scene. Little charming animals seek shelter from the rainfall with a happy melody—"drip, drip, drop, little April shower . . ."

But this is no *Bambi* happily ever after . . . this is fucking hell.

Chapter Forty-Two

. . . juggling grenades

MY PHONE IS RINGING YET AGAIN WHILE A DETERMINED knocking echoes from my front door. I stumble out of bed, a pounding headache and sharp stinging in my eyes making it difficult to see. Damn, I've slept with my contacts in. Grimacing, I navigate the sea of wine bottles that litter my living room. Harsh sunlight invades the apartment, causing me to squint.

I pull open the door to reveal Jeannie, my assistant, and an unfamiliar man in the hallway.

"Charlotte, I've been calling you all morning," Jeannie says as she breezes past me into the living room. "You missed the ten a.m. Zoom call with marketing, and we have another meeting in ten minutes with *Women's Wear Daily.* Where's your laptop? Is it charged?"

I motion to my computer, suddenly aware that Jeannie is there to salvage the situation. Taking a deep breath, I straighten my posture and refocus on her. "We'll set up on the kitchen counter," I say. "Throw up a green screen. I'll be right back."

Moments later, I reemerge in a red silk blouse, my hair

swept into a ponytail, cheeks flushed and lips tinted. It's a far cry from my usual polished look, but it will have to do.

Forty-five minutes later, the meeting's concluded, and I thank Jeannie for stepping in to manage it. I don't offer any excuses or explanations. That's the beauty of hiring professionals—you can rely on them.

Unlike me, I think wryly. Duane couldn't trust me. I had deceived him about the book, and then lied again by delaying my confession.

"I can handle the rest of the day's calls and meetings from here," I tell Jeannie. "I'll be back in the office tomorrow."

"Is everything okay?" Jeannie asks, concern edging her voice now that the emergency is over.

"Yes, why? Did someone mention my absence this morning?"

"Well, Duane stopped by with Oliver on their way to the airport to DC. Oliver wants you to call him. I guess he's been trying to reach you, too. And who's that man waiting outside your door?"

The strange man. I had almost forgotten about him. As I open the door to say goodbye to Jeannie, he's still there, standing like a soldier in the hallway.

"Excuse me," I call to him, "but who are you and why are you here?"

"Ms. Gordon-Lennox, I'm Chris. I was told you should call Mr. Mitchell at Riverbank. He'll explain."

I frown, confusion swirling. Is this related to Duane and the book? That doesn't seem likely. This man is clearly security, clad in a standard suit, discreet earpieces. Duane and Oliver seemed to be ramping up their security even as they brought me closer to their workspace.

Having switched my phone back on after the meeting, I notice a flood of missed calls and text messages. My phone lights up mid-scroll. Oliver.

"Security's in place. You with Chris?" No hello, just orders.

"Yes. He's here. What's happening?"

"Layers on layers. DC is one layer. Your book is . . . adjacent. Duane and I are in the war room planning strategy."

This is beginning to sound like they're mounting a campaign.

"So is it about the book?"

"Not really. Complicated, GL."

"You're a terrible liar, Oliver. Coming from a professional, that's saying something."

"Save your confessions. I'm not judging. Stay put. Chris doesn't leave your side."

"He won't talk to me again, will he?"

"Relax. He's pissed, not gone. Give him time to process."

"I'm not exactly a blind-trust kind of girl."

"You trusted him once. Start there. He trusts you more than he'll say while we're juggling grenades."

The battle references are beginning to alarm me.

"I know Congress is essential. He has to do this."

"Yeah—and there's more. He'll brief you when he's back. Sit tight."

"Okay. And . . . thank you. For believing in me."

"I do. He does. He just speaks fluent rage when the stakes are high. Let him cool."

"Tell Duane I'll wait to talk. Actually—don't. I need to say it myself."

"Attagirl. We're back in forty-eight."

The call leaves the kind of silence that precedes a strike in my living room, prompting me to escape to the gym. Chris insists on driving me in his special edition SUV and waits for me outside.

"I got you a freshly made green juice from the juice bar," I offer as I climb back into the car after my workout.

"Thanks, Ms. Gordon-Lennox, but I can't accept," he responds.

"I understand," I reply, the gravity of the situation sinking in. He is here to protect me, prepared for any unforeseen incident. Uneasiness continues to seep up my spine.

I manage to push through the day, taking the necessary calls and signing in to Zoom meetings. My senses are dulled, my emotions suppressed. I feel like I'm sleepwalking, tasting a bitter fear at the back of my throat. Why hadn't I confessed to Duane earlier? I'd been foolish. I'd allowed this thing between us to evolve, only to shatter his trust and my own heart.

At seven p.m., a knock on my door jolts me from my thoughts. It's Chris.

"I'm going off duty now. This is Mark, who will take the next shift," he announces, gesturing to the man beside him.

Mark nods in acknowledgment. "Ms. Gordon-Lennox." He's a stout man in his forties with cropped hair. His nondescript suit does nothing to hide his large stature and muscular frame. "Please keep your windows and the balcony door locked, and let me know if you hear anything unusual."

"I'm not sure what or whom you're protecting me from," I say with a weak smile. "But I'm glad you're here."

The next day, back at Riverbank, the pieces of the puzzle start to come together.

Chapter Forty-Three

. . . no details at this time

"HEY, DAD, YEAH, I'M IN THE MIDDLE OF SOMETHING. HOW are you?" I say, leaning back in my chair at the Riverbank headquarters desk, wincing at the lie.

Actually, I'm having a quiet morning while Duane, Oliver, and their entourage are in Washington, DC, but I don't want to entertain my dad's explanation, his spin, about why he couldn't show up at the Met Gala when I asked for his support. This is just who he is. I remember Duane's casual comment, that it doesn't always have to be an older man you can count on, even as my dad speaks.

"You know, Charlie, I'd do anything for you." For once, this doesn't ignite my anger. I know he believes it. He loves me, just not in the way I need him to show it.

"It's fine, Dad," I reply. "I know you would. Let's have dinner when I'm back in New York next week. You can tell me more about Sabrina."

"Great, kiddo. Will do. So glad you understand. Love you."

"Yes, I love you too, Dad."

My attention is abruptly drawn by the rising voices around me to the large screen high in the corner of the office.

Concern escalates into shouts as words runs along the bottom of the screen: "Cofounder of Riverbank, a cryptocurrency trading platform, has been shot on the steps of the Capitol."

"Who's been shot?" someone shouts as people gather in front of the screen.

"Turn it up!"

"Is it Oliver?"

"Is it Duane?"

We watch as an ambulance pulls away, police car lights flashing, as a reporter says, "No details at this time, but we do know the Riverbank founders had been testifying moments before in front of Congress. The company was here to advocate for cryptocurrency regulation and to educate legislators about digital gold."

The room is a mix of disbelief, fear, and shock. My heart is somersaulting in my chest. The sting of cold sweat and panic seizes me. *No, no, no, oh please, no.*

Jeannie rushes up to me. "Charlotte, it will be okay."

As she places both hands on my shoulders, my phone rings. Oliver's name lights up the screen, and my stomach drops. Duane. It was Duane who's been shot. Duane, shot on the steps of the Capitol. He has to be alive. Please let him be alive.

"Oliver, how . . . how is he?" I struggle to get the words out.

"Charlotte, he's been shot. His bodyguard managed to deflect the bullet, but he's been hit in the shoulder. They're taking him to surgery now at Washington Memorial. I'm sending the jet for you. It should be there in two hours."

"But how is he, Oliver?"

"The surgeon said he won't know until he gets in there and sees what the damage is."

"Do we know who did this? Are you safe?"

"We're still waiting for more details from security. Kurt

took down the gunman, so we'll find out who's behind this soon. Don't worry, Charlotte. We're on top of this. You just need to be here for him. And remember, you need to do exactly what the security team tells you at all times."

Chapter Forty-Four

. . . cybersecurity and defense

I'VE BEEN PACING THIS FLUORESCENT PURGATORY FOR two hours while Duane's in surgery. Oliver keeps buzzing in and out, his phone welded to his ear. A guard I don't recognize stands across the room; another waits at the door to guard Duane's recovery.

A gentle hand lands on my shoulder.

"He's out of surgery," Oliver says, voice low and steady. "Good news. Less damage than we feared."

I throw my arms around him as he pulls me into a hug.

"Oh, Oliver—thank God. I need to see him. I need to tell him everything I've been holding back. I was terrified he didn't want me. Maybe he won't now. But he has to know I love him." I grip his forearms. "Can I see him?"

"Yes, but I need to talk to him first."

"Don't burden him with all this now. He needs to focus on healing."

"He'll ask," Oliver says, tiredness roughening the edges. "We have unfinished business."

The dread I've been swallowing climbs back up. "Do

you know who did this? Was it my book? Did I put him in danger?"

"No," he sighs. "He went ahead with the Hill testimony knowing something might happen."

"He knew?"

He pauses, looking at me, his expression hard. "That's why I have to speak to him. We thought we had them in our sights."

And suddenly all the pieces slide into place—extra security, Oliver glued to my side, the abrupt move to the Pit.

"Now that they know about him, they know about you," Oliver adds, grim.

"Bloody hell, Oliver. Why didn't you tell me?"

"We were tracking them. Waiting for them to move while we were ready. And they did."

"But he was shot. He could have died!"

"I know. He knew. It was his call." Oliver's voice thins. "Not mine."

"Why would he risk his life?" Tears slide down my face.

"He's tired of hiding."

Our conversation is cut short as two men enter the room. One wears an impeccable Armani suit exuding authority and confidence. The other is more casually dressed in a tweed blazer, a quieter power on display. The room's dynamics shift in their presence; a sense of maturity fills the air. Oliver makes short introductions.

"Charlotte, this is Gerald and Gabriel, Duane's uncles. This is Charlotte, Duane's girlfriend."

Gerald wears the Armani. He looks like he's in his early fifties, broad shouldered, silver-laced sable hair, intense light blue eyes that drill into you. Professorial Gabriel in tweed, younger looking, has a softer edge and a faint note of pipe tobacco.

They nod at me, no handshakes.

"His condition?" Gerald asks, his clipped British voice turning the question into an order.

"Duane just got out of surgery. It went well. We're waiting for him to wake," Oliver says.

"What about security?" Gabriel interrupts.

"Two Force men are here, two at the hotel."

"Make it two more." Gabriel steps away, phone already to his ear, his quieter, Oxfordish lilt belying the steel in his tone.

Gerald turns to Oliver. "We agreed on this, Oliver. Duane wasn't supposed to testify. What happened?"

"Look, I know what we decided," Oliver responds hurriedly, "but Duane wouldn't stick to that plan. He doesn't want to hide anymore."

"He told you that?" Gerald pushes.

"He didn't have to. Press release with his picture, the Met Gala, testifying on the Hill—he's been burning bridges to his old life."

"What's gotten into him?" Gerald asks, visibly frustrated.

Both of them look at me.

"I wrote the book about him before I really knew him," I say, heat creeping up my neck. "I didn't see why he should shy away from those activities. I always wondered why he was always in the shadows. He's passionate about crypto—"

"Charlotte, you have no idea," Gerald cuts in, flat. "Davos is off the table. Our security can't handle that."

It hits me that I don't actually know who Gerald and Gabriel are. This is disruption of the worst kind, but disruption offers opportunity.

"I know you're not his real uncles. He obviously respects and cares for you. Who are you to him, really?"

"Not the time, Charlotte," Oliver says, cutting me a look.

Gabriel lifts a hand. "No—she's in this. She should know.

"We aren't family by blood," he adds. "We were close to his parents—especially his mother. We're in cybersecurity and defense. When they died, we stepped in."

The realization strikes with lightning clarity. The

professionals who effectively erased Duane from the internet.

"You scrubbed his past," I say. "Thorough—maybe too thorough. Nothing exists before boarding school."

Gerald nods once. "It was a bit clumsy. It's easier to bury a past than to fabricate a parallel life."

Heat rises in my chest. His parents were murdered—none of that explains why he was shot.

"And exactly what were you burying?"

Silence.

"There's some information I can give you, but that part has to come from him." Gerald checks his phone. "The surgeon's ready to brief us. We'll share what we learn."

As they leave, I collapse back onto the couch. "Oliver, I need to close my eyes for a few minutes. Now that Duane's out of surgery, I can finally breathe."

Oliver settles into the chair next to me. "Let the 'uncles' do what they do best. We should both get some sleep until we can see Duane." He squeezes my hand, then, leaning his head back, he closes his eyes.

Several hours later, I'm in the surgical ICU, holding Duane's hand as he sleeps. He's off the respirator, but his face looks worn, pale, and aged. My breath hitches, tears threatening to spill as I first lay eyes on him.

A large man stands security outside his room, another at the ICU entrance. Privacy is a luxury we don't have. Medical staff bustle around, adjusting his IV, taking blood samples, hanging new medication bags, and quietly checking his vitals. The room is filled with the steady beeping of his heart monitor, creating a trancelike rhythm. I'm watching the nurse hook a new bag to his IV when I feel his gaze on me.

"Duane." I smile, my heart bursting with relief.

"Lola, I'm so glad you're here. Don't leave me."

Gripping his hand tighter, I lean in to give him a gentle kiss, whispering, "I love you. I'll never leave you."

Chapter Forty-Five

. . . cryptocurrency . . . that's what happened

"HE'S GETTING BETTER," I TELL DANNY OVER THE PHONE, MY voice echoing the weariness from my long hours at the hospital. "They moved him from step-down to a regular room yesterday. The physical therapists are optimistic about his recovery—he should have normal use of his shoulder pretty soon."

Danny has been checking up on me ever since he heard about the shooting. While I waited to discuss discharge plans with Oliver, his calls kept me moored to daily life.

"Duane being young and healthy is working in both your favors. I may not know him very well, but I've noticed a change in you since you two met," Danny observes. "You've become more open during our conversations, even started sharing memories of Mom that we haven't touched in years. I've missed that about you, Carlie."

"I do feel different, I admit," I say softly, a knot forming in my throat. "It's—it's a good feeling, Danny. I want to see this through. But I've got to go now. Oliver wants to talk. Give my love to Kate and the kids."

As I approach Oliver, his fatigue mirrors my own.

"Charlotte," he begins, looking at me through tired eyes, "we believe Duane will be safer back at the hotel, so he's being discharged today."

"Is he medically stable enough to leave?" I ask, concern creasing my brow.

Oliver nods reassuringly. "Yes, it's all good. We can provide the necessary medical care he needs at the hotel."

Entering the presidential suite is like walking into a high-tech surveillance hub. Half a dozen people are glued to large monitors, their fingers dancing on keyboards, voices whispering into headsets. The suite is buzzing with an undercurrent of tension.

Security is everywhere—elevator entrances, exits, even the floor below has been converted into a dwelling space for the men, adding another layer of protection to the top floor. The only familiar face among all this is Kurt, deep in discussion in the war room.

In this whirlwind of confusion, I find solace in one of the suite's few quiet places—the bedroom. Oliver has suggested I sleep there. Does that mean he expects Duane and me to share a bed? Do I expect that? More importantly, what do I want?

I try to step back, to think objectively, but I'm overwhelmed by my feelings. I know I want to be with Duane. He's been there for me repeatedly. But am I confusing gratitude with love? No, it is gratitude, but for the first time in a long while, I feel I can trust someone. I trust him. I feel more open, hopeful that my life can become what I want.

Regret washes over me as I think about my failed marriage to Matthew. I hadn't given it the time it deserved, hadn't been as involved in Matthew's life as I should have been, even as I still hear my therapist's voice asking why I feel solely responsible for our failed marriage.

I'm caught in an all too familiar cycle of self-blame, with Matthew constantly insisting that it wasn't his fault but mine. I remember agreeing to join him on his business trips, only for him to later tell me it wasn't a good time because he'd be too occupied with meetings. But when did that start? Was it after he'd begun his affair? Overwhelmed, I lean forward, my head in my hands. I just can't remember. I rise from my seat and venture into the suite's bustling living area. The constant flux of men moving to and from the elevator and the war room is oddly soothing.

One of them approaches me, juggling several shopping bags. "These came for you. We had to go through everything," he says, his tone apologetic but firm.

"I understand," I respond, grateful to see the familiar department store bags. I had asked a personal shopper at Neiman Marcus to send over clothing, shoes, and toiletries, since my stay had been longer than I had planned.

Over the next half hour, I find some normalcy in the routine of dressing in my new Veronica Beard blue sweater and jeans, pulling my hair into a casual ponytail, and applying a light touch of makeup.

As I emerge from the bedroom, I spot Duane stepping off the elevator, flanked by a team of security, Oliver, and his uncles. Despite the sling on his left arm, he looks as strong and determined as ever. I move toward him, halting at the sight of his injured arm before laughing softly and throwing my arms around his neck. He returns the embrace with his free arm, pressing a swift kiss to my lips before pulling away.

"I'm glad you're here," he says, his voice carrying a note of exhaustion that tugs at my heart.

I nod, acknowledging his need to focus on the threat at hand before we can address our relationship. "Always, always. When you're ready, we'll talk."

As the day drags on, I find myself confined to a new phone

and devoid of my laptop for security reasons. I'm stuck in my thoughts, wrestling with questions of forgiveness and betrayal. Has Duane forgiven me? It seems so, but why?

Our age difference is a looming concern—the fear that one day he might want someone younger. But isn't that the risk in any relationship, regardless of the age gap? The true challenge is making each other a priority, never taking one another for granted. It was a commitment my father had never given to his family. He had never made his family a priority.

I yearn to talk to Duane, to lay my fears and realizations before him, to assure him of my commitment to our relationship.

After several hours, Duane joins me in the bedroom, taking my hand and leading me to the couch. "Oliver and I have to leave tomorrow for about a week. You can wait at Riverbank or in New York, but you'll have security either way," he explains.

"Wherever you're going, I'm coming with you. We should be together," I insist.

"I'm going to Davos. I can't put you in that danger," he says firmly.

"Davos is one of the safest places in the world, with all those dignitaries and billionaires. Let me come with you," I plead.

"No, Lola, I can't risk it," he refuses again.

"Why did someone want to kill you? Please, I need to know what's going on. Have you forgiven me for that terrible book? Did that have anything to do with this?"

My words tumble out in a rush. "Duane, what happened?"

"What happened?" he repeats, his voice edged. "Cryptocurrency. That's what happened."

Chapter Forty-Six

. . . what they started fifteen years ago

"HAVE YOU EVER QUESTIONED HOW OLIVER AND I MANaged to secure enough funding to launch our own cryptocurrency trading platform?" Duane queries. "We raised capital a few times, but it was nowhere near what giants like Coinbase or Gemini collected."

I move on the couch, shuffling to create some room for him. He sits.

"Are you going to clue me in? Contrary to what you might believe, I, your muse, am not a mind reader. More often than not, you're the one reading *my* mind," I joke, attempting to give him some breathing space.

"You keep your feelings under wraps, Duane, but I want us to be a team," I continue. "I want to truly know you. The good, the bad, all of it."

He sighs and picks up my hand, bringing it to his lips for a quick kiss as he continues.

"Oliver and I made a lot of money with our personal cryptocurrency investing, but not on the scale of wealth needed to start a crypto platform. We were able to launch Riverbank so quickly because I had personal access to a large sum of bitcoin," he explains.

"Where did that come from?" I ask with interest.

"Well, my mom had an affinity for cryptography. More than that, she was exceptional at it. She was devoted to using cryptography, cipher codes, to forge a new type of digital currency. The biggest obstacle was this thing called the 'double-spend problem.' She, along with other brilliant minds, grappled with that for years. But she was the first to crack it, and in 2008, she published her protocol for cryptocurrency and blockchain," he says.

As he leans toward me on the couch, his gaze is intense, waiting to witness the moment of realization light up my face. I can feel my breath quicken as his words start to sink in, and then, my eyes are locked onto his.

"Hold on, Duane . . . cryptocurrency, a protocol, 2008? That's when the bitcoin white paper—your mother, are you saying your mother . . ." I stutter and then fall silent.

"My mother was Satoshi Nakamoto," he confesses softly.

I spring up from the love seat, spinning around to face him. My movements are erratic, swift.

"What the fuck, Duane? What the actual fuck?" is all I can muster.

His mother had invented bitcoin. She had coded the software that was being used by nodes worldwide to mine bitcoin. I'm struggling to wrap my head around the enormity of it all.

"Your mother? When did you find out? What happened?" I can't quite process the revelation.

"Both my parents had advanced degrees in computer science. They emigrated from Romania in the 1980s and accepted teaching roles at a mid-level college computer science department. It gave my mother the free time to pursue her lifelong ambition.

"She wanted to establish a digital currency that would

empower individuals rather than rendering them reliant on banks or their country's economy, especially during periods of inflation or recession," he continues.

"She dreamed of providing the world's unbanked population with opportunities we often take for granted here, given our stable and mostly reliable banking system. I knew she was on to something. She would always refer to it as her 'double-spend project.' She taught me so much," he shares.

"Did you know when she published the protocol?" I manage to ask.

"Yes, she told me back then, but it took quite a while for people to catch on. For the first two years, she was the only person mining bitcoin. She mined over a million bitcoin," he reveals.

"Wait a minute." The reality of what a million bitcoin would be worth in today's market hits me—a staggering sum, at least a billion dollars.

"I know," he responds, watching as I grapple with the magnitude of the numbers. "And that wealth led to my parents' murder. They were executed for their bitcoin.

"They'd surrendered the safe combination, which housed the private keys to about fifty thousand bitcoin." His voice is hoarse, but he continues speaking. "We believe they were killed so the remaining bitcoin would be taken out of circulation, assuming the location of the private keys perished with them. It was the early days of bitcoin. The murderers didn't understand that my parents would have been more valuable alive. They didn't realize the sheer amount of bitcoin my parents actually owned."

I slip my arm around his waist, mindful of his sling, and pull him as close as I can. We sink into a heavy silence.

"I'm so sorry, Duane. I had no clue," I murmur. My lips brush the rough line of stubble along his jaw.

"No one does, apart from my uncles, Oliver, and now you," he says.

"But why are they after you now?" I question, eyes searching his.

He swallows. I see the motion of his throat. "I don't think they knew about me. They probably hadn't done their due diligence. I doubt they realized my parents had a child.

"When I found my parents, I called Gerald. He took me away, and I never returned to my childhood home. I didn't even attend my parents' funeral. Gerald and Gabriel didn't want anyone to be aware of my existence. They erased all traces of me, keeping my name out of the media," he explains.

I lace our fingers on his good side. His palm is hot and steady.

"I was a wreck for nearly a year," he continues. "My uncles were my lifelines. They ensured I had someone to talk to, to help me process the horror that had happened. Once we agreed I was ready to tackle school again, they created a new identity for me and enrolled me in boarding school."

"What was your old identity?" I smooth my thumb over the ridge of a small scar at the base of his finger.

"Duane isn't my real name. My birth name is Romanian: Ciel. I picked Duane because, as you guessed, my mother was a fan of Duane Allman."

Tears silently begin coursing down my cheeks, as the weight of his revelation overwhelms me. I press my forehead to his temple, careful of his shoulder.

"I'm so sorry. It's unthinkable what you've had to endure. How did you manage? How did you rebuild your life after such devastation?"

"Lola, please don't cry. I'm better now. I have incredible people in my life. My uncles, Oliver, the team at Riverbank, and now you," he says, gently wiping my tears away with his free hand.

"But I betrayed you. I wrote such terrible things about you and convinced myself I was being humorous, entertaining . . . but in reality, I wanted to hurt you," I confess.

"I could tell. Your book is brutal, but I was awful to you. I get why you wrote what you did," he admits.

"But I hid the book from you. I should've been honest from the start. How can you ever trust me again?" I ask.

"I do trust you, Lola. You've been so honest with me, even when no one else was. You are my muse; you've inspired me to come out of the shadows, to stop hiding. You've pushed me to reclaim my life and embrace who I truly am. Now I'm prepared to face those who took my parents from me and make them pay. I wasn't ready before," he declares.

"My uncles have urged me to take action, but I could never comprehend the long-term implications," he continues.

"The long-term implications?" I echo.

"The reality is, I can never truly be me until I finish what they started fifteen years ago. The people who did this will be at Davos. We're headed there to get more information and plan our next move," he explains.

My fingers catch his sleeve, and then release it. "Please don't go, Duane. I'm terrified that something might happen to you."

"No, Lola, as you pointed out, Davos is the most secure place on the planet during the World Economic Forum," he says, grabbing my hand.

"But what if, because it's being held in June instead of its usual time in January, the conference routine is disrupted and security isn't as tight?" My voice is forced, too high.

"Security will be just fine. But what about us? You mentioned earlier that you want us to be together. Do you mean in a committed relationship? Can you see a future with me? Because I can," he says, searching my face.

"What . . . what are you trying to say?" The words trip; my tongue feels too big for my mouth.

"Charlotte, I've yearned for a family since I was fifteen. I've never shared that with anyone. You now understand why family is so crucial to me, and that's not going to change. I've never told anyone my secret before. When I was lying on the Capitol steps, overwhelmed by my anger, my fear, my pain, it all became clear to me. We should get married."

A small sound leaves me—half inhale, half protest.

He drops to one knee. The soft thud of it against the rug feels louder than it should be. He looks up at me, scanning my face. "Charlotte, will you marry me?"

"Duane, I . . ." My mouth is dry, the rest of the sentence breaks apart. I press my free hand to my chest, as if I can calm the flutter there. "You want to marry me? This is all so sudden. Are you certain?" My voice comes out thin.

"Yes, I am. It's the one thing in my life I'm sure of." He steadies himself on one knee with his hand fisted. "You know I don't consider our age difference an issue. Besides that, what are your reservations?"

"So many things." The words rasp; my throat tightens as I count them off on my fingers to anchor my thoughts. "I work for you. I penned a derogatory book about you. I . . . I didn't even know your real name." My voice frays to a thread as I see a grin spreading across his face, followed by a soft chuckle.

"Nice try, Lola," he says, and opens his right hand. Light spills across his palm—an emerald-cut sapphire wreathed in diamonds. Eight, maybe ten carats; storybook big.

"I heard cornflower sapphires are your favorite," he says simply.

My lips part; my pulse lifts to my throat as I gasp. "You . . . know? You've been planning this?"

"Yes, Lola, yes, I have. Give me your left hand." Adeptly maneuvering the ring one-handed, he slides it on my ring finger. The Ceylon blue pulses with an inner fire bending the light like liquid cobalt. "Consider my proposal. No rush. This is your ring to keep, regardless. I'll be back in a week, and we can discuss it further."

He stands, pulling me up with him, using his good hand. The movement brings me to his chest. I steady myself there as a laugh catches in my smile because of the joy bubbling up, overwhelming my heart and soul.

"Say yes. You complete me. As my muse, as my wife. I need your inspiration in my life forever. You told me it was my time to step into the light. I want you there beside me."

Chapter Forty-Seven

. . . love and crypto thrive on volatility

THERE I AM, STANDING WITH HIM ON THE TARMAC, AS HE'S about to board the jet.

"Consider us, Lola. I will always be there for you," he whispers in my ear as he bends to kiss me, pulling me closer, holding me tighter than ever before.

His kiss tastes warm, fresh, pulling me deeper into the intoxicating aroma of his male, bergamot scent. Kissing him back, being cautious not to hurt his injured arm, it takes every ounce of my strength not to simply yield, to whisper, "Yes, I'll be yours."

My ring shimmers under the sun's spotlight, reflecting off the jet's sleek metallic body. As I pull away, Oliver approaches and steps between us, putting a hand on Duane's good shoulder and one on mine. He looks at each of us and says, "Take heart, you two. Love and crypto thrive on volatility—if it's too stable, it's probably dead."

We laugh with Oliver at his humor and charm, unaware it's an invocation. And then they're gone.

Over the next couple of days, I feel his physical absence

more than his words. Though the phone is quiet from his end, it rings frequently with calls from Danny and incessantly from Viv. Every time I answer, I'm greeted by yet another reason from Viv on why I should agree to marry him. Most are reasons I've already considered.

I know my answer will be yes. The certainty struck me the moment he asked the question. All this charade was nothing but an attempt to convince myself that I was being rational, reasonable, weighing the pros and cons of a life changing decision with equanimity. But deep down, I know it's all pretense, as artificial as my ring is real.

"Think about how incredibly intelligent your kids will be, inheriting his IQ and your brilliance," Viv points out, marking reason number fifteen on her persuasive list.

"Oh Viv, that's not the point. I'm choosing to marry him because I love him and because when it counts, he shows up. I kept doubting he really wanted marriage and children—he's young; it sounded like a line. But now that I know what happened to his parents and how he carried that loss for fifteen years, I see it: Family sits at the center of him. He's steady. He wants a home. I believe him." I can't help but laugh at the straightforwardness of my decision, and Viv joins in, echoing my joy.

"That settles it," I say. "I'm heading to Davos. I can't delay this. I need to let him know."

"Whoa there, Charlie. Let him know when he gets back. I'm sure he's got his hands full over there with networking, business deals, making plans for Riverbank's future."

"All the more reason to be there, Viv. To be part of his life at this moment. That's what my intuition tells me, and I'm going to trust it. I need to figure out a way to get there. Remember, I still have the pass he had made for me when he intended for me to join him," I muse aloud.

"Well, you're in luck. Stacy and Rich Delvaney are jetting

off to Davos tomorrow. I ended up sitting next to her at a fundraiser last night, and Davos was all she could talk about. They were supposed to go last year but it got canceled. You could probably hitch a ride with them," Viv suggests.

"That's just wonderful, Viv! What are the odds of you knowing someone heading there? It's as if it's meant to be. Should I give Stacy a call?" I query.

"Absolutely, and remember, she's a hopeless romantic. So if you mention it's a love mission, she'll be more than happy to offer you a seat," Viv says.

Tracking down Stacy proves to be more challenging than I'd anticipated, but eventually, I manage to snag her number from a mutual friend. At first, my conversation with her feels a bit awkward, but I press on. "Stacy, you'd be doing me a huge favor. I need to reach Davos urgently to deliver an answer that could be the key to two people's happiness," I implore.

Stacy's voice dips low, a quiet intensity enveloping her words. "Oh, Charlotte, do tell," she commands.

"Well, you haven't met him yet, but if everything pans out as I hope, I promise I'll introduce you. Could you do me this favor?" I ask.

Chapter Forty-Eight

. . . one perfect, ridiculous, glorious moment

ENGADIN AIRPORT IS ONE OF THE HIGHEST AIRPORTS IN Europe, and our jet descends to breathtaking views of the snowcapped peaks of the Swiss Alps, with vibrant green valleys below. The atmosphere in the cabin is slightly tense as the plane passes through the narrow space created by the valley, but the pilot expertly navigates the plane until the runway comes into view with mountains reaching up on both sides. We quickly disembark to enter the modern terminal designed with wood and stone, reflecting alpine architecture.

"Wow, the air is so fresh," I remark, descending from the plane. I breathe in deeply, the quiet surroundings punctuated by the sounds of aircraft landing.

"We'll guide you through security," Stacy offers. "Things are a bit topsy-turvy this year after the break."

I nod gratefully, musing on the strange alliances and newfound relationships that love can inspire. The Delvaneys had been amicable and engaging during the flight, maintaining a pleasant balance between conversation and privacy. Together, we passed an agreeable five hours discussing mutual acquaintances and social events. We'd departed at the crack of dawn and had landed in Davos just in time for cocktails.

Never in my life have I pursued a man before. They had always been the ones to gravitate to me. Now, the roles are reversed, and it leaves me a touch apprehensive. Is his proposal serious, or is it just a spur of the moment reaction to his near-death experience? I'd have my answer soon enough—all I had to do was watch his reaction when I told him yes.

This is my first time at the World Economic Forum in Davos, and the town feels oddly exposed in summer. No blankets of snow to soften the edges, no winter fog to blur the sightlines—just sharp green slopes, glaring sunshine, and security that has nowhere to hide. The streets hum with black cars and badge wearing delegates, but above them, men in monochromatic gear patrol the rooftops like hawks, their silhouettes etched clean against the sky. Their gazes sweep ceaselessly, scanning 360 degrees. I can't tell if the rifles are really there or if it's only my nerves inventing them, but the air carries the metallic taste of watchfulness.

I turn to the Delvaneys, offering warm hugs goodbye—a small, normal gesture against the surreal stage of hidden rifles and invisible trip wires. Davos in June is meant to feel like renewal, but it hums with vigilance.

Stepping through the revolving glass doors of the hotel, I notice the scent of fresh pine, the sound of soft jazz piano overlaying the rustle of newspapers, the clink of espresso cups, and the quiet hum of multilingual conversations. There's a vibe of calculated calm. Tall men in sober suits with earpieces stand at the corners of the space, eyes scanning calmly. The lobby buzzes with the presence of CEOs, tech founders, journalists, and NGO leaders. Some are deep in animated conversation, others tap out emails with intense focus, while others sit calmly as aides hover nearby. Paparazzi aren't allowed inside, but a few photographers wait outside, hoping to catch a glimpse as attendees enter and leave.

I dial Duane and then Oliver, but both calls go unanswered. Settling down on a luxurious couch to wait, I pick up a newspaper headlining a recent suicide at the conference—an attendee who happened to be a Chinese businessman, the founder of a prosperous offshore cryptocurrency trading platform, a veteran since the early days of bitcoin. A sense of disquiet washes over me, and I dial Duane once again. No response, just an automated voicemail greeting. I send him another text.

Nearby, two individuals engaged in a hushed discussion catch my attention. From their conversation, it seems they are part of the press, deliberating about the man who had tragically ended his life.

Details about him and his company are scarce. He'd seemingly emerged out of the blue around 2010, engaging heavily in bitcoin trading before launching his platform, Nakamoto, without any investor funds. Rumor has it that he'd amassed wealth on the darknet, laundering it through bitcoin transactions on his platform. No suicide note had been found.

"Well, we'll have to dig elsewhere for a story. Police have deemed it a suicide. Case closed. Feels like a hasty attempt to avoid further scandal for the forum. This entire year feels off-kilter—Davos in spring, now a suicide. Something doesn't sit right," one journalist comments.

A surge of anxiety swells in my chest, escalating into an almost paralyzing panic. The conversation leaves a lump in my throat as I struggle to swallow around it. I quickly scan the lobby for a server to fetch me some calming tea.

"Ms. Gordon-Lennox, can I assist you?" It's Kurt, Duane's personal bodyguard. My relief is immediate, and I smile gratefully at him.

"Kurt, I'm so relieved to see you. I've been trying to reach Duane, but I keep getting his voicemail. Do you know where he is?"

"Yes, I'm just going back now, I'll let him know you're here. Please be prepared for a scan for security when we enter the suite," he says.

"Yes, thank you so much. I'm really glad you found me," I say as we enter the elevator. Having Kurt around means I am able to navigate without incessant security checks. The suite is located on the fourth floor. It's amusing to think there likely weren't enough luxury suites to accommodate all the high profile guests in town, but Riverbank had somehow secured one. One of Kurt's men greets us at the door and conducts the routine security sweep on us and our devices.

My phone cleared, I leave them and step into the living area, bustling with security and Riverbank staff. The atmosphere hums with tension—watchful eyes, hushed radios, subtle movements of men trained to spot threats before they happen.

And then I see him—no, see *them*.

Duane and Oliver sit apart from the crowd on a low couch, heads bent together in hushed intensity. Their posture is off, not casual colleagues but coconspirators. Oliver leans forward, his hand gripping Duane's good shoulder. It looks congratulatory, but my gut twists. That gesture—too firm, too solemn—reads like *a seal on something irreversible.*

The businessman's death. The rumors swirling. Instantly, I know. My stomach lurches.

In that single snapshot, their bond is illuminated: chosen brothers, yes, but also partners in shadows. I freeze, my certainty a blade in my chest.

And then Duane looks up.

His eyes widen, surprise slicing through his mask. He rises instantly and strides toward me with the urgency of a man starved. His arm pulls me in, enveloping me, commanding me.

"Lola, darling, what brings you here? I wanted you to wait for me back in the States."

The shock fractures; all the imaginings crumble. My body betrays me, clinging to him, whispering against his chest, "I couldn't bear to be apart from you. I couldn't wait."

Oliver joins us, that wry half smile tugging at his lips. His gaze lingers on me, strangely knowing. "Glad to see you made it after all, GL. Well done. Black-tie dinner tonight. You'll be radiant."

Duane cuts him off, voice edged. "Don't plan our evening, Oliver. We may have other plans involving no one else."

Continuing Oliver's lighthearted banter, I say, "I happen to have brought something stunning to wear—but Duane may keep me occupied until then."

Oliver chuckles and retreats. "I've got this, Duane, no worries. Catch you two later," he says casually.

I squeeze Duane's hand. My "What does he mean by that?" goes unanswered as he guides me through the room, answering questions from staff with a nod here, a clipped order there, as if batting away the outside world. He leads me down a corridor, every movement infused with urgency.

The bedroom is bright with mountain light. A wide bed, a desk, an open laptop. He halts me in the center of the room with a tug, and then he's on me—kissing me like a man who has been parched for years and has finally found water.

He cups my face with one hand as if he needs to make sure I'm real. His touch is trembling at first, then strong, claiming. I feel the heat of his relief pour into me, fierce and unguarded. The pressure of his mouth as his tongue finds mine sends a shiver straight through my chest, winds down my spine, and explodes in my core. I gasp softly, but he swallows the sound as my knees threaten to give way. I kiss him back, lost in the physical domination of my mouth, an unspoken ache building. Every nerve sparks, every inch of my skin is tuned to him.

We break, gasping. His forehead rests against mine, voice ragged. "Why are you here? I need you to say it. Say it, Lola."

The laughter spills out of me like bubbles breaking to the surface. "Yes. Yes, Duane, I'll marry you. Yes."

His smile detonates—blinding, boyish, almost unbearably beautiful. He awkwardly lifts me up with one arm around my waist, spinning me until I'm dizzy, our laughter braided together. The kiss that follows is tender, reverent, almost disbelieving.

A knock at the door interrupts. Duane curses under his breath, but admits a hotel staffer carrying a tray: champagne on ice, two waiting glasses.

"How—how did you know?" I breathe.

He gives a sly smile. "Oliver knew. He said the night I proposed that if you came to Davos, it could only mean yes."

I laugh, shaky, dazzled. "You and Oliver—despite appearances—sometimes I think you're twins, reading each other's thoughts."

He shakes his head, a glint in his eyes. "No. He sees only the surface. You see all of me. I've seduced my muse . . . and now I want to seduce my fiancée."

The champagne glasses are forgotten on the desk. Duane kisses me hard, then pulls back with a groan.

"Damn it—sling," he mutters, glaring at the strap holding his arm in place.

I laugh, breathless. "Well, I wasn't planning on a threesome with medical equipment, but if it's part of the deal . . ."

His grin flashes, wicked and boyish all at once. "You're impossible." With his good hand, he tugs at the buckle, trying to free himself, but the fabric catches. I reach up to help, our fingers fumbling over the straps until the thing finally drops to the floor in defeat.

"There." I brush his hair back from his forehead. "Liberated."

He leans down, kissing me again, deeper, urgent, but when he shifts his weight, a strangled groan escapes him.

I freeze. "Are you all right?"

He laughs, shaking his head. "I'm fine. Just . . . not my most graceful performance." He lowers himself carefully, his good arm braced above me, his body hovering in a precarious dance between passion and injury. "You may need to do most of the work here, fiancée."

I bite my lip, giggling, then deliberately roll my hips against his, drawing another groan—this one definitely not from pain. "I think I can manage that."

The awkwardness dissolves into laughter as we shift and rearrange, finding angles that don't strain his shoulder. Every time he tries to take control, his body betrays him, and I end up laughing against his mouth.

He hums his dissatisfaction. "Careful, fiancée. I may be down one arm, but I'm still dangerous in bed."

"Dangerous?" I tease. "You're useless."

"Useless?" he growls, and with a sudden, reckless movement, he flips me beneath him. Pain flickers across his face—he curses under his breath—but then his mouth crashes onto mine, hot, claiming. "Still useless, Lola?"

I'm laughing against his lips, breathless. "Fine. Half useless. But the good half is very good."

We fumble, adjust, rearrange, each groan of pain from him turning into a gasp of pleasure from me. At one point he tries to pin both my wrists but forgets he can't use his bad arm, leaving me half free.

"You can't even hold me down properly," I whisper, giggling.

"Then stop wriggling and help me out," he retorts, biting at my collarbone until I squeal.

The laughter lingers even as desire overtakes us, each groan and gasp tangled with murmurs of love. His touch, though one-handed, is no less commanding. He traces every line of me as though he's memorizing, branding, owning. And when finally he moves inside me, slow and careful, I arch against him, tears pricking my eyes at the sheer beauty of it—of us.

His forehead drops to mine, his voice rough, breaking. "Even half broken, I'd fight every shadow in the world to have this. To have you."

Joy floods me, uncontainable, spilling out as I laugh and cry in the same breath. "You do have me, Duane. Always."

We move together, the awkwardness gone, replaced by something pure and radiant—pleasure, yes, but also relief, release, the unshakable truth that we've found each other again.

He kisses me gently, reverently, his hand stroking my hair. "Not useless after all, was I?"

I grin through tears and laughter, breathless. "Infuriating. Impossible. And mine."

For one perfect, ridiculous, glorious moment, we're a mess of tangled limbs, bruised laughter, and raw love. Sling abandoned on the floor, danger forgotten.

It feels like we've outrun every shadow in the world.

Chapter Forty-Nine

. . . not until you

WE'RE LYING ON OUR SIDES IN BED. SHEETS TWIST AROUND our tangled bodies, our skin still slick with heat and pleasure. The air is thick—heavy with the scent of warm champagne and the intoxicating musk of sex. My body is still humming, my pulse just beginning to steady, but my mind is racing. Duane's fingers move lazily over my bare hip, tracing slow, possessive circles that make my stomach tighten all over again. Even though his breathing is even, his body relaxed, he's just waiting—waiting for me to speak.

"Duane," I murmur, my voice still rough from the pleasure he just wrung out of me.

He shifts slightly, and I watch as the low light catches on the strong lines of his chest, the deep grooves of muscle, the soft dusting of stubble along his jaw. He's devastating—all sharp angles and restrained power, a man sculpted from raw, smoldering intensity.

A slow smile tugs at his lips. The kind that makes my core tighten, my thighs clench. "Is this the part where you ask me when we're getting married?" His voice is smooth, teasing, but the hand on my hip tightens just enough to make my breath hitch. "Or how many children we'll have? Where we'll live?" His fingers skim lower beneath the tangled sheets, stroking just to remind me I'm already undone for him. "My answers are—whenever you want, as many as you want, and wherever you want."

Heat pools in my stomach, a deep aching pull that I should be immune to by now—but never am. I let my hand slide over his chiseled abs, feeling the tension beneath my touch, feeling the way his muscles twitch at my deliberate, featherlight strokes.

But I can't let him distract me.

Not yet.

I shift, propping myself up on one elbow, the sheets slipping down my body. Espresso eyes smolder as they drop to my bare skin. He watches me like he's about to drag me right back under him, back into the delicious chaos of his touch.

I force myself to focus, swallowing hard.

"No, darling, we'll decide on those things in time," I murmur, dragging my fingers along his jawline. His stubble scrapes against my skin, rough and delicious, a stark contrast to the way his soft lips part under my touch. "I need to know about the Chinese businessman who recently died."

The warmth between us, the teasing, the slow, simmering tension—it all shatters in an instant. His fingers still in my hair, his playful caresses gone. His muscles lock beneath my hands, and then the man before me isn't just Duane, the lover who whispers dirty commands against my skin.

He's Duane Blacklock, Shadows and Edges. The architect of digital empires, forged in vengeance.

"You don't need to know about that," he says, his voice dropping lower, ominous.

I sit up, ignoring the cool air that skates over my skin, as I lean in to make sure he looks at me. "But I know you and

Oliver are involved in something." I press my voice sharper now. "We're in this together, Duane. Keeping things from me doesn't protect me—it puts me in harm's way."

His jaw clenches, muscle ticking, but he doesn't look away.

For a long moment, I don't think he's going to answer.

Then something cracks.

He moves so fast I barely have time to gasp before he's over me again, pushing me back onto the bed with one hand on the side of my face, his body caging mine, his heat pressing into me, his presence drowning me.

"You are the only thing in this world that could retrieve me from the shadows," he murmurs, his breath hot against my lips.

The words aren't poetic. They're raw. Bitter. A confession that tastes like pain.

My heart pounds, my breath quickens as his lips ghost along my jaw, down my throat. He drags his teeth over my pulse, just enough to make me whimper, before soothing the spot with a slow open-mouthed kiss.

"You don't understand, Lola." His voice is molten sin, rolling over my skin, sinking into my bones. "I never wanted to be in the light. I built a kingdom in the dark because the dark was safe. It's where I survived. But then you walked in—all fire and fight, all beauty and defiance—and ruined me."

His hands slide lower, fingers dragging over my waist, my hips, gripping hard enough to make my thighs clench. He shifts, and I feel the full, hard proof of his need pressing into me, making my breath stutter, making heat coil low in my core.

"I should have stayed away," he growls, dragging his lips over my collarbone, down to my breasts.

"But the moment I had you, I knew—I would never want anyone else the way I want you."

I arch into him, my nails raking down his back, and he hisses between his teeth, biting down on my skin just hard enough to make me softly cry out.

Then, just as suddenly as he took control, he stills.

Foreheads pressed together, our chests heaving, he pulls back just enough to look at me. His gaze is unreadable, but I see it—the war inside him, the battle between the man he was and the man he's becoming.

"I spent fifteen years hunting them," he murmurs finally, his voice raw, like gravel coated in silk.

I swallow hard. "Your parents' killers?"

His jaw flexes, muscles tightening beneath my fingers.

"It wasn't just the men who pulled the triggers," he says, his voice like steel, edged and cold. "It was him. The man who ordered it. The Chinese businessman greedy for crypto, who destroyed my life."

I shiver beneath him. Not from the cold, but from the chill of what he's saying.

"He didn't even understand what he was stealing," Duane continues with a hoarse, bitter laugh. "Back then, no one did. He exploited the private keys to access tens of thousands of bitcoin. When bitcoin started to soar, he sold enough to kick-start his cryptocurrency trading platform."

I frown, searching his face. "Because there was more, wasn't there?"

Duane tilts his head slightly, studying me like he's deciding how much to give. His fingers skim along my jaw, down the column of my throat, sending a delicious shiver through me despite the serious conversation.

"More than anyone ever realized," he says finally. "My mother wasn't just Satoshi Nakamoto. Remember, she was the only one mining bitcoin in those early years. The only one. And she mined millions. She hid it away—something the killer knew nothing about, making her the single wealthiest person in the world, if she had lived."

A chill creeps up my spine at the weight of it. "So they killed them, thinking they had taken it all."

He nods. "It was only years later that they realized how much had been left behind. He used what he stole to start his empire and the trading platform to launder money, buy influence, and move power into the shadows."

His voice hardens again, his fingers pressing into my hip. "As his power grew, he accumulated more and more enemies, which gave us an opportunity to track him. It took years of persistence and patience. A few times we were close, but I never made my move." His lips brush over my temple, his next words a confession against my skin.

"Not until you."

My breath catches.

He pulls back, his eyes like obsidian as he searches my face.

"You were the tipping point, Lola," he murmurs. "You woke something in me—something I didn't even realize had gone dormant." He drags his fingers through my hair, his touch reverent, almost worshipful. "You made me want more than vengeance. You made me want a life. A future. A reason to stop hiding."

My chest tightens with emotion, with the depth of what he's saying. I press my palm against his heart, feeling the steady, unshakable rhythm beneath my fingers.

"Only in the last month did everything fall into place," he continues. "I was off site training, yes, but also planning. It was a race against time. I found out about Chiang before he knew about me, but he acted faster. And got to me first. After that, we had to assemble a team to eliminate him while he was here."

"I never meant to change you," I whisper.

A slow, dangerous smile tugs at the corner of his lips. "No, baby. You didn't change me. You reminded me who I was supposed to be."

I don't realize I'm shaking until he tightens his arm around me. Protective. Unyielding. As if he can hold me together with just his presence.

We sit in silence. Even as I ache for the boy who found his parents murdered, I feel slightly sick at the thought that he planned someone's murder. *Is this the life I want? The violence, the threats, with a man who is capable of having someone killed?*

"This is me," he continues. "The desire for vengeance for my parents' murder has been my motivation for over a decade. They were denied the opportunity to live, to love me, to guide me. The son I might have been under their care—that's a story untold. Their death forced a different narrative."

"But why kill him?" I question.

His response is solemn. "As long as he was alive, he posed a threat to my safety, and yours, too. No amount of protection would have been enough. This was a necessary course of action."

"But what if it's not over?" I whisper, hating the fear creeping into my voice.

His expression hardens instantly. "It is."

I swallow. "How can you be so sure?"

His fingers slide down my spine, slow, deliberate, making me ache despite the gravity of the conversation.

"Because there's no one left to come after us," he murmurs, trailing kisses down the side of my neck, making me dizzy. "Because I won't let anything touch you. Ever." His lips hover just above my skin. "Because you're mine, Lola. And I protect what's mine."

A shudder rolls through me. Not from fear.

From the way he says it.

From the absolute certainty in his voice.

Still, my mind won't quiet.

I search his eyes. "Can I ask you another question?"

"Sure, but we need to get ready for this party. There's some crypto business I need to negotiate at this conference."

"Actually, that's related to my question. Will I be able to

continue working at Riverbank once we're married, or should I be networking tonight to secure a new job?"

Duane leans back slightly, amusement flickering through the intensity in his gaze. He lifts my left hand between us, twisting it just enough for the dim lamplight to throw sparks off the sapphire.

"That ring looks exquisite on your finger," he murmurs, brushing my knuckle with his mouth.

"Why don't I share with you some of my other favorite gems," I tease. "No need to spy."

"I don't need intel," he says, smiling against my fingers. "I have the source." He kisses the inside of my wrist—slow, distracting. "As for work: Stay if you want, build what you're building. Or start something of your own and let me back you. Tonight the only person I want you networking with is me."

I arch a brow. "Still not an answer."

"Fine." He shifts closer, thumb circling my pulse. "Then how about this—we'll figure it out?"

I groan, flopping back against the pillows. "You and your 'we'll figure it out.'"

He chuckles, a deep, sinful sound that vibrates against my skin as he rolls on top of me.

"And yet, every time I say it, things seem to work out just fine, don't they?" His voice is low and knowing, his lips brushing over mine, teasing but not quite kissing. "Or do you need more convincing?"

I hate that I already know I'm going to give in.

But I love that he knows it, too.

His mouth finally claims mine, deep and devastating, and whatever lingering thoughts I had about my job, my fears, our future, dissolve under the heat of his touch.

Because right now, the only future that matters is the one I see in his eyes.

Chapter Fifty

. . . a fever dream of movements

THE KIRCHNER MUSEUM STANDS BEFORE US, ITS SLEEK glass panels reflecting the dusky violet hues of the Swiss evening sky. The entrance, framed by smooth concrete and glass, glows under the soft golden hue of the museum's recessed lighting. As we pass through the security check, there's the scent of fresh alpine blooms and expensive perfume, the kind that clings to silk gowns and crisp tuxedos. A discreet yet formidable security presence flanks the groups of guests, sleek earpieces barely visible beneath their sharply tailored suits.

I take a slow breath, feeling the steady presence of Duane's palm against my lower back as we step forward. He moves as if he owns the world, as if nothing could touch him, as if he weren't the most dangerous man in the room.

Inside, the museum unfolds with clean, open expanses and high ceilings, a hallmark of the Kirchner Museum's design. The space is intimate yet bold, designed to showcase the raw energy of German Expressionism rather than overpower it. The smooth white walls act as a silent stage for the vivid chaos of Ernst Ludwig Kirchner's art. The colors are electric—blazing oranges, raw reds, pulsing blues, and jagged strokes of neon violet and acid yellow. It's a fever dream of movements, wild and unrestrained, a world away from the polished elegance of the guests milling about.

Everywhere I look, there's wealth wrapped in effortless sophistication. Men in tailored tuxedos and women in couture gowns weave through the open exhibition halls, champagne flutes glistening between their fingers. The soft strains from a string quartet float through the space, the acoustics of the museum amplifying the music into a haunting, ethereal presence.

We move around the room, meeting people from the cryptocurrency realm. At one point, Oliver joins us, greeting us with warm hugs and showering me with extravagant compliments about my appearance. He looks extraordinarily handsome tonight in a jet black tuxedo, his rich brown hair slightly tousled, his warm eyes sparkling with amusement as he looks back and forth at us.

"I didn't see much of you today. What were you up to?" His innocent manner does nothing to hide the sexual innuendo.

Duane ignores his question, turning to me. "You do look absolutely breathtaking tonight, Lola. The way your hair cascades down to your shoulders, and this strapless gown . . . is it Balenciaga?"

Taken aback, I let out a surprised laugh. My dress, with its vibrant tropical flowers in shades of red and royal blue against a yellow backdrop, and layered ruffles at the bottom, was indeed a Balenciaga.

"I'm impressed you recognize the designer."

"No, you're the one who's impressive in that dress." He admits with a wink, "I checked the label while you were getting ready."

He tracks the hollow of my throat with a focus so searing I feel the pulse jump beneath my skin; the room simply ceases to matter. I force myself to look away, letting my eyes skim over to Oliver, who lowers his head in a slight bow as he moves away.

I fix my gaze on the man standing before me: devastatingly handsome in a tux, the expensive fabric molding to his broad shoulders, crisp and clean against his sharp jawline, his bronzed hair brushed back above his turbulent brown eyes.

"I hope you also figured out how to get me out of it. I wore this just for you to take it off," I tease, as I feel the pressure of his hand across my open lower back, warm and firm, grounding me to this moment.

A Harry Styles song drifts in from a nearby room where couples sway in rhythm to the rich and haunting melody.

"Dance with me," he says. It's not a question. It's a command.

His hands find mine, fingers threading together as he guides me onto the polished marble dance floor. I let him pull me in, into the heat of his body against mine, feeling the way every inch of him is tension wrapped in control.

He has given me so much.

Not just his secrets—the ones no one else in the world knows, the ones that explain why he spent years in the shadows, why he lived every day waiting for war. Not just his protection—a promise made without hesitation, with a certainty that still shakes me.

No. He has given me himself.

Fully. Completely. Without walls.

"You're staring," he murmurs, his lips just inches from mine.

"You're smirking," I counter, but my breath is unsteady.

He leans in, his words a serrated whisper against my skin.

"I was always going to have you, Lola. You're mine."

The words hit deeper than they should, wrapping around and melting something buried inside me. The pain, the disappointment, and the betrayal from all the men in my life. I tip my head back slightly to let my gaze sweep the room—the glittering chandeliers, the flickering candlelight against the gold-rimmed glasses, the blurred reflections of bodies moving on polished marble.

His voice breaks through the moment, smooth and teasing. "You're thinking too much."

I scoff. "Thinking is very good for me, actually."

"Hmm." He spins me slowly with his good arm, then pulls me flush against him again. "You're sure about that?"

"Duane, I hate to be the one to tell you, but not all of us can survive on sheer arrogance and unholy good looks."

He chuckles deep and low, shaking his head as he drops his forehead briefly against mine. "It's not arrogance if it's true."

I laugh despite myself, my chest filling with something warm, something shimmering, something dangerously close to happiness.

The entire scene feels untouchable, suspended in time.

A moment I want to hold on to.

And then—a presence moving too fast.

A voice cuts through the music, sharp and urgent.

"Duane! Security—NOW!"

The shift is instantaneous.

Duane's body goes rigid against mine, every muscle locking into something lethal. His hand tightens at my waist, pulling me in as his head snaps toward the sound.

I barely have time to register Oliver's panicked sprint through the crowd, his phone clenched in his hand, his face twisted in urgency.

Then—impact.

Something—or someone—slams into me.

A sharp, piercing sting explodes in my arm, white-hot and burning.

I gasp, looking down, confused not to see blood on my arm, then stumble as the room violently spins.

Duane catches me, his grip clumsy, but suddenly, I feel like I'm slipping through his fingers.

"Lola."

His voice is wrong. Low and raw and shaking.

I try to lift my arm, but I can't.

I try to breathe, but the air feels thick, syrupy, too heavy in my lungs.

A strange coldness spreads through me, curling around my limbs like smoke, sinking into my bones.

I blink up at him, but my vision is already starting to blur, the golden lights of the museum flickering like dying stars.

I hear Oliver shout for an ambulance, but it's far away now, like it's happening on another plane of existence.

No.

No, this wasn't supposed to happen.

We were supposed to be safe.

Duane cradles my face with one hand, unshakable, his eyes—God, his eyes.

"I've got you," he breathes, but there's something desperate in the way he says it.

I want to tell him I know.

I want to tell him I believe him.

But my lips won't move.

My body feels weightless now, even as I lean against his chest, but not in the fantasy, floating way it did moments ago.

This is different.

This is cold.

This is wrong.

And the last thing I hear as the world becomes a tunnel is his voice—breaking, unraveling, pleading.

"Lola, stay with me. This isn't the end."

Chapter Fifty-One

. . . whatever truth he's about to give me

I FEEL THE DARKNESS. IT'S WARM, NOT COLD, NO LIGHT around me and something, something else. Where was it? It's at the edges; it's there, for me, pulling me from the black, there at the edge, where it's still empty.

A shift. A change. A scent.

Something, pulling me from the void. It smells like comfort, warm, soft, surging in me, coming from the edge. It's—*him*. And I reach for it, desperate.

Voices breaking through. Too loud. Too sharp. I just want the warmth. I want the scent. I want—

"Call the doctor. She's moving."

The void trembles. My body is weightless, yet something presses down on me, keeps me from floating away. I try to move, but everything is distant, unreachable.

"Charlotte. Charlotte. I want you to squeeze my hand. Go ahead. Squeeze my fingers."

I feel the cool, dry skin and squeeze as hard as I can.

"You can do it, Charlotte. Just squeeze as hard as you can."

I try. I think I do. But the effort drains me. The voices blur, melt away. And then the warmth is back, wrapping around me, and the scent is there, as well as emptiness.

"Charlotte, I want you to open your eyes. Open your eyes, Charlotte. Open them now."

It's a command. Gentle, firm. I want to obey, but everything is so heavy. My eyelids, my thoughts. But then—there. The warmth again, pressing close. A whisper, lower, coaxing.

"Open your eyes, Lola. Open your eyes for me."

Duane.

His voice anchors me. My fingers twitch, aching for something solid. I force myself up through the thick weight dragging me down, my lashes fluttering against the oppressive brightness. The light is blinding, cruel, but I fight against it.

And I want that smell, I want it so much and I lift the heaviness to see a face, his face, near mine, and this is him, this is his smell before the heaviness descends and he is gone but he's still there because I can still smell him.

The ceiling is white. A faint humming comes from a distance. I feel something on my middle. I reach out and touch his hair. His head is lying on my stomach, and there's a movement. I see his face: disheveled hair, tired eyes, tight lips. He whispers *"Lola!"* as I feel his arms around me, hugging me to him, and all I can make myself say is *"Duane."*

I open my eyes and smile faintly as Duane steps into the room, his broad frame filling the space like a shadow made real. He's clutching a bouquet—white bells and bright green leaves—my favorite. Their scent floods the room, sweet and intoxicating, like spring after a storm.

I lift my arms, reaching for him, and he's enveloping me, pulling me close to him. The bouquet slips onto the tray table in the rush, as he gathers me in his arms. I laugh, breathless, but he doesn't. He holds me tightly, like he's afraid I might disappear.

"Lola," he groans, his voice raw against my ear, his breath warm, ragged. His entire body shakes as he buries his face in my hair. He's crushed by something. I can feel it in his grip, in the way his chest rises and falls too fast, like he's drowning and only now, only now, is he breathing again.

After a moment, he pulls back just enough to sit beside me on the bed, keeping an arm around me. I try to shift to make more space, but my body is too weak; it barely obeys me. He feels it—feels how little strength I have—and it makes something flicker across his face. A shadow of torment.

Then in a whisper barely above a breath, he says, "I didn't protect you."

I blink at him, confused.

"I brought you into this, and I failed." His voice tightens, rough with regret. "I thought I had it under control, but I didn't. You almost died, Lola. You were gone, and I—" He stops, his throat working around words he can't say. "I'm so sorry. I will never forgive myself."

I shake my head, rushing to reassure him. "Duane, no. I'm *here*. You're here. It's okay—"

His hands come up to my arms, gripping them just hard enough to still me. Anguish floods his face. "No, it's not okay." His voice is sharp, almost furious. "You were dead for nearly three minutes. Three minutes where I—where I—" He swallows hard, his jaw clenched so tight it looks painful. "It was a syringe filled with poison. An injection in your arm. I almost lost you. You were in a coma for five days. And we are still not safe."

The warmth of the moment is gone.

His words crack something open inside me, and the full weight of everything that's happened begins to seep in like sepsis in a wound.

The memories rush back in fractured pieces—the music, the warmth of Duane's arms around me as we danced, the sudden jolt, the sharp sting in my arm, the way the world tilted, then . . . *nothing.*

My stomach clenches.

I almost died.

For the first time since waking, I realize how little I know. I've been floating in the simple relief of being alive, but now reality crashes down. I don't even know *why* I almost died. I don't know *who* tried to kill me, or *why.*

And Duane does.

I see it in the way he's watching me, the way he knows I'm finally catching up to what he's been living with for hours—days. The agony of it. The guilt.

My thoughts are racing. Of course things are not okay. I don't even know what's going on. I almost died. I'm like a child, just wanting to believe the nightmare didn't happen. I want to shake myself, but instead my heart sinks as a growing numbness slowly spreads over me. What the actual fuck did happen?

"Then tell me, Duane," I say, my voice low, steady. It's not a question. It's my demand. "No more hiding. No more omissions. Explain to me why I almost died."

Something shifts in his expression. For a long moment, he doesn't move. Then slowly, he stands and walks away from the bed, as if he needs distance before he can say the words. He runs a hand through his hair, his movements rigid, controlled.

I want to ask him to stay next to me. But I don't. Instead, I lower my gaze to my hands, as if surrendering to whatever truth he's about to give me. I know it's going to hurt.

"I've been tracking the men who killed my parents for fifteen years," Duane says quietly. "I told you that much. We found the ones who pulled the trigger. They're gone. But the man who gave the order? Chiang. Finding him took longer.

With the bitcoin he stole from my parents, he built an empire. He became untouchable."

His voice is cold. Detached. Clinical.

It terrifies me.

"And then, you did find him," I say, not encouraging, just enough to pull him back from wherever his mind has gone. His voice is empty, and I need to hear him—not some hollowed out version of himself.

He glances down, his posture still. "Yes. We found him and then I was shot."

My breath is tight in my throat.

"How did he find you?" I whisper. "Why now? Why come after you now?"

And then a question that has gnawed at me for a long time, a paralyzing fear: "Did my book expose you? Did I put you in danger?"

His head snaps up. "No, Lola." His answer is immediate, fierce. "That wasn't because of you. I did this to myself."

He takes a step closer, then another, his voice no longer empty. It's filled with something else now. Conviction. Passion. Resolve.

"I stepped out of the shadows. I stopped hiding. I chose to become the man I was meant to be, for you. I wanted you next to me, and I knew I couldn't remain at the edge of things but had to be front and center. Because I wanted to stand beside you. I wanted the honor of being yours."

His fingers tighten around mine. "You are my true north, Lola." His lips brush mine, a whisper of warmth. "My muse."

Something hot presses against the back of my throat, a wave of emotion I don't know how to control.

"Duane . . ."

"I could finally see a way forward," he murmurs. "A way to be with you. But that meant stepping into the light. Once I did, I was seen. And that set the next part in motion. Chiang found me. He never knew my parents had a son. When I went public—when I became someone to watch, someone with power—he saw me as a threat. A loose end."

His grip tightens. "At the same time, we were closing in on him. We tracked him to Davos. And we made our move."

The weight of his words presses against my ribs.

"But he's dead now," I say, as if saying it aloud will make it final. "So why—why did they come after you but get me instead by mistake?"

"Because his death set other things in motion," Duane's steady voice becomes measured. "His organization still lives. His second-in-command wants to finish what Chiang had started. And they don't just want me dead, Lola." His thumb brushes my palm. "They want revenge."

The nausea rises before I can stop it. Deep inside me, I know. Duane doesn't blink. Doesn't look away. This conversation isn't the worst of it.

He's about to tell me something even worse. And I don't see it coming.

Chapter Fifty-Two

. . . that little girl again

"THAT POISON INJECTION WAS MEANT FOR ME, LOLA. They're still after me, and I have to end this. I can't risk anything happening to you. I failed to protect you once, and I won't let it happen again, no matter what it costs, or what I have to sacrifice. That's why I've come to tell you I need to go away for a while."

His words drop like stones into the fragile silence between us, each syllable heavy, final, shattering something inside me. My breath stalls, my ribs locking around my lungs like iron bars.

He's leaving?

No. No. No.

I shake my head slowly at first, then violently, trying to knock the words from existence. My hands fist my gown over my heart like I can keep it from breaking.

A low moan tears from my throat before I can stop it, swelling into a panicked wail. "No!"

Duane reaches for my hands, gripping them tight, anchoring me to him. But I don't want an anchor—I want to tear the world apart, to rip down the walls, to make everything stop.

"I have to finish this, Lola." His voice is steady, infuriatingly calm against the storm inside me. "We won't be safe until they're gone. You won't be safe. I need to do this so we can be together."

I can't focus. My thoughts slip away, frantic, scattered, but all I can grasp is one thing, one blaring, unbelievable fact—he's leaving me.

Just like before. Just like when I was eight years old.

"No, Duane, no, please don't leave." My voice is raw, splintering. "Take me with you. Whatever you have to do, I understand, but let's do it together."

His mouth tightens. Not cruel. Worse—resolved.

"It's not possible." His fingers cinch around mine, firm, but he doesn't say yes.

Then he draws back, careful, the motion constrained by the sling, as if even leaving me has to be done in pieces.

"Trust me. We will be together. I don't know how long it will take—weeks, months, I don't know. Oliver will stay behind to run Riverbank. I've gathered the best people with an unlimited budget to track what's left of Chiang's organization down and eliminate them." He swallows, the words scrape on the way out. "Trust me, Lola, I will come back to you."

He leans in for a soft brush of his lips against mine, so soft, so gentle, but I don't want soft. I want certainty. I want to burrow into his chest and anchor myself there, to make him promise, to make him stay.

"Do you trust me, Lola?"

My face is stinging from the sloppy, salty tears streaming down my face. I should wipe off my face. I'm a mess, but I don't care. "Duane, I do. I do trust you."

"My muse, my love." His voice drops, calm with urgency. "You see me, we see each other, who we really are. The darkest parts." His good hand cups my cheek, thumb sweeping once, as if he can wipe away what he's about to do. "You have to be nothing to me until you can be everything. You know this will not be the end."

But he's already moving—slipping out of the moment—and panic detonates in my hands.

First I clutch his wrist. He shifts, and the sling strap tugs across his chest.

So I grab the strap instead—fingers curling into it like a handle, like an anchor. "Please—Duane—"

His jaw flexes. "Lola . . ."

I slide down to his shirt, fisting the fabric, knuckles white, pulling him toward me with a strength borrowed from terror. "I love you, I love, I can't—"

For a flash, I'm that little girl again—clutching my father's sleeve, digging my little fingers into his coat, trying to hold him there, to make him stay—to make him love us enough to stay.

And then Duane does the same thing my father did.

Not with violence. With inevitability.

He peels my fingers open one by one. Until my grip fails and my hands drop, useless, to my sides.

A sound rips out of me—raw, animal.

He takes one step back.

He pulls away.

I lunge forward, but it's too late. The door closes behind him.

The sound is deafening.

My body shakes as I clutch the sheets, my nails scraping against the smooth fabric as if they might find something to hold on to. Because this is the moment my life always seems to circle back to—the moment someone chooses a mission, or a secret, or a cleaner life without my mess in it.

I've spent years telling myself I always find strength. I always push forward.

But right now all I can feel is the terrible, humiliating fear that maybe my strength is just what people count on while they walk away.

Chapter Fifty-Three

. . . so this is how it's going to be

VIV APPEARS IN MY ROOM AFTER I RETURN FROM MY PHYSical therapy session twelve days into my hospital stay. My muscles tremble with exhaustion as I lower onto the bed for my post-rehab rest. Beneath the usual sharp scent of antiseptic, I catch the faint trace of Viv's perfume—something bright and gentle, like powdery vanilla, an odd contrast to the dull ache in my bones. She bursts in, all warmth and energy, as if willing me back to life through sheer force. "Charlie, look at you," she says, voice rich with pride and forced cheer. "Looking so strong. What's the good news?"

Viv has been my constant. While Danny, Oliver, and the Mitchells arrived in waves, their visits brief and full of well meaning reassurances, Viv *stayed.* Day after day, she worked from my bedside, her laptop balanced on her knees as she maneuvered through my tests, my treatments, my recovery. Always present, always bringing fragments from the outside into this sterile world—celebrity gossip, page-six news, books she swears will distract me, updates from the trading group.

She tries so hard to make me laugh.

I want to laugh for her.

"The good news," I manage, stretching my aching limbs, "is that they're going to discharge me in two days. I've regained enough strength to travel and can continue my physical therapy back in New York."

"Excelsior!" Viv exclaims, throwing her arms up in mock celebration.

I let out a soft, tired chuckle, but it barely reaches my lips. "Excelsior," I echo, letting my head sink against the pillow, my eyelids fluttering shut.

For a moment, there is only silence. The kind of silence that stretches thin, pregnant with the weight of words unspoken.

Then, quietly, I ask, "Where is he?"

No answer.

My breath catches, my voice coming stronger now, insistent. "Where *is* he?"

Viv is next to me in an instant, grabbing both my hands, her grip firm and grounding. Her brown eyes meet mine—full of worry, of understanding. She's bracing for this.

"He left so quickly after I woke up, Viv. He was here, but only for a moment. He just—" My voice falters, but I push forward, determined to make sense of the ache gnawing inside. "He made sure I was okay, and then he was *gone*. It's been too long. No calls. No texts. Nothing."

I shake my head, my chest tightening. "I know he loves me. I know he said he had to finish this. That he wants to keep me safe. But why can't he at least—" I break off, my breath shuddering. "Why can't he at least tell me *he's* safe? That he misses me?"

Viv squeezes my hands, hard.

"Charlie," she whispers, her voice thick with a certainty she doesn't quite believe, "he'll be back. You *know* he'll be back."

I let out a breath, shaky and unsure, as Viv pulls me forward, wrapping her arms around me. I press my forehead against her shoulder, gripping her like she's the only thing tethering me to the present. To certainty. To something I can count on.

But nothing is certain. Not anymore.

The next two days slip by in a haze. My balance has improved enough that I can walk short distances on my own. The doctor runs through my follow-up instructions with Viv and me, his words crisp, clinical, practical.

Viv takes notes, scheduling appointments before I can even think to ask. She's already arranged visits with a neurologist, with my doctor, and for additional PT sessions back in New York. She's handling everything. Of course she is.

After the doctor leaves, something in me cracks. I turn to her, throwing my arms around her, in a tight hug.

"Thank you, thank you, thank you," I whisper fiercely. "I could never have done this without you."

She exhales against my hair, her laughter warm but tired. "We're not through this yet," she reminds me, pulling back just enough to meet my eyes. "But you're on track. Let's get you home."

She presses a kiss to my cheek before grabbing her things. At the door she pauses, turns around with a knowing look. "I'll be back at nine a.m. sharp to pick you up to go to the airport. Be ready."

I nod, forcing a smile. "Viv, I am so ready."

Later that night, cocooned in my hospital bed, I listen to my favorite playlist through my headphones. As the first notes of "I Hear a Symphony" by the Supremes rise, the soft, lilting melody pulls at something deep inside me, something fragile, something on the edge of breaking. The scent of antiseptic and fading flowers lingers in the sterile air, mixing with the distant echo of footsteps in the hallway. My body is sore, every muscle aching with the ghost of trauma, but it's the hollow space in my chest that aches the most.

There's a presence. A shadow at the door.

I pull my headphones down just as a familiar voice, steady and grounding, fills the space.

"Charlotte."

My breath catches. "Oliver."

His name leaves my lips in a mix of relief and expectation. He strides toward me, his long coat damp from the rain outside, the scent of the cold night air and deep woods clinging to him. His arms wrap around me in a fierce, steadying embrace, the gabardine of his Burberry trench coat rough against my skin. When he pulls back, his eyes scan me, assessing, searching.

"I've heard good reports from the doctors." His voice is calm, but I hear the undercurrent of tension beneath it. "You're ready to leave, so I've come for you and Viv. The jet's waiting. We're taking you back to New York tomorrow." He reaches out and cups my chin lightly, his fingers warm against my cold skin. "You don't have to do this alone. We're here for you."

I swallow against the tightness in my throat, trying to find words that won't betray the sinking feeling in my chest. My gaze flickers past him, toward the doorway, the hallway beyond.

"Is Duane here?"

Silence.

The answer is on Oliver's face before he even speaks.

I don't try to hide my disappointment as I whisper, "Well, I see one of you, anyway."

Oliver exhales sharply, then gently tilts my chin so I meet

his gaze again. "Duane isn't here," he says, his voice firm, but not unkind. "But I am. He sent me."

Something inside me twists. I try to steady my breathing, but it comes out uneven, raw. "Where is he, Oliver?" My voice cracks—pleading, desperate. "Where is he?"

He hesitates. Just for a moment. But I see it—the weight of something unspoken, something heavy. He steps back, as if putting space between himself and the truth.

"He'll be back. He promised you. He's got to settle things so that you're both safe."

Safe. The word feels foreign now, like an illusion I once believed in. I stare at him, but his eyes won't hold mine for long. He shifts, inhaling deeply before continuing.

"Duane has paid off your remaining personal loans and debt, Charlotte. He doesn't want you to have that burden any longer. He wants you to be able to focus on your physical therapy, on getting stronger. You'll have benefits from Riverbank, so nothing to worry about money-wise."

What? My debts are gone? Anticipation of this day infused my daydreams over so much of the last two years as I imagined how I would celebrate: a night out at a club, a private dinner party, a spa day? All that background worry and anxiety gone, with one conversation. My heart is racing, I feel flushed, thinking how Duane has given me this gift even as he disappeared. I want to hug Oliver in gratitude. Someone should get hugged. I realize he's still speaking even though his voice has slowed, as if he's bracing for impact.

"It's necessary you have some financial stability because . . . we don't want you to come back to Riverbank. Not even after you've recovered."

A chill crawls down my spine.

"What?" My voice is barely a whisper. There's a pause, my emotional high slowly receding as I register his meaning.

"It's not safe." Oliver's assumes a placating tone. "You need to distance yourself from Duane and Riverbank until he's eliminated Chiang's organization. There've been cyberattacks on the Riverbank platform. We're on high alert. So far, we've managed to keep everything intact, and trading continues. No accounts have been hacked. But it's a constant battle. Duane's team is rewriting code twenty-four seven, tracking down malware before it breaches the system."

I shake my head, trying to process the walls closing in on my life. "So this is how it's going to be?" My voice is bitter, sharp. "Me separate from Riverbank?"

Oliver's jaw tightens, but his eyes stay resolute. "This is how it *has* to be for now. Go back to New York. Recover, get stronger. Let Duane do what needs to be done."

His words sink into me like stones. The truth is an iron weight pressing against my ribs.

Duane is gone.

Again.

On the jet back to New York, I stare out the window as the sky swallows us whole. The roar of the engines is deafening, but not enough to drown out the memories.

I think of the first time I was on a Riverbank jet, the way Duane had claimed me with his hands, his voice, his body. The way he *knew* me—knew the parts of me I had paved over, the secret cravings I never dared give voice to. He showed me he knew my longings. He took them, molded them into something that wasn't shameful but *wanted, desired.*

I close my eyes, pressing my forehead against the cool glass.

His voice echoes in my head, rough, commanding. *You're mine, Lola. Don't run from it.*

But I am running. Or maybe he's the one who ran first.

My heart aches, a slow, deep pain that has nothing to do with the poison that nearly killed me. I feel cut off, severed from the dark intensity that he wraps around me like a second skin. He is my shadow, my constant, even in absence.

I whisper into the silence, into the space between my breaths.

"Oh, Duane. Where are you?"

A cold sense of premonition prickles at my skin, a whisper of uncertainty. Because Duane is still out there.

And I have no idea what that means for either of us.

Chapter Fifty-Four

. . . "safe" is the radical choice

MY LIFE BACK IN NEW YORK QUICKLY FALLS INTO A RHYTHM. Mornings spent in crypto Zoom trading sessions. Afternoons in physical therapy, pushing my body toward recovery even as my mind remains stagnant, unwilling to move forward. Evenings with Viv or Danny or sometimes Danny and his family. I rarely see my father or even talk to him. I don't feel the usual clutch of pain as much when I realize we will never be close. Coming to Switzerland when I was hospitalized was so outside his comfort zone, but I was grateful he had come. He had never done anything like that before. Although I did almost die, so there's that.

Surprisingly, it's Oliver who refuses to fade into the background of my life. Every few weeks a text. "In town. See you?" Simple words that chip away at my resistance as his drop-ins begin. Ten minutes later he rings my bell, joining Danny, Kate, and the kids already there for dinner at my place. By dessert he's explaining "digital treasure" in kid terms and promising to bring a puzzle next time.

Another Saturday he appears while Viv is perched on my

counter with a glass of Sancerre. He brings deli flowers and a ridiculous key lime pie. Viv gives him a once-over and a slow grin. "Finally, someone who knows their role: dessert."

Then on a rainy babysitting afternoon, I open the door after his text and he calls, "Look who I've brought to see you"—Lily breezing in from a conference, dropping her tote, and hugging me like a sister. As he leaves, the kids shout down the hallway, "Bye, Uncle Ollie." And I don't correct them.

It's been four months since Davos, as my people slowly become his people. We never talk about Duane. At first, I asked. But each time, with the subtle drop of his gaze, the hesitant shake of his head—I learned to stop. The absence of an answer spoke louder than the question itself.

Having completed my physical therapy after a week home, I follow up on a recommendation from a stylist friend and accept a job teaching at the Fashion Institute of Technology. It isn't full-time, but it is a new challenge. Viv and the trading group embrace and cheer my decision. We linger to chat about my news at the end of a trading session.

"You are riding the wave," Natasha says as she swivels in her chair.

"Metaverses, cryptocurrency, and fashion tied up in a Gordon-Lennox bow," comments Marta.

"Now the next step is for you to start dating," announces Viv, and there is silence. Did she really just say that? And then there is a deluge.

"The best way to get over a man is to get under a new one."

"Unfollow the ex and follow the next."

"Why cry over spilt milk when you can have a new cocktail?"

Then Marta calls out, "Ghost the old flame and DM a new crush." The laughing slowly stops as the significance slips in.

I speak up. "Well, it's more like the old crush ghosted me first." Awkwardness. It's too quiet.

"Fuck it. It's fine," says Viv, and we all start laughing again.

My thoughts lift with the laughter. These are my chosen family. People I can count on. Who make me laugh at reality. Especially when things don't feel funny.

But I don't want to start dating again. I am going to turn thirty-eight in a couple of months. And Duane is thirty now. He had celebrated a birthday in August, perhaps alone, out there in his lifelong quest to slay the dragons who had changed the course of his life. I had known but am more accepting now: Everyone has their own path to follow. Can't I just be happy my path had crossed his, even for a short time?

Last year was another lifetime. From starting at Riverbank to becoming engaged, the agony of Duane being shot and then Davos, learning about Duane's secret unfinished pursuit of his parents' killers—and where I almost died. Did all that really happen? Yes. A shudder passes through me. I almost died.

We sign off, and I find myself shaking my head, trying to make sense of all that has happened. Four months without a word from Duane. No texts, no calls. For all I know, he isn't alive. He decided I don't get to know. Everyone says move on. Danny keeps offering to set me up with a colleague from the hospital. A doctor: steady, unexciting, safe. Maybe "safe" is the radical choice now. I'm tired of holding my breath.

My previous meandering weeks are quickly replaced with a focused, full schedule blocked out to write lectures. FIT wants me to be a guest lecturer in some of its existing fashion business courses. I've been asked to speak about how fashion will play out on the new metaverse platforms, which are under rapid development by the social and gaming media sites.

I find I have my work cut out for me. I had been an English major and had marketing expertise, but did I know how to tell a compelling story in lecture form? More challenging is crafting a one hour talk that explains the concepts of crypto-currency, blockchain, and metaverses melding with fashion. I write and rewrite to come up with the clearest explanation. Finally, I am satisfied that the audience will understand how a player in a metaverse or gaming world could use tokens to outfit their avatar in designer fashions. And finally leaving Duane, Riverbank, and Oliver behind, I venture on a new path.

My lectures go well, with many students staying to ask so many questions I remain for an hour after each presentation. It feels good to have a connection with a group so eager and enthusiastic about all the things that are important to me. The department chair notices, and in November asks me to teach a course in the spring. Of course, he wants to review my syllabus and presentation notes by the end of December before the semester starts in January.

It's going to be a lot of work, but I embrace the idea with relish and a hefty dose of trepidation. As I work six, eight, nine hours a day to pull together an informative but entertaining course, I'm thankful not to have the stress of high-risk trading now. It gives me much-needed emotional freedom to focus on the course. And draws my thoughts back to Duane, as ever, to how he has given me a last gift: emotional relief from monetary stress.

But there will never be freedom from the constant, slightly sick-to-my-stomach feeling. It's always there, even when the episodes of sudden panic from thinking I'll never see Duane again have abated.

Chapter Fifty-Five

. . . the siege begins

SOMETIME TOWARD THE END OF THE CHRISTMAS HOLIDAYS, with snow and sleet pelting my apartment window, I sit writing the last of my course lectures. It's only early afternoon but daylight has been whitewashed out. As I take a break and walk into the kitchen, I glance at my phone and read the news notifications announcing that the World Economic Forum in Davos is to begin back in its original time slot in January.

Sipping hot tea, I lean against the kitchen counter, and I'm pulled back to that hotel room in Davos as I walk in and see Oliver and Duane sitting on that couch, Duane's arm on Oliver's shoulder, the look that passed between them. And suddenly I'm flooded with remembering it all, all those things I thought I had successfully pushed down, not to be remembered again. The experience of Duane crushing me to his chest as I said yes, I would marry him, when we were alone in his bedroom. A cry escapes my lips as the intensity of that moment and the moment in his arms at the dance—the last moment I remember being truly happy. "Oh, Duane," I whisper.

There's a knock at my door. It's Viv, back from her holiday in the Maldives with her new love, Ian. She's bubbly, and her eyes shine as she throws her arms around me, happily announcing, "I'm back. Where's the wine? I'm in love, girlfriend." I hug her tightly, happy for her, drawing her close to me, desperate to squeeze some of her happiness into myself. And then my phone rings.

"Good afternoon. This is Flower's Delight. We have a delivery for Charlotte Gordon-Lennox. Are you available to receive our delivery? Someone must be able to accept the flowers."

"Yes," I say hesitantly. "I'm here. When would you like to deliver?" We agree on delivery within the next hour, but then I hurriedly ask, "Who are they from?"

"I'm sorry, Ms. Gordon-Lennox. I can't answer that. It will be in the sealed card."

That's so strange. Is it the trading group? Maybe Danny, but what's the occasion? The low-level sick feeling in my stomach churns stronger.

I buzz the delivery person in a short while later. Viv has left to unpack, planning to return later for a glass of wine. He enters with another person carrying a large bundle wrapped in floral paper between them. I rush to the round entry table and move things to the floor to make space for them to set the bundle down. They maneuver the parcel onto the table and turn to go. I call out, "Wait." One man turns upon seeing my question and says, "There's a card," and points to something white attached to the paper and then leaves.

I pull the envelope off but don't open it. Instead, with shaking hands, I strip open the large bundle looming unknown on the table, flinging the paper and cellophane into heaps on the floor. "Of course." My entire body flushes with warmth, my hands shaky, my pulse rapidly pounding in my head. It's from him.

It's a cascading, overflowing arrangement evoking a lush

shade garden with moss, ferns, and hundreds of lilies of the valley. Their fragrance quickly permeates the apartment. Viv walks through the door as I slowly circle the table in a trance.

"Holy fuck," she says, bringing me out of my trance. "Who's it from?"

I look at her blankly, unable to focus my thoughts. I look around and point to an envelope on the floor. She pushes aside the papers and grabs it, straightening up, and hands it to me.

"Open it," she commands.

"I don't want to," I plead. She rips open the card and shoves it into my hand. I slowly look down, a tight vise in my chest, as my thoughts tumble. I manage to focus on the writing and read: *I'm coming home.*

I feel like someone has struck me. I stumble back to fall onto a small couch near the table. Viv rushes over and reads the card. "This is it, Charlie. What are you going to do?"

Her question snaps me out of my confusion.

Do? What am I going to do? Nothing. I'm going to do nothing. It's over. It's been over for a long time. I have a new life now. I got through the worst. Mourning and missing him and what we could've had. I'm fine. He can come home, go back to Riverbank and his life, but it won't be with me. I let myself feel the anger I've suppressed for so long. Rage rises up from its hidden depths. I no longer feel passive or resigned. Indignation, dissatisfaction, betrayal take hold of me.

And I remember his words now. I was his everything, his muse, his true north. It all meant so little to him that he could leave me since June without a word, message, or anything—216 days? I cannot let him back into my life. What if it isn't over? What if he's only taken care of part of the problem and things still aren't safe? *I almost died.*

A shudder passes over me, and I grab Viv by the shoulders. "I am going to do nothing," I say, shaking her a little. My voice is loud and harsh. "It's over. He is nothing to me." She grabs my arms, and I drop them to my side as she moves me to sit on the couch.

"Nothing," she repeats. "That's good, Charlie. You do nothing. Nothing is good," she says. Her calm voice is a soothing balm spreading over my raging emotions as she sits next to me and gently rubs my back.

The phone rings the next day. I don't recognize the number, but as I'm negotiating a sidewalk crowded with people, I answer without thinking.

"Lola," Duane says.

The sound of his voice is a gut punch. My breath catches, a sharp intake I can't disguise. I bite down hard, but the gasp slips out anyway. I quickly press my palm against the cold brick of a building to steady myself.

"Duane," I manage, forcing my voice into something flat, neutral. If he hears even a trace of longing curling hot and cold through me, I'll shatter.

Silence. Thick and unbearable.

"How are you?" he asks. His voice is deep, quieter than I remember, but still with that magnetic pull that makes my chest ache.

A laugh bursts from me, brittle, too loud in the stream of city noise. *How am I?* For two hundred and seventeen days I've been hollowed out by the absence of this voice, every day like glass in my lungs.

I swallow, but bile stings the back of my throat. "I'm okay, Duane." The lie tastes like metal. My heart is pounding against my ribs, every sense alive and screaming.

Another silence. I hear the faint movement of a chair, or maybe he's pacing. Then—

"Lola, I want to see you. I have to see you." The urgency in his tone sparks down my spine, igniting every dormant synapse that has gone cold these past eight months.

"No." The word slashes out of me, harsh and immediate.

I clutch the strap of my bag tighter, my knuckles white. "No, Duane. I don't want to see you." My voice is rising now, breathless, but I don't care if people on the sidewalk glance at me like I've lost my mind.

"I've moved on," I continue, sharper, louder, trying to convince myself as much as him. "I have a new life now. I survived you leaving me. I got through the silence, the endless nights wondering if you were even alive. Please don't call me again."

There's a pause. I can feel him there, on the line, wanting to speak—but I don't let him. I hang up, my thumb slamming the red button with more force than necessary.

My hand is trembling, my chest heaving. The city presses around me, and I feel the cold, a stranger's shoulder shoving into mine as they pass. I nearly retch from the acid in my throat. My legs keep moving out of sheer instinct, carrying me toward FIT, toward the waiting classroom of eager faces who expect me to lecture about NFTs and fashion in the metaverse.

But inside, I'm unraveling. My pulse still echoes with the syllables of my name in his voice. *Lola.*

The next day, the siege begins.

At first, it's a knock on the door, and when I open it, a courier is holding a Harry Winston box. Inside, sapphire and diamond earrings sparkle against the velvet. The card reads: *The color of your eyes.*

My breath hitches. I snap the lid shut and shove the box back into the courier's hands.

Then a book arrives—a first edition of *The Beautiful and Damned* by F. Scott Fitzgerald, the same one we'd argued about late one night in the Caymans, our voices stretched thin between disagreement and laughter.

Next, a photograph, framed, intimate—the shot from the Met Gala that went viral: me gazing up at him, my smile alight with excitement and attraction.

Each gift is a needle pressed into my skin, threading me

back to him. I can't breathe when the case of Billecart-Salmon champagne arrives: *The Mark Hotel, the night I seduced you.*

Enough. The memory of our first time, skin on skin, his touch and attention to me, my needs, giving me something no one else had ever been able to give me. He hadn't been hesitant. He knew what he wanted to give me. He had really seen me and understood what I wanted and hadn't ignored my desires like Matthew or backed away from me like David. And then taking it further, giving me what even I didn't know I wanted. More pleasure, more pain, and the relief his acceptance granted me that this was what we both wanted, no shame, no overthinking it. And that was one of the hardest parts of the relationship to let go of, because who could ever replace that?

What am I supposed to do with these feelings—the physical longing, the aching need to be with him even knowing it might not last? I do the only thing I can do. My hands shake as I dial the courier and demand every package be returned. All of it. I need it all gone before I lose my grip entirely. I just need to block and tackle my way down this minefield until he grows tired and leaves me alone.

Chapter Fifty-Six

. . . until you could be everything

BUT THE UNIVERSE WON'T LET ME OFF THAT EASILY.

The following evening, I answer the knock on my door, expecting another courier, another memory wrapped in a ribbon. I open it—and the world tilts.

He's there.

Duane.

All six foot three of him, filling the doorway like he owns it. He radiates health with burnished skin and lighter and longer bronzed hair falling in untamed waves around his temples. A plain black T-shirt stretches tight across his chest, his arms cut and corded, veins rising over the sinew of muscle, his jeans hugging his muscular thighs, so goddamn good-looking I can't look him in the eyes. Not yet.

My vision tunnels to black—black like the cotton stretched across his chest, black like the void in my heart, black like the numbness rushing in as blood pounds through my head. The air between us tightens, too thick to inhale. *Breathe, Charlotte. Breathe.*

For a beat, neither of us moves. Panic, elation, anger,

joy—everything collides as my gaze stays pinned to his chest, unable to climb to his face. The silence between us stretches, heavy, alive. And when I finally lift my eyes, his stare hits mine—sharp as a blade. His expression gives me nothing. That signature poker face intact.

He seems calm and cool compared to my screaming thoughts: *Step away. Shut the door. Don't look at him.* My body betrays me first. I turn away, not rejection, instinct—like I'm trying to shield myself from his gravity. But somehow, without thinking, I step just far enough for him to enter.

His voice cuts through the silence, rough like sandpaper. "Lola." One word, full of bite. "You've ignored my texts. Blocked my calls. You send back every gift. We need to talk."

"There's nothing to talk about, Duane." My voice should shake, but it doesn't. Instead, it slices through the space between us, stark and sharp. Blood pulses in my ears, and my heart wrenches free in my chest and starts somersaulting.

His hand closes around my arm—firm, not brutal—heat through fabric. I break free and step back.

Distance. I need distance.

His exhales a controlled release. His eyes flash, a hairline fracture in his poker face. "I'm sorry I left you. I had to. You almost died, Lola." His voice falters on the word "died."

I flinch. That night. The dance floor. The injection. The blackout.

"I had to make it safe for us. To find them. And end it once and for all.

"My uncles. A team. We tracked them for months. We chased shadows, ran into dead ends, went underground. We waited, and when they finally surfaced—we got them."

My throat tightens so hard it aches. "And not once"—my voice trembles now, sharp with something between fury and grief—"not once could you send me a message? One call from a burner phone? Something to say *I'm alive, I still want you, wait for me?* A whisper that we were still real?" My breath stutters. "Do you have any idea what that silence did to me?"

My words come faster now, louder. I hear myself losing control. Duane's jaw tightens. He sees me breaking apart, unraveling before him. My breath is shallow and rapid. I'm shaking. Everything is blunted, like I'm in a soundproof room.

He moves before I can spiral further. His tone drops, commanding me. "Stop, Lola. Listen."

My body stills before my mind does.

He steps closer, filling my space, the scent of him—citrus and smoke, and something unmistakably him—rolling over me like a wave, like a wave from the Cayman surf.

"You had to be nothing to me," he says, controlled, threaded with anguish. "So I could do what I had to do. I couldn't let myself think of you. Couldn't let you be my weakness. If I had, I would've run back to you a thousand times over. You had to be nothing—until you could be everything."

His arms close around me.

For one devastating moment, I let myself fall—forehead against his neck, body turning into a live wire: tingling, burning, wanting. His hands stroke through my hair with slow, careful pressure, like he's soothing a frightened animal.

"I've missed you," he murmurs. "My love, my muse . . . my true north."

And then—I push away.

Because the fear returns. The memory of near death. The knowledge that danger doesn't vanish—it just changes shape.

"Tell me, Duane," I whisper, voice raw, "are we safe? Can you promise me I'll never have to look over my shoulder again?"

His hands tighten on my arms, his gaze shuttered. "There are no absolutes, Lola. I'm Satoshi Nakamoto's son. No matter how deep I bury it, one day, the truth will surface." His voice steadies, fierce. "But I will do everything—everything—to keep you safe. I won't let anyone hurt you again."

The words sink into me, heavy as lead. A thud in my chest.

I sway. His hands reach, but I slip away, crumbling to the floor.

I feel sick with fear. It must show on my face. No poker face here. "I can't do this." My voice is barely there. "I've made a new life. I finally recovered physically from the poisoning, but the stress of the experience—it just won't go away. I feel it all again when you're here. When you're close."

He drops to his knees in front of me—eyes locking onto mine, stormy, desperate. "You're scared," he murmurs. "I get it. But let's face this together. You're not alone, darling. You've lived in my head the entire time. Every breath I took—you were there. I survived because I imagined us." His voice tightens. "Now, all I want—all I need—is to make us real."

His voice drops and turns rough, making warmth rise low in my body, spreading like heat through a locked room. "All the things I want to do to you. All the things you want me to do to you. The pleasure and the pain." His fists clench on his thighs. "Let me help you through this."

And I want to.

God, I want to.

His pupils are blown wide now, his mouth tight, restraint fraying. He looks so good, like the god that he is, leaner, harder—power packed under skin.

Tears spill down my face. Kneeling there, he pulls me close, calming, stroking, soothing me as if I were a child. "Lola, Lola, everything's okay, baby. I'm here now. I'm here now."

I quiet in his arms for a few silent minutes. Then, I pull back and stand to grab tissues. Duane rises next to me, an intensity, a hunger rolling off him. He's too close.

It would be so easy to turn an inch and fall into his arms. My body starts to rotate like there's a tracking beam pulling me to him. I ache for him—the undertow, the connection of a muse to her lover—until it tangles with the old panic:

Being with him is dangerous. Something bad could happen. Something deadly.

I force myself to move. Toward the door. Away from him.

"Duane," I say, voice trembling, "I want you to leave. What we had is over. I don't feel that way about you anymore."

His gaze doesn't flinch. "Those are just words. Your feelings haven't changed. I felt it when we touched, when I held you." Quiet certainty. "This isn't over, Lola. You know it. I know it."

He steps past me but pauses—just long enough to take my chin between his fingers, just long enough to crush his mouth to mine.

It's searing. Urgent. My lips part, and he takes everything—breath, control, resolve—fire and ruin, and everything I shouldn't want.

And then he's gone. Footsteps retreating down the stairs.

I touch my fingers to my lips—bruised, burning, still his.

Chapter Fifty-Seven

. . . it's an intervention

I LIE IN MY BED AND LET MYSELF REPLAY HIM—BECAUSE MY body doesn't care about separation that turns love into a wound. I remember the weight of Duane's chest under my cheek, his muscles hard and warm, the heat of him through his shirt. And, infuriatingly, he looks even hotter than before. Leaner, stronger, all sharp lines and quiet power. Handsome AF.

And oh my God, I tried to forget him. But how many nights did I turn him into my only escape? My private highlight reel on a loop leading to touches that were never enough despite the endorphins exploding in my head. Because it was all fantasy, and when it was over, and the fleeting high vanished, I was all alone. And I'd curled inward, moaning his name.

And now he's back—alive, solid, wanting me the way I want him, which should feel like salvation. My body reacts like it's been waiting for the moment, like it has no memory of fear. But I do. I'm responsible for my life and, ultimately, my own happiness. There will always be a threat hanging over any life I have with Duane, my days edged with vigilance. I don't want that. I don't want to live my love story on top of an anxiety attack.

The next day I'm explaining to Viv everything that happened, but something is off. Normally, she gives a running commentary on everything I say. Usually, I can't shut her up. But now she's quiet. Her silence isn't empty. It's heavy. It has the feel of folding chairs and concerned faces, of a circle you didn't agree to sit in. I keep talking anyway, filling the space. She finally speaks as she leaves, her voice is soft but aimed.

"Don't let your fear keep you from the love of your life, because, Charlie, he's exactly the love of your life."

And as if on cue, the advice continues. It's like my entire support system has formed a committee, and I'm the agenda item.

By the time I'm having dinner at Danny's with Kate and the kids, I'm braced for it. Sure enough, he doesn't even let the plates land.

"Hey, Carlie," he says, too casual. "I hear Duane's back."

I freeze, fork halfway up. "Danny . . . this is starting to feel like an intervention: Viv and now you."

He doesn't deny it. He just gives me that look—the one that says *We're doing this because we love you*—and jumps in. "Have you talked to him?" he asks. "It's your life, and I only want what's best for you, but despite everything—I mean everything, including the poisoning—he's the best thing that happened to you."

"What exactly makes you say that?" I snap, feeling rattled. "I want some hard facts."

"You smile more when you're with him," he says like he's been collecting evidence. "You're calmer. It's obvious you adore him. It's the way you look at him."

"How do I look at him?" I demand.

He ignores the bait. "And you laugh. You laughed very little with Matthew. And never with that deadbeat David."

"Yes, I laughed," I say harshly, "right up until the time I collapsed after being injected with poison."

"But you don't remember the actual events, right?" Danny challenges.

"I remember dancing with Duane," I say slowly, "and then waking up in the hospital."

"Exactly. It wasn't like you experienced incredible pain or torture. It's the idea of it that haunts you."

We sit there for a moment while my chest tightens around the word "idea."

Danny's voice softens. "Ideas can change. They fade. They even disappear with time." He pauses. "You're the most courageous person I know. From falling off that runway platform to Matthew's betrayal, and death, and losing the baby—you held steady. Hold steady now, Carlie. What you have with Duane is worth it."

When I leave, I hug Danny close and say, "I'll think about what you said." He's never weighed in like this about a man in my life. Not like he's trying to save me from myself.

Okay. Fine. It's an intervention.

I can practically hear the next voice in the circle clearing their throat, waiting for their turn. So when his number appears on my screen after so many months, I'm not surprised. I sigh. *Of course.*

"Hey, Oliver."

"GL." His voice is velvet steel, calm but warm, like a diplomat taking the floor. "Tell me the truth. How are you? Not the polite version."

"My strength's back. Body's fine."

"And your heart?" His pause is deliberate. "Still in recovery?"

I flinch. "I'm busy. Teaching. Consulting. It keeps me moving forward."

"That's what you do. Always forward." His tone dips, then

steadies. "But forward isn't always healing. Sometimes it's just running."

The silence cuts deep. I deflect. "Oliver, why are you calling?"

"You know why." His sigh carries the authority of someone who has brokered peace and war alike. "It's Duane."

"Does he know you're calling me?"

"Fuck no. He'd never forgive me."

"You have two minutes," I say, moving back and forth in the room.

"He's unraveling, Charlotte. Since he came back . . . he barely eats. Barely sleeps. The platform's under siege with security threats, and he can't focus. Do you know what he does? He hunts me down just to talk about you. Always you. You're haunting him."

I feel my face flush. "That isn't my intention."

"I know. But intentions don't matter here. He's a storm without you." He stops, then continues, voice taut with loyalty. "I've stood beside Duane in war rooms and boardrooms. I've seen him bleed and rise, win battles no man should have survived. But the moment he lost you, it was as if his compass shattered. You're his muse, the obsession he can't shake. Without you, he's not a warrior, not a genius—he's wreckage."

"Oliver"—my voice cracks—"I'm exhausted. I've had to let him go to survive."

"He's here now," Oliver presses, gently but firmly, like he's guiding a negotiation. "Here wanting your life woven with his. Even when he disappeared, it was for you. The question isn't whether he'll keep coming after you. He will. The question is whether you'll finally let yourself be caught."

Silence strangles me. I glance at the clock.

"I'm sorry, Oliver, but I have to go," I say. "You know there's a big crypto conference in town, and I'm expected at a panel in thirty minutes. I'll think about what you've said. Give my love to your family."

Great, I'm officially the problem in my own story—and everyone has notes.

The tears start, hot and unwelcome, blurring the lines of neat eyeliner. I rush into the bathroom to press tissues to my eyes, whispering to myself like a drill sergeant—*Stop it. Not now. You can fall apart tonight.* I lean over the sink, staring blankly at my reflection, as my breath evens out.

When I enter back into the quiet of my bedroom, I stand perfectly still, listening to the faint hum of the city beyond the windows, trying to gather myself for the panel. My hands ache with the need to do something—shuffle notes, zip my bag, grab my keys—anything to relieve the throb Oliver's words have left inside me. *He still loves you. He's unraveling without you.*

And yet, hasn't love from him already cost me nearly everything? My body. My safety. My peace of mind.

I gather my things, ready to leave, but my steps falter. Almost against my will, I turn to the bedroom, to the back of the closet, to the box I haven't touched in months. My fingers close around it, trembling.

The ache inside me swells—longing tangled with dread. I slip the box into my bag, not knowing if I've chosen armor or surrender.

Chapter Fifty-Eight

. . . panel discussions

I ENTER THE PRESENTATION ROOM AT THE JACOB JAVITS Convention Center a few minutes ahead of the panel discussion. I'm surprised to see the room crowded, with most seats filled and people standing along the back. This was going to be a generic discussion about what the average person living today will experience when they log into a metaverse. Not a very hot topic in the cryptocurrency or metaverse worlds. These are probably outsiders here at the conference to learn more about this ecosystem, I think, as I make my way to the front.

I take an empty seat up onstage next to the discussion moderator, greeting him as the other panelists grab the open seats lined next to ours. There's a stale, artificial air in the conference room, thick with the mingling scents of coffee, electronic equipment, and the tension-fueled sweat of the panelists shifting uncomfortably. I know Jack, the moderator, from other crypto conferences I've attended and lean over to ask, "Why are so many people here?"

"Didn't you check the conference app with the panel

discussion update?" he asks in between greeting the other panelists.

"No, what update?" I ask as I look over, acknowledging the others. I sigh as I remember that last panel three years ago. They're wearing the same standard tech garb as they did then: hoodies over T-shirts with jeans and Nikes. There's been so much progress with crypto platforms, metaverses, and even fashion entering the space, but the tech uniform remains unchanged.

And suddenly I remember how Duane had looked that time, on that panel, so different from these brilliant but casual, comfort-first tech wizards. He was in midnight blue slacks, a crisp white button-down, and loafers without socks. Had I noticed him because he was well dressed and my world is fashion or because of his mysterious demeanor and movie-star-handsome face?

Remembering his good looks and the way his muscular build had filled out those slacks and shirt, I regain focus to pick up on Jack's words. I notice he's furrowing his brow. "I thought you would know. Didn't you two work together a while ago at Riverbank?" he asks.

"What?" I ask, his words finally registering.

"The guy who just agreed to join the panel today," and as he says his name, Duane Blacklock, I see the man in person moving toward me on the stage. He stops in front of the person sitting next to me and leans down to say something to him. The guy gets up from his chair and moves to the empty one at the end as Duane slips into the vacated seat next to me.

Bloody fucking hell. Every internal siren I own goes off at once—danger, danger, danger.

He turns to me and says, "Charlotte, good to see you."

"What are you doing here?" I seethe.

"Panel discussions are our thing, Lola," he answers casually, stretching his legs out in front of him, relaxed and unperturbed for all the world to see. "If you remember, it's where I get to say very personal things about you. To be sure, I said personal things about you on that first panel, not knowing you at all, but this time I can say so much more because I do know you."

There's a playful note to his statements as I dig my fingers into my thighs, my nails pressing against the fabric as I try to suppress the burn of old wounds resurfacing.

"I don't want you here," I lean in and whisper-shout—then that familiar trace of him reaches me and my body instantly sabotages me—like it's Team Duane and I'm just the unpaid intern.

"Well, I have to use any chance I get to see you since you don't answer my calls. I'm not giving up on us," he says as his gaze lingers on my hand.

He says all this as he calls out hellos and greets the other panelists, making his statements to me smoothly, unruffled. Our conversation halts as Jack introduces himself and welcomes the audience. He then goes down the line, introducing each panel member. He begins the discussion with a question for a panelist who works on one of the large metaverses.

I quickly lose track of what the speaker is saying as Duane slides his palms to rest on his thighs. His strong hands with his long fingers stretch out before me, and I remember how he touched me that last time, lying in his bed in the hotel suite. His hand pressed against my thighs as he commanded me to keep them open and trailed bites along my skin to punish me for my disobedience in coming to Davos, giving me the pain that he knew I needed to feel the pleasure.

I'm on fire, and I swear Duane feels my intensity as I press my thighs together. He shifts in his chair next to me, leans over, and whispers, "Squeezing your thighs is not going to relieve the ache. You need me to do that for you." I inhale a sharp breath, on the brink of combusting from his words alone.

Jack notices me then. The others have been speaking for the last twenty minutes without any participation from Duane or me. With each attempt to get Duane to speak, he brushes the question off to another speaker to answer.

For once, I'm happy to be left out of the discussions, satisfied to have the men vying to grab and answer the questions first. I'm too occupied trying to control my physical need for Duane, attempting different deep and shallow breathing techniques to shut down the heat growing in my core.

Realizing the discussion is wrapping up, I start to breathe more normally until Jack turns to me to announce with clean, sharp scalpel strokes cutting open old healed wounds: "So Charlotte, you and Duane worked together at Riverbank with you coming onboard to bring fashion into the crypto world. In the emerging metaverse, how do each of you see relationships evolving from the real world versus relationships in the metaverse?"

"Relationships in the metaverse versus relationships in the real world," I paraphrase as I struggle to keep incredulity out of my voice. Of all the un-fucking-believable questions to ask me, at this time, in this place: me, the unfulfilled muse of the tarnished king beside me.

A dishonorable king who pursued me, seduced me, sacrificed me, left me.

I keep my voice steady, audible but firm.

"I would say it will allow many of the nefarious interactions of the real world to continue—the deceit, the lying, people telling each other things they don't really believe in order to cultivate a relationship to get what they want from someone. The same as what happens and is to be expected in the real world. But much more so in the metaverse because it's so much easier to hide who you truly are, from your physical appearance being replaced by whatever avatar you want, to pretending to have virtuous qualities. In the metaverse, as in the real world, you can pretend to be someone trustworthy, someone to rely on, someone constant."

"Whoa, that's a pretty harsh view," Jack says, shaking his head. "What about you, Duane, do you agree with Charlotte?"

"No, Jack, I really don't, because I think the same issues will be at play in the metaverse that exist now between two people in a relationship. Issues best solved by communication. If there is dialogue, open and necessary conversation, whether in the real world or virtual world, relationships will be stronger and couples can overcome misunderstandings."

"Misunderstanding?" I repeat, my disparaging tone slightly louder than it should be. His remarks are obviously intended to minimize what has happened between us. And without thinking it through, my need to call him on it takes over. "Mr. Blacklock, when two people have a relationship and one person is not truthful, leaves the other person alone to try to figure out what's going on between them, essentially abandons the other—that's more than a misunderstanding." I can feel my cheeks burning.

The moment I hurl my accusation at Duane, a flicker of something unreadable—pain, regret—flashes across his features before his jaw locks. Sweat glistens on his forehead, subtly visible under the dim panel lighting, as my words seem to strain his patience.

"If the other person had no choice, if he didn't want to leave, but did what he did to protect the other person and keep them safe . . ." As Duane's voice lowers to a growl, the microphone catches the change, adding an eerie crackle, making his emotion feel raw and exposed.

With that, Duane is standing, towering over me, his knuckles white and clenched. He shoves both hands into his pockets as if to keep from touching me. There's an audible ripple of whispers traveling through the audience.

Restrained power mixed with desire radiate from him like

a heat wave, making me feel small and wanting his protection, wanting him to own me. I feel cornered, restrained. I can't breathe.

The entire room misreads the moment—his intensity, his stance, his unflinching stare—and they think he's threatening me. I catch sight of Jack shifting in his seat, his forced smile slipping into one of visible discomfort as he glances between Duane and me, sensing a volatile history unraveling before a room full of strangers. The other participants are making comments among themselves, obviously confused about what's going on.

A gray-hoodie guy reacts instantly: "Step back, man. You're making her uncomfortable."

Another panelist joins in. "Dude, she just said you abandoned her. That's more than a misunderstanding. Maybe let her speak for herself."

A spilled drink leads someone to yell curses as they frantically try to pat dry their lap.

Jack scrambles to regain control, but in his rush, his mic falls off, hitting the floor with a thunderous thud—the final trigger that sets off pandemonium.

A woman in the front row stands and screams "Somebody call security."

Voices rise in shouts and questions as everyone moves toward Duane and me.

"Leave her alone."

"What's going on?"

"Is everything cool here?"

Duane, visibly agitated, turns toward the people closing in on him and barks, "Fuck. Off."

The room is unraveling around me. I hear Jack's voice trying to steer things back on track, but it's useless. The moment has spiraled out of control. Chairs screech against the floor as the panel collapses into chaos, voices overlapping in violent protests, urgent concerns, and frightened confusion.

I should be outraged. I should be humiliated. Instead, I feel something dangerously close to relief.

He came. He found a way to be near me, to pull me back into his kingdom, just as he always has. And I want to be there.

I hate the way my body betrays me, how even in the midst of this madness, I can feel the slow, measured way he watches me—not with anger, not with frustration, but with a radiating heat.

I thought I wanted him to stay away. I thought I wanted to prove that I was over this—that I could sit beside him on this stage and feel nothing but cold detachment. But I was wrong.

I want to fight with him. I want to argue until we run out of breath. I want him to grab me, shake sense into me, force me to admit all that I couldn't confess: That I miss him. That I still ache for him. That I have spent every second of his absence trying to pretend I'm fine when all I've done is wait—wait for him to come back, to prove me wrong, to prove us right.

But this isn't the way it's supposed to happen. Not here. Not now.

Not with a room full of strangers dissecting us like a spectacle.

Panic surges through me, burning through my chest, igniting my pulse into a frantic rhythm. I can't let this happen here, like this. The thought of it—the sheer, unbearable weight of so much emotion condensed into this one moment—becomes too much.

I push back my chair violently, the legs screeching against the stage floor. Someone calls my name, but I barely hear them. I move on instinct, breaking free from the tangled mess of voices, of bodies closing in on me, of Duane's presence looming too large, too consuming, too undeniable.

I don't look at him as I leave.

Because if I do, I know I won't go.

I need air. I need distance. I need to think.

But Duane—he knows me too well. And he's not going to let me run.

Chapter Fifty-Nine

. . . ancient kings and their muses

THE COLD AIR OUTSIDE THE CONVENTION CENTER HITS MY skin like a slap, sharp and bracing, but it does nothing to cool the fire sweeping through me. My heels click against the pavement, my pulse hammering so loud in my ears it drowns out the voices, the footsteps, the chaos I left behind.

I don't know where I'm going—only that I need to be anywhere but there.

Anywhere but in front of him.

But I should've known better.

Because he finds me. He always does.

"Lola."

His voice cuts through the late-afternoon air like a sharp steel blade. It's not a name; it's a command. A shiver rushes down my spine—not from fear, but from knowing what comes next.

Before I can take another step, his hand wraps around my wrist, pulling me back, forcing me to turn. His grip isn't rough, but it's unyielding. Just like him.

I don't fight him. Not really. Because part of me wants this.

Part of me has been waiting for it. We stand in the dim glow of the late afternoon, with the rush of traffic in the distance, the faint hum of voices drifting from the convention center behind us.

It's just us here at this moment.

His jaw is tight, his eyes molten, searching for something in my face, something he's desperate for me to say.

"Don't run from me," he orders.

I catch my breath and don't answer. I don't trust my voice.

He steps closer, his tall body wrapping me in his protective shadow.

"I'm not letting you go," he murmurs, his deep voice a slow moving electrical current inside my body. "Not after everything. Not after eight fucking months of hell without you."

I squeeze my eyes shut. Eight months. The number sits between us, heavy and immutable.

He lifts his hand, his knuckles grazing my jaw, tilting my face up to his. His touch is gentle, reverent, but there's an intensity in his eyes, those mesmerizing eyes that pin me in place.

"I love you, Lola. I never stopped loving you," he says, his voice dropping lower, more urgent. "Tell me the truth. If you don't want this, if you don't want me—say it now, and I swear I'll walk away."

My lips part, but nothing comes out. Because I can't say it.

I don't want him to walk away.

I don't want a life without him.

I don't want another night in my bed, reaching for someone who isn't there. I don't want to pretend my body doesn't ache for him in a way it never has for anyone else. I don't want to keep lying to myself, to him.

His fingers brush over my cheek, trailing lower, tracing my jaw, and I feel myself tremble.

"I wanted you to chase me," I whisper, the words falling out before I can stop them. "I wanted you to prove you wouldn't let me go. That this wasn't the end."

His lips press into a hard line; his exhale is sharp, pained.

"I'll never let this end, Lola," he says. "Not for a second."

He leans in, his forehead brushing mine, our breath mingling, his fingers tighten at my waist, pulling me against him like he's afraid I'll disappear.

I can't take it anymore.

I grip the front of his shirt and pull him down to me.

Our mouths crash together, desperate, starved—months of longing, of silence, of wanting, all colliding into this moment. His hands slide into my hair, fisting it, tilting my head back as he devours me.

I feel his body—the solid weight of him, the heat of him—pressing into mine, and I know this is it.

I don't want to fight anymore.

I break the kiss, gasping, my lips swollen from the force of him. His eyes are harsh, guarded, but I don't let my gaze drop.

"I love you," I whisper. "I love you, Duane."

Then he moves, pressing me against the wall, his fingers gripping my waist, his breath hot against my ear.

"Show me, show me the ring you're wearing," *He's so bossy . . . it steals my breath.*

And I bring my left hand up between us as he moves to look down to see the ring I had taken out of its hiding place at the back of my closet today and slipped on for the first time in six months.

The blue cornflower sapphire sits like a royal seal upon my finger, an emblem of power and elegance, whispering stories of ancient kings and their muses. The celestial blue pulses with an inner fire.

"Say yes, Lola. Right now." He's here for it.

And suddenly it's clear. It's always been clear.

I've been waiting for him to fight for me, but I've been

fighting, too—against myself, against what I already knew, deep down. I'm here for it.

I don't need time.

I don't need space.

I just need him.

"Yes," I breathe. "Yes, Duane. I'll marry you."

A strangled sound leaves his throat—a sound that isn't quite a laugh, isn't quite relief, but something in between—before he kisses me again, fierce and hungry, as I fall into his shadows and edges.

Epilogue

. . . and I believe you now

Cannes—a year later

THE LIGHT IN THE SUITE IS RIDICULOUS—GOLD AND SOFT, the kind that makes everything look like the lily garden in a Sargent painting. I'm standing by the window in a black slip, barefoot, one diamond earring in, the other dangling from my fingers, forgetting what I'm doing because the Mediterranean outside keeps catching the light just right. The air is thick with salt and jasmine from a bouquet someone left on the marble console. My gown of emerald green silk with a high slit waits on the nearby armchair. I'm waiting, too.

Married now, a son sleeping serenely in the next room under the care of our trusted nanny. A loyal bodyguard outside the suite and two others detailed in the hotel. Here to support my friend Grace's directorial debut. I feel safe, the way Duane promised I would, and I'm waiting.

Earlier this afternoon we'd met Oliver for drinks at the Carlton terrace. Sun-browned in a linen jacket, he looked both satisfied and restless as he talked about Riverbank's new metaverse project. Then he told us he'd set up "the Muse fund" in my name that offers microgrants to fashion-tech founders.

"First grant goes to a woman in Lagos building virtual ateliers. I hope you'll review the finalists, GL."

I could only nod and pull him into a quick hug as Duane signaled for champagne. "To new worlds," Duane said, touching his glass to Oliver's and then mine. We lingered there in the salt-soft light, in sea-washed contentment—future bright, unhurried.

As we're returning to our hotel, Duane's phone buzzes. He has an upcoming Zoom call with Riverbank's cybersecurity team about a possible platform threat he wants to take back at the hotel.

He glances at the screen and chuckles. "Lily," he says, showing me the name. Lily's voice spills through in a rush of her trademark stumbling, intense sentences—a breakthrough in her AI research, relationship conflicts, complicated post-doc positions. She promises to explain everything over dinner the next time we're together, her words tumbling so fast they blur into laughter before the line goes dead.

Grace's star rising, Oliver building something vast and untested, Lily pushing into uncharted frontiers, and us . . . steady, scarred, alive.

And I'm so grateful to be here, waiting.

I feel him behind me before I see him—his energy in reverent silence pulling me to him even as he comes closer, heat spreading over my body.

"You are breathtaking," he says.

"Don't start with me," I warn lightly, not turning around, breathing rapidly. "We have thirty minutes before leaving. We have to be on the red carpet on time if we want to meet up with Grace. If you mess up my makeup . . ."

He doesn't let me finish. His lips brush the top of my shoulder. One hand slides around my waist; the other lifts my hair. He begins to kiss the back of my neck. Slow. Intentional. The way he does everything when he wants to ruin me.

"You always did talk too much when you were nervous," he says as he slowly turns me, breathing onto the pulse point of my neck. "Am I making you nervous, Lola?"

I look into those dreamy, luminous eyes and I'm breathless. Not because of what he looks like—though God, the man is walking temptation in his tux, the intensity rolling off him—but because of what he *is*. Mine.

"I'm not nervous. Excited. For Grace. This is her night. Because the film industry might finally acknowledge her with a hard-won award," I say.

"Every night we're together is our night," he says.

I glance at him over my shoulder. "Oh?"

His voice lowers, velvet, unyielding.

"Because every night I get to touch you, to look at you, to kiss you—it's a miracle. Do you know how many times I thought I'd lost you? Bleeding out on those Capitol steps, nights I thought I'd never make it back to you, nights I pictured you moving on with someone safer, someone older, someone who didn't carry shadows at his back. And still—somehow—here we are. That's why every night we have is ours, Lola. We fought for this. We paid for it in scars, in sleepless nights, in silence and sacrifice. And we won. We're here. Together."

His fingers trace the straps of my slip, loosening each so it falls away in a silent whoosh at my feet, and he presses between my legs to make me step out of it. He can't volunteer anything. If he wants this, I want him to take it. To work for these intimate moments, so hard won with past mental anguish, past physical violence.

Each time I called him Mr. Shadow and Edges, it was safer than admitting what he truly was—light carved out of darkness, relentless in his pursuit of me. Every word strikes me like a match, heating my blood, pulling my body to his.

He kisses me like he's apologizing, one slow kiss at a time, sinful step after sinful step on the road to Santiago de Compostela, pious restraint gradually adding oxygen to the embers.

He murmurs all the hardships.

"I was shot."

Kiss.

"You were poisoned."

Kiss.

"Apart for eight months."

Kiss.

"I dreamed of this every night—every fucking night I was gone."

His mouth stops moving along my neck as his lips reach mine. And he pours all the pain, fear, uncertainty, into our kiss. My desire rushes from the same place as my love: from knowing he bled, fought, and endured, just to stand here with me, to kiss me like this.

And then he's commanding me, the way he needs to, the way I crave, and it's like that first time in a flurry of a sapphire dress, tuxedo, and flashbulbs.

"Let me remind you of what this love costs," he growls. "Strip. Now." And as I discard my lingerie, he lifts me onto the bed and kneels between my legs, parting my thighs as his head lowers, and he uses his mouth, his tongue. His touch electrifies my body in all directions until the lights explode in my head and I fracture into a thousand pieces. He's in control. I fall apart.

He moves up my body, kisses me, and I taste myself as he continues the assault on my mouth. Then he thrusts forward, giving me pleasure with just enough edge to make me feel alive. "Lola," he groans, his forehead dropping to mine, sweat slicking his brow, his breath shuddering. "I told you it wasn't the end."

And later as I lie draped across his chest, our bodies tangled in sun warmed sheets, clarity filters through the orgasmic shimmering and I whisper in his ear:

"And I believe you now."

Acknowledgments

I LOVE WRITING THANK-YOU NOTES. THERE'S SOMETHING deliciously unhurried about the experience: a small, quiet pause to savor what has been before rushing into what will be. And elegant, luxurious stationery makes me swoon. So here I am, on modest paper in commercial font, trying to make my gratitude feel as lush as it actually is.

First, thank you to Joanna Penn. She's someone I've never met, never had the chance to talk to, and yet who has been a mentor and steadfast adviser, giving me the skills and confidence to follow her personal belief: *Everyone should write a book.* If you're reading this, Joanna, consider this my bouquet, delivered to you in *the book I wrote.*

More personally, Maria, Ashley, and Lauren have individually moved through this story with me, each offering me their greatest strengths, collectively becoming my creative and emotional shield as I pushed through the writing gauntlet. You helped me to keep going when "keep going" felt like an unreasonable request.

Publishing salvation arrived in the form of Emilie at Girl Friday Productions, along with her team of editors and book experts, Adria and Katherine, who took my work to the next level. Kudos to them for a job well done. You made this book tighter, stronger, and far more itself.

Another important and equally unknowable influence who waited in silence, Georgette Heyer, ambushed me with extraordinary delight. Her exquisite Regency romance plots, historically researched dialogue, and devastating restraint give you full romance tingles even when the couple kisses only once in three hundred pages. If any of that delicious tension found its way into my bloodstream while I was writing, blame her. With gratitude . . . and possibly a faint blush.

About the Author

FRANCESCA FROST IS A ROMANCE OBSESSED AUTHOR WHO believes every great love story is a negotiation—a meeting point where hard-earned defenses, deep desires, and raw vulnerability shape the bond between two people. She delights in slipping readers into unexpected worlds, most notably the high-stakes, enigmatic world of cryptocurrency. She writes complicated characters shaped by emotional wounds—and the unforgettable love powerful enough to transform them.

www.ingramcontent.com/pod-product-compliance
Lightning Source LLC
Chambersburg PA
CBHW061416160726
47995CB00003B/625